He climbed a gate, and from Ashleigh Wood on his left, a girl's voice hailed him.

'Hi! Young man!'

David turned. Just inside the wood and framed by a tangle of white-flowering hawthorn was a girl. The girl looked trapped.

'What's up?' called David.

'Me dress, that's what!' she yelled. 'It's caught up, so come and 'elp me.'

'Coming,' said David, going towards her.

'Shut your eyes, d'you 'ear?'

David, closer now, clearly saw her predicament. The skirt of her dress was obviously caught up behind her, causing its front to be dragged up above the tops of her blue stockings, and her clutching hands pulled down again on the hem of her dress. He reached around the girl with both arms and his fingers found the source of her embarrassing predicament. The hems of her dress and slip at the back were hooked high by thorns. 'Got the little devils,' he said.

'Oh, I'm goin' to hate you in a minute,' she breathed.

'Hope not,' said David, and managed to free her. She ran a hand through her hair, ruffled it, shook it and let a relieved breath escape.

BRIGHT DAY,
DARK NIGHT

Mary Jane Staples

CORGI BOOKS

BRIGHT DAY, DARK NIGHT
A CORGI BOOK : 0 552 14708 7

First publication in Great Britain

PRINTING HISTORY
Corgi edition published 1999

1 3 5 7 9 10 8 6 4 2

Set in 11/12pt New Baskerville by
Phoenix Typesetting, Ilkley, West Yorkshire.

Corgi Books are published by Transworld Publishers Ltd,
61–63 Uxbridge Road, London W5 5SA,
in Australia by Transworld Publishers,
c/o Random House Australia Pty Ltd,
20 Alfred Street, Milsons Point, NSW 2061,
in New Zealand by Transworld Publishers,
c/o Random House New Zealand,
18 Poland Road, Glenfield, Auckland
and in South Africa by Transworld Publishers,
c/o Random House (Pty) Ltd,
Endulini, 5a Jubilee Road, Parktown 2193.

Reproduced, printed and bound in Great Britain by
Mackays of Chatham PLC, Chatham, Kent.

To Sandra and Alan's Three Graces,
Caroline, Emma and Samantha

THE ADAMS FAMILY

Daniel Adams = Maisie Gibbs = (2) Edwin Finch
b.1873 (d)   b.1876   b.1873

Emily = Robert = (2) Polly   Lizzy = Ned   Tommy = Violet   Sammy = Susie
Castle   (Boots)   Simms   b.1898 Somers b.1900 Coles   b.1902 Brown
b.1898 (d) b.1896 b.1896   b.1895   b.1900   b.1904

Matthew = Rosie   Eloise   Tim
Chapman b.1915 (A) b.1917 (B) b.1921
b.1911

Annabelle = Nicholas   Bobby   Emma   Edward
b.1916   Harrison   b.1920   b.1922   b.1924
            b.1912   =
                                  Jonathan
                                  Hardy
                                  b.1919

Philip   Linda
b.1936   b.1938

Alice   David   Paul
b.1925   b.1926   b.1930

Daniel   Bess   Jimmy   Paula
b.1927   b.1928   b.1930   b.1935

(A) – *adopted*
(B) – *by Cecile Lacoste*
b. – *born*
(d) – *deceased*

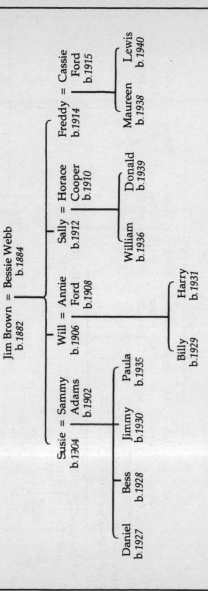

THE BROWN FAMILY

Jim Brown = Bessie Webb
b.1882   b.1884

Susie = Sammy Adams
b.1304   b.1902

Daniel   Bess   Jimmy   Paula
b.1927   b.1928   b.1930   b.1935

Will = Annie Ford
b.1906   b.1908

Billy   Harry
b.1929   b.1931

Sally = Horace Cooper
b.1912   b.1910

William   Donald
b.1936   b.1939

Freddy = Cassie Ford
b.1914   b.1915

Maureen   Lewis
b.1938   b.1940

Prologue

Mid-September, 1939

'Durn me, is these 'um?' asked Jake Goodworthy, clumping over the stone floor of the kitchen to lay dark eyes on the three evacuees who sat at the table with his wife, son and daughter. Their tied cottage was large, with five bedrooms, built in the 1880s when families were large too. Beth Goodworthy had offered to take two evacuees, but at the village hall yesterday afternoon she had so liked the look of two brothers and their sister that she'd offered to have all three. Mrs Grierson, the squire's wife, regarded her in astonishment. All three, Mrs Goodworthy, all three? Maybe I'm taking up a cross, said Beth, but best for them to be together. I'll manage, she said, even if that old cross gets a mite weighty.

Beth Goodworthy was thirty-three, her husband Jake thirty-eight, with the black curly hair and black eyebrows of a Spanisher. That was what the Devon people had called the men of the Spanish Armada, whose great galleons had been scattered and wrecked by storm and the English fleet three hundred and fifty years ago. Many of Spain's soldiers and sailors managed to reach the shores of Devon, and some stayed and married Devon girls.

Jake's dark looks belied his mild nature.

'Is these 'um, Beth?' he asked again.

'These be 'um, same this morning as last evening,' said Beth, brown-haired, rosy-faced and comely.

'Don't look the same,' observed Jake.

'They're fresh-washed and not so tired as last evening,' said Beth.

'Ah, that be it, then, fresh-washed,' said Jake. His children, ten-year-old Posy and eight-year-old Abel, took a look at the evacuees for the umpteenth time. Posy giggled. The evacuees ventured cautious smiles. Jake pulled his chair out and sat down.

'You're ready now?' said Beth.

'That I am,' said Jake, and Beth got up and took from the hob of the wood-burning range oven a platter containing thick slices of toast and a mound of fried eggs. She served a slice of toast and an egg to each of the young ones and herself, and two slices of toast and two eggs to Jake, who thereupon said grace. 'We be grateful, Lord, for this thy provender and thank you according.' A smile showed. 'Tuck in, little 'uns.'

The evacuees cast glances. They were the children of Tommy and Vi Adams of Denmark Hill, south-east London, namely fourteen-year-old Alice, thirteen-year-old David and nine-year-old Paul. Alice was slim, fair-haired and engagingly precise. David, dark-haired, was a supple, quick-moving and adventurous boy. Young Paul was a likeable scamp. They were already fighting the pangs of home-sickness, brought about by the decision of their parents to send them into the safety of the West Country, away from the threat of German air raids. The United Kingdom had been at war with Hitler's Germany since early September.

Alice decided to make a point.

'Excuse me, Mr Goodworthy,' she said, 'but we're not little any more, except for Paul.'

'Me?' said Paul. 'I'm young, but I ain't little.'

'Ah,' said Jake solemnly.

'If you see what I mean,' said Alice. Well, she was fourteen and growing very nicely, and David at thirteen was already springing up.

'Ah,' said Jake again, with Beth hiding a smile, 'that's it, is it, big 'uns as well as little 'uns. Well, tuck in, big 'uns and little 'uns.'

They all tucked in.

'Cows all right, Jake?' enquired Beth, pleasantly homely in a jumper and skirt.

'Pasturing up in the long field now,' said Jake. It was Saturday morning, and he had gone out early to see to the cows. The large herd was important, very important, because of the war, and Jake was chief herdsman for Squire William Grierson, whose estate and farm employed the best part of the local labour. The Goodworthys' cottage was on the outskirts of the village of Ashleigh, through which ran a stream, a little tributary of the river Exe. The countryside was agricultural in every direction, and on a summer day its farmhouses, nestling hamlets and cosy villages looked as if they had been

11

set down as much by the hand of God as the hand of man.

While Alice, David and Paul had not been brought up in the crowded streets of inner London, but in the suburban-like atmosphere of Denmark Hill, the heart of Devon was a world of wonder to them. Their breath had been taken by what lay outside the cottage, a winding country lane, hedgerows lush with honeysuckle and blackberries, the sound of horse-drawn farm carts, and fields ripe for harvest. And behind the cottage was a vegetable garden, full of carrots, turnips, cabbages, parsnips, lettuce, runner beans and outdoor tomatoes. There were no flowerbeds, and nor was there a lawn. Like many other villagers, Beth and Jake put their ground to practical use. However, from the dry stone walls surrounding the garden sprang colour. Buttercups, daisies, dandelions and cow parsley all made their home there. At the far end was a wired-off chicken run with actual chickens that laid eggs while the lordly cockerel strutted.

Yesterday evening the evacuees had been tired out from the long train journey and the hustle and bustle of their arrival in Ashleigh. They went to bed early, following a nourishing supper and the arrival home of Mr Goodworthy from a twelve-hour shift on the farm. Alice was given a bedroom to herself, so was David, and Paul shared with Abel.

At breakfast, they'd been given cereal while waiting for Mr Goodworthy to join them for breakfast proper. Now they were enjoying their toast and fried eggs, the eggs morning-fresh and, in a manner of speaking, home-grown. Large mugs of hot tea stood beside each plate. The square kitchen was bright with light flooding through the large window above the sink and draining-boards. A huge zinc bath hung by one strong handle from an iron hook in a far corner, and against the wall below it was an old but still serviceable butter churn, which would be out of action when wartime priorities reduced the supply of the farm's dairy produce to its workers.

Above the range hung pots and pans of iron or copper, and at a right angle to the chimney breast stood a wide, high-backed settle with a storage compartment under the hinged seat. A commodious Welsh dresser fitted comfortably into the recess on the other side of the range.

Beth smiled at the evacuees.

'It be suiting you?' she said.

'Beg your pardon, Mrs Goodworthy?' said Alice.

'Your breakfast be satisfactory to all of you?' said Beth.

'Oh, yes, Mrs Goodworthy, very satisfactory,' said Alice.

'Better than that,' said David.

'Mind, I like fried bread best,' said Paul.

'Who said that?' asked Jake.

'Him, he said it.' Abel, dark like his father, nodded at Paul.

'Paul, where's your manners?' said Alice.

'He's probably sitting on them,' said David.

'Won't do much good there,' said Posy, apple-cheeked. She giggled again.

'I only said I like fried bread best,' protested Paul.

'Well, you fathead, you're not supposed to say it in someone else's home,' said David.

'And not when you've been given a nice slice of toast,' said Alice. 'I do beg his pardon, Mrs Goodworthy.'

'My, don't she have a funny way of talking?' said Abel.

'Well, she's a girl,' said David, 'she's the same at home.'

'Seems to me, Beth,' said Jake, 'that there's talking going on.'

'So it is,' smiled Beth, 'and I be certain sure there's more to come.'

'Yes, I don't actu'lly unlike toast,' said Paul, devouring the last of what was on his plate.

'That be clear to you, Beth, he don't unlike it?' said Jake, a twinkle in his eye.

'Clear enough,' said Beth, 'but he can have fried bread come tomorrow.'

'Oh, you mustn't go to any trouble, Mrs Goodworthy,' said Alice.

'It's not any trouble to me,' said Paul, and Posy, a kindred spirit, giggled yet again.

'Looks like Posy's got a potful of giggles on the go this morning,' said Jake. 'Let's see, names be a useful thing to know, so who's going to speak them?'

'I spoke them for you last evening,' said Beth.

'Slipped from my mind,' said Jake, 'so who's going to speak up now?'

'I will,' said Alice. 'That's David, that's Paul, and I'm me.'

'Alice,' said David.

'Alice, Paul and David, that's it, is it?' said Jake. 'Well, you young 'uns up from London, 'tis a fine old family Mrs Goodworthy and me have got ourselves now. This be where all of you have come to live for a while, maybe a tidy while, maybe a tiddly while, and it's our pleasure to have you. But we'll thank you not to go racketing about, not while there's some crops not yet harvested. Best you don't go treading and trampling, nor make holes in hedges and leave gates open, nor go fighting and yammering. And it'll be obliging of all of you to do as Mrs Goodworthy asks, seeing she's going to feed you and look after you, and won't take kindly to vexations. It's our pleasure to provide for you, the London Parliament being fair about that.' The Government was paying a subsistence allowance for all evacuees. 'All that being spoken, Mrs Goodworthy and me, and Posy and Abel, say a kind welcome and all.'

'Oh, thank you, Mr Goodworthy,' said Alice, 'we won't do any of the things we shouldn't, and I'll see David and Paul help with washing-up the breakfast things before we go out, shall I?'

'Us?' said Paul.

'I hope she's not going to be a worry to us,' said David. 'Still, we'll help if Mrs Goodworthy would like.'

'I've already made my bed, Mrs Goodworthy,' said Alice.

'I'm thanking you for that, Alice,' said Beth. It had been a shock to Jake, finding she'd taken on three evacuees when he came home last evening.

15

Too much for her, he said, seeing they might all turn out to be young London demons. They'd heard about the rowdy behaviour of earlier evacuees in other villages. Beth had a feeling, however, that maybe she and Jake were going to be lucky. Jake wasn't a man of tempers, but he knew how to put his foot down with ructious children. Maybe he wouldn't have to with these three. The girl seemed very well-behaved, the elder boy looked a good-natured smiler, the younger one, well, if he looked a scamp, Abel was one for sure. 'I don't think I'll need any help yet, not as it's Saturday and your first morning.'

'I'll take all of you up by the long field,' said Jake, 'and from there Posy'll show you round the farm. Will that be your pleasure, Alice, Paul and David?'

'Crikey, not half,' said Paul.

'I'm on,' said David.

'It'll be nice,' said Alice. It would give them things to look at and take their minds off the woe of being hundreds of miles from home and their mum and dad.

'I'll look after you,' said Posy to Paul.

'Ta,' said Paul, 'except I usually look after meself. Usually.'

'You'll find things a tiddly bit different here for a while,' smiled Beth.

'I'll look after everyone as soon as we're used to everything,' said Alice, serious-minded.

'That's what I'm afraid of,' said David, hardly ever serious.

    'I be going with Pa now,' said Abel. 'Is all of you coming?'

    'Yes, we're coming,' said Alice.

    That was how the children of Tommy and Vi Adams began their time as evacuees from London in the green fields of Devon.

Chapter One

July, 1941

The war with Germany had been going on for nearly two years. Hitler's iron hordes had conquered most of Europe, and his bombers had devastated London, Plymouth, Coventry, Glasgow and other towns and cities in Britain. In Russia, his massive war machine was grinding up the disordered armies of Joe Stalin, and in the Middle East, General Rommel and his Afrika Korps were across the border from Cyrenaica and threatening the British hold on Egypt.

Prime Minister Churchill, the lion at bay, was nevertheless still an inspiration to Britain and its Empire. In a speech, he dwelt on the necessity of continuing the struggle. The speech included a typical passage.

'When I look back on the perils overcome and on the mountain waves in which the gallant ship has striven, when I remember all that has gone wrong and remember all that has gone right, I feel sure we have no need to fear the tempest. Let it roar, let it rage. We shall come through.'

During the worst days and nights of Germany's

aerial onslaught on London, Mrs Susie Adams, wife of Sammy Adams, had said she was sure Mr Churchill would one day repay the Germans for their war on women and children. Susie was exceptionally fond of Mr Churchill and believed wholeheartedly in his growling determination to use the growing might of the RAF in a way that would turn Hitler grey, reduce Goering's bombast, and send the Germans running for their shelters.

Her belief had not been misplaced. Since the middle of June, RAF bomber squadrons had been ranging far and wide over German occupied territory and Germany itself. Much to the chagrin of the German High Command and the disbelief and discomfort of the German people, many of the raids were carried out in daylight, when the bombers were escorted by swarms of fighters. Bremen, Kiel and Oldenberg were dealt devastating blows from out of sunny skies. And at night, death rained down on the industrial towns of the Ruhr.

This onslaught, seen by the British people as a reprisal as well as an offensive in strength, was still going on.

'Wizard show, what?' said RAF public relations officers to the Press.

'Bleedin' gorblimey hooray,' said the bombed cockneys of London to each other. People of other devastated towns and cities let go their own expressions of satisfaction about the biter being bitten.

Pacifists deprecated this enjoyment of revenge, and disapproved of revenge itself, but Churchill took the view that if tactical bombing was also seen by most people as deserved chastisement of a nation that had unleashed terrifying air raids on all and sundry, so be it. Churchill was a man for the people, and understood their need to strike back, human emotions being what they were.

Men and women who had suffered blitz from the air again and again were happier now, although Goering's bomber squadrons still made periodical raids. London and other cities were kept on a constant alert, and that meant parents insisted on evacuated offspring remaining safely in small country towns and villages untouched by bombs.

Apart from devastated Plymouth, Devon seemed at peace with the world.

The path across the fields from the bus stop to the village of Ashleigh was a right of way, its trodden surface a dry, light russet, the russet of Devon soil. The day was fine, the sky a clear blue, the air a warm caress. The weather had been perfect for a week, and the land was lush and verdant. A rich profusion of daisies, buttercups, dandelions and cowslips showered the grass of meadows with white, yellow and gold. In the cool shade of hedgerows, wild roses nestled, and in sheltered nests a smug preening of feathers by parents of fledgling birds indicated all was right with their world, providing ravenous sparrowhawks or bullying magpies kept their distance.

A girl in a school dress of green and white check was running fast over the path, her straw boater at the back of her neck and held there by its elastic band, her satchel swinging from its shoulder strap. Posy Goodworthy could have stayed on the bus until it reached Ashleigh's Post Office Store, but she'd jumped off at the earlier stop in order to chase after a torment in the shape of one Daisy Ricketts, an evacuee from Bermondsey, now running ahead of her. The path would take Daisy over the fields to the outskirts of Ashleigh village. But would she ever get there alive? Not if Posy could help it.

The sun poured its light over the scene of two girls running, one in spitting chase of the other, gingham dresses whipping, legs in rapid motion. Posy, now twelve and a madcap, was slim and athletic, bent on pulling Daisy's hair out. She was gaining on the London girl, the same age as herself, and no more of an angel than she was. Daisy was actually running for the fun of it, not because she was scared.

'You stop there!' yelled Posy, boater bobbing. 'I'm going to pull all your hair out, you see if I don't!'

Daisy fled onwards, shrieking with laughter. Posy, sprinting, caught her up and, dropping her satchel, she grabbed her. Both girls went down. Daisy yelled.

'I'll tell yer ma, I'll tell yer pa!'

'See if I care,' panted Posy. 'I heard you say that rhyme on the bus in front of everybody. You're always saying it.'

The rhyme ran as follows:

'Poor old Posy, what a shame,
With a face like hers and a soppy name.'

Posy's apple-cheeked face was actually quite nice and she liked her name. So did her pa.

'Gedorf me,' gasped Daisy, 'or I'll punch yer nose in.'

'Like to see you try,' said Posy. 'You stay still now, so's I can pull your hair out.' Daisy yelled again, and the two girls rolled over and over, Daisy kicking and Posy vengeful. Legs in white socks threshed about. 'Oh, I be going to learn you a thing or two, you see if I don't,' breathed Posy.

'I'll bite yer,' gasped Daisy, and over they rolled again. Posy finished on top and took hold of Daisy's hair. 'Leggo,' yelled Daisy, 'or I'll kick yer leg orf!'

'Talking don't be doing,' said Posy.

A shadow fell across them, and someone spoke.

'Well, I'm blowed, are you two at it again?'

Posy turned and scrambled to her feet. Daisy only giggled a bit.

'Where'd you come from?' Posy demanded of the third party.

'I got off the bus as well,' said David Adams, elder son of Tommy and Vi. 'I guessed you were after scragging Daisy. Posy, you're a terror.'

'Me?' said Posy, flushed and indignant. 'What about her? She be a cat, saying that rhyme about me so's everyone on the bus could hear.'

'Crikey, ain't you touchy?' said Daisy, getting up. Posy elbowed her. She and Daisy were alternately giggling friends and yelling enemies. Posy was a country saucebox, Daisy was a cockney girl with the ready tongue of her kind. Many of the evacuees from London had managed to settle into village life after months of being awkward, obstreperous or downright nuisances. A few still didn't like their circumstances, and continued to hanker after bricks and concrete, pavements and puddles, street markets and the chance to do a bit of nicking from stalls.

'What's the idea of all that punching, kicking and hollering?' asked David, hiding a smile. On his way to sixteen, he was a typical Adams of the male gender with his long legs, dark brown hair, grey eyes, infectious grin and an ambition to do well for himself. 'D'you two want to end up scalping each other?'

'Ain't yer business,' said Daisy.

David actually felt a bit sorry for Daisy. He, Alice and Paul, and other evacuees, were looked after very well by kind villagers, but Daisy wasn't so lucky. She lived with Mrs Mumford, a stiff and sharp-tongued woman, and Daisy hardly enjoyed a happy existence. It was no wonder she had moments when she was more of a torment than a friend to Posy, who herself could be provoking.

'Why can't you two girls be friends every day instead of only once a week?' he asked.

'Me be friends with that fat thing?' said Posy, her sparks still flying about.

'Fat? Who's fat? I ain't,' said Daisy. She was a little plump in places, that was all. 'It ain't my fault you got a soppy name, and it wasn't me that made the rhyme up.'

'It was your fault you sang it on the bus,' said Posy, 'and you be a cat and all.'

'What a carry-on,' said David. 'I've never heard the like, knock me over if I have.'

23

'Corblimey, listen to you,' said Daisy. David grinned. 'Star turn, you are,' said Daisy. 'Still, I like yer bruvver Paul. 'E kissed me once.'

'He never did,' said Posy. 'It was you that kissed him and made him nearly sick. I saw you, didn't I?'

'Crikey, ain't yer got big eyeballs?' said Daisy. 'And a soppy name?'

Posy yelled and went for her again. Daisy took off, shrieking with new laughter as she ran. Posy hared in pursuit. David let them go. He picked up Posy's satchel and sauntered, his school jacket under his arm, his cap stuffed into a pocket. He was attending Westbury Grammar School. His sister Alice was at the girls' establishment. So was Daisy, quite bright in a classroom, and so was Posy, along with a few other promising village girls.

In having ambitions, David was aware he took after his Uncle Sammy who, while still a schoolboy and a bit of a ragamuffin, had begun a determined campaign to make every farthing count in his desire to become a successful businessman with money in the bank. He emerged victorious.

David was well past thinking of farthings. He was well into the desirability of pounds and shillings, and to acquiring sufficient to start his own business after the war. He was a little vague about what sort of business. He only knew he wouldn't mind making some kind of a go of it in Devon. Devon suited him, and although he and Paul and Alice missed their parents and the familiarity of their own home, Mr and Mrs Goodworthy had been so kind to them that the cottage was all of a second home to them, their caring hosts now known as

Aunt Beth and Uncle Jake. The area was one of farms and woodlands, totally quiet and peaceful, although there was some kind of military establishment three miles away, standing alone and enclosed by a high wire perimeter, with smart, straight-backed soldiers on guard at the gates. But there weren't a lot of comings and goings of military vehicles, so it didn't interfere much with the peace and quiet. It wasn't like an Army camp.

Brown from the outdoors he enjoyed summer and winter, David looked more like seventeen than fifteen, just as his Uncle Sammy had at that age. The saucier girls of Ashleigh were quick to smack his lips with kisses at dances in the village hall. Devoted to healthy activities, especially those that earned him money, he couldn't think why some girls wanted to go in for cheeky talk and what they called pash kisses instead of helping to split logs or clean a neighbour's windows. You could get a shilling for cleaning windows, and one-and-six for splitting logs.

He watched the running girls fade into the distance, and felt sorry again for Daisy. Her parents didn't seem to bother much; they'd never been to see her, and Mrs Mumford wasn't known to be a motherly body. Well, according to the Goodworthys, she was a mite bitter about what life had done to her, poor woman, her husband having walked out on her nine years ago. It was a terrible shock to her, and to make things worse, her old collie dog, Jackie, died not long after. She'd doted on that dog, apparently. Mr Goodworthy, Uncle Jake, said maybe that was the reason why Barney

Mumford took himself off, that Dora Mumford gave all her affection to her dog, and Barney had found a woman who had affection to spare. In any event, Mrs Mumford let it be known years later that she'd been granted a divorce for desertion. In the meantime, she'd acquired another collie, which Daisy said got fussed over more than she did. Still, Daisy admitted the old cow did have some kind moments, about one every six months.

In the distance, Ashleigh Hall was visible. A mansion of brown stone and rose-coloured brick, its clusters of chimneys spilled dark wood smoke into the sky every winter. The sky retreated in outrage, but every summer it forgivingly returned and on summer days it framed the dark red chimneys with pure blue. Ashleigh Hall was the home of the squire, Mr William Grierson, Uncle Jake's employer. The produce of his fields and his dairy farm contributed handsomely to the war effort, and his labourers were kept busy, especially in the summer. David was always willing to lend a hand, and Mr Grierson himself had once put his hand into the pocket of his breeches and given him half-a-crown just for being there.

He climbed a gate, and from Ashleigh Wood on his left, a girl's voice hailed him.

'Hi! Young man!'

David turned. Just inside the wood and framed by a tangle of white-flowering hawthorn was a girl. Ashleigh Wood represented a trap in that nature was allowed to proliferate, and an unwary intrusion could find one suddenly surrounded by all kinds of unfriendly growth. The girl wasn't surrounded, but she looked trapped. Her summer dress of sky blue was rucked, and she was pulling down on its hem.

'What's up?' called David.

'Me dress, that's what!' she yelled. This is turning into one of those yelling days, thought David. 'It's caught up, so come and 'elp me.'

'Coming,' said David, going towards her. Another yell arrived.

'Shut your eyes, d'you 'ear?'

'I can't see with my eyes shut,' said David.

'Well, you'd better try or I'll faint.'

David, closer now, clearly saw her predicament. The skirt of her dress was obviously caught up behind her, causing its front to be dragged up above the tops of her blue stockings. Dainty white suspenders peeped, and her clutching hands pulled down again on the hem of her dress.

'Bless me, very unfortunate,' he said. He was reading *David Copperfield* this term.

'Crikey, you a vicar's son or something?' she said. 'Here, you're lookin', you worm. Didn't I tell you not to?'

'Don't worry,' said David, dropping his jacket and the satchel, 'yours aren't the first legs I've seen.' Some of the village girls were as saucy as cuckoos in spring. 'Not by a long shot.'

'That makes me feel better, does it?' said the girl.

'What happened?' asked David.

'What 'appened? What 'appened?' The girl sounded as if she couldn't believe her ears. 'Are you tryin' to start a conversation, you dummy, at this moment in me life?'

'Not a good moment?' said David.

'What a specimen,' said the girl. 'Can't you see that if I let go of me dress, it'll run right up and make your beady eyes fall out?'

'Got you, yes, I do see,' said David. 'That's different,' he said. 'Yes,' he said decisively, 'you're in a fix all right. The trouble's all behind you, is it? Let's have a look.'

''Ere, don't you dare,' gasped the girl, still clutching her dress, 'don't you dare get behind me.'

'I can't, anyway,' said David, who supposed her knickers were showing, poor girl. 'The hawthorn's in the way.'

'Well, reach, can't you?' said the girl, her exposed legs looking as if they belonged to a saucy seaside postcard.

'Right,' said David. Here was a cockney girl new to him, large green eyes hot with exasperation and dark auburn hair touched with fiery tints. He thought of his late Aunt Emily. She'd had green eyes and the same kind of auburn hair. He reached around the girl with both arms and his fingers found the source of her embarrassing predicament. The hems of her dress and slip at the back were hooked high by thorns. 'Got the little devils,' he said.

'Get off me,' she said. He was very close to her.

'Hold still, don't jump about,' he said.

'Oh, I'm goin' to hate you in a minute,' she breathed.

'Hope not,' said David, and did some helpful work with his fingers until he was able to carefully draw her dress and slip clear of thorns. 'There, how's that?' he said as the garments fell into place behind her.

'Thanks, but I didn't know it was goin' to take you half an hour,' she said, and David stepped back. She let go of her hem and smoothed her knee-length dress down. She ran a hand through her hair, ruffled it, shook it and let relieved breath escape. 'Is me dress torn at the back?' she asked, turning.

David took a look.

'No damage, just a couple of pulled threads,' he said.

'Well, blow it,' she said. 'Still, it could be worse.' She looked him over. 'What's your name?' she asked.

'Adams.'

'Adam?' she said.

'Adams, David Adams.'

'Well, you'd pass with a push, except for your beady eyes,' she said. 'You a country bloke?'

'No, a South London cockney,' said David.

'Not the way you talk,' she said, but she liked the look of him, tall, healthy and with a bit of a cheeky grin on his face.

'Well, my parents are cockneys,' he said, 'and so are some of my close relatives.'

'You don't sound as if you are,' she said accusingly. 'Still, we all 'ave to put up with our drawbacks. I'm Kate Trimble. What're you doing 'ere in Devon?'

'I've been living in Ashleigh with my sister and brother since we were evacuated in September, 1939,' said David, thinking her a pert and lively young female. 'With Mr and Mrs Goodworthy.'

'Crikey,' said Kate, 'you're a bit old to be an evacuee kid, aren't you?'

'I used to be a kid, years ago and well before the war,' said David. 'I'm a feller now, if you'd like to make a note of it. How about what you're doing here? I've never seen you around Ashleigh.'

'I'm from Camberwell,' she said.

'What a coincidence, so am I,' said David. 'Denmark Hill.'

'That's middle class,' said Kate scornfully. 'I can see now, you're middle class yourself, you poor bloke. Don't you hate yourself sometimes?'

'No, I like me most of the time,' said David.

'Now you sound stuck-up as well,' said Kate. 'Are you?'

'No, not much,' said David.

'What d'you keep smirkin' for, then?' asked Kate.

'You're funny,' said David.

'No, I'm not, I've got a serious mind, specially as the war's serious,' said Kate. 'I bet you're smirkin' because you saw me legs and stockings.'

'Well, I can't say they didn't look pretty,' said David.

'Don't get saucy,' said Kate.

'What's brought you to Ashleigh?' asked David.

Kate made a face, went sober and said her mum and dad had been caught in an air raid when they were up West one night. It was in the early days of the blitz and a bomb had dropped in the street when they were running for a public shelter. It killed them and several other people. That was

October last year, and it made an orphan of her.

At that point, David, remembering his Aunt Emily had been killed in an air raid, said how sorry he was. Kate said she was just about getting over her parents' death now, and that her Aunt Hilary, who lived near St John's Wood and was a distant cousin of her dad, had taken her in. Aunt Hilary wasn't married, she was a writer and had been living in Paris until the Germans invaded France. She managed to get back to England just before Paris fell. She was very kind but a bit devoted to her writing, and sometimes didn't know if it was lunchtime or teatime or suppertime. She wrote books about foreign places that were attractive to visit for well-off people, except with the war on people couldn't travel much. So she was writing now about places to visit in Britain for ordinary people, hoping to get the books published after the war. Kate said her late dad hadn't been keen on her, that she was proper middle class, which wasn't to his liking, him being one of the country's striving workers that the middle classes oppressed. Her mum had always spoken kindly of her, though, saying it was nice Dad had a distant relative who was a writer.

The reason, said Kate, why she and her aunt were now living in Ashleigh was because her aunt got fed up with the air raids and having to spend so many nights in a shelter. So when she heard about a cottage up for rent in Ashleigh down in Devon, she fastened all her teeth on the prospect of a bit of country peace and quiet. She wrote a letter to the owner and enclosed a deposit to tempt him. He wrote back giving her permission to rent the cottage for the duration of the war. Kate said she herself gave up her job as a junior clerk in a factory, and she and her aunt arrived in Ashleigh yesterday. Her aunt meant to do her writing there, to go out a lot on her bicycle and look at places that were a bit special.

'Well, bless my soul,' said David, 'a real live writer's come among us?'

'What d'you mean, bless your soul?' said Kate. 'You sound like some old geezer in a museum. Be your age, you dummy. And of course me aunt's a real live writer, she couldn't do it or go out on her bike if she was dead, could she? She's probably famous to rich people that travel. What does your mum do?'

'Well, she's not famous, she just looks after our dad,' said David.

Kate's dress rippled to the advent of a playful breeze and the light turned its blue into a shade that matched the midsummer sky.

'And what does your dad do?' she asked.

'He's just our dad, he looks after our mum,' said David. 'He's not famous, either.'

'Oh, well, not to worry, it's not your fault,' said Kate. She was just sixteen and counting it something of a lark to have met this manly-looking boy with a bit of dash about him. It might be entertaining to have him as a regular acquaintance while she was living in the country. It could help to make sure country living didn't get too boring for a girl who liked the lively atmosphere of towns and cities and street markets. Of course, the absence of bombs was a relief, but a girl needed a bit of entertainment as well. 'Come on, you can walk me to the village, if you like, but don't try anything.'

'Anything?' said David.

'Like trying to kiss me,' said Kate, 'because I've got boyfriends back 'ome that'll come and murder you if you fancy your chances.'

'I don't know why you girls go on so much about kissing when you could be out riding your bikes or doing the Monday wash for old ladies with rheumatics,' said David.

'Me do what?' said Kate.

'The Monday wash for—'

'Yes, I heard,' said Kate. 'You're a sad case, you are. And it's boys that go on about kissing. Anyway, come on if you want to walk with me.'

David picked up his jacket and Posy's satchel, and began to walk the path with his new acquaintance.

Chapter Two

Their walk was a saunter.

'How'd you manage to get caught up on that hawthorn?' asked David.

'Oh, glad you asked, I'm sure,' said Kate. 'I was standing on an old log, trying to break off a sprig of the blossom when I heard some yells so I turned and saw these two girls running by. They were both yelling, what a palaver! Me feet slipped off the log, and me dress caught up on some thorns. Crikey, me legs, I nearly died.'

'Don't see why,' said David, 'you've got very nice legs.'

'Listen, don't you mind about a girl's blushes?' asked Kate.

'Did I see any?' asked David.

'I forgot,' said Kate.

'Forgot?' said David.

'Yes, I had all these worries about my dress getting torn, and it made me forget to blush,' said Kate.

'Can a girl forget to blush?' asked David.

'Yes, course she can,' said Kate. 'I did, didn't I?

Look, suppose I was having a warm bath without nothing on in a tropical river and some bloke with beady eyes like yours came along at the same time as a crocodile swam up with his big jaws open, I'd forget to blush then, wouldn't I? I'd jump right out of the water into the bloke's arms in case me legs got bitten off.'

'If the bloke was me, I think I'd do all the blushing,' said David.

'I bet,' said Kate. They were still sauntering, their progress unhurried in the sunshine. 'Listen, what's there to do in Ashleigh?'

'Well, you can muck out the cowsheds—'

'Do what?' said Kate.

'It can be a bit smelly, but it'll earn you a bob or two,' said David.

'Oh, you dummy, me muck out cowsheds?' said Kate. 'I'd love that, wouldn't I?'

'Not your idea of something to do?' said David, opening a gate leading to the next field. Kate went through and he followed, closing the gate behind him. 'Well, you could try a bit of gardening for some of the old ladies in the village. Nearly everyone's growing vegetables, digging for victory, as the posters say. Mind, you help old ladies out of kindness, not for wages, although they always insist on paying if you clean their windows.'

'Did I say I was looking for odd jobs, did I?' asked Kate.

'No, just for something to do,' said David. 'How'd you feel about helping to herd cows?'

'Crikey, you're a case for a doctor, you are,' said

35

Kate. 'D'you have lots more brilliant ideas about how to pass the time here?'

'There's a dance in the village hall about once a month,' said David.

'Blimey, that's wild,' said Kate.

The quiet sky was suddenly invaded. A buzzing sound quickly turned into a roar. They looked up. A tight little formation of three RAF fighter planes hurtled across the blue, and so low that their markings could be plainly seen. They came, they passed and they went, faster almost than the eye could follow. The roar faded, the planes became mere smudges of colour in the distance and then vanished.

Kate expelled excited breath. David thought of cousin Annabelle's husband Nick, who had won his RAF wings about a month ago.

'Flash of daytime lightning,' he said.

'Oh, me thumping heart,' said Kate, 'were they Spitfires?'

'No, Hurricanes,' said David. 'The tips of their wings are blunter than Spitfires.'

'Crikey, would they be on their way to fight German planes?' asked Kate.

'There's an RAF training establishment near Exeter,' said David, 'and they're probably from there. You'll see others from time to time.'

'I can't wait,' said Kate. 'Well, I've never seen anything like them over Camberwell or St John's Wood, I've just seen barrage balloons over the Thames. Listen, about the war, when you going to join the RAF and be a famous fighter pilot?'

'I'd join tomorrow if they'd take me,' said

David, 'but they won't until I'm eighteen. You can volunteer then.'

'What a shame you can't volunteer tomorrow,' said Kate. 'I wish I could. Oh, well, I daresay we could try one of the dances sometime if you want to invite me.'

'Sounds all right,' said David.

'Well, I like a bit of socializing,' said Kate. They approached another gate, the one that led to the lane on the outskirts of the village, close to the Goodworthys' cottage. Two village boys were sitting on the top bar of the gate.

'Here be that London ninny,' said Billy Crump.

'Girl as well,' said Georgie Shuttleworth.

'Another ninny, only female?' said Billy.

'New face, that's her,' said Georgie.

'Up from London, you reckon?' said Billy.

'So I heard,' said Georgie.

'What's she doing with him?' asked Billy.

'You can search I,' said Georgie.

'Are these dafties real?' asked Kate of David.

'I can't always tell for sure,' said David.

Billy and Georgie looked at each other and grinned.

'The Adams ninny's got lip,' said Billy.

'Not much else,' said Georgie.

'That be gospel?' said Billy.

'So I heard,' said Georgie.

'I like her better,' said Billy.

'Well, she's prettier,' said Georgie.

David smiled. He'd had some of Billy and Georgie before. There were still occasions when a few of the village boys gave the evacuees a hard time.

'Billy, d'you mind letting us through?' he asked.

'Did he say summat?' asked Billy.

'Not as I heard,' said Georgie. 'Did you?'

'Can't say, except it worn't nothing much,' said Billy.

'You'd better open your ears,' said Kate, 'and this gate.'

'Is she saying summat now?' asked Georgie.

'I worn't listening,' said Billy.

'Here, look at that,' said David, 'it can't be a barrage balloon up there over Ashleigh Hall, can it?'

Eyes flashed upwards. David lifted the gate catch and pulled the gate open. Billy and Georgie tumbled backwards and fell off.

'Crikey,' said Kate, 'how'd they get down there?'

'Any bones broken, d'you think?' said David.

Bruised, Billy and Georgie sat up and looked at each other again.

'You knowing what happened?' asked Billy.

'No, I ain't,' said Georgie, 'but I'm knowing what's going to happen next.'

Up they scrambled, boys of the same age as David, and rugged with country life.

'What do we do now, David?' asked Kate, although no-one could have said she looked concerned. She was summing up David's chances if she did a bit of kicking in support. 'Come on, what do we do now?'

'You conk them with this satchel, one at a time,' said David, 'and then start running.'

'Oh, right you are, mate,' said Kate, and took the satchel by its strap. Cheerfully, she swung it.

Georgie caught a biff, Billy ducked, Kate began to run and David hared after her. Billy and Georgie were left gawping. David caught up with Kate and passed her. "Ere, wait for me, David!' she called.

David stopped and let her come up with him.

'What's the idea, fighting with the natives?' he asked.

'You said conk them, didn't you?' she countered.

'Didn't think you would,' said David, shaking his head. 'What a girl. Start running again.' Billy and Georgie were beginning to move. Kate ran, and David ran with her. Billy and Georgie gave up. David stopped when he reached the Goodworthys' cottage. Kate stopped too. 'Glad you didn't leave the satchel behind,' he said and took it from her.

'Listen, are you a coward?' asked Kate.

'No, a good runner,' said David. She looked at him. His eyes were as cheeky as his grin. Crikey, it was all a lark to him, as much as it had been to her. 'They're all right, Billy and Georgie, they don't bite,' he said, 'but best not to get into a fight.'

'I don't know for sure, but I think I might get to like you, even if you are a bit stuck-up,' said Kate. 'You can come and 'ave a cup of tea with me and me aunt now, if you want. I don't think she'll mind.'

'Thanks,' said David, 'but I've got a bit of work to do for the Goodworthys.'

'That's the people you're livin' with?' said Kate.

'Yes, them and their son and daughter,' said David.

'You gone on the daughter?' asked Kate.

'Not yet,' said David, 'she's only twelve.'

'Well,' said Kate, 'I'd come and meet them all, only I'm a bit late. Never mind, I suppose you'd like to see me again tomorrow, wouldn't you?'

'Well,' said David, 'I—'

'All right, then,' said Kate, 'see you tomorrow. Same time, same place.'

'Same place?' said David. 'You'll be stuck to the hawthorn again?'

'Blimey, you're a laugh a minute,' said Kate. 'Anyway, don't be late.' Off she went, young, lithe and swinging. She turned and waved.

'So long,' called David, and went round to the back door of 'Home Cottage'.

'What kept you, Davy?' asked Beth Goodworthy when he appeared in her kitchen.

'I met a girl,' said David. 'Can I have a glass of water, Aunt Beth?'

'Help yourself,' said Beth, and David fetched a glass from the dresser and filled it from the cold tap. He drank thirstily, Beth watching him and thinking what a good-natured and nice-looking young chap he was, with a lot of healthy go, and growing apace. 'What girl?'

'Kate Trimble, just arrived in the village with her aunt,' said David.

'Oh, yes, m'dear, they be renting old Mr Hacker's cottage,' said Beth. 'He's gone up by Yorkshire to his sister. Grown up and pretty, is she?'

'Who, old Mr Hacker's sister?' said David.

Beth smiled.

'No, the girl,' she said.

'Well, she's as grown up as Alice, I can tell you

that,' said David, 'but she's had some hard luck.' He explained about Kate.

'I see.' Beth sighed for the girl, then smiled again. She had a very soft spot for David. 'Did you say if she were pretty?'

'A bit more than that,' said David.

'You not having a girlfriend, you be thinking this one might do?' said Beth.

'No, I'm not thinking that right at this moment,' said David. 'I'm thinking about the war and all my relatives who are doing their bit to help win it. And I've got a feeling it'll last long enough for me to volunteer to do my own bit. D'you think it will, Aunt Beth?'

'I hope it won't, Lordy I do,' said Beth.

'Well, I'd like to start my own business when it is over, if I've got enough capital,' said David.

'What sort of business?' asked Beth, preparing what was left of a roast chicken for a stockpot.

'Can't make up my mind yet,' said David, 'but I sometimes wonder if farming would suit me. That's if I could buy a farm.'

'Buying a farm'll cost 'ee a tidy sum,' said Beth, 'but you be thinking, say, of one here in Devon?'

'I like Devon,' said David, 'and I like you and Uncle Jake.'

'Well, a pleasure that would be, Davy, not to lose you back to London,' said Beth, 'but how would your parents feel?'

'We all have to go our own ways sooner or later, don't we?' said David. 'But it wouldn't be like going off to Canada or Australia.' He thought then about his paternal grandmother, known to the family as

Chinese Lady. 'My grandma wouldn't allow that, not much she wouldn't.' And she'd have something to say, he knew, about Devon. Devon would be foreign parts to her. His mum had mentioned in a letter that his grandma was a bit upset that his cousin Rosie, just married, would live her life in Dorset. 'By the way, where's Posy?'

'Came home looking like I don't know how,' said Beth. 'Little devil she be for larking about, and she's up with Abel and Paul by the chickens now, so I be watching out for feathers flying. Alice be doing her homework early.' Alice was an earnest scholar, with ideas about higher education. 'Do you have homework, Davy?'

'I'll do it later,' said David. 'After a cup of tea, I'll get on with building the new chicken coop.' Aunt Beth always made a pot of tea when everyone was home from school. 'And again after supper.'

'That coop be more like a small shed from what I've seen of it,' said Beth. 'Regular young carpenter, that you are. Let's see, what did Mr Goodworthy say he'd pay you?'

'Half-a-crown out of his harvest bonus, Aunt Beth.'

'So he did,' said Beth, 'and what was it you said?'

'A tanner would do,' said David.

'There's a tidy old difference between sixpence and half-a-crown,' said Beth.

'Oh, well,' said David.

'Oh, well,' said Beth fondly. 'Now don't 'ee forget your parents will be coming next Saturday for one of their weekend visits, when I daresay you'll get more pocket money.'

'It'll be gratefully received,' said David, 'but it's not the same as money you earn yourself.'

'No, not quite the same,' said Beth. 'A regular busy bee you are at earning your sixpences and shillings. And all for saving?'

'Well, yes,' said David. He was definitely treading in the footsteps of his Uncle Sammy in his keenness to acquire capital. Most of what he had so far was lodged with the Government in war bonds in his dad's name, and earning 5 per cent interest. The rest was in a Post Office Savings Account. Well, a feller could make deposits of as little as sixpence a time.

'I'll make tea now,' said Beth, 'if you'll call the others.'

Earlier, on her way to Rose Cottage, where she was living with Mrs Mumford, Daisy Ricketts ran into Stevie Clark, a Bermondsey boy of thirteen who, on seeing his first fox, thought it was a wolf that had escaped from Russia on account of all the cold Russian snow. He had a kind of *Just William* look, tousled of hair, innocent of eye, careless of socks and shoelaces. It hid the cockney belligerence that had earned him the village's disapproval during his first months as an evacuee, but he'd calmed down to some extent, although he still occasionally chucked stones at the wrong kind of targets.

'Watcher, Daisy,' he said. ''Ere, I ain't 'ad nothing to do lately, so what say we start our gang up again?' He and Daisy had been prime movers of warfare with the village boys.

'I ain't in the mood for no more gangs or fightin',' said Daisy.

'Why aincher?' asked Stevie.

'I dunno, I just ain't,' said Daisy.

'You gettin' soft?' said Stevie.

'No, course not,' said Daisy, 'I've just 'ad six punch-ups wiv me best-friend Posy Goodworvy, ain't I?'

'Corblimey,' said Stevie, 'you're a pair of funny friends, always jumpin' and treadin' on each other.' He frowned. 'It ain't decent,' he said.

'What'dyer mean?' asked Daisy.

'Showing yer legs like yer both do,' said Stevie, 'yes, and yer knickers as well sometimes. You ain't six years old, yer know, nor's Posy. You're both nearly girls.'

'Nearly girls?' said Daisy. 'You gone daft, Stevie Clark? We ain't nearly girls, we are girls.'

'I mean you ain't kids no more,' said Stevie, 'and it ain't right, jumpin' on each other and showin' yer washin'.'

'Crikey, you're sweet on Posy, that's what it is,' said Daisy.

'Me?' said Stevie.

'Yes,' said Daisy, who actually wished he wasn't, because she liked him herself, a lot.

'Me?' said Stevie again.

'Now you're blushin',' said Daisy.

'Me?' said Stevie yet again.

'Crikey, a blushin' boy, what a laugh,' said Daisy.

'I ain't blushin', I just got a touch of fever,' said Stevie.

'Corlummy,' said Daisy, 'is it love fever?'

''Ere, give over,' said Stevie, 'I ain't old enough to 'ave love fever. And what's love fever, anyway?'

''Ot blushes,' said Daisy.

'Daisy, I'll 'ave to bash yer brains out in a minute,' said Stevie.

'Mind, I got to admit Posy's ever so pretty,' said Daisy thoughtfully.

'I ain't noticed,' said Stevie.

'Bet you 'ave,' said Daisy.

'No, I ain't,' said Stevie.

'What yer blushin' again for, then?' asked Daisy, and went on her way to 'Rose Cottage' before Stevie had a chance to roll up his sleeves. She walked round to the back door, from where the garden looked neat with its square lawn, its flower borders and its vegetable beds beyond the lawn. It was one of the gardens not wholly practical in its output. Mrs Mumford kept it looking nice.

The lady looked up from her kitchen sink as the girl entered.

'You're late, missy,' she said.

'Me, Mrs Mumford?' said Daisy.

'I don't be talking to myself,' said Mrs Mumford, a tall woman of forty-two, with a firm body, a fine head of dark brown hair and searching hazel eyes.

'I just stopped to speak to some friends, like,' said Daisy.

'Boys, I daresay,' said Mrs Mumford, scraping the light skins off new potatoes lifted from her vegetable plot.

'Only Stevie Clark,' said Daisy.

'A rapscallion and a troublesome boy, I'm always hearing,' said Mrs Mumford.

'Oh, 'e don't trouble me, Mrs Mumford,' said Daisy.

Mrs Mumford glanced at her and frowned.

'Why's that school frock of yours looking like it's been through a hedge?' she asked.

'I fell over by Ashleigh Wood,' said Daisy. 'I was walkin' across the fields. I s'pose I shouldn't 'ave, I s'pose I did wrong like I'm always doing.'

'Now then, missy, no backchat, if you don't mind,' said Mrs Mumford. 'I be set on taking care of your frocks and other things. I daresay you understand they cost money.' A charity set up on behalf of poverty-stricken evacuees helped to provide for Daisy, since nothing very much could be extracted from her mother. 'Missy, isn't your birthday about this time of the year?'

'Yes,' said Daisy, looking a little bitter. Her twelfth birthday had been two days ago, and she hadn't received a card or a nice present from her mum, just a brief pencilled note wishing her a happy day and enclosing a battered threepenny bit.

'I remembered you had a birthday about this time last year,' said Mrs Mumford, who worked in the Post Office Store from nine until four as assistant to Mr Pennicot. 'There be something on the table for you.'

'A present?' said Daisy.

'To your liking, I hope,' said Mrs Mumford.

The something was wrapped in shop paper, and Daisy opened it, revealing a book, *Swallows and Amazons* by Arthur Ransome. Daisy's eyes sparkled. She might be a terror, but she loved books.

'Mrs Mumford, 'oo give me this?' she asked.

'To my way of thinking, everyone should have something for their birthdays,' said Mrs Mumford. 'The book suits you, missy?'

'Oh, crikey, yes,' breathed Daisy, and gazed in perplexity at the stiff and straight-faced lady who looked after her. 'Mrs Mumford, d'you mean you give it me?'

'It was in the shop ready to be bought,' said Mrs Mumford.

Daisy could hardly believe that Mrs Mumford, a sort of stern country guardian to her, had honoured her birthday like this. The book must have cost at least half-a-crown. She gulped.

'Mrs Mumford, I – well, I – oh, thanks ever so much.'

'You be welcome,' said Mrs Mumford, washing the scraped potatoes under the tap. 'On Sunday you can have two friends to tea, if you want. I'll bake a carrot cake.'

'Mrs Mumford, a birfday tea?' gaped Daisy, open-mouthed and open-eyed.

'Be sure your hair's properly brushed, and put a clean frock on,' said Mrs Mumford. The charity had helped her provide clothes and underwear for her sparsely funded evacuee. 'But I won't have any scallywags sitting at the table, if you don't mind, so be careful who you invite. Just two.'

'I'll just 'ave Stevie Clark and Posy Goodworvy, could I?' asked Daisy. Mrs Mumford frowned.

'That boy's a downright scallywag,' she said.

'Oh, he is a bit,' said Daisy, 'but he's 'ad a lot of 'ard times at 'ome, and I'll see 'e behaves, Mrs

47

Mumford. I'll kick 'im if he – I mean, I'll talk to 'im if 'e plays up.'

'H'm,' said Mrs Mumford, looking dubious. 'All right, if that's what you want, the boy and young Posy Goodworthy.'

'Oh, thanks, Mrs Mumford,' said Daisy. 'Can I 'elp yer shell them peas?'

'I be able to manage,' said Mrs Mumford. 'You get your hands and face washed, then do your homework.'

'But me 'ands ain't dirty, Mrs Mumford, nor me face.'

'I be seeing different,' said Mrs Mumford, 'so do as you're told, missy.'

'Yes, all right,' said Daisy. Crikey, she thought, she don't half fuss about soap and water. Still, giving me a tea party and this book, I'd best do what the old girl wants. With the book clasped to her chest, a new wave of rapturous gratitude swept her, and she said breathlessly, 'Mrs Mumford, I do like me present, thanks ever so much again.'

'Well, I'm glad you do like it,' said Mrs Mumford.

Later that evening, Daisy called at the Goodworthys' cottage and asked Posy to come to her birthday tea. Posy demurred. Her mum gave her a look, and that brought her round. She and Daisy were friends again.

Daisy found Stevie Clark after that, and Stevie, on receiving the invitation, together with the fact that there'd be a birthday cake, said he'd be highly pleasured to come and to get acquainted with the cake.

'And I like yer for thinkin' of me, Daisy,' he said.

'Well, we've both had 'ard times at 'ome,' said

Daisy. Stevie came of a quarrelsome family. 'But mind you wash yer face and brush yer hair, or Mrs Mumford won't let you in. And besides, me and Posy won't want no birfday kisses if you ain't got a clean face.'

'I ain't special at kissin',' confessed Stevie.

'Well, you'll just 'ave to learn, won't yer?' said Daisy. 'Specially if you want to kiss Posy.'

'But it ain't 'er birthday,' said Stevie.

'Oh, that won't matter,' said Daisy, 'and I'll 'elp to learn yer.'

That was if Mrs Mumford allowed birthday kisses. Daisy was pretty sure she wouldn't.

She was also pretty sure that if Stevie tried to kiss Posy, Posy would kick his legs to bits.

Crikey, what a lark, though, birthday kisses from Stevie.

Chapter Three

Lieutenant Rosie Chapman, formerly Adams, knocked on the door of Major Robbins' office in the headquarters of 21 Armoured Brigade at Bere Regis, Dorset.

'Come in, come in.'

Rosie entered.

Major Clarice Robbins, commanding officer of the ATS contingent, was thirty-three, hearty, outgoing and a deliverer of barks worse than her bites. She looked up from her desk.

'Ah, there you are, Lieutenant Adams,' she said, 'haven't seen much of you lately. Something happened?'

'Yes, ma'am,' said Rosie, 'my marriage to Mr Matthew Chapman of Bere Regis a week ago last Saturday.'

'So that was it,' said Major Robbins. 'Yes, of course. Slipped my mind. It's all this bloody bumph that keeps landing on my desk. All my eye and Aunt Fanny, most of it. Good wedding?'

'Lovely,' said Rosie.

'Glad for you. I found mine a bit of a fag, but I

made sure it was over by midday. Well, I'd fixed up to ride point-to-point in the afternoon. Didn't want that mucked up. Happy to see you back, Lieutenant. Thought it was odd you weren't around. Subaltern Maclean did mention something to me about a wedding, but that gel mumbles so much in her Welsh accent.'

'Scottish, ma'am.'

'Well, one or the other, she mumbles,' said Major Robbins. 'Talk to her, will you, Lieutenant? Tell her to get rid of her tonsils. Good man, leave it to you. Hold on, is that more bumph you're going to give me?'

'Tomorrow's orders for the day, ma'am,' said Rosie. 'The Adjutant has had his copies.'

'Chuck it over,' said Major Robbins, and Rosie placed it on her desk. 'Look here, did I mention to you I was thinking of recommending your promotion to captain?'

'I can't recall you did,' said Rosie.

'Not last Thursday?'

'I was on marriage leave all last week, ma'am.'

'Ah, yes, but can't think why it slipped my mind,' said Major Robbins. 'Hope I'm not losing my head. Well, I'm going to get you promoted to captain, Lieutenant Adams—'

'Chapman now, ma'am,' said Rosie, a little hint of amusement in her blue eyes, and as trim as ever in her uniform.

'Eh? Oh, quite so. Where was I? Yes, with the rank of captain you can attend to all the bumph that lands on my desk. It takes up too much of my time. Never did think a lot of Army paperwork, anyway.

You can look after it. You can manage that?'

'Yes, ma'am,' said Rosie, 'and thanks for the promise of promotion.'

'Don't mention it, you're a smart gel,' said Major Robbins. 'I've been at Corps headquarters for most of today. Only just got back. Glad to be out and about, though. Need to keep myself in trim, y'know. Used to a horse normally. Nothing like a half-mile gallop for shaking up a lazy liver, and it keeps my legs fighting fit. Can't stand fleshy legs and fat thighs, y'know. Don't suit a woman. Well, at Corps, I met Colonel Adams, and found out he was your father. That's right?'

'Right,' said Rosie.

'Splendid chap, and good family connections, I daresay,' said Major Robbins. 'D'you mind if I say he's a regular dasher?'

'Do you mean he's got sex appeal?' asked Rosie.

'That's it. Damn fine pair of long legs, I thought. Ought to look first-class on a horse. Wouldn't mind swapping him for my old man, who always looks as if he's about to fall off, poor sod. Have you finished duty for the day?'

'Yes, ma'am,' said Rosie. It was five-forty.

'Buzz off, then. By the way, how'd you like having a husband?'

'I've no complaints,' smiled Rosie.

'That's the stuff,' said Major Robbins. 'Glad to hear it. I liked it myself for a couple of months. But be firm, be your own woman. Don't want to lose you.'

In other words, thought Rosie as she left, don't have any babies.

It was the fourteenth of July, she'd been married for just nine days and had discovered exactly what it was like to have Matthew make love to her. Well, of course, they were both so ready and so ardent for each other that there was a risk of attempting the ultimate before they even went up to bed. Fortunately, Matthew said the bed had to be a better venue than the fireside rug, and she said she'd never had the rug in mind herself. So up they went, and after cleaning their teeth and so on, into bed they went. From thereon Matthew took charge, sending her mad with prolonged love play, which included doing things to her that made her think of rows of dots in novels that were telling only up to a point.

'Oh, my God, Matthew, must you?'

'Shall I stop?'

'No, do it some more, no-one's looking.'

Eventually, the ultimate arrived. She was twenty-six, but it was her very first time, and Matthew knew that. So he had taken his time, and Rosie simply abandoned herself to being receptive.

Utter bliss.

No, she had no complaints, far from it.

She was in a hurry to get home now, to their attractive stone-built cottage close to the village of Bere Regis. It was today that Matt had gone to Bovington to be given the result of his Army medical examination, and to be told if it meant he could enter REME, despite having a gammy ankle. Arriving at what her unit termed her official billet and she called her home, she found he wasn't back yet. It was disappointing, but she felt better late than early. The longer he was at Bovington, the better the pointer, surely.

She went up to their bedroom, where everything looked so fresh. Matthew had redecorated throughout, and given particular attention to the bedroom, where the wallpaper was a delicacy, her dressing-table lovely. Much of the furniture throughout the cottage was new. Rosie stripped and took a shower. The shower was new too, Matthew having fixed one above the bath. That's my man, Rosie had thought at the time, he's making the work a labour of love.

At six-forty, in a dress, she began to prepare supper. She interrupted the preparations fifteen minutes later to go up to the top of the garden and feed the chickens. She still had to get used to her domestic timetable. The chickens, strutting in their large wire cage at the top of the garden, received boiled potato peelings and other kitchen scraps as if they represented the equivalent of a henhouse banquet.

The pan emptied of food, Rosie came out of the cage and fixed the wire gate. She was just a little anxious now about Matthew's absence. Had he been turned down, and was he drowning his sorrows in a country pub?

Someone whistled. She looked up. Matthew, as long-legged as Boots, her father, was coming through the open back door at a limp. His misshapen ankle, the result of a bad break years ago, was always going to make a limping man of him.

'Rosie?'

Rosie dropped the pan and ran. He saw her

coming, her hair shining in the evening light of
summer, her body springing, the skirt of her dress
flouncing, her face warmed by the sun.

'Matt, lovely you're home,' she said, and wound
herself around him. He kissed her. Mobile lips and
firm lips performed a happy meeting for a good ten
seconds. 'Oh, that's better,' said Rosie, 'I've been
finding out that when I come off duty I don't like
you not being here.'

'You've only been back on duty a day,' said Matt.

'Not a good comment,' said Rosie, and searched
his eyes and face for a sign. She was dying to
know, but almost afraid to ask. Heavens, if love
brought on cowardice, love needed talking to. But
because she knew how much it meant to him, entry
into the Army, and because she so much wanted it
for him, she was sure she wasn't going to bear disappointment. Her pulse jumped a little as he let a
smile surface. 'Oh, come on, you beast, tell me,' she
said.

'I'm in, Rosie, as a second lieutenant. I've been
measured for my uniforms and I'll take up my
duties next Monday. There'll be some instructions
concerning King's Regulations that apply to
officers, but my gammy ankle was dismissed as of
no account in relation to the kind of work they want
from me, and a REME cobbler will do any necessary
reshaping of my footwear.'

'Then I'm blissed all over for you,' said Rosie,
and hugged him.

'Blow my hat and shirt off, Rosie, I'm a happy
man,' said Matt. 'Well, it's a tidy old piece of good
fortune that's fallen my way out of God's sky.

First you and now an Army commission.'

'I like to know I'm first,' said Rosie.

'Rosie, you're first now and always, and if there comes a day when I don't live up to that, it'll only be because I'm ninety and can't tell one woman from another, or a pork chop from a Dorset cheese.'

'Lovely stuff,' said Rosie. 'You're happy, I'm happy, so what comes next?'

'Well,' said Matt, 'I did happen to notice new potatoes, garden peas and fresh mint coming up to the boil in saucepans, and two lamb chops from Farmer Bettles sitting in a pan in the oven, so let's have supper first.'

'And then?' smiled Rosie.

'Ah, well, your choice, Rosie.'

She hugged him again and laughed.

'My choice is you and me,' she said.

Over supper, she told him she was going to be promoted to captain as a reward for taking on some of Major Robbins' work, which would enable that horsy lady to spend more time in the saddle. Her horse was stabled at headquarters, one of the perks of a commanding officer.

'Captain, eh?' said Matthew. 'How's that going to affect me as a second lieutenant?'

'You'll have to salute me, but only if I'm wearing my cap,' said Rosie.

'If you're only wearing a cap—'

'I didn't say that.'

'—you can expect something extra to a salute.'

'I didn't say only a cap.'

'The ATS wouldn't allow any officer to appear in just a cap, would they?'

'Go on, make me fall about,' said Rosie.

'Have you still not heard from the solicitors about your inheritance?' asked Matt.

Rosie had been left twenty-five thousand pounds by her natural father, killed in action at Tobruk. She had seen the solicitors and established her identity with them.

'Well,' she said, 'they're arranging to credit me, but only when probate has been granted. Lord knows how long that will take.'

'Are we bothered?' asked Matt.

'No, we're not, are we?' said Rosie. She was, in any case, investing the money in the family firm, in the property company her Uncle Sammy was forming. 'Matt, what time off will you be getting at Bovington?'

'Sundays, generally,' said Matt.

'With a permit to travel?' said Rosie.

'Home Saturday evenings, back Sunday evenings,' said Matt.

'In that case,' said Rosie, 'have I got to settle for a once-a-week husband so early in our marriage?'

'Look at it this way,' said Matt. 'That's twice as much as a once-a-fortnight husband.'

'And four times as much as a once-a-monther,' said Rosie.

'Then there are overseas men who only get home leave once a year, if that,' said Matt.

'So what do you think about once a week?' asked Rosie.

'Under the circumstances, I think lucky old me,' said Matt.

'That makes two of us,' said Rosie.

'Except you're a mite different from me,' said Matt. 'If you weren't, what kind of a marriage would we have?'

'Peculiar,' said Rosie, and they laughed. Then she said, 'Matt, shall we have a phone installed?'

'Fair old idea,' said Matt, 'but our application would go to the back of a wartime queue. Never mind, I know George Sylvester, area supervisor.'

'Is it playing the game to jump the queue?' asked Rosie.

'No, it's bad form,' said Matt, 'but as I didn't go to Eton I can live with giving some rules a miss. How about you, Rosie?'

'I'll play Nelson at the Battle of Copenhagen,' said Rosie. 'Well, I didn't go to Eton, either.'

Sammy Adams said, 'Susie, my one and only—'

'There, did you hear that, Paula?' said Susie to her six-year-old daughter. 'Did you hear your daddy say I'm still his one and only? Let's hope he means it.'

They were at supper in the well-equipped kitchen of their handsome house on Denmark Hill. Susie's other children, Daniel, Bess and Jimmy, were still evacuees in the West Country.

'If I might be allowed to continue?' said Sammy, now thirty-nine and in what he considered his coveted prime as a husband. Well, it was true that Susie, nearly thirty-seven, was a wife who did covet his prime, she being a healthy woman not given to

58

saying she had a headache on certain occasions.

'Oh, yes, pray continue, dear sir,' said Susie.

'Pray what?' said Sammy. 'Where'd you get that from?'

'I'm reading a Regency novel by Georgette Heyer,' said Susie, 'it's lovely.'

'Well, I don't mind what you read as long as it's not the *News of the World*,' said Sammy, 'but could you keep to good old-fashioned English?'

'Sammy, you couldn't have anything more old-fashioned than "pray continue, dear sir,"' said Susie.

'It beats me, Plum Pudding the Second, what your mum picks up out of books,' said Sammy.

'Daddy, I like my mum, she's nice,' said little Paula.

'I like her too,' said Sammy, 'and I try to forget she's always giving me the run-around. Where was I?'

'No idea,' said Susie, 'but whatever it was, pray continue, my lord.'

'There she goes again,' said Sammy, and little Paula giggled. 'Anyway, Susie, I had an hour with our accountants and solicitor today, and the firm of Adams Properties Ltd is now what you might call in being and off the ground.'

'Oh, I'm honoured, dear sir, to have you confide such exciting news to me,' said Susie.

'That's done it,' said Sammy. 'We've got to face it, Plum Pudding, your mum's gone off her rocker. What's this barmy book that's doing it?'

'A Regency romance,' said Susie, 'and it's about—'

'Hold on,' said Sammy, not enthusiastic about Regency novels, which in his opinion were heavy on bowing, curtseying, villainous rakes, swooning females and smelling-salts. 'I didn't mean I want details.'

'Yes, it's about a lord who's sort of arrogant and cynical,' said Susie. 'He's the—'

'I don't want to hear,' said Sammy.

'He's the guardian of the young lady who's the heroine—'

'I'm not listening,' said Sammy, eating his supper in the resolute fashion of a man with a will of iron when it came to establishing who was boss in the household.

'She's sort of rebellious with lots of spirit and he's sarcastic and worldly,' said Susie, 'and they exasperate each other. Every time—'

'I'm not listening,' said the man with a will of iron.

'Well, you should be,' said Susie. 'Every time Judith – she's the heroine – asks her guardian, Lord Worth, for advice, he tells her—'

'I don't want to know,' said Susie's lord and master – some hopes. He raised his voice a little. It was a matter of principle now, letting her know who was wearing the trousers. 'You hear me, Susie, I don't want to know.'

'He tells her she probably won't take any notice of what advice he does give her, anyway—'

'I'm not listening,' said Sammy loudly.

'Of course, he's really falling in love with her,' said Susie, 'which makes everything—'

'I'm not listening!' bawled Sammy.

'Oh, dear,' said Susie.

'Oh, crikey,' breathed little Paula.

'What's wrong, darling?' asked Susie.

'I think Daddy's having a fit,' said little Paula.

'Never mind, pet,' said Susie, 'he'll be all right tomorrow. He's always all right the day after.'

Sammy nearly gave up. But he was excited about the new company. The first transaction had taken place. The freehold of the Southwark brewery site had been transferred from Adams Enterprises to Adams Properties. It was only a site, the brewery having been bombed to total destruction months ago, but as a site it was perfect for post-war development.

'Doesn't anyone want to hear about Adams Properties Ltd?' he asked.

'Yes, of course,' said Susie. 'We both do, don't we, Paula?' Alas, she then added wickedly, 'Pray, do continue, dear Mr Adams.'

Sammy fell off his chair. It did his will of iron a grievous injury.

Chapter Four

Captain Polly Adams, wife of Colonel Robert Adams, received a personal and private memo from her immediate superior, Major Harriet Jordan, the following morning. It told her she was to apply at once for her discharge.

Oh, well, she thought, what must be has to be. She was well into her third month of giddy expectancy. On the day a doctor in Corfe Castle village confirmed she was pregnant, she fell into a temporary stupor, a not unreasonable reaction in a woman of forty-four, who would be forty-five by the time the baby was born in December. However, Boots brought her out of her state of confusion and uncertainty by declaring himself delighted and expressing a conviction that she could count herself on equal terms with a miracle.

Polly knew who was chiefly instrumental in forcing her discharge from the ATS. General Sir Henry Simms, her father. Well, the dear old lad had her best interests at heart, and was set on becoming a grandpa for the first time, never mind the demands of war. The war. It was a stinker that those idiot Germans had fallen hook, line and sinker again for a warmongering figurehead. The years of peace between 1918 and 1939 now seemed almost Utopian to Polly, despite the economic depressions and her very personal frustrations. To have Boots's child was going to be an event of wonder, but how much lovelier if it were born with the world at peace, and they were able to really enjoy the years he and she would share with their son or daughter.

Then there was the question of what was going to take the place of her ATS admin work. Certain civilian ladies wanted her as the new president of the local WVS. That had little appeal for her. It would be a natural part of the pattern of the life of her stepmother, now a diligent Red Cross officer, but not of her own. She thought of something then, and a little smile touched her mouth.

One of the ATS sergeants knocked and entered.

'Good morning,' said Polly.

'Morning, ma'am. Um, Major Jordan asked me to tell you that if you want to see her, she'll be in her office till O-ten-hundred.'

'Right, got you,' said Polly. She knew what it meant, and she took a written application for discharge to her commanding officer ten minutes later.

'Any regrets, Polly?'

'Only that it's going to be a wartime infant,' said Polly. 'Permission to go off duty for an hour?'

'Granted.'

*   *   *

Lance-Corporal Higgins, batman to Boots and Polly, was tidying up their requisitioned cottage when Polly walked in.

'Ah, Corporal Higgins,' she said.

'Yes, ma'am?' said her man-of-all-work.

'Come into the garden with me,' said Polly.

'Eh?' said Higgins, startled.

'Yes, come on, be a sport,' said Polly, 'I need you for five minutes.'

'Beg yer pardon?' said Higgins, blushing a bit.

Polly laughed.

'No, it's nothing like that,' she said, 'it's to do with the garden.'

'Oh, right,' said Higgins, and accompanied her out of the back door of the kitchen into the large, well-kept garden. Boots kept it so in his spare time. He was fond of gardening, and Polly had begun to take an interest. She walked to the top of the garden, to where the lawn ended and a narrow border of flowering plants existed. Higgins gave them an admiring look.

'Yes, very nice, ma'am, I like flowers meself,' he said.

'Tell me,' said Polly, 'if part of the lawn at this end of the garden was dug up, we could grow vegetables, couldn't we?'

'Us, ma'am? Me as well?'

'Are you any good at digging up part of a lawn and preparing the ground for planting?' asked Polly.

'To me everlastin' regret, ma'am, no, I ain't,' said Higgins.

'You sure, or are you trying to dodge it?' asked Polly.

'Dodge it?' said Higgins. 'I forgive yer for using that word, ma'am, which don't apply. Me gifts point me to kitchens and cookin' and 'ousehold jobs.' His household jobs didn't include tidying up the marital bedroom. Polly saw to that, because it was a private place and out of bounds to the batman. 'I'm feeble in a garden, ma'am, but if yer really want a bit of this lawn dug up, I'll get a GD squaddie to do the work.' GD meant general duties, and usually fitted a bloke not particularly bright up top but well able to perform manual labour.

'Good,' said Polly.

'Could I ask who's goin' to plant the vegetables and look after them?' enquired Higgins cautiously.

'I am,' said Polly.

'Eh?' said Higgins.

'Me,' said Polly. 'I'm leaving the ATS.'

'Leaving?' Higgins looked sorrowful. 'You've got reasons, ma'am?' he asked, as if he didn't know.

'Yes, reasons,' said Polly.

'Consequent on you and the Major – I mean the Colonel – being a married couple, like?' said Higgins.

'You could say that,' said Polly.

Officially, only her commanding officer knew the reason, but Higgins, of course, being batman to Boots and his ATS wife, had put two and two together weeks ago, and was admiring of what they'd accomplished, considering Captain Polly was in her forties.

'Well, you'll still be livin' 'ere with the Colonel, eh, ma'am?' he said.

'And making myself useful,' said Polly.

Higgins, not too keen on what that might mean, said, 'Might I ask if I'm goin' to see a bit of you in me kitchen, ma'am?'

'Only if I'd like you to show me how to make jam or bake a cake,' said Polly, who knew Higgins regarded the kitchen as his own private territory.

'Ah,' said Higgins, looking dubious. Polly smiled.

'How about the good egg who can dig up part of this lawn?' she said.

'I know just the bloke,' said Higgins. 'Ginger Harris, very useful GD bloke, ma'am. I'll get me bike and cycle to HQ and rustle him up.'

'Thanks,' said Polly.

'Eh?' said Private Ginger Harris, GD.

'You 'eard,' said Lance-Corporal Higgins, 'you ain't that gormless.'

'Dig up a lawn?' said Ginger, broad, sturdy, and slow on the uptake.

'A bit of it,' said Higgins. 'What job you on at the moment?'

'Dunno,' said Ginger.

'What d'yer mean, you don't know?' said Higgins.

'I forgot,' said Ginger. 'No, wait a tick, I got gravel to rake.'

'Well, forget it again,' said Higgins. 'Grab a bike and foller me.'

'Well, I dunno I—'

'Don't make me cross,' said Higgins, 'or I'll split you down the middle.'

''Ere, that'll hurt,' said Ginger.

'You're right,' said Higgins, 'and it'll last a week.'

'Well, all right,' said Ginger. He landed up in the cottage garden a little later, where he was given a personal introduction to Captain Polly Adams, an ATS officer of vivacious looks, well-preserved figure, long lashes and high-class legs. He blushed as she gave him a sporting hello and a welcoming smile. She explained what she wanted him to do. Ginger surprised her then, and Higgins too, by pointing out he'd have to cut turves out, that a bloke couldn't actually dig up a lawn. You'd got to cut it out and lift each turf with a spade. The turves could be piled and left to rot down for use as rich earth.

'You sound like a gardener,' said Polly.

'Well, wasn't I a public park gardener in me home town of Chelmsford?' said Ginger.

'Capital,' said Polly, 'you're just the useful cove I'm looking for. There are spades and things in the shed, and they're all yours.'

'You leave it to me, mum,' said Ginger, 'I'll sort out what I need. What's under the grass is virgin soil, so you won't need no manure, not this year.'

'Here, watch your mouth,' said Higgins, 'don't use them kind of words to a lady that's also an officer.'

'If I might say so, which I will, them's gardening words,' said Ginger.

'Yes, very agricultural,' said Polly. 'You must teach me more. Look after him, Corporal Higgins,

67

he's a splendid bloke. Give him some refreshments.'

'Will do, ma'am,' said Higgins.

'I'm going back to HQ now,' said Polly, and left them to it. Ginger sighed.

'You got a problem, Private Harris?' said Higgins.

'Well, course I have,' said Ginger, 'I've just fell in love, ain't I?'

'Unfortunately for you, Private Harris, Colonel Adams saw her first,' said Higgins. 'So ruddy 'ard luck.'

In a military convalescent hospital near Farnham in Surrey, Lieutenant Felicity Jessop, blinded in an air raid, regarded her rehabilitation as a kind attempt by the experienced staff to make her believe she could still live a happy life. They were all first-class, and one gentle-speaking bloke was particularly good in the patient way he gave her lessons in Braille. Her favourite person, however, was Clara, her own specially caring nurse. She read letters to her and wrote letters for her. One from Lieutenant Tim Adams had just arrived. Tim, the son of Colonel Robert Adams, was her fiancé and a young man of courage and resolution who had made a name for himself with 4 Commando of Troon in Scotland. He'd expressed a determination to marry her and take her up to his billet in Troon, where he and his motherly landlady, Maggie Andrews, could help her in her wish to become a useful wife.

'Ready?' said Clara, nicely plump in the right places as far as men were concerned, although she had a dietary campaign of a reductive nature going.

Felicity, seated in the summer sunshine, said, 'Ready, Mother.'

'Thanks a bundle for Mother,' said Clara. 'Here goes. *Dear Felicity*—'

'Is that all?' asked Felicity. 'Nothing about "Dear Light of my Life"?'

'Not this time,' said Clara. '*Dear Felicity, I'm not angry about the news I've just received from you, telling me you've been refused permission to discharge yourself when we're married. I'm simply sorry. But I understand why, that you still need more time before the specialists are satisfied you can reasonably cope. Well, Puss, you and I must swallow the pill, especially as it's been prescribed by learned doctors. But at least I note the marriage can still go ahead as long as I give my word to deliver you back to Clara and the other caring professionals. We'll face up to the delay in being together under Maggie's roof. So no real worries, just a waiting time, and we're not too old to wait. Hope you don't feel too upset.*'

'Well, I do, I feel bloody upset,' said Felicity.

'Understood,' said Clara, and continued the reading. '*I'm fighting my own disappointment by beating the hell out of recruits who need to be shown how to stay alive on forced marches in full kit and a bit more. It's still killing me as much as them. Well, you know what I'm like when my feet are twice their normal size and my legs want to lie down and pass away, I'm not fit to live with, but it's the war, of course, and being resigned to the fact that the Commandos alone can win it. My chance to relax comes only when I'm tucked up in bed and trying to think of you in a grass skirt on a windy beach.*'

'That's his perverted self at work again,' said Felicity.

'Well, I agree with you, his perverted self has a lot going for it,' said Clara. 'I mean, I like a man who uses his imagination in a sexy way, don't you?'

'Listen, Mata Hari,' said Felicity, still trying to come to terms with the setback, 'do me the favour of finding one of your own.'

'Some are hard to come by,' said Clara, and went on with the letter. '*Ailing feet aside, I want you to know that despite the upset, I'm still looking forward to our special date on the ninth of August at your registry office, with your parents and mine in attendance. I'm tickled you're having Clara as your bridesmaid, as I owe her a lot for being your most invaluable nurse and will do all I can to show my appreciation, as well as taking advantage of my entitlement to give her a smacker or two.*'

'Look here, Goody Two-Shoes,' said Felicity, 'if I hear anything in the way of smackers going on between you and him, it'll be the end of our beautiful friendship.'

'Believe me, Felicity, I'll put up a desperate fight before I give in,' said Clara.

'He's a Commando,' said Felicity, 'so watch out for your dress and hang on to your knickers. Read on.'

'*There's only a few weeks to go now, and I'll be getting some obliging squaddie to make sure my buttons are polished, and I'll make sure myself that they're all done up in the correct order at the right time. If that's a weak joke, put it down to my condition. Everyone's always got some kind of condition bothering him up here, where there's still a lot of muttering going on about the casualties we took in*' *the last raid. If Clara's reading this, tell her to keep that comment to herself. Tell her to clasp it confidentially to her bosom and hold it there.'*

'What a prize lemon,' said Felicity lovingly.

'A girl hardly knows what he'll say next,' murmured Clara.

'Is his mention of your bosom doing something for it?' asked Felicity.

'Not a lot, just a giggle,' said Clara, and continued. *'I told you, didn't I, that my sister Eloise suddenly went overboard for my detachment commander who, like my dad, has just been promoted from major to colonel and second-in-command here. Eloise is now going about with a glazed look, as if she's jumped the gun, which Maggie tells me is happening with other engaged couples up here. She gets her information from other landladies who form Troon's gossip club. As you know, a number of the Commandos are engaged to Troon's Scottish sexpots, and the landladies don't miss a thing. It's just as well, for the sake of your honour as a Croydon Old Girl, that you're down there and I'm up here.'* Clara coughed.

'Are you reading the letter or making it up?' asked Felicity.

'Word for word, it's all here,' said Clara.

'I'll have him arrested one day for being pornographic,' said Felicity. 'God knows why I'm daft about him. Any more?'

'Yes,' said Clara. *'Eloise is getting married in October, which is just as well in my opinion, and I only hope another op doesn't get in the way.'* Felicity made a face at that. She inferred Tim was letting her know another Commando raid was being planned. What he refrained from mentioning was the fact that

71

Commando-style raids were taking place in the desert against Rommel's Afrika Korps, and that 4 Commando would probably be supplying reinforcements. '*But I mean to be with you in front of the registrar on the given day, and carry you off to my home for the weekend, where we'll do something to pass the time. Any ideas? Let me know. God bless, all my love, regards to Clara. Tim.*'

Felicity's brittle façade faded away and she let go a little sigh, her blind eyes in strange pain behind her dark glasses.

Clara heard the sigh and felt for her suffering but courageous patient.

Chapter Five

David Adams again alighted from the bus at the same stop as yesterday, and made his way over the fields, whistling as he went. At the gate close to Ashleigh Wood, Kate Trimble was waiting for him, this time in a white shirt-blouse and blue skirt. The day was full of July warmth, the sun just as bright. Its light played over her auburn hair and fiery tints danced.

'So you're here again,' she said from the other side of the gate, 'but you're a bit late.'

'The bus wasn't, so I can't be,' said David.

'Well, I've been waiting hours,' said Kate.

'You sure?' said David.

'Well, nearly hours,' she said, which meant ten minutes.

'Decent of you not to push off,' said David.

'Are you being cheeky?' asked Kate.

'No, I'm pleased to see you again,' said David.

'I should hope so,' said Kate, 'I'm not any girl, y'know. When I was only fourteen I won first prize as Venus in a swimming costume at a holiday camp.'

'At only fourteen?' said David. 'What a girl.'

'Oh, don't mention it,' said Kate, 'I grew up quick, that's all.'

'Quick, yes,' said David, and eyed her top. 'Yes, I've got the picture.'

'You'll get a black eye next,' said Kate, and laughed. 'Anyway, come on, let's go and sit down. I want to read you something.'

David opened the gate and went through to join her. He walked with her to the woods, where she sat down with her back against the foremost tree. She had a cardboard folder with her.

'I've got some time to spare,' he said, sitting down beside her. He thought her colourful and summery, and that the quality and style of her clothes were first-class. He supposed her aunt was well-off as a writer. 'What's the something you want to read to me?'

'You remember I told you me aunt's a writer?' said Kate. 'Well, I'd like to do writing meself, only not about places. I want to write about exciting things to do with the war.'

'You could start with a very exciting account of how you went to war with a hawthorn bush yesterday,' said David, 'and how it nearly got the better of you.'

'Oh, you dummy, call that exciting?' said Kate.

'Well, it was up to a point,' said David.

'Embarrassing, more like, seeing you were looking,' accused Kate.

'Not me, I've been brought up to look somewhere else when a girl's showing her undies,' said David.

74

'I bet,' said Kate. 'Anyway, stop talking about yesterday. Honest, you're a bit puerile sometimes.'

'I don't see how you can say that,' said David, 'you've only known me for about an hour.'

'It don't take an hour to find out someone's a bit puerile,' said Kate. 'Listen, I've written a sort of imagin'ry account of how I stole Hitler's secret plans.'

'What secret plans?' asked David.

'I hope you're not going to be a waste of time,' said Kate. 'Hitler's bound to 'ave all kinds of secret plans, isn't he? Just listen.' She began. '"*How I Captured Adolf Hitler's Secret Plans* by reporter Kate Trimble. It was evening when I found meself in Hitler's iron fortress looking down a corridor that was all dark and eerie in the faint light of a flickering German candle."'

'A what?' asked David.

Kate ignored that unnecessary question and went on. '"Holding me breath I ventured forth from me hiding-place and much to me anguish the towering figure of a Nazi Prussian Guard appeared which made me heart jump into me mouth but fortunately being in me disguise as a German tank commander with a moustache I was able to walk up to him in a highly confident way and wait for his challenge with a stern warlike look on me face and in me expression which made him draw himself up very cautious and polite—"'

'Half a mo',' said David, 'what about some commas and a few full stops?'

'What for?' asked Kate. 'You've got to get on with your writing if you want to make it exciting, and you

75

can't read it slow like a prayer for the dead. You don't want full stops holding it up.'

'Did I hear you say you're disguised as a tank commander?' asked David. 'I mean, you're wearing trousers, jackboots and false moustache, and pistols in your belt?'

'Well, of course I am,' said Kate, 'I couldn't 'ave got into Hitler's fortress dressed in me Sunday frock, could I? Use your loaf, David.'

'But wouldn't it be better to be a beautiful spy in a slinky black gown with a long fag holder?' asked David.

'Crikey, where you been all your life, in a nursery?' said Kate. 'Beautiful spies went out with flappers and fag holders years ago. My report's about me using me intellect more than me beauty, which I've got as much of as any feller, I'll have you know.'

'OK,' said David, 'I'll admit I don't have much beauty myself.'

'Brains, you dummy,' said Kate, 'and stop aggravating me or I'll knock some of your teeth out. The war's serious, y'know, and so's the way I'm writing about it.'

'Carry on,' said David. Kate carried on.

'I got to where I made the Prussian Guard draw himself up very cautious and polite. Well, from there it says, "and click his heels. He said halt who goes there, and I said Colonel Fritz Winkelhof—"'

'Pardon?' said David.

'Well, that's a German name, isn't it?' said Kate. 'Stop interrupting me and listen. "And I said Colonel Fritz Winkelhof tank commander weary from battle so take me to our great leader this minute as I have grave news for him and he said the leader was in his secret abode and not to be disturbed and I said take me to his secret abode immediate or I'll have you shot and with that I drew out me machine-gun and looked him in the eye with it although me heart was still in me mouth despite me brave posture and then he said very good at once Herr Tank Commander and I stiffened me resolve and followed him down the dank and gloomy corridor with me gun pointing very steady at his back despite me trembling hand. I knew I was—"'

'That's good, that bit,' said David.

'What bit?' asked Kate.

'Where you put a full stop in,' said David, 'or at least where it sounded as if you did.'

'D'you want to listen or don't you?' asked Kate.

'I'm hooked, honest,' said David, 'I can't wait for the end.'

Kate continued.

'"I knew I was in grave danger as the towering Prussian Guard went down other flickering corridors with me following and all me nerves jumping but determined to lay me hands on the secret plans I'd heard about in a Berlin night club where Hitler's confidential officers often went to be entertained by skimpy-dressed trollops in—"'

David strangled coughs. Kate gave him a vexed look.

'Sorry,' he wheezed.

'You've 'eard of trollops, haven't you?' said Kate.

'Well, yes—'

'Just listen, then,' said Kate, and continued. '"Where Hitler's confidential officers often went to be entertained by skimpy-dressed trollops in pink garters and where the officers often spoke very indiscreet when they were flushed with wine and where I was present meself one night and disguised as one of the gaudy ladies."' Kate paused for breath. '"At last the Prussian Guard reached a secret door which he opened with a secret key but then told me to wait while he went to ask the great leader if he would see me which I knew he probably wouldn't because my name as a tank commander was one I'd made up so as the Prussian Guard turned to go in through the secret door I stunned him with me machine-gun and he fell to the ground. I stepped over his body and went in and found meself in a secret filing chamber that I guessed had all Hitler's secret plans hidden away and which were now at me mercy, well, how lucky I was because the first file I opened contained just the ones that I'd been hoping to find so I snatched them up and just at that moment I heard Hitler himself speak which made me tremble very agitated—" David, what's up with you?'

'Oh, just another cough,' said David.

'Well, take something for it, can't you?' said Kate crossly. 'It's getting on me nerves.'

'Sorry,' said David, 'carry on.'

'Yes, "I heard Hitler himself speak which made me tremble very agitated because he shouted who's that in me secret filing chamber, answer up at once on pain of death but I didn't answer, I rushed out leaping over the body of the stunned Prussian

Guard to hurl meself through the glowering corridors and out of the iron fortress at the same place where I'd come in which I'm not permitted to reveal by the orders of me editor who has to answer to our head of Government whose name I can't reveal in secret matters like these but I can say was very pleased when I handed him the secret plans and he bowed to me when I left with a compliment'ry escort of Grenadier Guards. Yours faithfully, reporter Kate Trimble." I think reporters have to say yours faithfully, don't they, just to show they're not making it up.'

David said, 'Well, I – well, I—'

'Now what's up with you?' asked Kate. 'You've gone all hoarse.'

David fought the fight to keep his face straight and won by a whisker.

'I'm just lost for words,' he said.

'Oh, what d'you think, then, was it exciting, did it sound as if I've got some of me aunt's writing gifts?' asked Kate.

'It sounds as if you've got gifts of your own,' said David.

'Crikey, are you admiring of me story?'

'Never heard anything like it before,' said David.

'Oh, thanks,' said Kate.

'Just one thing, though,' said David, 'I'm not sure about your disguise as a tank commander. I mean, you're only about five feet five, and a German tank commander with a moustache would probably be a husky six-footer with ice-cold blue optics. Yours are green, like dewy parsley.'

'Oh, you wet week,' said Kate, 'whoever heard of

eyes like dewy parsley? Besides, this is about me as a daredevil woman reporter properly grown up.'

'See what you mean,' said David. 'But wouldn't you be a bit improperly grown up to act the part of a trollop in just pink garters?'

'Take that,' said Kate, and hit him with the folder. 'It wasn't *just* pink garters, you wooden-head. You'd better do something about your vulgar imagination or one day it'll land you in a bit of trouble.'

'Well, I'm very admiring of yours,' said David.

'Honest?' said Kate.

'Honest,' said David. 'By the way, did you read that report to your aunt?'

'Well,' said Kate, 'first she told me not to bother her at the moment, then she changed her mind and read it and said I'd got a lot of promise. Of course, I daresay me writing itself could be improved a bit.'

'Oh, just a few commas and some full stops would do it,' said David.

'I'll write another one some time and read it to you,' said Kate. 'D'you think I'd make a good reporter when I'm a bit older?'

'Not half, especially if the war's still on and you're sent on secret missions,' said David.

'Well, thanks,' said Kate. 'I'm glad you're admiring, and I expect you'd like to be one of my boyfriends, wouldn't you?'

'Not if your others would murder me,' said David.

'Oh, you dummy, they wouldn't know unless I told them,' said Kate, 'and even if I did, you don't

80

suppose they'd come all the way from London to bash your 'ead in, do you?'

'OK,' said David, 'we'll see a bit of each other, then.'

'All right, now you can come and have tea with me and me aunt,' said Kate. 'I told her I might bring you and she said all right.'

'I'll pop in to see Mrs Goodworthy on our way and let her know,' said David.

He did just that, and took Kate in with him, to introduce her.

'My,' said Beth, studying the pretty young lady, 'so you be Miss Martin's niece. I met her today in the Post Office Store. Mr Goodworthy and me hope you'll both be happy in Ashleigh.'

'Oh, thanks,' said Kate. 'We're already happy about it being a lot more quiet at night, for a start. Aunt Hilary got a bit chronic about all the bombs in London. Well, I'll take David to have tea with us now, and I'll come and have tea with him here one day, if you'd like.'

'You be welcome,' said Beth, thinking the girl bright as well as attractive, even if she did do funny things to the King's English, unlike Devon people. Apart from that, she'd rival any farmer's daughter.

'Aunt?' called Kate, as she entered Yewtree Cottage with David.

'I'm in here,' called Miss Hilary Martin from the little sitting-room next to the parlour.

'Come on,' said Kate to David, 'come and meet me aunt.' She took him into the sitting-room, already turned into a study by Miss Martin, who was sitting at a table under the window, a typewriter in front of her. She was using it, a cigarette between her lips. An ashtray held several butts. Some typed sheets of paper lay in a wire basket, another contained blank sheets, and beside the typewriter was a book with a faded jacket that bore the title, *The County of Devon*. The lady, in her early thirties, had a mass of black hair that she wore looped over her forehead like a divided curtain, a pale complexion, aquiline features and a brightly lipsticked mouth. 'This is David, Aunt,' said Kate. 'David, this is my aunt, Miss Martin.'

'How'd you do, Miss Martin,' said David.

The lady stopped typing, turned her head and removed her cigarette.

'Don't care much for Miss Martin, but how'd you do, young man,' she said in a throaty voice, and the cigarette went back between her red lips.

'I'm fine,' said David, noting that the bodice of her loose-fitting dress had a deep V, which he supposed would be called a bit Bohemian. 'How's your good self, might I ask?'

Out came the cigarette again.

'Oh, my good self is doing a spot of recuperating now we've left those infernal bombs behind,' said the sexy-voiced lady.

'You look as if you've settled in already,' said David. 'D'you like it here?'

'Haven't seen much of it yet,' said Aunt Hilary, 'but I've a feeling it's going to be a bit too quiet for Kate.'

'No worries,' said David cheerfully. 'Some of the

village lads'll make things a bit noisy for her when they get to know her.'

'Oh, thanks a lot, I don't think' said Kate.

'No, you'll find they're a lively bunch,' said David.

'Like those two we met at the gate? You can keep them,' said Kate.

Aunt Hilary smiled, and it made her look an alluring if slightly languid woman.

'Well, David,' she said, 'you might be able to help Kate find something agreeable to do, as I don't suppose she'll find a job easy to come by here.'

'I did notice your front garden looked a bit in need,' said David.

'In need of what?' said Aunt Hilary, putting her fag back.

'In need of tidying up,' said David.

'Excuse me,' said Kate, 'it was like that when me and Aunt Hilary moved in a few days ago, and the back garden's just the same.'

'Well,' said David, 'if you'd like, Miss Martin—'

'I beg you, not Miss Martin,' said the alluring lady, cigarette between her fingers again. 'As you're a friend of Kate's, Hilary will do.'

'Er?' said David.

'Very well, young man, Aunt Hilary. Definitely not Miss Martin. Too stodgy.'

'OK,' said David. 'Anyway, I'll show Kate how to do gardening. That'll be useful work till she finds some kind of job.'

'Look, I didn't come all the way here to do gardening,' said Kate. 'D'you know, Aunt, he told me yesterday I could 'elp to muck out cowsheds.'

'Oh, dear,' said Aunt Hilary, and stubbed out her fag.

'It can be a bit smelly, I admit,' said David, 'but it's a kind of honest country smell. Still, if Kate could bring herself to have a go at gardening, I daresay it would suit her better than mucking out.'

'Crikey, what a bossyboots,' said Kate. 'I can sort out me own life, if you don't mind.'

'I'm busy myself with my writing and exploring most days,' said Aunt Hilary.

'Yes, Kate told me you write books for travellers,' said David. 'She's proud of you, and so would I be if you were my aunt. It's a flag day for me, meeting an authoress.'

'Listen,' said Kate, 'can't you do something about sounding like Lord Muck?'

David could have said her aunt sounded like a sexy Lady Muck, but didn't, of course.

'You're a little slapdash yourself, Kate,' said Aunt Hilary. 'David, what d'you know about Dartmoor?'

'That it's got a prison, a lot of bogs, some wild ponies and is supposed to be a bit eerie at night,' said David.

'I must go there and explore,' said Aunt Hilary, 'I must take a long look at Devon while I'm here. On my jolly old bike. Let's see, about the garden, I asked a forthcoming lady in the shop this morning if she knew someone who could attend to it once or twice a week. Alas, she said casual labour was hard to come by on account of the war.'

'She was right,' said David, 'most of the villagers able to work are employed by Mr Grierson, the squire, so I'll be pleased to show Kate what to do and how to do it.'

'That's it, lead me to it,' said Kate, 'I'm nearly falling over meself to do digging.'

'Well, think about it and let me know,' said David breezily. 'The Government wants everyone to dig for victory.'

'There's other things, y'know,' said Kate, 'like comforts for the troops.'

'Hello, d'you knit socks for soldiers, then?' asked David.

'I'll go off bang in a minute,' said Kate. 'Listen, I'm not doing any knitting till I'm an old lady. I meant making up Red Cross parcels for our soldiers and sailors. Aunt, can we 'ave some tea now?'

Aunt Hilary, lighting herself another fag, said, 'I'll leave it to you to make a pot, while I finish a paragraph or two. Find some biscuits. There should be some in the tin.'

'Yes, all right, Aunt,' said Kate. Aunt Hilary wasn't fanatically domesticated, but she did keep her in good clothes and was her safeguard against being sent to an orphanage.

'I'll have a look at your back garden,' said David.

Kate, taking him through to the kitchen, said, 'Listen, you bossy ha'porth, I hope you're not going to be an aggravation in me life.'

'No, just one of your boyfriends,' said David.

'Tell me,' said Kate, filling the kettle, 'what d'you think of me Aunt Hilary?'

'Sexy,' said David.

'Sexy? Aunt Hilary? You're off your rocker. What about me, then?'

'You're young and pure,' said David, 'but I daresay you'll be sexy enough as soon as you're a woman.'

Kate shrieked with laughter.

'What about when I was showing me legs?' she said. 'Didn't I look sexy then?'

'Pretty,' said David. 'Well, I'll have a look at your back garden. I like the idea of helping you to get it in order.' He went quickly out of the back door just in time to escape having her chuck something at him.

Kate thought that in a few years he'd be the kind of young man who'd try to run a girl's life for her. Well, he'd be lucky if he thought he could run hers.

Later, over the pot of tea in the kitchen, David said the back garden wasn't too bad, that it was a conventional garden with a lawn that needed mowing and flower borders that needed weeding. Kate said she didn't know anything about mowing or weeding, and that she didn't want anybody to learn her. Aunt Hilary, languidly poised over her cup of tea, said she thought David was being helpful. David said he might be able to do the work himself, by putting in an hour now and again. Aunt Hilary gave him her alluring smile, and in her throaty voice said she'd want to pay him, and hoped he wouldn't take offence if she did. David said he wouldn't be a bit offended, but that as Kate was a friend of his he'd only charge a shilling an hour. Aunt Hilary said he'd be robbing himself, and David said it would be in a good cause.

'Well,' he said blithely, 'a feller's got to do what he can for two helpless ladies just up from London.'

'Aunt Hilary,' breathed Kate, 'can you believe he actu'lly said that?'

'I can believe our young man is a humorist,' said Aunt Hilary, whose ivy green dress, hitched while she was seated, was short enough to give her legs an airing. 'Yes, a humorist.'

'Bumptious more like,' said Kate. 'Listen, bumptious,' she said to David, 'how would you like it if one of us 'elpless ladies gave you a fat eye?'

'Count me out, Kate dear,' said Aunt Hilary with a faint show of distaste.

'And what's more, Lord Muck,' said Kate, 'what sort of a friend are you? Don't think you can make me second best to mowing and weeding when you come round. What am I going to do when you're out in the garden?'

'You could write some picture postcards of Devon to your boyfriends in London,' said David.

'Oh, yes, I could do a lot of that, couldn't I?' said Kate.

'Or you could write another reporter's story,' said David.

'Another interesting example of your own kind of talent, Kate,' said Aunt Hilary sweetly.

'But I don't want to do it all the time, do I?' said Kate, and expounded bitterly on what a feller owed a girl who'd done him the favour of making him one of her boyfriends. David said he'd take her for country rambles at weekends when he wasn't busy doing jobs for old ladies or helping Mr Goodworthy up at the farm. Mr Goodworthy worked long hours in the summer and liked a bit of help with the cows. How did Kate feel about helping with cows? Kate said she felt she couldn't wait, that she loved cows, of course, and would go mad if she couldn't bring one home with her.

Aunt Hilary interceded to say that as David probably knew Devon better than she did, perhaps he could offer a different kind of help by recommending places of interest that were worth a detailed mention in the book she was currently putting together for travellers. David said he didn't know what his recommendations would be worth, but thought she might find Buckland Abbey, Widecombe and Dartmoor very interesting.

'How kind,' said Aunt Hilary. 'Would you have heard of any of my books, David?'

'Well, much to my regret, I can't say I have,' said David.

'I don't suppose he hears anything much except cuckoos,' said Kate.

'There were some up to their tricks in April,' said David. 'Well, I think I'll push off now, I've got some work to do on a new chicken house for Mr Goodworthy.'

'Oh, really?' said Kate. 'What's he want to live in a chicken house for when he can live indoors with Mrs Goodworthy?'

Aunt Hilary laughed. David grinned.

'See you tomorrow, Kate?' he said.

'Yes, all right, but don't get too keen on me,' said Kate.

'All right, I won't,' said David, 'I daresay you've got affections for a bloke back home. So long, Miss – um, Aunt Hilary – thanks for the tea and biscuits, and I might be able to do a bit of mowing for you in a day or so. Afterwards, I could show Kate how to clean the mower.'

'That's done it,' said Kate, and chased him out of the cottage. Off he went, whistling, but she was laughing as she watched him go. When she re-entered the cottage, Aunt Hilary was already back at the typewriter and smoking another fag. Kate began thinking about what to prepare for supper. Well, Aunt Hilary might be a good writer of books for travellers, but she was no cook. And she'd never married. Kate's late dad always said his distant cousin liked men but not the bonds of marriage.

Chapter Six

The first thing Colonel Robert Adams, known as
Boots, noticed when he arrived home from duty at
six-thirty was a large bare patch at the top of the
lawn. He observed it from the window of the little
dining-room.

'Corporal Higgins?'

'Sir?' called Higgins from the kitchen.

'What's happened to the lawn?'

'Dug up, sir.'

'Dug up? What for, suspicion of a UXB?'
Unexploded bomb.

'No, sir. Instructions from madam.'

'My wife instructed you to dig up half the lawn?'

'Not me, sir, no. I ain't much cop at diggin' up
lawns, me forte being an interpretation of Mrs
Beeton's cookery recipes, which I trust don't give
cause for complaint. Have to report, sir, that
Captain Adams instructed Private Harris of the GD
squad, and Private Harris dug it up accordin'.'

'For what reason?' Boots entered the kitchen.

'Vegetables, sir.'

'Come again?' said Boots.

'Your lady wife says she's goin' to grow vegetables, sir.'

'Repeat that, Corporal Higgins, and look me in the eye this time.'

'Yes, sir. Right, sir.' Corporal Higgins looked his officer squarely in the eye. 'Madam clearly informed me, sir, that she's goin' to grow vegetables.'

'Well, damn me,' said Boots.

'Yes, sir,' said Higgins. 'It's consequent, I understand, on her retirement from the ATS.'

'I see,' said Boots gravely. 'Is madam at home?'

'Upstairs, I believe, sir, and supper'll be on the table in about half an hour.'

'What a splendid bloke you are, Corporal Higgins.'

'Yes, sir, thank you, sir.'

Boots left the kitchen, and from the small hall of the cottage he called.

'Polly?'

'Up here, old love,' called Polly, and appeared on the landing. She was in skirt, shirt and tie, her smile reminding him of the moment when he first met her, an ex-ambulance driver of the Great War, a vivacious young woman heading into the Wild Twenties in an attempt to find the promised fruits of victory, fruits that proved to be bitter. He could not honestly say she had had an immediate appeal for him. In fact, he had thought her slightly absurd, and although she appeared and reappeared in his life, always in a beguiling mood, at no time had he seriously considered being unfaithful to Emily, his wife. All the same, over the years Polly had grown

91

on him more than he realized, and after absenting herself from his life following the death of Emily in an air raid, she reappeared. There she was, still beguiling, but in a different way, a woman gently appealing to him to end her long impatient wait in the wings. It seemed then the most natural of gestures to ask her to marry him, to be his wife. She had done so in a way that surprised him, showing that beneath her flippancy there existed a warm, loving and feminine woman. Together they had achieved the totally unexpected, the conception of a child.

'Polly?' he said again, and Polly, looking down at him from the landing, saw his smile and its familiar note of whimsy. She wondered how she had managed to endure the years of being on the outside of his life.

But she said lightly, 'Something tickling you, old sport?'

'I understand from Corporal Higgins that you're relinquishing your commission in order to grow vegetables,' said Boots.

'Well, I had to apply for my discharge sooner or later,' said Polly, 'but I must find something to do. I'm not going to sit around or join a ladies' knitting circle.'

'You've had a good part of the lawn massacred,' said Boots.

'I know, darling, but I don't think vegetables grow through grass, do they? Some very accommodating GD private did the work for you.'

'For me?' said Boots.

'Yes, wasn't that obliging of him?' said Polly. 'Oh,

you owe me five bob, by the way. I felt I had to give him something for his labours. You don't even have to dig the ground over, he did that as well for you. Over supper I want to pick your brains about what seeds to plant. Ginger said that with the summer so advanced—'

'Are we talking about Private Harris of the awkward squad?' asked Boots.

'Yes, he said that with the summer so advanced it's too late for some kinds of vegetables, unless we can still get certain seedlings, like leeks, from a nursery. You don't mind, do you, that I'd like to have a vegetable plot to look after?'

'I thought you were going to interest yourself in cooking,' said Boots.

'Oh, I'm all for learning how to serve up a meal, but—' Polly dropped her voice a little. 'But Corporal Higgins simply won't let me into the kitchen. He'll be happier if I'm in the garden, creating my vegetable plot.'

'You'd like to do that?' said Boots.

'I can't wait to begin,' said Polly.

'Come down here and let me salute you,' said Boots.

'At once, O Great Sultan,' she said, and she was quick in her descent of the stairs. Boots thought her too quick. Her right heel caught in the carpet runner halfway down, and she tripped. Boots leapt and held her as she tumbled into his arms, her head striking his shoulder. He thanked God that her quickness had alerted his reflexes. He felt a little shiver run through her body. She clung, her face on his shoulder. 'Silly me,' she said muffledly.

'Don't ever make haste on stairs again,' he said, and lightly caressed her hair.

'No, darling, I won't, I promise. Thanks for being where you were.' She lifted her head, her expression rueful. 'Nearly did it in, do you think?'

'Oh, I think you're tougher than you give yourself credit for,' said Boots reassuringly. 'You'd have absorbed a few bruises.'

But they both wondered, of course, what a fall down the stairs would have done to the child of twelve weeks, especially as Polly was in her forty-fifth year and had never carried before.

Lance-Corporal Higgins was lucky enough to be billeted with his wife in a nearby farmhouse. Mrs Higgins worked for the farmer, along with Land Army girls, but wasn't sure if the billet was lucky for her. The farmer, a slightly bow-legged widower of fifty, fancied her something chronic, and her daily safeguard was in the form of a pair of Land Army breeches that, going spare, she'd fastened onto like a drowning woman to a lifebelt.

As a batman, Higgins was on duty from seven-thirty until eleven each morning, and from five to eight-thirty each evening. Arriving in the presence of his wife on this particular evening, he gave her a smacker and his latest piece of news.

'Me lady's leavin', Molly.'

''Ere, what d'you mean, your lady?' asked Mrs Higgins. She was twenty-four, he was twenty-eight, they were both from Battersea and had been married a year. Higgins was lean and wiry, she was happily buxom. She believed a buxom state was what nature intended for all women, but that it had careless moments and didn't pay enough attention to every woman's development. 'Your lady, you said?'

'Me lady captain,' said Higgins.

'Well, Charlie,' said Mrs Higgins, round face rosy from her outdoor work, 'kindly remember I'm your lady wife.'

'And ain't you been that for a year, me love, and ain't I yer proud 'usband?' said Higgins.

'Saucy more like,' said Mrs Higgins, and giggled. 'Me mum never told me nothing about saucy 'usbands, she only said to shut me eyes and think of Christmas. Anyway, I suppose your lady captain's leavin' the Army on account of what you told me in secret about 'er condition.'

'Regulations mean she's got to leave,' said Higgins. 'Army personnel ain't allowed to 'ave babies in an orderly room or on a battlefield. Mind you, Molly, as soon as Captain Adams told me she was gettin' her discharge, I 'ad worries about not 'aving the kitchen to meself, but much to me relief she's goin' to grow vegetables.'

'She's what?' said Mrs Higgins.

'Carrots and beans and stuff,' said Higgins. 'Ginger Harris dug up part of the lawn for 'er.'

'But what about 'er condition and being over forty?' said Mrs Higgins.

'Me lady captain's a goer, a reg'lar game gal,' said Higgins, 'and even if she was sixty I'd lay yer odds she'd still be able to dance a livelier hornpipe than any sailor.'

Mrs Higgins, demurring, made a little sceptical sound between pursed lips.

'I don't know I'd like to see 'er doing anything like that now, not the way she is,' she said. 'I don't know she even ought to be workin' in the garden. A nice quiet lie-down ev'ry day, morning and afternoon, that's what she should treat 'erself to at her age and in 'er condition.'

'She'll be all right,' said Higgins. 'Well, gardening ain't like doing the high jump. I've got admiration for me lady captain as long as she don't interfere in me kitchen. Which reminds me, me love, 'as Farmer Bickers been a trial to yer today? Interfering with yer?'

'I'm safe while I've got me breeches on,' said Mrs Higgins, 'but I've got to admit he's been standin' a bit close to me jumper just recent, and breathin' very 'eavy.'

'I'll send Corporal June Cooper round to see 'im,' said Higgins. 'She's six feet and don't believe in not 'elping out if there's a bloke in need close by. Mind, old Bickers'll probably pass out and expire by the time she's finished givin' 'im her kind of help. That reminds me, I feel I'd like to be close to you meself on account of certain ideas that've come over me.'

'Oh, certain saucy ideas?' said Mrs Higgins, and giggled again.

'See that, me love?' said Higgins, and pointed a finger at his right eye.

'It's nothing I don't see every day,' said Mrs Higgins.

'You ain't lookin' 'ard enough,' said Higgins. 'Can't yer see me twinkle? You know what a twinkle means, don't yer, me love?'

'Oh, me gawd,' said Mrs Higgins, 'you've got your lady captain's private condition on yer saucy mind, but didn't we say we didn't ought to start a fam'ly with a war on?'

'Well, I'll admit we did, but me twinkle's overcoming me prudence,' said Higgins, and carried her buxom self forthwith to the bedroom.

Being married to her, he had no trouble with her breeches, except it naturally took a lot longer to get them off than a skirt.

Polly would have laughed had she known that her condition had put a twinkle in the eye of Lance-Corporal Higgins and resulted in him giving Mrs Higgins a terrible blushmaking time.

'Charlie – oh, yer saucebox!'

Chapter Seven

Over breakfast, Boots read a letter from Eloise, his daughter by a Frenchwoman, now dead.

Dear Papa, I'm in despair, yes, what do you think, my fiancé Colonel Lucas is being transferred to the Long Range Desert Group in the Middle East. Colonel Lucas was a rugged and purposeful fighting soldier. The Long Range Desert Group, known as the LRDG, was a Middle East formation of selected officers and men proving highly capable of harassing Rommel's Afrika Korps. They were striking at the enemy with the same kind of hit-and-run tactics as the Commandos, blowing up German fuel dumps and destroying German fighter planes on landing strips. They were now asking for experienced home-based Commandos to join them and help extend their operations. Churchill, always quick to encourage something original, was in favour. Eloise, however, wasn't in favour of Colonel Lucas going. *I have told him he can't go, that we're to be married in October, that he must tell London so, but he says he can do no such thing and that if he did London would order his court-martial and execution. Isn't that utterly despairing for me?*

He has to select twenty-four officers and men from among the best here in Troon, and to take them with him. He says the Middle East Command will be drawing similar contingents from other Commando groups. Although he's put Tim on the list, he hasn't included him in the draft that's to embark in two weeks. He wanted to, he thinks so much of him, but knowing how important it is for Tim and Felicity to be married soon, he's managed to defer his transfer until after their wedding. As you know, Tim fractured his collarbone during the last raid, and Colonel Lucas is using that as an official reason for deferring his departure. He insists Tim will have to follow soon after the marriage, that his commitment to the Commandos will be the more important then. Tim's swearing about things, yes, but have you heard the latest news on Felicity? The hospital authorities are refusing her permission to discharge herself after her marriage to Tim. They say she needs a few more months with them, and they're able to compel this because she hasn't yet been discharged from the ATS. She's still under orders, would you believe.

Colonel Lucas says that under these circumstances, Tim's departure won't be as traumatic for her as it would have been if she were living with him in Troon. I suppose it is better for her to remain in hospital while he's overseas. But, Papa, what about me? No marriage, and no husband. My despair is very real. Can't you do something for your devoted daughter? Tim says everyone in the family knows you are the best fixer ever. Is that right, best fixer? I send you my love and my hopes, also much love to Stepmama Polly. Kisses, Eloise.

Boots passed the letter to Polly.

'From Eloise, our despairing daughter,' he said.

'Thank you, darling, for saying she's mine as well as yours,' said Polly, 'but despairing?'

'Read it,' said Boots, and Polly perused the letter in thoughtful fashion from start to finish.

'I feel for Tim and Felicity,' she said, 'but yes, under the circumstances, it probably is better for Felicity to remain in hospital to continue learning how to cope with the worst of her limitations. It doesn't surprise me that there's a call from the Middle East for Commandos, and that both Tim and Colonel Lucas will be going. But does it worry you?'

'All our young men are at risk, Polly,' said Boots. 'Tim, Bobby, Jonathan, Nick Harrison, Freddy Brown, they're all serving, but I don't allow myself to worry too much.' A little smile came into being. 'Vera Lynn keeps my pecker up.'

'Some pecker,' said Polly. 'As for Eloise, what young lady in love wouldn't despair at such a turn of events? But couldn't the marriage take place by special licence before her beloved Luke embarks?'

'It probably could,' said Boots, 'but some men don't like the idea of marrying a woman one day and going off to face shot and shell the next. Bobby, for instance, confided to me that he won't marry Helene until the war's over. I can understand that. Well, is there anything less recommendable than making a woman your wife and your widow all in the space of a few weeks if the fates are against you, as they often are? Wouldn't Colonel Lucas have that in mind?'

'That kind of wartime marriage would depend

on the woman,' said Polly. 'Let me tell you that if you'd given me the chance to marry you in 1916 when we were both in Albert, I'd never have said no, even if you'd been going up the line to the trenches the day after.'

Boots looked doubtful.

'Are you seriously saying that if we'd met in Albert, you'd have married me within the space of my short time there?' he asked.

'Darling, you still don't know your Polly, you still don't realize that when I first met you in Sammy's grotty junk shop I'd have jumped over the moon for you.'

'H'm,' said Boots.

'You think that's absurd?' said Polly.

'Men are known for their imperfections, women for their absurdities,' said Boots, 'and I'm devoted to yours.'

'Exceptionally devoted?' said Polly.

'Exceptionally,' said Boots, 'so don't part with them.'

'Now you've made my day,' said Polly. 'But what about Eloise and your reputation for being the family's best fixer?'

'Well,' said Boots, and mused a bit while spreading marmalade on a slice of toast.

'Oh, come on,' said Polly, 'you can wangle a way round for our young French lady, can't you?'

'There's one possibility,' said Boots.

'Has there ever been a time when you haven't seen a light, you old sport?' said Polly.

'It's like this,' said Boots, and went on to say that with the continuing reinforcement of the Eighth

Army, contingents of ATS admin personnel were regularly departing for places like Cairo, Alexandria, Port Said and Beirut. A posting to any of these Middle East sites of Army administration would put Eloise as near to Colonel Lucas as she could hope for, and there was no reason why she couldn't be included in one of the drafts, providing a military figure with the right kind of influence pulled a few strings.

'You?' said Polly.

'To the War Office, I'm nobody,' said Boots.

'To me, darling, you're everybody,' said Polly.

'But you're not the War Office,' said Boots.

'God forbid I should ever come to look like a Whitehall building,' said Polly.

'Amen to that,' said Boots. 'However, this is the point where you come in.'

'Ask anything of me,' said Polly, 'I can always kick and scream.'

'I'll only ask you to speak to your father,' said Boots.

'Dear Sir Henry?' said Polly.

'A much respected military figure with undoubted influence,' said Boots. 'Mention Eloise and her despair, let him know you cherish her happiness and that you'll never fail in your devotion to him if he'll get her on a draft to the Middle East. Weep a few appealing tears, of course—'

'Say that again,' said Polly.

'I think you could manage to speak to your father with a caring stepmother's sob in your voice,' said Boots.

'If I didn't know you, I'd think I was listening to the man in the moon,' said Polly. 'Look, old scout, you're the father of Sir Henry's expected grandchild and accordingly the apple of his eye, so why can't you speak to him yourself?'

'I've had too many favours from him, Polly,' said Boots, 'mostly favours that have kept you close to me against all the regulations concerning serving husbands and wives. So I think you're the one to speak to him about Eloise. All things considered, you're an exceptional woman as well as being Sir Henry's one and only daughter. In short, too irresistible to be denied.'

'In short, so are you, you old darling,' said Polly, and laughed.

Higgins made himself heard.

'Colonel Adams, sir, beg to inform you it's O-nine-hundred, well past your usual getaway time. Also, ma'am, Private Harris is 'ere with a bunch of what 'e says is advanced seedlings that could grow into winter cabbages if you planted 'em today with a drop of nourishing water.'

'And what'll happen if they're planted tomorrow?' called Polly.

'Might grow into bananas instead, ma'am.'

'I'll plant them this morning,' said Polly, 'and forget about bananas.' She smiled at Boots as he came to his feet. 'Ask Sir Henry if he can find time to phone me, will you, darling?'

'I think he's overseeing manoeuvres of our new armoured division today,' said Boots, 'but I'll ask him if he can phone you before we leave for the field of battle.'

*   *   *

Sir Henry did phone his daughter. Polly made known her wish for Eloise to be posted to the Middle East, and why. Sir Henry enquired if he was being asked to pull strings. Polly said yes, that was what some fathers were for, especially fathers who were generals.

'Damn me,' said Sir Henry, 'I'm to—'

'Yes, thanks so much, you've always been an obliging old sport,' said Polly. 'Neither of us wants to see two lovers thousands of miles from each other, do we?'

'Thousands of lovers have to suffer that,' said Sir Henry.

'I know, darling,' said Polly, 'but there are exceptions, and in my delicate condition I don't think I could share my stepdaughter's despair, and you wouldn't want me to, would you?'

Sir Henry laughed.

'Minx,' he said.

'Love you too, dear old thing,' said Polly.

'I'll see what I can do,' said Sir Henry.

The dialogue in an innocuous London office was in French, and aimed at Helene Aarlberg and Bobby Somers.

'Your name, *mademoiselle*?'

'Claudette Dubois.'

'Papers?'

'Here.'

'You come from Lyons, I see.'

'Yes, I was born there.'

'At what address?'

'Twenty-four Rue de Marseilles.'

'Your birth date?'

'January 5, 1919.'

'Your present address?'

'It's there, in my papers.'

'Your present address?'

'Such fussiness. I'm living at eleven Avenue du Parc, Lys.'

'Lys?'

'In the Haute Garonne.'

'Your work?'

'I keep a millinery shop, below my apartment in Avenue du Parc. Do you wish to buy your wife a hat?'

'My wife has enough hats. Do you have an assistant?'

'A manageress.'

'Her name?'

'Madame Simone Clair.'

'Is she Jewish?'

'No. A good Catholic.'

'Everyone these days is a good Catholic. What was your father's trade?'

'Profession. He was chief clerk to a lawyer, Raymond Valery, well-known and much respected.'

'Who is this man you're with?'

'My fiancé. He's—'

'Let him answer up. Your name, m'sieur?'

'Henri Beaumonte.'

'Papers? Thank you. You're from—'

'Marseilles.'

'Born where?'

'Marseilles, as my papers show.'

'Some papers, m'sieur, don't always show the truth. Do you know your date of birth?'

'Of course. July 15, 1918.'

'So you are twenty-two?'

'No, twenty-three.'

'What was your mother?'

'A woman.'

'Don't be insolent.'

'My mother was a nurse until she married my father, an engineer employed by Citroën.'

'What is your work?'

'I'm a freelance journalist.'

'Living where?'

'I have a room in my fiancée's apartment.'

'Did you serve in the Army?'

'Yes, from 1938 until 1940, when—'

'Never mind. Take your papers back. And here are yours, mam'selle.'

'Well, sir, how was that?' asked Bobby of Major Buckmaster, head of SOE (French Section).

'Yes, how did we do?' asked Helene, the young Frenchwoman whom Bobby had brought to England from her home in France not long after the Dunkirk evacuation. Helene was now an officer in FANY, Bobby had recently been promoted to captain, and the two of them had volunteered to be sent to France to help the growing Resistance. 'We were better than before?'

They had been examined a week ago in respect of their new identities, and been found just a little wanting. Since then they had, by extra application, fully taken on their identities as Claudette Dubois and Henri Beaumonte.

Major Buckmaster, more than satisfied with the progress made by these two adventurous young people, said, 'You were both excellent, except never advance any information that isn't asked for. Be like most people when stopped, resentful rather than forthcoming. Resentment is natural to the innocent, eagerness to please a sign of the guilty.'

He then advised them that Helene would be known to the movement only by her code name of Lynette, and Bobby by his code name of Maurice. That restriction included the way they addressed each other in the presence of other agents or French members of the Resistance, and they were to remember that the moment they began their journey to France.

'When will that be?' asked Bobby.

'I can't give you an exact date at the moment,' said Major Buckmaster. 'Have either of you ever heard of the small town of Lys?'

'Yes,' said Helene, 'it's in the Haute Garonne, not far from Toulouse, although I've never been there. But it's where you have placed us in our identity papers. Is it where you are going to send us?'

'We are planning to, yes,' said Major Buckmaster. 'We have information to the effect that the Vichy authorities have set up a concentration camp for French Jews in Lys, and that they are processed there before being sent to German camps, from which, it appears, they are unlikely ever to emerge alive.'

'No, no, *mon Commandant*, this cannot be happening in Lys, not in France,' said Helene. 'I am against the Vichy government and the traitors who form it, but I cannot believe any French authorities would conspire against their Jewish citizens by delivering them into the terrible hands of Hitler's Nazis.'

'Regrettably,' said Major Buckmaster, 'our French contacts inform us that Petain has promised his German overlords a gradual round-up of all French Jews. Lys is one of the assembly centres. We would like you two to meet a man who needs your help in gathering all kinds of informa-tion concerning this centre, particularly routines. This man is a Jew himself, working underground from Carbonne, not far from Lys. He can't go into Lys himself. He's known there, and as a Jew, he'd be picked up. We've provided him with an RT operator, a Scotswoman, code name Marcelle. I'll let you have further details when the time comes to send you on your way. Do you both feel you would like to undertake this mission of assistance?'

Helene and Bobby looked at each other. Helene, a statuesque Latin brunette very much in love with Bobby, nodded. The stalwart elder son of Lizzy and Ned Somers, Bobby thought Helene the choicest and gamest young lady who had ever come out of France. He gave her a little smile, then turned to Major Buckmaster and said, 'Yes, we'd like to go.'

'Good,' said Major Buckmaster. He was dealing with the unusual. SOE preferred agents to know nothing, or very little, of each other. This meant that in the event of capture no agent, even under torture, would be able to disclose any worthwhile facts about others. If both these young people fell into the hands of Gestapo units operating in Vichy

France, thought Major Buckmaster, how long could the man endure the sight of the woman being subjected to torture before giving the right answer to every question? The particular risks of their mission would always be present. 'I'll see you again in the near future. By the way, to enable you to work together as you asked, and to make it natural for you to be seen together and to reside at the same address without arousing suspicion, we thought it a good idea to send you out as an engaged couple. You've no objections?'

'Bobby will have none,' said Helene. 'How could he have? It will give him the privileges of a fortunate man.'

'Let me know sometime what fortunate means,' said Bobby. 'I'm a simple bloke generally.'

'You still make terrible jokes,' said Helene.

Major Buckmaster smiled.

While the German armies were preparing for the advance that would threaten Moscow, RAF Bomber Command was at its now regular work of aerial attack. A daylight raid by Blenheims on the German-held port of Rotterdam shattered seventeen enemy ships and severely damaged others. The Blenheims flew in at mast-height to make their attack, and were clearly seen by Dutch people out on the streets. Just as clearly, the bombers' crews observed the welcoming upraised arms of these people, evidence of their support for the RAF, and the confidence they now had in the general accuracy of the British bomb-aimers.

In the Western Desert the British Eighth Army

was at war with General Rommel and his Afrika Korps. The British had been enduring hair-raising battles, in which Rommel had come out on top all too often. He was over the border of Cyrenaica into Egypt, and Churchill was relying on General Auchinleck, Commander-in-Chief of the Eighth Army, to complete the preparations for an offensive and throw him back.

Friday, July 19

Vi and Susie were sharing a pot of afternoon tea with their redoubtable mother-in-law, Mrs Maisie Finch, known to her family as Chinese Lady for various reasons, including the fact that she had almond eyes. Vi and Susie left the war alone to begin with, since Chinese Lady said she always got more than she wanted of that from her cantankerous wireless. She was quite convinced that other people's sets weren't as aggravating as hers in the way it dispensed news she didn't want to hear.

Vi and Susie having informed her they were making their monthly visit to their evacuated children this coming weekend, she produced some money from her purse and asked them to share it out amongst the young ones.

'Mum, there's three pounds here,' said Vi.

'Well, yes, ten shillings each for your three and the same for Susie's three,' said Chinese Lady, always a generous grandmother. 'I expect with their summer holidays coming up they can do with an extra bit of pocket money, poor lambs. All this time away from their fam'ly homes, ever since the war started. I just don't know that it's natural.'

'It doesn't feel natural to me and Sammy,' said Susie, 'and if we didn't take Paula with us each time, she'd be growing up a stranger to her sister and brothers.'

'Tommy's always growling about not havin' a proper fam'ly to come home to,' said Vi. 'If only those Germans could be trusted to leave London alone for good, he'd bring our three back tomorrow. Me dad says bombing civilians is a – well, I can't repeat what he actu'lly said, but he meant it was a shockin' way to try and win a war, and never ought to be allowed. My, the language he used. Mum nearly had seven fits, but I'm glad she didn't.' Vi smiled. 'Well, she always says seven's an unlucky number.'

'It's the war,' said Susie, bringing it to the fore now that Vi had mentioned the air raids.

'The war, Susie?' said Chinese Lady, wishing it would go away.

'Yes, Mum,' said Susie, 'it's making everyone use language.'

'Well, Susie, I hope no-one brings any language into this house,' said Chinese Lady. 'Vi, how's that growing son David of yours? I heard from your Alice in her last letter that he's nearly as tall as his dad.'

'Yes, he is,' said Vi. 'Oh, I had a letter from him only this morning saying that when he's mature he might buy a farm and take to farming.'

'Buy a farm?' said Chinese Lady.

'That's what he said, Mum, but not until he's got enough money, of course,' said Vi. 'He's savin' hard, like Sammy did when he was young.'

'I can't think there's any farms round here,' said Chinese Lady. 'There might be some in Dulwich. I'll ask Edwin, he'll know.'

Vi forbore to mention David had Devon in mind. She knew her mum-in-law didn't approve of anyone in the family being out of convenient reach. She was sad enough as it was to have Rosie living her married life in Dorset, which she considered on a par with a foreign country.

'Oh, David also mentioned he's met a Camberwell girl with a lot of imagination—'

'Imagination?' smiled Susie.

'I don't like the sound of that,' said Chinese Lady, who considered imagination not the sort of thing any girl should have a lot of. It was bad enough some young men having ideas about being lords and masters when they were married.

'David said Kate probably gets it from her aunt, the one she lives with and who writes books,' remarked Vi.

'Oh, that sort of imagination is different,' said Chinese Lady, willing to believe that writers of books were held in high regard by respectable people like vicars. 'And we mustn't forget a lot of nice girls come from Camberwell.'

That set the tone for the remainder of the homely chat.

112

Chapter Eight

Saturday morning

At a little after eleven, David stopped to speak to Miss Hilary Martin's engaging if scatty niece on finding her at the gate of the cottage her aunt was renting. He had seen her every day since his original encounter with her last Monday. She always looked as fresh as morning, a gift of appearance with which some girls were born, whatever their background. A typically pert and perky cockney girl, he liked her, even if she did consider him lah-di-dah, which he wasn't.

'What-oh, Kate, how's it going?' he asked.

'How's what going?' asked Kate, morning-pure in peach.

'Your writing, for a start,' said David.

'Oh, a bit at a time, according to me artistic mood,' said Kate. 'Writing is called a form of art, did you know that?'

'Like cooking?' suggested David, dressed in a sports shirt and belted trousers, his head bare, his face tanned.

'What d'you mean, like cooking?' asked Kate suspiciously. She'd quickly come to find him a bit of a leg-puller, the saucy lump. 'Yes, what d'you mean?'

'Well, at school once during a science lesson, our class was having a discussion on whether it was gas cookers or electric cookers that turned out the better food, and why,' said David. 'Old Bunsen-Burner Bidwell—'

'Old who?' said Kate.

'Yes, our science master. He said not to forget something was always owed to the cook. He said cooking was a creative art practised daily by our mums, and not to forget it.'

'Crikey, d'you 'ave to talk so posh?' said Kate. 'I feel sorry for you sometimes. Down the London markets, you could get kids chucking things at you.'

'You sure?' said David. 'Only I've met all kinds down markets, funny old gents, retired teachers and haughty old ladies, all talking posh. But I've never seen kids chucking things at them.'

'Only because they've got respect for old people,' said Kate. 'Oh, well, you can't help it, I suppose, poor bloke, and I'm learning to live with it instead of giving you the push.'

'Well, you're living daily with your posh-talking aunt,' said David.

'Yes, but she's been in foreign parts,' said Kate, 'and she's older than you.'

'I can't see why they're reasons for—'

'Well, they are,' said Kate. 'Listen, are you going to mow our grass again today?'

David said it wouldn't need another mow until next week. He had done the honours with a mower found in the garden shed, and Miss Aunt Hilary had paid him with a handsome silver florin and a beguiling smile, for which he said he'd do it next time for just ninepence, or a bob, if she liked. What a kind young man you are, she'd said, and quite dashing too. He told Kate now that when the school holidays started next Tuesday he'd come and show her how to use the mower and weed the flowerbed. Kate said she hadn't been brought up to use mowers or weed flowerbeds, and if he tried to show her how she'd do him a serious injury. It wasn't work for a girl who wanted to be a reporter, she said, and besides, at her old Camberwell home, there'd been a nice back yard that didn't need any mowing or weeding.

'Can't you come round and do our flowerbeds yourself this afternoon?' she asked.

'No, sorry, my parents are coming,' said David.

'Oh, is it today they're coming for the weekend?' asked Kate.

'They'll be arriving any minute now,' said David, 'they always leave home early. They'll be with an aunt and uncle of mine, who'll go on to spend the weekend with their kids in Broadclyst, then pick up my parents on their way back tomorrow. By the way, Mrs Goodworthy says you can come and have Sunday tea with us.'

'Oh, pleasured, I'm sure,' said Kate, 'and I'll be honoured to meet your posh parents, won't I?'

'They'll be leaving before tea,' said David, 'they always like to get home before a raid starts.'

'Oh, I hate those raids,' said Kate.

David said he'd look forward to seeing her arrive in her Sunday frock, and that even if his posh parents were still there, they wouldn't look down on her. Nobody would, considering she was the niece of an authoress and had once won first prize as Venus in a swimming costume.

'Well, I do 'ave my own special qualities,' said Kate. 'Hello, who's this?'

An open car was entering the village, having turned off the main road half a mile back. It passed the Post Office Store and reached the first cottages.

David, taking a look, said, 'Here they are, my parents!'

'What, in that posh car?' said Kate.

It was Sammy's car. He was at the wheel, Susie beside him. Tommy and Vi were in the back, little Paula between them. The men were bareheaded, the ladies in spring coats and fetching hats. Sammy brought the car to a stop close to David.

'Is that you I'm looking at, David?' he asked.

'And with a young lady, if I ain't mistaken,' said Tommy.

'Hello, David,' smiled Susie, and glanced at Kate. My, she thought, she's a bit special.

'David, you're browner every time we come,' said Vi, thinking how tall he was growing and how attractive the girl was. She was probably the Camberwell girl he'd mentioned in his last letter. 'You're getting to be a real young man, I must say.'

'Just ageing gradually,' said David. 'Hello, everybody, and how's my best girl?'

'Me?' said Vi.

'Me?' said Susie.

'Mummy, it's me,' said Paula.

'Not half,' said David, 'so how's yourself, Roly-

116

Poly, how's your cotton socks?' Paula giggled. 'And how would you like to meet a new friend of mine?'

'Let's all 'ave the pleasure,' said Tommy. Handsome, honest and down to earth, he eyed Kate with frank interest. 'Might we be introduced, me lad?'

'This is Kate Trimble,' said David, 'she's new here.'

'Nice to know you, Kate,' said Tommy. 'I'm David's dad, this lady is his mum. That's his Aunt Susie, the driver bloke is his Uncle Sammy, and this little pickle name of Paula is theirs, if I've got me fam'ly facts right.'

'Hello, everyone,' said Kate.

'Pleased to meet you, I'm sure,' said Vi, liking the girl.

Kate blinked. David's parents really were cockneys. Not loud and hearty, but cockneys all right.

'Oh, mutual,' she said.

'Granted,' smiled Sammy, thinking David was already showing good taste. The girl was a picture, her dark auburn hair as striking as poor old Emily's had been. 'You an evacuee?'

'No, me and me Aunt Hilary came down from London just a week ago for some peace and quiet,' said Kate.

'Her aunt's a famous writer,' said David, 'and Kate once won first prize as—'

'They don't want to hear all that,' said Kate, 'so kindly don't mention it.'

'David givin' you trouble?' smiled Tommy.

117

'Tommy, our David wouldn't do that,' said Vi.

'Oh, I never let boys give me trouble,' said Kate cheerfully. 'Like my Aunt Hilary told me, you put your foot on troubles before they rise up and get to be a headache.'

'Know what you mean,' said Tommy.

'Yes,' smiled Vi, 'me and David's dad know he's a bit of a lad that can make himself heard.'

'I know someone else like that,' murmured Susie.

'Bermondsey Town Crier, I expect,' said Sammy. 'Well, nice to have met you, Kate, and if you'll excuse me, Tommy, I'll push on and drop you and Vi at the pub.' Tommy and Vi always put up at the village inn.

'Carry on,' said Tommy. 'We'll see you at the Goodworthys' in a bit, David.'

'Yes, I won't be long, Dad,' said David.

'Goodbye, Kate,' smiled Vi, always agreeable.

''Bye,' said Susie.

''Bye,' called Paula, and Sammy drove away. Susie and Vi waved.

'Well,' said Kate to David, 'I don't think your parents are a bit posh.'

'I did tell you they weren't,' said David. 'Glad we've got it settled. By the way, I was thinking that in the autumn, you could find space in your garden for some blackcurrant bushes.'

'Oh, I like blackcurrants,' said Kate, 'I'll tell Aunt Hilary you'll plant some for us, which could earn you a just reward.'

'What's a just reward?' asked David.

'Cup of tea and a cucumber sandwich,' said

Kate. 'I make nice cucumber sandwiches.'

David grinned.

'I thought you meant a smacker from Aunt Hilary,' he said.

'Crikey, you don't want a smacker from a woman nearly old enough to be your mum, do you?' said Kate.

'Not if she's smoking a fag at the time,' said David, and Kate laughed. 'Don't forget Sunday – oh, I daresay your aunt could come too, if she'd like to. Mrs Goodworthy'll be pleasured.'

'I'll ask her,' said Kate.

'Come about half-four,' said David. 'So long till then, Kate.'

'So long,' said Kate, and went in to tell Aunt Hilary about the invitation to Sunday tea with the Goodworthy family. Aunt Hilary gave a delicate shudder and asked to be excused from the horrors of a Sunday tea. 'Horrors?' asked Kate. 'But it might be nice.'

'Nice can sometimes be boring,' said Aunt Hilary, studying a map of Devon. 'You go, but count me out. I'm thinking of taking a bike ride tomorrow, anyway, to explore some Ancient Briton monuments, like Nembury Fort. I'm also going out this evening.'

'Yes, all right,' said Kate, thinking her aunt could sometimes be a bit offhand about people. She didn't seem to need them, and as for friends, she'd said she left them all behind when she escaped from France and the invading Germans. She liked getting out and about by herself, but Kate acknowledged she did sometimes remember to thank her for preparing most of the meals and doing most of the housework.

She went airily off on her bike that evening to look at the countryside. Kate did some writing while wishing David would come round. The village didn't offer a lot of excitement to a girl who liked the bustle and buzz of London, especially with its wartime atmosphere and its many uniforms. She liked the RAF uniform best. Lots of its wearers had done deeds of daring in the sky.

She did some more writing, and was soon smiling over it.

Tommy and Vi had a very enjoyable weekend with their offspring and the Goodworthys, the two families sharing a mutual liking as well as a Sunday dinner of which the high point was a large roast leg of Devon lamb. Beth said Jake had come by it in a way that hadn't done any damage to their ration books, which meant, of course, that the squire had allowed him the natural perks of a valued employee.

Vi became aware during the weekend that Alice was so keen on her education she was hoping she could win entrance to a university in time. Bless us all, thought Vi, imagine if me and Tommy had a daughter at university.

Paul, she thought, was still a bit of a scamp, just like young Posy. He was much more likely to give a rabbit a run-around than feed it lettuce leaves. He was also given, apparently, to the old Walworth trick of collecting beetles in matchboxes and handing the boxes to young evacuee or village girls, who shrieked and jumped a mile when they opened them.

As for David, he was an Adams all right. He took after his dad in his good looks, after his Uncle Boots in the way he talked, and after his Uncle Sammy in his ambitions. He was an admirer of Sammy as a self-made man. He'd been delighted to receive ten shillings from Grandma Finch, and had quickly dashed off a letter of thanks to her, telling her it was a boon to his savings.

There was another family wedding in the offing. Boots's son Tim to a young lady called Felicity Jessop in August. There was to have been yet another, that of Boots's daughter Eloise to an Army officer in October, but that had been postponed because the officer, a Colonel Lucas, was going overseas shortly. Tim's wedding was to be a quiet one, with just Boots and Polly there, on account of the unhappy fact that Felicity had been blinded in an air raid, which was dreadful for her, and for Tim too in a different way. Vi had agreed with Tommy that even if all the family had been invited, they still wouldn't have let the children come home for it. There were still air raids.

Tommy, having been taken with the girl Kate, had a man-to-man talk with David about her. David conceded she was a bit special.

'Well, if she's your girlfriend,' said Tommy, 'me and your mum wish you luck.'

'Oh, I'm just one of her several boyfriends,' said David.

'Up to you to see off the opposition, sunshine,' said Tommy.

'I'd like to remind you, Dad,' said David, 'that I've still got my schooling and my work.'

'If you mean you've got a job, that's news to me,' said Tommy, 'and how'd you manage it, anyway?'

'I mean my work helping on the farm, doing gardening for old ladies, cleaning people's windows and other odd jobs,' said David. 'It all helps me with my savings, which I look on as capital for my future.'

'Takin' after your Uncle Sammy, are you?' said Tommy.

'I do have ideas about getting to be his kind of self-made man after the war,' said David.

'Well, you've got me best wishes there, son,' said Tommy, 'but don't forget all work and no play ain't supposed to be all that bright for a feller. Like your grandma's always saying, young people ought to grow up knowing how to be sociable.'

'I'm sociable, Dad,' said David.

'I know you are,' said Tommy. 'But peaches like Kate don't grow on gooseb'ry bushes, y'know.'

'Got you, Dad,' said David, 'but it's nothing serious, not at our ages.'

'At your age,' smiled Tommy, 'I had a soft spot for your mum, she being just as young as Kate, only her own soft spot at the time was for your Uncle Boots. Fortunately, she came to recognize me sterling worth.'

'Fortunate for me as well,' said David, 'or I'd never have been born.'

Tommy laughed and clapped his elder son on the shoulder.

'You'd have arrived somehow, young feller-me-lad,' he said.

On Sunday afternoon at four, Sammy and Susie, with Paula, turned up to collect Vi and Tommy for the drive home. Off they all went five minutes later, everyone else calling goodbye to them.

Posy then departed for Daisy Ricketts' birthday tea, and at four-thirty Kate arrived for tea with the Goodworthys. Aunt Hilary, she said, wasn't able to come, she'd had to go out.

'Well, you be very welcome yourself,' said Beth.

'More than a tidy bit,' said Jake, noting that Kate looked a rare young sprite in primrose.

Paul and Abel made themselves known in boisterous fashion, then Kate met Alice.

'Oh, how'd you do, pleased to see you,' said Alice.

Kate smiled.

'Oh, thanks,' she said.

'David told us your aunt writes books,' said Alice.

'Yes, about foreign places,' said Kate, at which Paul said the best idea for a good book would be about ferrets catching rabbits and having them for tea.

'Gruesome boy,' said Alice, 'I wouldn't read a book like that.'

'Well, you're a girl,' said Paul, 'you only read soppy books.'

'Excuse me, if you don't mind,' said Alice, 'I'm reading a Charlotte Brontë novel this term.'

'There y'ar, told you,' Paul said to Abel, 'soppy books.'

'Well,' said Beth, smiling at Kate, 'Mr Good-worthy and me hope Sunday tea will be a mite better than soppy.'

It proved a very pleasant tea, enjoyed around the parlour table, Beth having overcome all kinds of wartime shortages to make sure such goodies as home-made blackberry jam, blackcurrant jam tarts and a large jam sponge were provided for the hungry young. Beth's larder contained a hand-some stock of pre-war home-made jams. There were blackcurrant bushes in the garden, picked every summer, and hedgerow blackberries in profusion, picked every autumn. Beth used precious wartime rations of sugar as wisely as she could, which meant saccharine went into tea, and diluted honey on porridge. Up at the farm, as else-where, fields of sugar beet were proliferating, to help with the country's own sugar yield.

Jake made sure Kate was well looked after, and everyone made sure there was no lack of talk. It seemed to Kate that the Goodworthys and the evac-uees were all one family, they were so in tune with each other. She herself talked about what a change it was to move from London to Devon. She asked David if he liked country life.

'All the time except when we hear about bombs on London,' said David. 'Then we're all waiting for letters from home to tell us if everyone's all right.'

'We lost our Aunt Emily in a daylight bombing raid last August,' said Alice, wincing a little at the memory.

'Oh, I'm sorry,' said Kate. 'I lost me mum and dad in a raid in the autumn, they died together.'

'My, that were terrible, you poor lamb,' said Beth, and became sympathetic and sorrowful. Alice, Paul and Abel fell silent. David, sitting next to Kate, gave her arm a little squeeze, which made her swallow a bit, and Jake spoke with feeling.

'Kate, I be certain sure they Germans be devils for what their bombs do to women and children,' he said. 'It were a downright piece of devil's work, robbing you of your parents.'

'Oh, I'm over the worst,' said Kate, although she sometimes woke up at night to find herself tearful. 'And Aunt Hilary's been very kind, takin' me in and lookin' after me. I'd just like to see the Germans get beaten to make up for me losing Mum and Dad.'

'Well, they Russians might be running backwards right now,' said Jake, 'but there'll come a day when they'll stop and turn round, like they Old Contemptibles did at the Marne in 1914, and then, I reckon, the beating of they Germans will begin. Ah, and we'll be coming at their backs, us and our Empire cousins. We owe our Empire cousins, that we do, eh, Beth?'

'It be something this country shouldn't ever forget,' said Beth. 'When you be older, Posy and Abel, and you, Paul, you remember Australia and Canada and the like.'

'Indian soldiers too,' said Jake.

'I won't forget,' said Paul. 'And I won't forget you, Uncle Jake, nor you, Aunt Beth, nor Posy and Abel.'

'Bless the boy,' smiled Beth.

'We're away from home, Aunt Beth,' said Alice, 'but we all feel it's as much family here as at home.'

125

'Good on you, Alice,' said David, liking his sister for saying that.

'Well, this family be all the better for having you three,' said Jake, who knew there were people in Ashleigh and other villages whose resident evacuees still gave them a tidy amount of headaches.

Alice introduced a different note.

'Kate, you've got lovely hair,' she said, gazing in sincere admiration at Kate's auburn waves. She was fair-haired herself, like her mum. 'Our Aunt Emily's was just like yours, really lovely.'

'Oh, thanks,' said Kate.

'Old Mrs Passmore down by Church Lane wears a wig,' observed Abel solemnly. 'Fell off in church once, when her was kneeling. Hat fell off too.'

'Old Mrs Passmore don't be wanting everyone to know, young Abel,' said Jake.

'Vicar knows,' said Abel, 'he saw it.'

'Was she bald underneath?' asked Paul.

'Abel's not saying,' said Beth.

'But, Ma,' said Abel, 'I saw too, and—'

'You're not saying, you hear?' said Beth. 'Now, might I be cutting more cake for anyone?'

Anyone turned out to be everyone, and the large sponge cake took such a beating that it ended up as if it had never been.

Chapter Nine

After tea was over, David took Kate for a walk in the evening sunshine.

'Where're we going?' she asked.

'Here and there, round and about, anywhere your legs fancy,' said David.

'Never mind me legs,' said Kate, 'if you think you're going to find a place where you can kiss me, you can think again.'

'I never think about kissing—'

'I bet,' said Kate.

'Still, if you're keen yourself, I'll consider it,' said David.

'I'm keen on giving you a poke in the eye, more like,' said Kate.

'Well, if you change your mind,' said David, taking in the fresh air, soft and summer warm, 'I charge at the rate of two for sixpence.'

'You what?' said Kate.

'It's an old family custom,' said David, 'started by my Uncle Sammy.'

'I don't believe this,' said Kate. 'You actu'lly saying you charge a girl for kissing her?'

'Tanner for two, five for a bob,' said David. 'If she's keen.'

'I'm dreaming,' said Kate. 'I mean, what girl's going to pay for being kissed by a Lord Muck?'

'I thought I'd mention it just in case,' said David, keeping his face straight, and accordingly looking as if he was a serious follower of what he called a family custom.

'Crikey, what a dummy, I never met a dafter one,' said Kate. 'You must've fallen on your loaf sometime. Oh, well, can't be 'elped, it's happened to other blokes. It's peculiar it's always blokes. Well, it's always blokes that go daft at an early age.'

'It only happens to girls when they're older?' suggested David.

'I didn't say that,' said Kate.

'No, I did,' said David.

'Girls aren't daft the way boys are,' said Kate.

'What way are girls daft, then?' asked David.

'Stop being clever and come to our cottage,' said Kate. 'Then I'll read you me latest imagin'ry report.'

'Leg it, then,' said David, 'I can't wait.'

Seated on the back step with her a little later, David was all intrigued ears as Kate began her reading.

'"*My Secret Journey to Adolf Hitler's Mountain Lair* by Special Reporter Kate Trimble exclusive. At the end of me intrepid flight in a plane that had been fired on several times by German guns I gave the controls to me RAF escort that happened to be a handsome and dashing admirer of me courage and beauty—"'

'Kate, I did mention about a few full stops,' said David.

'Never mind that,' said Kate, 'let's get on with it. "Holding me breath I jumped out wearing me parachute and landed on the mountain that was next door to Hitler's fortress lair which I was to blow up with the dynamite I was carrying as well as me machine-gun and gas mask and grenades——"'

'Wait a bit,' said David, 'you sure about carrying a machine-gun, a gas mask, a bag of grenades and a bag of dynamite all at once, and doing a parachute drop as well?'

'Everything was in one bag, wasn't it?' said Kate. 'Wake up, David, or you'll never be a famous fighter pilot.'

'Right, see what you mean,' said David. 'Carry on.'

Kate carried on.

'"As soon as I landed I released me parachute, rolled it up and ate it——"'

'Pardon?' said David. 'You ate the parachute?'

'Well, to keep it secret, of course,' said Kate. 'Eh? Ate it? No, course I didn't, you loony. How could anyone eat a whole parachute? Hid it, I meant, not ate it. Slip of me tongue. Anyway, "As soon as I landed I released me parachute, rolled it up and hid it, then brushed me Paris dress down to make meself look tidy and formal——"'

'I don't want to keep interrupting——'

'Well, don't,' said Kate, 'or you'll aggravate me again like you did before.'

'But you're not dressed as a tank commander this time?' said David.

'Well, of course I'm not, what's up with you?' said Kate. 'I was dressed for tea, wasn't I? It was afternoon and Hitler always has a sort of Devonshire tea with cream buns in the afternoons, and I thought if I was discovered lurking about I could always say I'd been invited and was looking for the tearoom.'

'Right, see what you mean,' said David. 'Carry on, Kate.'

'"I began to make me dangerous way up to Hitler's lair determined to overcome anyone that tried to stop me, well, me mission of destruction was highly important and I'd promised Sir Walter Scott—"'

'Kate, Sir Walter Scott's dead along with Dickens.'

'Not that one, you dummy,' said Kate, 'I mean Sir Walter Scott that's my imagin'ry head of our Secret Service who's a friend of my imagin'ry editor. Anyway, are you enjoying it so far?'

'I'm hooked, on my honour,' said David.

'Oh, that's good,' said Kate, 'I'll carry on, then. "I'd promised Sir Walter Scott I wouldn't fail so I set me teeth and climbed up to the balcony of the lair by me feet and fingernails and then one of Hitler's Stormtroopers appeared and demanded to know who I was and what I was doing, so I said I'd come to tea by invitation and he asked what was in my bag and I said a fruit cake, of course. Well, he still wanted to see what the bag contained so as he bent over it I stabbed him with me hatpin which made him sink groaning to the ground and gave me the chance to take out a grenade which I put inside his uniform and then threw him over the balcony and halfway down the mountain-side the grenade exploded and blew him up in mid-air. Then I stood and listened for a minute and caught the sound of teacups rattling from somewhere—"'

'Er, about chucking the Stormtrooper over the balcony,' said David, 'he'd have been a dead weight—'

'Oh, stop being finicky,' said Kate. '"So I made me way down to an underground chamber where I was to use me dynamite to blow Hitler's lair to bits and where to me delight there was already a big stack of dynamite and barrels of gunpowder as if fate was hand-in-glove with me. But then another Stormtrooper appeared and I said stand aside and let me pass but he just stood there staring at me Paris dress which I admit was very French so while he was struck deaf and dumb with admiration and desire I glided by only to have him suddenly come to and take brutal hold of me and lift me off me feet. To my 'orror I was carried body and soul into his bedroom with me Paris dress nearly falling off because of my desperate struggles and I knew the sickening beast meant to submit me to a fate worse than death which I knew would upset me. With a low evil laugh he threw me on the bed."' Kate halted in her flow of words and drew some needful air into her lungs.

'Are you short of breath?' asked David. 'So am I, and I'm not sure I can listen to what's coming next.'

'That's all,' said Kate.

'Can't be,' said David.

'I mean it's all for the time being,' said Kate. 'I'll

finish it tomorrow or the day after. Is it exciting up to where I've got?'

'Paralysing,' said David, 'but you sure at your age you ought to write about a fate worse than death?'

'Well, as I haven't actu'lly suffered it personal,' said Kate, 'I admit I'm a bit stuck. I thought you might be able to help.'

'Pardon?' said David.

'Well, you and girls,' said Kate.

'What d'you mean, me and girls?'

'Well, have you—?'

'Me?'

'Yes, with girls.'

'Listen, you monkey, at my age—'

'Yes, but you're tall and look as if—'

'How can anyone look as if—'

'Well, you do,' said Kate, 'and I need someone to 'elp me write about what I'm innocent about meself. I'm not a common girl about that sort of thing, y'know.'

'You're aiming to be a saucy one, though,' said David, 'but I can't help.'

'You mean you haven't—?'

'No, of course I haven't, and don't tell me again I look as if I have.' David examined her suspiciously then because Kate had let a giggle slip out. 'Blow me,' he said, 'you're having me on.'

'No, I'm not,' she said. 'I mean, how can I continue me exciting report if I don't know anything about – well, you know.'

'No, I don't know,' said David, 'but have you thought about asking your Aunt Hilary for help? I know she's single, but she looks as if—'

'Yes, doesn't she! A sort of worldly woman,' said Kate. 'Well, after she'd read all I'd written so far, I asked her if she could help, but she said although she'd suffered a fate worse than death several times herself without actu'lly expiring, she wouldn't dream of giving me any of the shocking details.'

'There you are, then, leave it out,' said David. 'Here, hold on, your Aunt Hilary wasn't serious, was she, about all that suffering?'

'Why not?' said Kate. 'When she was living in Paris, she met all kinds of exciting men, like glamorous Frenchmen, romantic Italians, handsome Germans, hot-blooded Spaniards—'

'Leave off,' said David, 'you're not going to get me to believe they all – um –'

'All what?' said Kate. 'Me aunt used to be very desirable in her appearance, and me dad often pointed out she was asking for trouble by living in Paris at the mercy of the kind of men that he himself wouldn't let past his doorstep. The trouble with me Aunt Hilary, he said, was that she was so middle class she couldn't mix with honest working people, and it was her own fault if she was meeting with fates worse than death in Paris.'

'You horrible girl, he didn't say anything like that to you,' said David.

'No, not exactly that,' said Kate, 'but I sort of read between the lines. Look, how far have we got now to me knowing how to write about what the evil Stormtrooper is set on doing to me?'

'Nowhere,' said David.

'Where?'

'Nowhere!' David let himself be heard loud and clear.

'Crikey, there's no need to shout,' said Kate. 'I'm only asking for someone to help me overcome my ignorance.'

'Well, I haven't overcome my own yet,' said David, 'and it's not bothering me.'

'Crikey, I hope you're not stuffy,' said Kate. 'Listen, though, I've just thought. The Stormtrooper's going to have a bit of a job with his evil desires, anyway, because don't forget I'm still clutching me bag of grenades and dynamite.'

'That's it,' said David, 'shove a stick of dynamite down his trousers while he's trying to tear your dress off. Then we can all sleep easy instead of worrying about what your imagination is doing to you.'

Kate shrieked with laughter.

'Crikey, drop a stick of dynamite down his trousers?' she said. 'What about your imagination, then?'

'It's nothing like yours,' said David.

'Not much,' said Kate.

'I still think you're having me on,' said David, and gave her a second suspicious look.

Kate had let slip another giggle.

And when he departed later, she was laughing.

Alice spoke to David while he was at work finishing the new chicken coop in the fading evening light.

'That girl Kate,' she said.

'What about her?' asked David, hammering in some final nails.

'She's nice,' said Alice.

'Well, I like her, I admit,' said David.

'It's rotten for her, losing her parents,' said Alice. 'What's her aunt like?'

'A bit like Pola Negri, the film star who used to play vamps lying on tigerskin rugs,' said David.

'Sort of sexy and exotic?' said Alice.

'I'm not up with that kind of language,' said David.

'Not much,' said Alice. 'I know you, you only admit to knowing the minimum about everything. Are you gone on Kate?'

David struck home the last nail and straightened up, and Alice thought how manly he looked considering he wasn't sixteen yet. That was the Adams look. Cousins Tim and Bobby had acquired it while still in their teens.

'She's fun,' said David.

That was another Adams thing. If somebody was fun, that was good enough.

'Wish you luck, then,' said Alice.

'Wish you luck too, sis, with your exams,' said David.

'Wish the war was over,' sighed Alice.

It was a fact that Hitler was doing his best to get the war with Stalin over double-quick, which wasn't what Churchill wanted, not by a long chalk. The Prime Minister was already arranging for arms to be shipped to Russia by regular convoys. It would be a deadly run to Murmansk for the merchant ships and their destroyer escorts. But Stalin was demanding aid, and Churchill was acceding, even if he thought the demand a bloody cheek on the part of a man who had refused to listen to warnings about Hitler's intentions to invade.

Chapter Ten

Meanwhile, Daisy Ricketts' birthday tea had taken
place without Stevie Clark doing anything to offend
Mrs Mumford, apart from his tendency to reach for
things instead of asking for them to be passed.
Generally, however, he behaved himself, didn't
break anything and was quite nice to Daisy, who
had given her face and hands a good wash, and
brushed her hair commendably.

After tea, the three young people were allowed
to play in the garden, although Daisy first asked Mrs
Mumford if she could help with the washing-up.

'I think not, missy.'

'I won't break nothing, honest, Mrs Mumford,
and you've been very nice givin' me a birfday
tea and all.'

'I'll feel happier handling all the china myself,
thank you,' said Mrs Mumford, but not unkindly.
'Join your friends in the garden.'

Mrs Mumford had a small lawn beyond which
was a fair-sized vegetable plot. Not being well-off,
she grew as many of her own vegetables as she
could, and the plot was now green with produce.

While she did the washing-up she was able to keep an eye on the antics of the boy and the two girls through her kitchen window. Her collie dog, Jamie, successor to her previous one, Jackie, was frisking about with them, emitting the occasional happy bark and chasing anything they threw.

The watchful lady called scoldingly from the open window.

'Don't you be encouraging him to ruck through the vegetables now!'

'No, Mrs Mumford,' said Daisy, who was enduring the awkwardness of feeling grateful to her humourless wartime guardian. She hissed to Stevie, 'Mind where you throw the sticks, can't you?'

'That boy can't throw, anyway,' said Posy.

'Course I can,' said Stevie, and hurled a stick to the very end of the garden. It landed close to the dry stone wall, in a corner. Joyfully, Jamie sped in chase. Reaching the stick, he seized it between his teeth and worried it. It didn't fight back, so he dropped it and began to dig. Mrs Mumford was now replacing dry crockery on the dresser.

'Come on, Jamie, bring it back,' called Daisy.

'That dog be daft between its ears,' said Posy.

'Betcher he's diggin' for a bone,' said Stevie, and they all went up by way of a centre path of flagstones to see what the collie was up to.

'Oh, crikey,' breathed Daisy, 'he's diggin' in the grave.'

The grave was that of the late lamented Jackie, a low mound with an oak plaque on which an epitaph was painted.

IN MEMORY OF JACKIE, A LOVED COMPANION

Jamie was digging away, bits of earth flying.

'Must've been a big dog,' observed Stevie, looking at the mound.

'Yes, it's a big grave, don't it be?' said Posy.

'Jamie, stop it,' said Daisy, taking hold of the dog's collar and pulling.

Out came Mrs Mumford then.

'How dare you!' Her voice was sharp. 'Come away this minute. I won't have you desecrating that grave. Jamie!'

Jamie stopped digging, and his tail went between his legs. Mrs Mumford called him again, more sharply. Jamie, low to the ground as if creeping up on sheep, sidled his way up to his mistress. Daisy, Posy and Stevie followed.

'Mrs Mumford, we only went up to see what Jamie was doing of,' said Daisy.

'Missy, you be knowingful that I don't allow interference up there,' said Mrs Mumford.

'Honest, we didn't do nothing, we only went to make Jamie come back,' said Daisy, looking a little sad at being misjudged.

'Well, Posy and the boy can go home now,' said Mrs Mumford.

'Please, can't they stay a bit longer?' begged Daisy.

Mrs Mumford looked severely inclined to deny the request, then relented.

'Very well, a little longer,' she said. 'I'll fetch a game and you can all play it out here on the table.'

'Could we have Ludo?' asked Posy.

'I be willing to fetch that if it'll keep all of you

out of mischief,' said Mrs Mumford.

'Oh, thanks,' said Daisy, and subsequently she, Posy and Stevie set to at Ludo around the table in the warm evening light. During the game, out came Mrs Mumford once more. From the garden shed she took a spade and went up to the grave, Jamie at her heels, and she used the spade to repair the damage.

Jamie came back with a bone between his teeth.

'There y'ar,' whispered Stevie, 'told yer 'e was diggin' for a bone, didn't I? She's dug it up for 'im. Blimey, what an old fussbag.'

'No, she ain't,' said Daisy, 'she's just respectful about the grave, that's all.'

'Daisy, she don't go to church,' whispered Posy.

'Well, nor don't I, and she don't make me, eiver, but it don't mean we're not respectful about graves,' said Daisy, and cast a glance. Mrs Mumford was using the flat of the spade to tamp the mound. ''Ere, whose go is it?'

'Mine,' said Stevie.

'No, it ain't, it's Posy's,' said Daisy. 'Go on, Posy.'

'Yes, all right, Posy,' said Stevie generously. He was sure it was his go, but he liked Daisy too much to argue with her at her little birthday party. It was Daisy who made him blush sometimes, much to his everlasting mortification. Well, the feeling could exist for a whole minute, which was as good as everlasting.

Posy threw a six and whooped with delight. Mrs Mumford came back, glanced suspiciously at the three of them, and said, 'Noise, noise,' before re-entering her kitchen.

'She ain't 'ardly the life and soul,' mumbled Stevie.

A few minutes later, Mrs Mumford came out yet again, with a tray.

'Here,' she said, 'I found some sweets and sherbet powder. There be two sweets and a glass of sherbet apiece.'

They each received two mint humbugs and a glass of sherbet water, happy acceptance of which was accompanied by another of Mrs Mumford's disappearing acts.

'I just dunno about her,' said Stevie.

'She be sweet on you, Stevie,' said Posy teasingly.

'Well, you're sort of pretty, Stevie,' said Daisy.

Stevie blushed to his roots.

'Pretty? Me?' he said. 'Course I ain't.'

Daisy whispered, 'D'you want to give us birfday kisses, Stevie?'

'Me?' gulped Stevie.

'You'll 'ave to be quick,' whispered Daisy.

'Yes, don't be taking all day, Stevie,' whispered Posy.

'Oh, blimey,' breathed Stevie.

The girls leaned, pursing their lips. Stevie plucked up courage and over the table he delivered a quick kiss on Posy's mouth, and attempted an even quicker one on Daisy's pink lips. Daisy's lips, however, pressed saucily and trapped the kiss. Stevie blinked and went red.

Mrs Mumford having observed nothing of this, Daisy giggled as they all sat straight up again.

'Crikey, look at you, Stevie,' she said.

Stevie was beetroot red, but somehow wasn't

suffering any mortification. In fact, he hardly knew he was blushing.

Posy's smile was impish.

'I be going to kick you for all that kissing, Stevie,' she said.

'I've got a feeling I won't feel it,' said the mesmerized Stevie. Well, for a thirteen-year-old boy who thought about being a boxer when he was older, it was mesmerizing getting a real smacker from young Daisy.

Young Daisy giggled again. She was having a lovely little birthday party.

Later, when Posy and Stevie had gone, Daisy spoke quite shyly to the stiff lady.

'Please, Mrs Mumford, could I thank yer ever so much for me birfday party?'

'Child, it was little enough, and how did you come by that stain on your best frock?'

'Oh, lor,' breathed Daisy, looking. 'Oh, crikey – oh, I just don't know, Mrs Mumford, it must've come when I wasn't noticing.'

'H'm,' said Mrs Mumford.

'Could it be a blackberry jam mark?' ventured Daisy.

'That or blackcurrant,' said Mrs Mumford, 'one be as stainful as the other.'

'Please, are you cross?' asked Daisy.

'Missy, we're all young once,' said Mrs Mumford, 'so no, I don't be cross.'

If she was cross at all, it was with Daisy's wretched parents. Their indifference to the girl was down-right shameful.

Stevie was living with Mr and Mrs Plackford, a middle-aged couple. They had suffered the devil's own job in trying to civilize the London boy during his first months with them. Eventually, Mr Plackford chucked the rules away and walloped the unruly lad for trying to set fire to a haystack. Stevie didn't write home to complain, he took the walloping and quietened down.

When he returned from Daisy's birthday party, he told the Plackfords what a fuss Mrs Mumford had made about the grave of some old dead dog being 'dessicated'. He explained how her living dog had come to start digging for a bone, which hadn't been no-one's fault except the dog's. And it wasn't half a big grave for a dog, a good six feet. No wonder Jamie, the live one, buried bones in it. Anyway, the old fussbag had tidied the grave with a shovel and found a bone there herself, which she gave to Jamie.

'Created, did she, Stevie?' grinned Mr Plackford, who helped look after the squire's greenhouses.

'First orf she did,' said Stevie. 'Still, she give us a swell tea wiv pilchards and bread and jam and cake before that, and sweets and sherbet water after, so she ain't actu'lly a bad old girl.'

'She be Christian at heart, I'm thinking,' said Mrs Plackford, 'even if she don't go to church these days.'

Later that evening, however, when she and Mr Plackford were in the parlour and Stevie was going after rabbits with Paul Adams from the Goodworthys', Mr Plackford said, 'Now there's an odd thing that's come to my mind, Maudie.'

'What thing be that?' asked Mrs Plackford.

'If that grave be six feet like Stevie said,' observed Mr Plackford thoughtfully, 'what's in it besides the remains of a collie dog?'

'You're talking about Dora Mumford's dog?' said Mrs Plackford.

'Well now, come to think of it,' mused Mr Plackford, 'I were a close friend to Barney Mumford, and he never said nary a word to me about wanting to leave Dora, nor wrote to me afterwards, not once.'

'Well, he deserted Dora,' said Mrs Plackford, 'and it were on his conscience.'

'Disappeared, that were what he did,' said Mr Plackford.

'With some woman, everyone said,' remarked Mrs Plackford, 'which meant Dora was able to get a divorce for legal desertion later on.'

'It's what we heard, but I don't remember her going to no court,' said Mr Plackford. 'Ah, well, it's a fact that she had a rare fondness for that dog, and were bound to give it a good burial, I rackon.'

Aunt Hilary was late back from her outing. It was dark, in fact, when she wheeled her bike up the front path, left it inside the porch and entered the cottage. Kate came out from the parlour.

'Did you get lost, Aunt Hilary?'

'Lost?' Aunt Hilary, in blouse, skirt and beret, laughed. Her pale complexion never seemed to be affected by the sun, it never took on a tan. 'I'm not in the habit of getting lost, Kate. I enjoyed a fascinating exploration of ancient monuments, and all I lost was count of time. I think I'd like a sandwich and a cup of tea.'

'Shall I do it for you?' offered Kate.

'Would you?' Miss Martin left most of the kitchen tasks to Kate, who hadn't yet come to suspect her aunt was making a servant of her. She was too grateful to even begin to think like that. 'There's a sweet girl. Has David been to see you?'

'Don't you remember?' said Kate, going into the kitchen and switching the light on. 'I went to tea with him and the Goodworthys.'

'Oh, so you did,' said Aunt Hilary, taking off her beret. She chucked it on a chair and ran her hands through her mass of black hair. 'Enjoyable?'

'Well, it wasn't boring, as you said it might be.'

'Have I earned a black mark?' asked Aunt Hilary with a languid smile.

'Oh, no-one complained about you not being there,' said Kate, taking some corned beef out of the larder.

'What's that stuff?'

'Corned beef,' said Kate.

'Is that all we've got for a sandwich?'

'Auntie, there's a war on,' said Kate, 'and being in Devon doesn't mean it's gone away.'

'What a wretched way of settling an argument,' said Aunt Hilary irritably. 'We all get dragged in, and there are bodies and blood everywhere. Deplorable. Well, I'll just freshen up and have a fag while you're making the tea and sandwich. A smidgeon of mustard on the corned beef, please, Kate?'

She went up then, leaving her beret looking like something carelessly abandoned.

Well, thought Kate, I suppose she's right, and I'm sure I don't know much about what makes governments go to war. But I do know I don't like Hitler and now we're fighting him, well, that's it, we've got to fight him till we win. I'm certain if me and David were old enough, we'd join the RAF together. I suppose being a bit of a Lord Muck, he'd be an officer and I'd be just anybody. No, I wouldn't, I'm never going to be just anybody and ordered about by Lord Mucks.

She thought then of what David's face had looked like when she came to the point in her story about a fate worse than death. What a laugh, he'd taken it all in with his mouth open.

She smiled as she cut two slices from a loaf of bread. The smile went as she remembered her dad had liked an evening sandwich with his last cup of tea of the day. Her dad had been a bit of a soap-box trade unionist in his time, but had a soft heart for her mum and for her. From somewhere came the feeling that he'd have liked David, even if David did talk a bit posh.

Now why would he have, seeing he didn't go much on anyone who sounded middle class?

'Crikey,' she said to the margarine dish, 'I'm askin' meself a question I can't answer.'

'Here, missy,' said Mrs Mumford on Monday morning, 'you can take this to school with you.' She handed Daisy something wrapped up in a paper bag.

'What is it?' asked Daisy, just about to leave.

'Two slices of your birthday carrot cake,' said Mrs Mumford, brisk and matter-of-fact. 'You can maybe give one slice to your friend Posy Goodworthy. That girl be as much of a scamp as that boy, but I've known worse. Off you go now, and mind that clean school frock of yours.'

'Oh, thanks, Mrs Mumford, it's ever so kind of you,' said Daisy, 'I never 'ad cake for school before.'

'Well, you have today,' said Mrs Mumford. 'And in the future, well, we'll see. You be a growing girl, needing a little something between meals, I'm thinking, and your schooling's special, a mite better than the village school, so make sure you get some good learning into your head. Shoo now, be on your way.'

Daisy went on her way, wondering if Mrs Mumford was actually getting to like her a bit.

Eloise received a letter from Boots expressing sympathy for her despair and assuring her that life, even in the Army, had its quota of good moments to make up for a percentage of the bad. As to doing something for her, although he wasn't in command of His Majesty's Forces, he had, with the help of her stepmama, reached the ear of a guardsman at Buckingham Palace and hoped accordingly that a word or two on her behalf would enter through the back door of the royal domain and end up in the ear of a high-ranking personage. If so, who could tell what might come of that? Boots suggested she put her despair aside and await events in a calm frame of mind.

'Not that your very expressive reactions to events aren't dear to me and the rest of your family,' he wrote. 'None of us would care to have you turn into a dull young lady, no, not at all, we cherish you as you are, my French chicken, and so, I'm certain, does Colonel Lucas. However, since losing the Battle of Hastings, this country has decided all its wars must be fought overseas, and this has meant partings and heartache for a great many people. Your stepmama and I fully understand separation from Colonel Lucas will be wretched for you, but hang on to the fact that while you're despairing we're hopeful. We send you our love and best wishes, and regards to Colonel Lucas.'

Eloise managed to use the officers' mess phone that evening.

'Hello?'

'Papa, is that you?'

'It is, and I'm sure that's you, Eloise.'

'Yes, and I have something to say to you. Papa, your letter, I've read it twice and I can see you are laughing at me.'

'Indeed I'm not, Eloise.'

'Indeed you are, yes, I can tell, but it isn't at all funny.'

'Well, I didn't want to write a gloomy letter. I thought an encouraging one would be welcome.'

'Papa, to be in despair isn't entertaining, it's natural, and I'm very cross with you.'

'I bow my head, but am still convinced you are one of the most entertaining members of your English grandmother's extensive family.'

'Well, thank you, Papa, you are very entertaining

yourself, and so is Stepmama, but you are not to send letters that laugh at me.'

'Perish the thought, my angel.'

'Why did you write such silly things about a guardsman at Buckingham Palace?'

'Ah, well,' said Boots.

'What do you mean?'

'It was a way of saying something might be done for you,' said Boots. His decision not to mention Sir Henry was simply to ensure his opportunistic daughter did not fasten on to the possibility that all kinds of favours could be asked of a general who was related to the family.

'But what is something, Papa?'

'Wait in hope, but take nothing for granted.'

'Papa, do you realize how much in love I am, and that I shall hate it here without the man I'm going to marry?'

Boots could have pointed out again that a great many people had to endure separation in wartime. Instead, he came up with a trite but comforting comment.

'Be of good cheer, Eloise, circumstances may change for the better.'

Eloise, who thought that happily comforting, said, 'Oh, I have much faith in you, Papa.'

Perhaps he was doing what he could to see that Luke remained in Troon. Her despair would be total if she had to exist thousands of miles away from him.

Chapter Eleven

The days went by. In Devon, Daisy was living a happier life under the care of Mrs Mumford, whose awareness of just how neglectful the girl's parents were had finally aroused a kinder attitude. Also, Daisy had discovered that Stevie, shy beneath his belligerence, did like her better than Posy. She thought that only right because, after all, he came from Bermondsey and she came from Rotherhithe, and the streets of these close neighbourhoods ran into each other.

Kate and David were building a relationship that was challenging on her part and happy-go-lucky on his. She was still suspicious of him as Ashleigh's Lord Muck, especially when she found out he had ambitions to run his own business. She asked him why he couldn't be an honest working bloke like her dad had been instead of wanting to grind the poor. David said he'd never thought about grinding the poor, that if he did come to employ people he'd pay fair wages. Kate said he'd probably be a real Lord Muck as an employer, and that his wife would probably be a real Lady Muck who'd treat her servants very haughty. David said he'd never thought about marrying a Lady Muck, haughty or otherwise, or of having servants. Kate said well, he talked already like someone who lived in a middle-class castle.

'What's a middle-class castle?' asked David.

'How do I know?' said Kate. 'I've never lived in one meself, 'ave I? Just me dad's rented house with a backyard.'

David couldn't think what to say to that. But he remembered his Uncle Boots once telling him he could expect everything of ladies that was worthwhile except logic. And you'll come to realize, he added, that you can't ask for logic when they're giving you everything else. David said he'd remember that. You'll get confused if you forget it, said Uncle Boots.

For the Adams family and its Somers branch, the war continued to be an inescapable factor in their lives.

Chinese Lady, the family matriarch, dwelt at home with her husband Edwin Finch, who still worked for a Government department. She spent much of her time writing letters to the absent members of her extensive family.

Boots was engaged in his staff work for General Sir Henry Simms, his father-in-law. In company with other specially picked officers, he was helping Sir Henry to create an effective corps from new divisions. Polly, her ATS commission relinquished on account of her expectations, was in a quite serious relationship with the good earth. Her new-found interest was of an earnest kind. It gave her healthy exercise and the promise of a reward when the plants were ready to harvest. She had bought seeds, seedlings and a book specifically put together as a guide for amateur gardeners, and with its help she established close contact with the large patch of virgin soil uncovered and broken up by Private Ginger Harris of the GD squad. Boots viewed her efforts with interest.

'Need any help, Polly?'

'No, this is mine alone, so go away.'

There she was, in rubber boots, some kind of smock, hair held in place by a bandeau, hands in gardening gloves, and face expressive of happy endeavour. He thought he'd come to know her well over the years, but she was still capable of surprising him. She was planting runner bean seedlings, leafy and flourishing, and beside the plot was a bundle of tall stakes to be used to enable the plants to climb.

'Like me to stick the stakes in for you?'

'Certainly not. Just let me know when supper's ready.'

Boots smiled. Polly, expecting a baby, was making another of her vegetable plot.

Up in Troon with 4 Commando, Tim was awaiting time off for his wedding and, subsequently, a departure to the Middle East. His left collarbone, fractured during the last raid, was subject to only a few twinges now, but it was these that had induced the MO, after a friendly consultation with Colonel

Lucas, to declare him unfit to be included in the draft headed by the Colonel. However, he would follow almost immediately after his marriage to Felicity. Colonel Lucas had felt it would do Felicity no good at all to be deprived of a ceremony that he correctly surmised meant so much to her, even if she had to wait to take her place beside Tim in whatever home they eventually found for themselves.

Tim, meanwhile, was making a hated name for himself by introducing new volunteer recruits to all the agonies he himself had suffered over a period of many months. They cursed him, made oblique references to the circumstances of his birth, and wished him a hideous death, but all out of earshot. Any man reckless enough at the peak of pain to let his expressions of hatred be heard found himself on a crime sheet that resulted in undergoing even worse agonies. The youngest officer of experience Tim may have been, but he knew the value of turning every new intake into a collection of rough, tough and disciplined fighters all too willing to get at the Jerries.

As far as his private life was concerned, he knew that sooner or later he had to let Felicity know he was due to leave for action overseas. He came to a decision one evening and made a trunk call to the hospital. It brought Clara on the line. They exchanged greetings like old friends, then Tim asked how Felicity was.

'Top of her form,' said Clara. 'I've just had supper with her at a table for two, and halfway through a diced whalemeat steak she said, "This tastes more like a fillet off Jonah's bum than the whale, but hooray, I finally don't have to guess where my mouth is. Haven't you noticed I've stopped putting food up my nose or in my eye?"'

'That's definitely top of her form,' said Tim.

'Would you like to speak to her?' asked Clara.

'I'd like to speak to you first,' said Tim, and told her he was embarking on an overseas draft four days after the wedding. 'Clara, how'd you think Felicity's going to take that?'

'Like a lady soldier,' said Clara. 'Well, she's still in uniform when she's not in something else, and she's been through the ATS military mill with all colours flying, I'd say. Am I right?'

'No-one could fault her,' said Tim. 'Her colours will still fly high, will they, if I break my news to her?'

'Well, Tim, after the wedding she'll know exactly what she is then – a soldier's wife,' said Clara. 'That may sound crummy, and a bit old-fashioned, but I think it'll fit. She's mentioned more than once the possibility of your going overseas after the marriage, and on the last occasion she added something else.'

'And what was that?' asked Tim.

'She said, "The bounder's a Commando, and if I know anything about any of them and their corpuscles, this one will leave me in the family way."'

Tim laughed.

'And what did you say to that, Clara?'

'I asked her how she would feel about it, and she said, "Bloody hard done by, but as I've come to believe in procreation, I'll grin and bear it." Note the witty allusion, Tim.'

'Grin and bear it?' said Tim. 'Noted. Shall I speak to her, then?'

'If you don't, and she finds out you've been on the line, she'll kill me,' said Clara. 'But can I say something first?'

'Go ahead,' said Tim.

'Felicity wants to be sure of you,' said Clara, 'so whatever happens, try not to let anything stop the marriage. You know you're her lifeline, don't you? I've told you that before. Without you, everything would have been ten times more difficult for her. Overseas or elsewhere, stay in touch with her, write to her as often as you can. Her best days are always the days when she receives a letter from you.'

'I think you've played your own part in all her days, Clara,' said Tim. 'You're a great girl. See you at the wedding. Can I speak to Felicity now?'

'Hold on and I'll fetch her.'

It was a little while before Felicity's voice came floating over the wire.

'Hello, sailor.'

'How's yourself, Queenie?'

'Blind as a bat,' said Felicity, 'but my hearing's first-class. Thanks for phoning. Is it to tell me something I'll like?'

'Well, d'you like the fact that I'll be with you on your wedding day?' asked Tim.

'Yes, be there in person,' said Felicity. 'Any substitute will get shot. What else is on your mind, lover?'

'Just you,' said Tim.

'No war at the moment?' enquired Felicity.

'Up here, only the usual quota of broken bones,' said Tim, 'and news to the effect that Eloise's number one bloke, Colonel Lucas, is off to the Middle East with a detachment in a week or so, probably to join the Long Range Desert Group.'

'I've heard on the radio that that's giving Rommel a headache,' said Felicity, 'but will it stop him taking over Egypt?'

'Not if the Eighth Army does its stuff,' said Tim.

'Tim, are you in the detachment?' asked Felicity.

'Good question,' said Tim.

'Answer up,' said Felicity.

'I'm going, yes,' said Tim, 'but not until four days after our wedding. It's a concession to you and me. Thought I'd better let you know.'

There was a little silence before Felicity responded.

'Well, curse it,' she said.

'Seconded,' said Tim.

'But I'm not surprised,' she said. 'I'd simply like to know, Tim, does it make any difference to you in regard to our special day?'

'How could it?' said Tim. 'I fancy you something chronic. I told you that ages ago. It's love, what else, so I'm keeping my appointment with you, and a team of elephants couldn't drag me away once I get there. You're my future. I told you that too, Puss.'

Another little silence, then, 'Oh, good show, I like all of that. Send me a card, won't you, when you get to where you're going.'

'One of a belly dancer wouldn't appeal to you, I suppose?' said Tim.

'Don't be a fathead,' said Felicity.

'Fell over my forgetful feet,' said Tim. 'Sorry about that, sweetie.'

'Keep off belly dancers,' said Felicity.

'Believe me,' said Tim, 'I don't fancy bouncing about.'

'Your perversion's showing,' said Felicity, and her laugh travelled over the line. It had a bit of a quiver to it, however, and Tim knew she was fighting emotions.

Felicity was a born fighter, he knew that too. He also knew he had to take precautions during love-making. One thing he couldn't do was to put her in the family way. That had to wait until she was 95 per cent adaptable to her blindness. There'd always be a 5 per cent margin at least.

Cousin Bobby was waiting, with his young French lady, Helene Aarlberg, for the call that would mean arrangements for their departure to France were in place. Helene was restless, Bobby outwardly calm.

They were living on the Kent coast, and in their civvies. They went walking every day to catch the sea breezes.

'Bobby, what are your nerves like?'

'Fairly steady.'

'Ah, you are a block of English wood.'

'Sorry about that.'

'No, no, I didn't mean it, and even if your nerves aren't troubling you, you're excited, yes?'

'Fairly. Well, in a nervous kind of way.'

'But you said your nerves weren't troubling you.'

'I'm just not sure exactly what we're going to be up against.'

'Yes, I feel like that too. Bobby, shall we make love?'

'Here, by the sea, with people walking about?'

'No, no, you idiot, not here. We can find a place somewhere. Bobby, you haven't made love to me since we've been in Broadstairs.'

'I'm trying to respect what I think your parents would expect of me.'

'But if we love each other, they would not mind, no.'

'Then there's Mrs Kepper, our landlady, who keeps her eye on us.'

'Of course she doesn't. She's one of us, we know that.'

'All right, my French pickle—'

'Don't call me that silly name.'

'Suits you.'

'French pickle? How would you like me to call you English onion?'

'Go ahead. It's great to be out on a day like this.'

'Bobby, it's beautiful, isn't it?'

They stopped to look out over the sea. The waters of the Channel were a sparkling reflection of the blue sky. Restless little waves were tipped with running white. On the other side of this world-renowned shipping highway, was the coast of France, only a little over twenty miles due east. North-east, and much farther, was Dunkirk, scene of the miraculous evacuation of the BEF in the summer of 1940, and the starting point of their own dash from France.

'Do you remember that night in the Channel, Helene?'

'Our time in *Fifi*? Will I ever forget, Bobby? No, never. How crazy we were. But I could not let you commit suicide by yourself.'

'As it ended up with you losing good old *Fifi*, I owe you. So when the war's over, my little one—'

'Little one? Little one?'

'True, you're a big girl now—'

'Big? Who is big? My figure is perfect, yes.'

'Well, we're both proud of it, of course, and I'll always do my best to keep a careful eye on it.'

Helene laughed, the breeze flattening her dress against her figure, except that neither dress nor figure looked at all flat.

'Bobby, how will you feel when we come face to face with the Nazi Boche again?'

'Frankly, I'm not sure.'

'But we will stand together, yes?'

'Against all-comers, count on it. And I was going to say that when the war's over I'll buy you another boat and you can call it *Daughter of Fifi*.'

'I should like that. We can sail it together. Are you glad we met as we did?'

'I think I've said before, that when we did meet, you looked around for your father's shotgun.'

'Oh, that lie is as terrible as your jokes.'

'Hope you'll be able to live with them when the war's over,' said Bobby.

'I will sacrifice myself,' said Helene, and they resumed their walk, arms linked, wondering what was in store for them between now and the end of the war.

*   *   *

Then there was Emma, Bobby's younger sister, married to her happy-go-lucky country chap, Sussex-born Jonathan Hardy. Jonathan had been airlifted home from the desert war with a smashed kneecap. An intricate operation had cleared the affected area of tiny bone splinters, and when healing was completed, another operation was intended, that of fitting a rounded metal cap to take the place of the smashed bone at the apex of the fibula. Jonathan counted himself lucky that the nature of the wound hadn't led to an amputation.

He was in the military wing of a hospital in Mitcham, and Emma came to see him twice a week.

'Hello, Emma.'

'Hello, darling.'

Kiss, kiss.

'I'm fair tickled to see you, Emma,' said Jonathan.

'So you should be,' said Emma, 'I'm wearing my best dress and stockings. How are you, Jonathan?'

'The first operation's been successful, I'm healed, and it looks like they'll be slipping in my tin cap tomorrow or the day after,' said Jonathan.

'Oh, that's wonderful,' said Emma. She glanced around the small ward. There were three other patients recovering from surgery, all men airlifted home. All three had visitors.

'Emma, you're looking a fair Sunday treat,' said Jonathan.

A whisper from Emma. 'Fancy me, do you, Jonathan?'

'Emma, if I could get out of this bed—'

'Jonathan!' A hasty interruption from Emma. 'Not out loud.'

Jonathan murmured, 'I should have said if I could get you into this bed—'

'Stop it, d'you hear?'

'Can't even start,' said Jonathan, 'my leg would fall off.'

Emma smiled. The war had broken out at just the wrong time for her and Jonathan, and it was an awful war with Britain and Germany bombing each other now, but although she felt for Jonathan and his crippled knee, she also felt extraordinarily happy that it was going to keep him on home service, that she wasn't going to have to say an overseas goodbye to him again. Bless his Sussex cheer, he didn't know what it was to be down in the mouth, he was an old-fashioned sunshine chap, treating life, even in wartime, as if it was a funfair. He had a lovely sense of humour and a very tolerant nature. She felt he got those qualities from his lovable Sussex parents. He was hers, her Jonathan, and dear to her, even if some of his conversation was of the kind that shouldn't take place in a hospital ward that was full of ears. For the sake of what she knew Grandma Finch would call proper, she became conventional.

'By the way, Mum and Dad send you their love and best wishes, and my Uncle Boots, in a letter to me, hopes your tin knee turns out to be a triumph.'

'Mind you, Emma, once I'm up and about—'

'Jonathan,' she whispered, 'nothing sexy, not here, if you don't mind.'

'Well, Emma, I reckon—'

'We haven't had an air raid on London for all of four nights, Jonathan, did you know that?' she said. 'It's utter bliss, four quiet nights in succession. I'm longing for you to get your posting to Somerset and to joining you there.'

'Well, for my part, Emma, I can't wait,' said Jonathan earnestly. 'I feel I'm going to like Somerset on my off-duty days. Let's see, the idea is for you to give up your job at the War Office and get you billeted with a nearby farmer and his wife who need help with their chickens. That's a fair wartime occupation, chicken farming. Or perhaps you could join the Somerset Land Army, except I don't be too certain I'd like you in a Land Army rigout. No, let's stick with a skirt and chickens and—'

'Wait a minute.' Another whisper from Emma as she decided to give in to the fun of being the recipient of the improper. That kind of talk allowed the imagination to take the place of the real thing, and they were both starved of the real thing. 'I think I want to know, after all, what your intentions are once you're up and about.'

'Come a fair bit closer, Emma, and I'll tell you,' murmured Jonathan.

'Lord,' breathed Emma, 'I hope it's not going to make me feel all sexy. I mean, what can we do about that?'

'Nothing very much until I'm right side up,' said Jonathan.

Boots's adopted daughter Rosie was waiting for the arrival home of husband Matthew after his first

162

week with the Bovington REME. It was Saturday evening, and he was motoring from Bovington to enjoy a 24-hour leave with her in their cottage, her official billet that was also her home.

She heard his key in the door a little after seven. Not given to being reserved, she flew from the kitchen into the little hall of the cottage, and there he was, in his cap and uniform, a single pip denoting his rank of second lieutenant. She was now a captain herself.

'Matt!' She was in his arms then. A warm healthy kiss alighted on her ready lips. Her dress engaged demonstratively with his jacket.

'Well met,' said Matt, and Rosie stood back a little to regard him. He looked an arresting Army man already, his tailored uniform fitting his long body so well. 'How have you been, Rosie?'

'Lonely,' said Rosie.

'That makes two of us,' said Matt, wondering, as he so often did, how he had come to win such a lovely and engaging young woman. 'I'm enjoying the work, and the set-up, but blow my boots off if I don't miss you every night, and you can take that as gospel.'

'But you're happy now that you're in the King's khaki?' said Rosie, who was delighted herself.

'Yes, I'm happy, Rosie,' said Matt, 'and a damned fortunate man all round.'

'Well, the chickens have been laying as if there's no tomorrow,' said Rosie, 'so I'm going to do lovely hot fluffy omelettes for supper, with a salad.'

'Is there some significance about that?' asked Matt.

'Yes, of course,' said Rosie. 'I have it on the excellent authority of a nutritional expert, in an old magazine article, that omelettes made from three eggs, and eaten with a salad, contain oceans of vitamins.'

'Who needs vitamins? I don't,' said Matt. 'Send the magazine to someone who does. But who can find three eggs per omelette in wartime?'

'We can,' said Rosie. 'You're forgetting our chickens. I think they knew you'd be arriving this evening.'

Matt laughed.

'Damn my old leg, Rosie, if you aren't a delight to come home to,' he said.

'I suppose you realize, do you,' said Rosie, 'that although we've only been married a short time, we're already a once-a-week couple?'

'I'm still counting my blessings,' said Matt.

The call came for Bobby and Helene, and they had their final briefing from Major Buckmaster in London. He advised the young couple that everything was now arranged for them to be flown to Vichy France and dropped by parachute in a selected area of the Haute Garonne. Their contact, the man whom they would know only as Paul, would meet them, and he would know them only as Lynette and Maurice. To the Vichy authorities and any Gestapo agents, their papers identified them as Claudette Dubois and Henri Beaumonte. Were they still confident they could command belief in these identities, while being fully in tune with their code names?

'Yes,' said Bobby.

'Yes,' said Helene.

'I'm confident myself that you can,' said Major Buckmaster. Once they were in contact with the man Paul, he went on, they would be guided by him in respect of all that was required of them. At some time they would meet their radio operator, a lady of Scotland. 'I gave you her code name last time I saw you. What was it?'

'Marcelle,' said Bobby.

'Good. She will transmit to us any necessary messages from you, and by necessary I mean only vitally important messages. Is that understood?'

'Absolutely,' said Bobby. 'No messages from Lynette asking for a packet of hairnets to be dropped.'

'Do you see, *mon Commandant*, how crazy this man is?' said Helene.

Major Buckmaster took that with a little laugh.

'In this organization, we're all crazy,' he said. 'The impossible can't be asked of sane and sober people. Next Tuesday, in six days time, then, a car will arrive at your Broadstairs boarding-house by twelve noon to take you to an airfield. I'll be there to see you off, and to wish you a safe landing and the very best of good fortune. If you feel you've had to wait a long time for the off, put it down to the unavoidable necessity of making sure everything is as it should be for you. Any questions?'

'None I can think of at the moment,' said Bobby, and Helene echoed that. They were both sure of themselves, even if flutters of nervous excitement existed.

Chapter Twelve

Subaltern Eloise Adams came out of the office of Captain Cary, senior ATS admin officer at Troon, with a look of delight on her face. Twenty-four, Eloise regarded herself as out of the ordinary in being the daughter of her impressive father. Certainly, she had enchanting looks and an extrovert personality that made her excel in company.

True, she was aware that Captain Cary didn't like her, but that, of course, was because Captain Cary was fairly ordinary herself. How sour she had been in telling her she was on a draft for the Middle East that would embark from Liverpool on the fifteenth of August, in exactly two weeks time.

She was going to be near Colonel Lucas, her exciting Luke, after all, she was sure of that.

Her English father had arranged it, she was sure of that too. She would write a letter telling him how grateful she was.

Luke was at home and coming to the end of his embarkation leave. In two days he would be sailing from Liverpool himself. She would phone him tonight and let him know she was following in two weeks. She had obtained 72 hours leave to spend last weekend with him at his parents' home in Sanderstead, Surrey. It was her first meeting with his parents, an extraordinary couple in their fifties, his mother tall and as thin as a rake, his father hugely fat. Mrs Lucas went about with a notebook, stopping every so often to jot down complaints about the condition of the house and garden, all of which she put together in a letter to her husband, which she handed to him for bedtime reading. Mr Lucas, a printer, went about hardly at all. Well, not in his own house and not during the weekend. He spent most of his time with his comprehensive miniature railway system that occupied the whole of a downstairs room of the modest semi-detached house. He said that he was too bulky to go in for a lot of movement while at home, and that it was his bulk that was responsible for cracks repeatedly occurring in the walls and ceilings, for stairs occasionally groaning and sinking, and for the frequent appearance of large holes in the lawn. But he chuckled at almost every word he spoke, and laughed loudly at himself from time to time, which made Mrs Lucas say it was like living with a barrel organ that never stopped playing 'The Laughing Policeman'. The eccentricities of both parents, who called their formidable son William, fascinated Eloise. They amused Luke, who treated them indulgently and assured Eloise that neither of them had ever been known to bite. His indulgence was at odds with the impatience he always showed for military personnel he considered inefficient idiots. In any event, Mr and Mrs Lucas received Eloise kindly, although Mrs Lucas, subsequently encountering her on one of her walkabouts, asked her who she was. Luke stepped in to advise her that Eloise was her future daughter-in-law.

'How nice,' said Mrs Lucas, 'yes, how very nice. But look at that, a hole in the skirting.' Down went the fault in her notebook. 'Not done by mice, I know that. I really must try to get Mr Lucas to live in the air raid shelter.'

Eloise felt relieved that one only married the man and not the parents. She had to say goodbye to Luke when he accompanied her to Euston on Monday morning, and she did so in a mood close to despair again, for nothing had come of her father's hint that wheels were being oiled. But for once she was not dramatic, she only asked Luke why they couldn't have been married during his embarkation leave.

'Not a good idea,' he said, 'marrying you and then leaving you. Let's wait until we can have the ceremony in Cairo.'

'Cairo? Cairo?'

'I've a feeling that's where you'll end up, my dear young lady,' he said.

'A feeling?'

'Yes,' he said, 'we're two people who are always running into each other. What was it your father said to you?'

'He told me to be hopeful.'

'Well, it seems your father shares my feelings, so let's both be hopeful. And let's get you aboard this train.'

Now hope had become happy reality, and

despair had taken itself off to skulk in the shadows and wait for another victim. How sad that there were all too many similar victims in wartime.

'Felicity?' said Clara, arriving at her patient's side. It was mid-morning, Felicity had just finished punishing herself with a laboured Braille reading, and was seated in an armchair in the recreation room.

'Is it still raining?' she asked, her dark glasses a perched permanency on the bridge of her nose during her waking hours.

'Afraid so.'

'Curse it, then,' said Felicity, who hated the feeling of being trapped by hospital ceilings and walls.

'But the clouds are breaking up,' said Clara. 'Listen, I'm told you've made extraordinary progress with Braille, that you've actually begun unassisted reading. You've caught and passed two other patients who've been here longer.'

'Extraordinary's right,' said Felicity. 'I've just started reading *The Hound of the Baskervilles*. I've read the first ten lines.'

'Hooray,' said Clara.

'Hooray my elbow,' said Felicity, 'it's taken me an hour, and I've worked out that by the time I finish it, I'll be fifty-one. What a life. Any letters?'

'Yes, the mail's just come,' said Clara. 'There's one for you, but it's not in Tim's writing.'

'I hope this isn't going to be a lousy day,' said Felicity. 'Oh, well, be a sport, Clara. Open it and read it.'

Clara opened it and read it.

Dear Felicity,
My compliments. I've had a word with Tim, and if it's
agreeable to you, my wife Polly and I will pick you up
from the hospital on the afternoon of the day before the
wedding and drive you to your home. I understand your
nurse is to accompany you. We'll also arrange to pick
you up from your home on the day itself, and drive you
and your nurse to the registry office.

Polly and I will be more than happy to do this, and
hope the day will be all that you wish. We send you our
love and look forward very much to seeing you again.
Sincerely, Robert Adams.

'I like that,' said Felicity, 'it's simple and unfussy.'

'And friendly?' said Clara.

'I like that too,' said Felicity, 'the prospect
of friendly in-laws who don't see me as a kind of
cripple. You can write a reply for me this afternoon,
will you?'

'Of course,' said Clara. 'It does call for a reply,
doesn't it? By the way, the rain's just stopped and
the sun's hitting the windows.'

'Jolly good,' said Felicity, 'let's go out for a walk
to get rid of my nerves.'

'You're suffering nerves?' said Clara.

'Well, of course I am, woman,' said Felicity, 'I'm
going to be married soon, and it's my first time.'

Clara experienced a familiar surge of affection
and admiration for this fine young woman whose
courage and strength of character were the chief

reasons why she was winning her fight to overcome her limitations in the world she could not see.

With the summer holidays in full swing, David knocked on the cottage door. Kate answered. She greeted him with a haughty look. David responded with a smile.

'Hello, Kate,' he said.

'Are you the paper boy?' she asked.

'No, a friend,' said David.

'Some friend,' said Kate. 'Where've you been, might I ask?'

'Mostly helping on the farm from morning to night,' said David. 'Mostly with the cows and lifting King Edwards.'

'What d'you mean, King Edward's? King Edward's what?' Kate was scathing. 'His coffin, for goodness sake? Well, he is dead, isn't he? Or d'you mean Mrs Simpson's King Edward that's now the Duke of Windsor, poor bloke?'

'No, not him,' said David, 'I don't think he's ever had much to do with potatoes, which are what I'm talking about. The ones I've been lifting were named after King Edward the Seventh, who was partial to good helpings of them. And yes, as far as I know he passed away a bit sudden years ago.'

'Crikey, what a show-off,' said Kate.

'King Edward the Seventh?' said David.

'No, you,' said Kate. 'I hope you haven't come round just to give me a history lesson.'

'No, just to mow your lawn now I've got time after doing my share of lifting potatoes,' said David.

'D'you mean to stand there and tell me our lawn comes second to mouldy old spuds?' asked Kate.

'I'll go round the side way to your back garden, shall I?' said David, dressed in an open-necked sports shirt, old blue shorts held up by a belt well past its best, and sandals on his bare feet. His hair was a bit untidy, his face warmly brown, his outdoor appearance redolent of summery Devon, and Kate wanted to kick him for looking so pleased with life when he hadn't been round for two whole days. 'I'll get the mower out and start straightaway,' he said.

'Wait a minute, you haven't answered my question,' said Kate, delicious in pastel green.

'What question was that?' asked David.

'Does our lawn come second to mouldy potatoes? And who's been messing about with your hair, one of the tarty village girls?'

'No to both,' said David.

'What?'

'Well, you asked two questions—'

'Stop being clever,' said Kate.

'D'you mind if I tell you I like you better when you're not ratty?' said David.

'That's done it,' said Kate. She turned, seized an umbrella from the hallstand and went for him. David vanished around the side of the cottage. 'Stop, you rotten coward!' called Kate, and hared after him. She caught him on the lawn and reached to grab. Her hand closed around the back of his belt, and tugged. The belt broke. David turned and down travelled his shorts at an alarming speed to his ankles, leaving his rumpled shirt doing its best to cover his brief underpants. It wasn't altogether

172

successful. Kate stared, then shrieked with laughter and pointed with the umbrella. 'Oh, crikey, look at you, you dummy, you're showing your knickers. Well, your pants, anyway. My, aren't they cute?'

David grinned.

'Shut the gate, there's a draught,' he said, and lunged at her. Unfortunately, his ankles quarrelled with his tangled shorts and he fell over, rolling onto his back, his shirt riding up to his waist. Kate shrieked again.

'Here, I'm going before I lose me eyesight,' she said, but she stayed there, laughing. 'My, I do like your lonjeray, David, and your legs.'

'Pleased with yourself, are you?' said David, sitting up.

'I'm getting me own back for you looking at me with me dress up that time,' she said.

'That's fair, I suppose,' said David. He came to his feet, pulled his shorts up and tucked his shirt in. He examined his broken belt. 'Got a piece of string?' he asked.

'I'm not giving you any string,' said Kate, 'I'm waiting for your shorts to fall down again.'

'I'll go and ask your Aunt Hilary if she's got a spare belt,' said David.

'Oh, dear, hard luck,' said Kate, 'she's out. Never mind. I'll find you one. I suppose I ought to really, after seeing you do a star turn. D'you do it a lot for the village girls?'

'Like me to tie your legs in a knot, would you?' said David.

'Fat chance you've got of doing that while you're still having to hold your shorts up,' said Kate. 'All

173

right, stay there, and I'll find a belt or something.'
Away she went, going into the cottage by way of the
back door. She reappeared after a few minutes,
carrying a ladies' belt of soft leather, and something else.

'What's that?' asked David, still immobilized to
some extent.

'A belt,' said Kate, standing off a bit.

'No, the other thing.'

'Oh, it's me Brownie camera,' said Kate. 'David,
could you do it again, let your shorts fall down, so
I can take a snap?'

'It'll cost you a bob,' said David.

'A bob?' said Kate. 'D'you mean I've got to pay
you a whole shilling just for taking a snap of you
with your shorts down? You'll be lucky. Not worth
tuppence. Give you a penny.'

'No, I'd better not,' said David, 'I've a feeling
everything'll fall down next time.'

Kate had hysterics then, and collapsed on the
grass.

'Crikey, you'll be me death,' she gasped. 'Here,
you can have the belt, I don't have any film in
the camera, anyway.' She offered the belt, David
took it, fitted it into the loops of his shorts and
buckled it.

'I'll mow your lawn now,' he said with his
engaging grin. 'That's if you could move off it.' He
gave her his hand and helped her to her feet.
Her green eyes were moist from laughter. 'Did
you know you've got mince pies like dewy parsley?'
he said.

'Dewy parsley, that again?' said Kate. 'I said

174

before, how can anyone have eyes like dewy parsley? That's the wettest thing I ever heard. Listen, when you've done the lawn, would you like to stay and have a cup of tea with me?'

'Not half,' said David. 'Any cake?'

'Aunt Hilary doesn't bake many cakes,' said Kate. Actually, Aunt Hilary didn't bake anything. Nor did she do much cooking. 'But there's some biscuits.'

'They'll do,' said David.

She sat on the kitchen doorstep and watched him cutting the lawn. He pushed the old hand mower with ease, and she liked the pattern he created up and down the broad stretch of grass. The day was warm, and clouds that had banked in the west were passing overhead, the prevailing west wind driving them eastwards, leaving the sky above a clear blue. How quiet the country was, she thought, and yet not quiet because there were the sounds of bees on the wing, the piping of blackbirds, the little crisp noise of the mower's cutters, and the faint chatter of magpies which, unknown to Kate, a girl of Camberwell, were forever manoeuvring to dive down on garden peas as soon as the coast was clear of humans. The air seemed to hum. It was, she supposed, the hum of summer in the country. And perhaps a garden did happen to be a bit prettier than a backyard.

David stopped mowing to take his shirt off. He threw it her way and she caught it.

'Crikey, you aren't 'alf showing yourself off this afternoon,' she said.

'It's hot,' he said, and resumed his work with the mower, the cut grass showering into the box.

Kate thought what a manly body he had. When he was nearing the finish of his work, she put the kettle on and brought the biscuits from the larder. She made the tea and they drank it sitting on the step, David with little patches of perspiration moistening his hair. She liked his warm outdoor smell, but told him to put his shirt on. He did so, and his shirt smelled warm too.

'It looks nice, the lawn,' she said.

'Well, that old self-sharpening mower is still a good one,' said David.

'It makes a nice pattern,' said Kate. 'Listen, I'm still trying to finish that report.'

'What, the bit about a fate worse than death?' asked David.

'Yes, I've got to work out if the Stormtrooper succeeds in his evil desire to overcome me,' said Kate, looking seriously thoughtful, 'or if I overcome him with me resourcefulness. I'm considering drawing me bayonet while he's trying to undo me corset.'

'Corset?' said David.

'Yes, me Paris one,' said Kate.

'I wish I knew about Paris corsets, but I don't,' said David. 'And you didn't mention a bayonet before. Where's it supposed to come from?'

'Out of me stocking-top, of course,' said Kate. 'It's where secret women agents keep daggers and bayonets, you dummy.'

'But compared with a dagger, a bayonet's half a mile long,' said David, 'and if you drew it out a bit quick you could cut your leg off.'

'Look, it's hard enough trying to work out how

to save meself without you making things difficult by trying to be funny,' said Kate. 'I can't put anything in that would sound daft, it's got to sound real enough for people to believe.'

'Like keeping a bayonet down your stocking?' said David.

'Yes, that's it,' said Kate. 'But I've just thought that if I wasn't able to draw it out because of me desperate struggles, I'd let 'im unlace me corset all the way and—'

'Unlace it?' said David.

'Yes, it's a lace-up Paris one.'

'I had a vague idea corsets were done up with hooks and eyes,' said David.

'Well, me Paris one isn't,' said Kate, 'it's laced up with silk cord. Now if I let the Stormtrooper draw the cord right out—'

'Kate, you can't do that,' said David, 'your corset would collapse, wouldn't it, and – and –'

'Yes?' said Kate, looking him in the eye.

'Well, as a grown-up woman,' said David, 'you'd be showing your – your – well, you'd be showing just how grown-up you were, wouldn't you?'

'Listen, brainless, it's got to be real, hasn't it?' said Kate. 'I'd have to suffer exposing me measurements for the sake of me desperate plan, which would be to seize the cord from his grasp and then strangle him with it.'

'Well, I'd rather that than you letting him overcome you,' said David. 'If he did, I wouldn't be able to listen. Go for strangling him. I could listen to that.'

'Yes, Stormtroopers are supposed to be 'orrible, aren't they?' said Kate. She mused and became sober. 'David, d'you think about the war a lot?'

'Yes, I do,' said David. 'Most people do, don't they?'

'I suppose so,' said Kate, 'I do meself.'

They talked on. Both were of a loquacious nature, but neither of them realized their growing compatibility was of a special kind.

Aunt Hilary returned from her outing, announcing her arrival by ringing her bicycle bell and then appearing from around the side of the cottage, wheeling her machine, in the carrier of which were a pair of binoculars. She was dressed in practical fashion, beret, blue jumper and cream skirt.

'Home is the weary one, home from the fields, and from scanning the vistas of glorious Devon,' she said. 'And it is glorious. Hello, David, cuddling up to Kate, are we, young man?'

'Aunt, we're just sitting and talking,' said Kate.

'My dear girl, I recommend cosy relationships,' smiled Aunt Hilary, leaning her bike against the cottage wall. 'Good for the young. Would there be some tea going?'

'What's in the pot must be stale by now,' said Kate.

'Kate dear, could you possibly make a fresh pot?' asked Aunt Hilary winningly. 'I'm fagged out.'

'Yes, all right, Auntie,' said Kate, getting up and going into the kitchen.

'Have you been to Dartmoor?' asked David of the lady who seemed better suited to a drawing-room than the saddle of a bike.

'No, not today, David,' she said.

'It's a good twenty-five miles from here,' said David.

'So my map tells me,' she said, 'but I won't be deterred. I must explore it sooner or later.' She cast a look at the lawn. 'Some divine young man has been at work,' she said, and hitching her skirt, she sat down in easy, uninhibited fashion on the step next to David. 'You, I think.'

'I promised I'd do it again as soon as I could,' said David.

'Well, you've earned a grateful kiss,' said Aunt Hilary, and kissed him. David blinked. She smiled, in an almost sleepy way, it seemed.

Kate, in the kitchen, said, 'Aunt Hilary, did I see you kiss David?'

'You did indeed, dear girl. Haven't you noticed what he's done to the lawn? It looks beautiful. Our young man deserves this as well.' Aunt Hilary pushed a hand into the pocket of her skirt, groped about and produced a florin. 'There you are, David,' she said and gave it to him.

'You keep giving me florins,' said David, 'and I did mention a bob would do.'

'A shilling?' murmured Aunt Hilary. 'Far too stingy, my young friend. No, mowing the lawn like that is well worth two shillings.'

'In that case,' said David, 'I'd better tell you I charge separately for kisses. It's an old family custom. But I'll waive it this time.'

In the kitchen, Kate, recovering from the shock of seeing her aunt kiss David, burst into compulsive laughter. Aunt Hilary, smiling, looked beguilingly feline.

A little later, when Aunt Hilary was taking a bath, David suggested to Kate that she might like to join him tomorrow up at the farm.

'What for?' asked Kate.

'Well, there's a bumper crop of those King Edward potatoes, and the squire can do with any amount of help in lifting them,' said David.

'Me dig up potatoes?' said Kate.

'You don't have to dig,' said David, 'they're turned up by a machine and you just pick them up and put them into sacks. But not in that dress, it's too pretty. Have you got something old and ragged you could wear, with gumboots?'

'Old and ragged?' said Kate.

'Anything old will do, including a pair of old gloves,' said David, 'and you get paid.'

'You'll get paid in a minute,' said Kate, 'with the frying-pan. Anyway, I'm starting in a job on Monday with the Red Cross in Westbury, in the packing room of their offices. It's only mornings, but I think I'd be doing my bit for the war, don't you? And I'll still be able to get the tea and supper for Aunt Hilary.'

'Can't she do that herself so's you could do your bit full-time?' asked David.

'She's too busy with her exploring and writing,' said Kate, 'and she's been so kind giving me a home that I like to be a help to her.'

'Yes, that's fair, I suppose,' said David. 'Well, I'd better be off now, I promised to clean young Miss Parkin's windows today.'

'Here, I met a Miss Parkin in the Post Office Store,' said Kate.

'That's her,' said David.

'But she's about seventy,' said Kate.

'Well, she had a sister who's dead now, but was a bit older,' said David. 'So the sister was known as Miss Parkin and the one you met was known as young Miss Parkin and still is.'

'Barmy,' said Kate. 'Look, are you saying you're buzzing off to clean her windows?'

'I did promise,' said David.

'I'm going to give you up as one of me boyfriends,' said Kate darkly.

'But we can still meet and talk, can't we?' said David.

'Hoppit,' said Kate. 'Hope your shorts fall down while you're cleaning windows.'

'See you tomorrow, when I might have time to tidy up your front garden a bit,' said David. Kate chucked a potato at him to see him on his way. 'Like a couple of kisses for a tanner, Kate?' he called.

Another potato made him duck. He went off laughing, and Kate began to prepare a potato, onion and cheese mixture for supper baking. A wartime recipe, of course, it was quite tasty as long as there was enough cheese in it, and Mr Pennicot of the Post Office Store had served her a generous amount yesterday, well over that which her and Aunt Hilary's ration coupons allowed. With the generous portion, Mr Pennicot had also donated a twinkle and a wink. He was a rosy-faced and chubby old gent, who had a woman assistant, a Mrs Mumford, who was very polite and helpful but didn't go in for twinkles and winks.

*   *   *

Luftwaffe bombers took off from their bases in Northern France to launch one of their retaliatory raids on London that night. It had come to that. The raids were not planned now as tactical warfare from the night skies, but were demanded of Goering by Hitler who, while happy with the progress of his invasion of Soviet Russia, was furious about that which was becoming intolerable on his Western Front, the RAF's regular bombing of Germany's industrial centres. His fury embraced Goering. Goering, a renowned fighter pilot with Baron Richthofen's squadron during the First World War, had lost his accredited lustre. His public declaration that no British bomber would ever be allowed to invade German air space had proved an empty boast, as had his promise to destroy London and compel Churchill to sue for peace. Alas, poor Hermann Goering, a man larger than life in more than one respect, the men of RAF Bomber Command were giving him the kind of headache he could well do without.

The raid itself gave Londoners one more frightful night. It was an angry and destructive assault. The East End, the West End, Lambeth, Walworth, Bermondsey, Camberwell and other areas were hit. Churches, houses, tenements, places of entertainment, shops and other buildings shuddered and collapsed as high explosives struck, and Sayer Street School in Walworth was completely destroyed. The maturer members of the Adams family knew that school well. Many of the friends of their young days had attended it.

Hardened though the people were to these raids, they were something nobody could ever get to regard simply as a nuisance. Every assault from the sky brought nerves to breaking point, and tested resilience to the limit.

Chapter Thirteen

Early evening in Devon saw clouds bringing a hint of rain. Mrs Mumford was at her sink, scraping the last of her new potatoes for supper, when her front door knocker sounded.

'Missy, do me the goodness to see who that be,' she said to Daisy, who was sitting at the kitchen table shelling garden peas. Daisy's frequent offers of help were now being accepted. Mrs Mumford was still matter-of-fact, but kinder generally, and Daisy was warming to that.

'Yes, I'll go, Mrs Mumford,' she said.

When she opened the front door, she saw Mr Plackford on the step, a heavy-looking sack perched on his right shoulder.

'Hello there, Daisy, how be your corns?' he said.

'Mr Plackford, I don't 'ave no corns,' said Daisy.

'Well, there's a blessing,' said Mr Plackford. 'D'you see this load I'm carrying?'

'Yes, what's in it?' asked Daisy. 'There's a smell.'

'It be ripe manure,' said Mr Plackford, 'the kind I occasionally bring for Mrs Mumford's vegetable plot. Would you ask her if she'd like me to take it up to the plot?'

Mrs Mumford appeared then from her kitchen.

'I thought it were you, George,' she said.

'Ah, it's me,' said Mr Plackford, 'with a sack of the good stuff. Shall I take it up to your vegetable plot instead of leaving it outside your kitchen door?'

'That'll be kind of you,' said Mrs Mumford, 'and it'll leave me grateful.'

'Yes, and it'll take the smell off our front doorstep,' said Daisy.

'That be the smell of the land, missy,' said Mrs Mumford.

'Oh, I know, Mrs Mumford,' said Daisy, now a girl wishful to stay in the lady's good graces, 'only I thought you wouldn't want it staying too long on yer front step in case it sort of crept into yer parlour.'

Mrs Mumford coughed. Mr Plackford grinned.

'Mebbe the little lady's got a point, Dora,' he said. 'I'll take it up right now.'

'I'm thanking you,' said Mrs Mumford.

'You're welcome,' said Mr Plackford, and took himself and the sack off the doorstep. He went around the side of the cottage and up to the vegetable plot. It was the first time he'd been this far up her garden, and he was all eyes. He left the sack near Mrs Mumford's enclosed compost heap that was in the opposite corner to her dead dog's grave. He saw her at her kitchen window on his way back. He smiled and touched his cap to her. He was pretty sure she'd been watching him.

'It's good for yer garden, that stuff, Mrs Mumford?' said Daisy.

'For the vegetable ground come the autumn and winter,' said Mrs Mumford. 'It puts back what growing takes out of it, and I'll need more come spring.'

'I could 'elp yer spread it, if yer like, only wiv a clothes peg over me nose,' said Daisy.

'I'll spare your nose,' said Mrs Mumford.

'I don't mind 'elping you wiv lots of things, honest,' said Daisy.

'I'm thinking, child, there be more good in you than I thought,' said Mrs Mumford. She heard a gulp. She turned from the sink. 'Well, bless my soul, there be no need for that,' she said. Daisy's eyes were visibly wet.

'Mrs Mumford, I – I –' Daisy gulped again.

'Now look at what you're at,' said Mrs Mumford, 'dropping tears into the peas. Ah, well, the tears of a young girl won't harm them, so come now, Daisy, dry your eyes.'

Knowing that was the first time the stiff lady had used her Christian name, Daisy said, 'Mrs Mumford, d'you – d'you like me a bit?'

'That be a question you don't need to ask, child,' said Mrs Mumford.

'Stevie were right, Maudie,' said Mr Plackford on arrival home. 'That dog's grave at the top of Dora Mumford's garden be all of six feet.'

'You still on about that?' said Mrs Plackford. 'More like you should take yourself under the pump and wash off what be smelling all over you.'

'Well, I reckon I left some of it on Dora's doorstep according to young Daisy,' grinned Mr Plackford.

'Be off with you, and stay mindful of your own business about that grave,' said Mrs Plackford. All the same, she mentioned it to one or two neighbours the following day.

The gossip spread, of course.

'Did you hear about the big grave Dora Mumford buried her dog in?'

'No, that I didn't.'

'It be a hugeous thing, I heard.'

'Well, I'd be telling a lie if I said I'd seen it. Dora Mumford never invites anyone into her place these days. Never got over the shock of Barney going off like he did and leaving her.'

'Some woman, weren't it?'

'Bound to have been, but do it matter, how big her first dog's grave be?'

'Mrs Plackford says Mr Plackford's puzzling over it.'

'Ah, well, I don't know I'd spend time puzzling over the size of a dog's grave.'

'Still, it makes a body think, the size of that grave, and no-one's ever heard from Barney.'

'Lordy.'

The old Lyceum Theatre in Wellington Street off the Strand had been converted into a dance hall for the duration of the war. It was crowded this evening, London girls and women, together with soldiers and airmen, defying the threat of another air raid to enjoy themselves. The escapist nature of the ballroom and the lively music of the band created an atmosphere that was almost akin to revelry.

Among the soldiers were a number of Canadian troops, up in town from their barracks at Caterham in Surrey, from where a regular train service brought them to the excitements of the capital in forty minutes. London might still be under siege from the air, but its galleries, museums, cinemas, theatres and other places of entertainment still offered the kind of atmosphere so coveted in wartime. Public shelters abounded for the safety of people in the event of any attack from the air.

Two good-looking cockney women in their thirties were having a great time at the Lyceum, vying with young women in their active participation in the new craze from America, the jitterbug. With their husbands on a night shift from six in the evening until two in the morning in a New Cross factory, they were free to join this infectious plunge into escapism.

They repaired after some breathless cavorting to the Ladies' to powder their noses.

'I think they fancy us,' said one to the other's mirror reflection.

'What's their names?' asked the reflection.

'They told us, didn't they?'

'Well, I've forgot, ain't I?'

'The dark one's Hubert, the other one's Gary. Which d'you fancy?'

''Ere, did we ought to talk like that?'

'Well, we've got to make up our minds, seeing they want to come 'ome with us. I don't mind my 'ome. Well, you've got lodgers.'

'Blimey, Winnie, they'd be first in the queue to tell me old man.'

'Now didn't we 'ear that your old man and mine get a bit of what they fancy from some of them fact'ry tarts? But all right, we don't want yer long-nosed lodgers talkin' out of turn. So my 'ome, then. Come on, Ellen, let's get back to the dancin', or Hubert and Gary will 'ave been pinched by some of the tarts 'ere.'

Mrs Ellen Mobsby and Mrs Winnie Ricketts returned to the ballroom and the company of two husky Canadian soldiers.

Stevie, like Daisy, wasn't expecting any parental visit during the school holidays. His mum and dad and his two brothers, both a lot older than him, made up a rowdy lot who liked a pub but got quarrelsome when they had a bit of drink inside them. Stevie out of family loyalty would have said they weren't actually neglectful, he'd have said they were forgetful more like. They all had skilled jobs in an important factory, which kept his brothers from being called up, and as he himself was an evacuee, he was out of sight and out of mind. Still, they hadn't forgotten to send him a postal order for a quid so that he could enjoy a spending holiday.

He was actually having an uneasy time at the moment, feeling he'd said more than he should about the grave of Mrs Mumford's dead dog. Mr Plackford was keeping on about it.

Stevie mentioned it to Daisy and Posy.

'What you talkin' about, Stevie?' demanded Daisy.

'It's what ev'ryone else is talkin' about,' said Stevie.

'Oh, and what might that be?' asked Posy. The three of them were outside the Goodworthys' cottage.

'About what's in the grave,' said Stevie.

'What d'you mean?' asked Daisy.

'I dunno, do I?' said Stevie.

'You Stevie, you best shut up, then,' said Posy.

'No, let 'im tell us what ev'ryone's saying,' said Daisy.

'No, I ain't goin' to,' said Stevie.

'D'you want a kick?' asked Daisy with some of her former belligerence.

'What for?' asked Stevie.

'For talkin' about what you won't tell us,' said Daisy, which was a perfectly reasonable response.

'Look, I ain't got nothing against the old fussbag,' said Stevie.

'Mrs Mumford's not an old fussbag,' said Daisy, 'and if you call 'er that again, I will kick yer.'

'But, Daisy,' protested Stevie, 'you used to call 'er all sorts of names.'

'That was when I was a wicked girl,' said Daisy, 'but I ain't now, and I don't fight with Posy no more, eiver.'

'Blessed if I don't be sad about that,' said Posy. 'It were fun sometimes, pulling your hair out.'

'You tried, but you couldn't pull none of it out,' said Daisy.

'Well, it be made of wire, that's why,' said Posy.

'Oh, yer mean cat,' cried Daisy. Posy put her thumb to her nose, Daisy yelled and Posy ran. Daisy went in hot-blooded chase. It was usually turn and turn about as to which girl ran and which one went in chase.

'I just dunno about girls,' sighed Stevie, forgetting he liked a bit of a dust-up himself on the occasions when village boys got saucy.

'What d'you think, Jake?' asked Mr Plackford up at the farm.

'That I don't want any part of it,' said Jake Goodworthy.

'I'm directly concerned about what might have happened to Barney,' said Mr Plackford.

'George, if you be that concerned, talk to Constable Brindle,' said Jake. 'I'm not your man. What's more, I've got work to do.'

'In a war like this, with them blamed U-boats sinking food ships every five minutes,' said Mr Plackford, 'we're all killing ourselves with work, which aren't going to please my Maudie or your Beth. Rightly, all I'm saying is that it were a mystery none of us ever heard from Barney.'

'It don't be bothering me,' said Jake.

The weather over France turned foul, and the departure of Helene and Bobby was postponed at the last minute while they were waiting to board an empty Whitley bomber. Quarters were found for them at the bomber station, where the eyes of young RAF men turned admiringly on the tall figure of the good-looking FANY officer. They edged up on her in extrovert fashion. Helene, of course, upbraided Bobby for allowing her to be so closely surrounded by these RAF gallants that she found it difficult to breathe. Bobby said he'd do his best to rescue her every time she called for help, but to remember he was outnumbered. She called him ten times an idiot.

Kate, doing morning work in Westbury for the Red Cross branch there, had finally given in to David's repeated offers to show her how to keep the flower borders free of weeds. Arriving one afternoon at the agreed time, he regarded her attractive dress dubiously.

'Excuse me,' said Kate, 'but are you looking me over?'

'Well, if we're going to do some gardening,' said David, 'how about wearing something old and ragged, with gumboots?'

'Old and ragged?' said Kate. 'Old and ragged? Didn't you suggest that once before?'

'Got anything like that?' asked David amiably.

'Oh, I've got a wardrobe full of old and ragged stuff, haven't I?' said Kate. 'Look, I'm not going to do any gardening on me hands and knees, am I? You said I just have to use a hoe.'

'A handfork today,' said David, 'and I can go back and find a spare pair of summer shorts for you.'

'Any more clever suggestions like that,' said Kate, 'and you'll find them that you're wearing will be round your ankles again.' With a wicked smile, she added, 'Would you happen today to be wearing something old and ragged under them?'

'No, not today,' said David, opening the shed door to look for weeding implements. He brought out a couple of small two-pronged handforks. 'Here we are, Kate, one for you, one for me.'

Taking one, Kate said, 'How do I use this, might I ask?'

'You dig the weeds out with it,' said David. 'You can see how some of them have grown.'

'Is that a weed?' asked Kate, pointing.

'No, that's a primrose that's died off,' said David. 'That's a weed, and there, that's a whole bunch of them. You'll have to get down on your knees.'

'I thought that's where I'd end up, on me knees, and didn't I say so?' said Kate.

'You won't be able to reach them standing up,' said David. 'Dig 'em up and chuck 'em in this bucket.'

'On me knees?' said Kate, who felt she was being treated too much like a would-be gardener and not enough as a girl with pride in her appearance. 'What about me dress and stockings, might I ask?'

'Well, I can't say they're not pretty,' said David. Kate looked at him. He gave her a smile. They were close. Kate's green eyes darkened with the suspicion that he was going to kiss her.

'Oh, no, you don't,' she said, but somehow they were closer, and there was a mesmerizing eye-to-eye contact uncommon to adolescents.

'Hello, what are you two up to?' It was Aunt Hilary's voice. 'Whatever it is, go ahead. I like to see young people doing what comes naturally.'

They jumped. Aunt Hilary was standing at the open kitchen door, her languid smile showing.

Kate, pink, said to David, 'You dummy, you were going to grab me and kiss me.'

'Just a birthday kiss,' said David.

'It's not me birthday till next June,' said Kate.

'Well, your aunt saved me from making a mistake,' said David.

'Saved you from getting a kick as well,' said Kate.

Aunt Hilary interposed again.

'Kate, when you and David have finished your tête-à-tête, will you make some tea, dear? I'd like a cup in my study.'

'Yes, all right, Auntie,' said Kate.

Aunt Hilary smiled and disappeared.

'I thought she was out,' said David.

'Lucky for me she wasn't,' said Kate, 'or I might be fighting off your evil desires by now.'

David laughed.

'That's a funny,' he said.

'Not much it isn't,' said Kate. 'Crikey, the way you look at a girl, you ought to be locked up.'

But she was laughing as she went into the kitchen to put the kettle on and to escape going down on her knees to dig up weeds. David started to lift the unwanted intruders, thinking Kate was being a servant again to her aunt, who could easily have made a pot of tea herself. He also thought he'd just experienced his first meaningful urge to kiss a girl.

Later, before she needed to begin preparing the supper, Kate said she'd managed to finish her report about Hitler's mountain lair. Would David like to listen to it?

Cautiously, he said, 'Is it about—?'

'Well, yes,' said Kate, 'I had to face up to that, didn't I?'

'Am I going to have to listen to the – er—?' asked David.

'David, don't be a wet,' said Kate. 'You're living in the real world, y'know, and you've got to realize it's not just about digging potatoes and cleaning old ladies' windows. There's a war on, and it's 'orrible, and this Stormtrooper with his evil desires, he's 'orrible too. You going to listen or not?'

'Well, all right,' said David, 'I just hope I don't have a fainting fit, that's all.'

'If you have a fainting fit, I'll give you up for good,' said Kate. 'Be manly and listen. You remember I got to where the Stormtrooper threw me on his bed with me Paris dress nearly falling off? Well, from there, this is what I've written.' She read from an exercise book. '"I stared up at him in 'orror and despair while he looked down at me legs and me Paris silks and satins which were showing and I could see his evil desires were going to overcome me if I didn't do something, so I pulled meself together and thrust me hand into me bag that I was still clutching and drew out a stick of dynamite which I hurled at him with all me might and much to my relief and like an answer to me prayers it struck him in his face and blew his head right off in front of me eyes."'

'Oh, jolly good,' said David.

'Jolly good?' said Kate scornfully. 'What d'you mean, jolly good? Fancy saying something like that about one of me characters having his head blown off. Anyone else would've said what an 'orrible death it was. I don't know why you have to sound all posh and soppy when your parents are nice common people like I am meself.'

'They're not common,' said David, 'nor are you. You're an eye-opener.'

'Are you referring to when my dress was caught up and your eyes went all beady?' demanded Kate.

'Oh, I've forgotten that,' said David.

'Well, thanks very much,' said Kate tartly, 'I'm sorry me legs and stockings turned out forgetful.'

'Not much,' said David. 'Never seen prettier.'

'Kindly don't be personal,' said Kate.

'That's a bit contrary, isn't it?' said David.

'I don't know what you mean,' said Kate. 'Just listen. "But even as the headless corpse fell to the floor in stormed four more Stormtroopers that had heard the explosion and they trembled with shock and rage as they saw what had happened which I admit wasn't a very handsome sight. Well, I was already off the bed and I drew out another stick of dynamite and ordered them to stand back or I'd blow their heads off too which caused them to turn faint and pale but one man summoned up courage and charged at me so I hurled the dynamite straight at him but to me bitter despair it didn't explode and they all charged at me then and I could only draw me bayonet out of me stocking-top to defend meself to the death for the honour of me country and me virtue."'

'Oh, gawd blimey,' said David helplessly and as common as muck, which was more to Kate's liking.

'"I stabbed the first man and he ran out clutching

196

his wounded chest but one of the other Stormtroopers got behind me and seized me, shouting that I was arrested in the name of Adolf Hitler and I was taken up to the balcony and into the room where Hitler was 'aving tea with his evil gang and some German ladies with large German chests which they have to have or they don't get invited." David, are you having a fit or something?'

'Yes, but carry on, I'll get over it,' wheezed David.

'Me story's still about the real world, y'know,' said Kate.

'I do know,' said David, 'and people do have fits in the real world.'

'You shouldn't have them at your age,' said Kate. '"The Stormtroopers threw me on me knees in front of Hitler and said I was guilty of murder. Hitler shouted 'orribly at me, then asked if it was true and I said no it wasn't, I said I didn't know the dynamite was going to blow the Stormtrooper's head off which still didn't make Hitler stop shouting and cursing, but then a man stepped into the room from the outside balcony and said very cool for everyone to put their hands up and that he'd shoot the first one that moved, oh, did me heart jump for joy because it was me dashing Air Force pilot who'd been with me on me flight to the mountain lair and was madly in love with me and desired me in an hon'rable way. Well, when everyone had their hands up and Hitler was red with rage we escaped and made our way to the plane where I adjusted me silks and satins and me gown before we flew off back to London and although I hadn't been able to blow up the mountain lair I had a medal pinned to me best frock in the House of Commons by our great leader in respectful honour of me bravery. Yours faithfully Kate Trimble special reporter." Well, what d'you think, David? David?'

'I'm having another fit,' said David.

'Honest, you're puerile,' said Kate. 'Can't you stand real life blood and thunder?'

'It's not the blood and thunder,' said David, weak and slightly hoarse, 'it's you adjusting your silks and satins on top of a mountain that's giving me a turn.'

'Well, I wasn't going to get on the plane with me Paris creations all untidy and blowing in the wind, was I?' said Kate.

'No, I suppose not, and I'll be all right in a minute,' said David. 'Er – shouldn't you describe your silks and satins?'

'What for?' asked Kate.

'Um – to make them sound real,' said David.

'Oh, you dummy, you don't suppose they're not real, do you?' said Kate. 'You don't suppose I could wear anything that was imagin'ry, do you?'

'Yes, but what are they?' asked David.

'Me French knickers and chemise, of course,' said Kate.

'Crikey,' said David, 'no wonder your dashing pilot desires you, but you sure it's honourably?'

'Don't be disgusting,' said Kate. 'Well, I'll have to start getting supper now.'

'And I'll have to get back for my own supper,' said David. 'I just hope me legs'll carry me. When you write your next story, could it be about a cricket match?'

'Cricket? Cricket?' Kate was 100 per cent not in favour of writing about cricket. 'What d'you want all that boring stuff for?'

'To stop me having fits,' said David, going on his way.

Kate giggled.

Chapter Fourteen

In the Western Desert, General Rommel was still besieging Tobruk, still building up supplies and armaments for a further general offensive against the British Eighth Army, while units of his crack troops were making periodical sorties to keep his opponents jumpy. General Auchinleck, in turn, was preparing the Eighth Army for an attempt to smash the Afrika Korps and hurl it back to Tripoli. If Rommel so far had proved superior in tactics, at least it was a fact that he had found the opposition tough. The British had learnt something from their fighting retreat to Dunkirk more than a year ago. Their only real need was a commander with as much tactical skill as Rommel.

In Russia, the victorious Germans were fortifying their stupendous gains while planning another massive attack. They would be aiming to capture Kiev, Leningrad, and Moscow itself, before the fearsome Russian winter set in.

In the Atlantic, German U-boats were hunting in packs, destroying British merchant ships at an alarming rate. Churchill ordered an increase in the protective rings of escorting warships, while the people of the United Kingdom tightened their belts further. In the United States, public figures like Charles Lindbergh were doing their best to keep their country out of the war by promoting isolationism, but young Americans were crossing the Atlantic to provide welcome reinforcements for the American Eagle Squadron of the RAF. Indeed, American pilots had fought in the Battle of Britain, and President Roosevelt, putting no discouragement in the way of a regular flow of volunteers, clearly showed where his sympathies lay.

Saturday, August 9

It was a quiet wedding indeed for Felicity and Tim at the Streatham registry office, with just their parents and Clara in attendance. Felicity and Tim were both in uniform. The war had brought them together, the war was still going on, and their khaki was representative of the many months, crowded with incident, in which they had come to know each other so well.

Clara, in a costume, was there as Felicity's bridesmaid, and Boots was his son's best man. If some members of the Adams family would have liked to attend out of natural interest and curiosity, they all refrained from appearing. Chinese Lady had ventured to suggest she and Edwin ought to at least have the pleasure of meeting the bride sometime before the wedding, and Boots had thought she'd get his stepfather, Edwin Finch, to drive her to the hospital one day. She might have done exactly that if Edwin hadn't succeeded in gently dissuading her.

He was sure, he said, that the young lady needed time to adjust to new relatives, of which, he pointed out, there were enough to be fairly overwhelming.

The service was simple but not unimpressive, and Felicity and Tim were prepared to make their brief responses clearly. Boots and Polly had their eyes on Felicity, noting her self-control and the dark glasses that hid her scarred eyes. The registrar, who had several weddings to conduct, one after another, forsook his usual formal approach in favour of a mellow and sympathetic attitude towards this particular couple.

Everyone had their own thoughts. Felicity's mother thought what a brave daughter she had, brave enough to go into a marriage when she must still be feeling awful about her blindness. It was hoped she would spend her time at home when she eventually left the hospital. At home, family care and attention would help her to adjust gradually to everything domestic until the day came when she could take up married life with the man she had chosen as her husband. Mrs Jessop conceded he was fine-looking and extremely agreeable, and she offered up heartfelt prayers for the two of them.

Mr Jessop thought well, I've come round to not being as worried about this as I was. I now believe that if this really is what Felicity wants, then it'll be more of a help to her than anything else I can think of. And having met Tim Adams a couple of times, I can't honestly say I'm doubtful about her choice. Look at her, she's smiling. She's completely blind, God help her, but she's smiling. That's got to mean something good.

Boots thought the smile an effort. He felt he knew what Felicity was going through. He remembered his own blindness when he and Emily were married, and how all through the service he was beset by the roughest of emotions. But Emily had never had any doubts about how to surmount the difficulties ahead, and he didn't think Tim would have dreamt of accepting an offer to withdraw if Felicity had offered it at the last moment.

Polly wondered at herself and her feelings. One simply couldn't escape the weakness of emotional involvement when belonging to the Adams family. They all lived such extrovert lives, in which they unashamedly wore their hearts on their sleeves in their attachment to each other. What one Adams did, every other Adams wanted to know about. The whole tribe regarded themselves as indivisible, and all paid their tributes to Boots's enduring mother, the matriarch. Ye gods, thought Polly, I pay my own, I'm one of them, I'm even a stepmother to some of them, including Tim. Look at him, perfectly happy about marrying Felicity and giving her something precious to live for. Bless that young man.

Clara thought about the fact that Felicity would return to the hospital after the weekend. I'm glad about it. It's too soon for her to leave, never mind how determined she and Tim were to make a go at it. She does need a few more months with us to make sure she's really capable of coping reasonably with everything. She's a lovely person and deserves as much happiness as she can find. I'm relieved the senior medicoes refused to approve her wish to discharge herself. My word, didn't she swear. But she came round, she saw how sensible it was to join Tim only when her rehabilitation was as complete as we can make it. And now she can't join him until he returns from overseas. That's a little sad.

The registrar smiled and advised Tim he could kiss his bride. The ring was on her finger, and she was now Mrs Tim Adams. Polly, of course, wondered if she had any idea of what it was going to mean, becoming an Adams. Whatever she was thinking, she received Tim's kiss as if happily willing to risk finding most of her in-laws either boring or freakish.

The marriage certificate, filled in, was signed, Tim guiding Felicity in her use of the pen. Her signature wavered a little and went off line a bit.

'How's it look?' she asked.

'Readable,' said Tim, 'and a lot superior to a couple of crosses. First-class, in fact.'

The certificate was witnessed, the registrar and his assistant were thanked, and the wedding party left, Tim driving Felicity and Clara in his Uncle Tommy's car, loaned to him for the weekend. Boots followed with Polly and Mr and Mrs Jessop. At the home of the Jessops in Streatham, the wedding breakfast, of a wartime kind but attractively presented by Mrs Jessop, was eaten around the dining-room table, on which were bottles of wine contributed by Tim's Uncle Ned, who had quietly asked if he might have the favour of doing so.

Felicity managed the intake of food and drink with only a little help, and conversation rattled along. Polly, Boots, Tim and Felicity herself were all naturals at setting a ball rolling. Mrs Jessop found it difficult to be light-hearted, but was relieved to have the atmosphere actually become festive.

'Is there going to be a speech?' asked Felicity eventually.

'Well, darling,' said Mrs Jessop hesitantly, 'we thought—'

'Mother dear,' said Felicity, 'even a quiet wedding should be graced by one speech. Off the cuff will do.'

Mr Jessop, chief cashier at a Streatham bank, was not given to the impromptu. A well-prepared speech was his forte, and it had to be particularly well-prepared for it to be suitable to this occasion.

'I'll forgo the privilege,' he smiled, 'if someone else would like it.'

'Over to you, Dad,' said Tim, whom Clara thought a wow in his best uniform.

'I pass,' said Boots.

'Back to you, Tim,' said Polly, 'off the cuff stuff from your father can be dangerous.'

'Dangerous?' said Felicity, keeping to herself all her feelings of bitter frustration. 'I like the sound of that. Go ahead—' She paused and managed a smile. 'Go ahead, father-in-law.'

'Heaven help us all,' said Polly, as Boots came to his feet.

'Allow me on this happy occasion,' he said, 'to recount what I believe is an apt story. At a certain wedding, the young bride and groom were both admirably virtuous, as of course are Felicity and Tim. They were innocent of all behaviour and experiences that might be called the reverse of innocent.'

'I'm getting suspicious,' said Tim.

'I'm getting alarmed,' said Clara.

'I'm listening,' said Felicity.

'After the reception,' continued Boots, 'the happy newly-weds set off for their honeymoon hotel, where at the end of the day they finally retired to bed, and where, in their innocence, they sat up all night waiting for their sexual relations to arrive.'

'Oh, my God,' said Polly.

Clara and Felicity shrieked with laughter, Mrs Jessop giggled like a girl, Mr Jessop smiled broadly and Tim roared.

'Regarding our own newly-weds,' said Boots, 'it's my personal opinion that Tim has acquired an exceptional wife, and Polly and I an exceptional daughter. We wish her and Tim an exceptional life, and I hope that any difficulties they have to face will relate only to the bothersome nature of Army rules and regulations. If they need any help in this respect, I recommend a phone call to Polly, who in her time has wangled her way round every regulation in the book. I now bow out.'

'With honours,' said Felicity, and Clara guessed how much she wished she could see exactly what Tim's father was like.

'Bless the man,' murmured Polly, and slipped a hand over his thigh as he sat down. She squeezed to let him know he had come up trumps. Somehow, he always did.

'How about a little something from you, Tim?' suggested Mr Jessop.

'Dad's a hard act to follow,' said Tim, but came to his feet. 'I'll chance a few words. Well, two questions, say. One, could my father's wife write down how to wangle a way round every Army rule and regulation? Two, could my father let Felicity and me know how to make our sexual relations arrive on time?'

'Tim, oh, my goodness,' blushed Mrs Jessop.

'What a bounder,' said Felicity. 'I'm married to him? I need a doctor.'

'A few more words,' said Tim. 'I owe thanks to everyone here. Thanks for being with Felicity and me today, thanks for all you've done for us in the past, and thanks for what I know you're all willing to offer in the future. What we'd all like most of all, I suppose, is for the war to end – no, correction, we all know what we'd first like, but failing that kind of miracle, join Felicity and me in looking forward in time to post-war blessings. We'll win.'

Clara knew which war he meant, the one he and Felicity would be fighting together.

Tim parked the car in the drive of the house on Red Post Hill, went round to the passenger door and opened it. He helped Felicity alight.

'This is it?' she said.

'Yes, this is my home,' said Tim, 'and it's ours alone for the weekend. My grandparents are staying with my Aunt Vi and Uncle Tommy. A hotel would have given us problems.'

'Yes, I know, Tim.' Felicity drew a little breath. The agreed arrangement was that she and Tim would spend the weekend here by themselves. His father and stepmother were on their way back to Dorset, taking Clara with them to drop her off at the hospital. She herself was to be driven back there by Tim on Monday.

Tim fished her valise out of the boot, and looked at the front door. A little silver-coloured wedding bell, a gesture of welcome, hung from the knocker. He glanced at Felicity, close beside him.

'This way to our honeymoon,' he said.

'Tim?'

'Felicity?'

'Stay with me.'

He took her hand.

She was laughing, actually laughing. They were in bed at last, in his bed. He had helped her in many ways since their arrival some hours ago in his house, a place whose geography she did not know, but on retiring she had claimed the right to undress herself by herself.

'I'm willing to stand by,' said Tim.

'You'll look,' she said.

'I thought modern women didn't mind,' said Tim.

'Blow that,' she said, 'I'm not doing a bridal striptease. Push off.'

Tim did the honourable thing and absented himself from the bedroom. When he subsequently joined her between the sheets, he wondered exactly how a man ought to behave with a sightless bride. Naturally, of course, since in the darkness he was as blind as she was. Further, she was just as exciting to him as she had been during their time in Troon. In any event, she had no reservations about this, that and the other. He kissed her with ardour, teased her, played about, made her kick and then said, when her breath was very quick, 'Someone's knocking, Felicity.'

'Oh, bloody hell, not now, surely.'

'Yes. It's our sexual relations, they're nice and early.'

That was when she laughed. That was when she truly relaxed and they made love in the darkness. Darkness was what she lived in day and night.

'Well, Mrs Adams the Fourth?' murmured Tim afterwards.

'Heavens, you don't expect me to talk about it, do you?'

'No, just say a few words.'

'Love you for marrying me.'

'My pleasure, Puss.'

Chapter Fifteen

They had a Sunday of necessary togetherness. While Tim understood her need to do things for herself, he had to be close by most of the time. She was at a loss on frequent occasions. She liked it when they went for a walk at eleven, for it took her away from the obstacles of chairs, tables and other furniture, and was a comparatively easy exercise for her. They had Sunday dinner at one-thirty. Chinese Lady had made her own contribution by leaving them a steak-and-kidney pie. With it she'd also left a note.

> *Dear Tim,*
> *Your Granddad and me send you and your bride our best wishes which come very sincerely from us with hopes you'll both be happy all your lives. I hope too you'll find this pie nice for your Sunday dinner, your Granddad brought the steak and kidney home with him from his Government place and said it was with the compliments of the Prime Minister which I took with a pinch of salt. The pie only needs putting in the oven for heating up and there's vegetables in containers in the bottom of the larder. Your Granddad and me hope you enjoy a nice weekend but if you turn the wireless on don't expect it*

to cheer you up as it is always very uncheering. Love from Grandma and give your nice lady wife our blessing.

Tim read it to Felicity, who thought it absolutely priceless.

'What a lovely old darling.'

'Agreed,' said Tim.

'And is there really a steak-and-kidney pie?'

'There's a pie with a lovely brown crust and crinkly edges,' said Tim, 'and if she says it's steak-and-kidney, it is.'

'I haven't seen steak and kidney since I don't know when,' said Felicity.

'Nor me,' said Tim.

'At least, I haven't encountered it,' said Felicity.

'Nor me,' said Tim. 'We're in the same war.'

'But not in the same boat,' said Felicity, and because of her smile Tim knew that was a whimsical comment, not a complaint.

'Well, your boat's a hard one to row, I know that,' he said, 'but I'm in it with you, Puss. I'm the one at the rudder.'

'Keeping me clear of the rocks?' said Felicity. 'True, we're both in it while we're together.' She was wishing togetherness could continue, that Tim did not have to go overseas and she did not have to go back to the hospital. Togetherness with Tim gave her a warm secure feeling. But she knew she was still fumbling and stumbling at times. 'About the pie, darling, I'll take charge of its reheating with just a little help from you, and we'll prepare the vegetables between us.'

'You sound like my wife,' said Tim.

'Yes, love it,' said Felicity.

The pie turned out to be delicious, and for afters they had fresh fruit in the way of apples. Felicity thought she'd peel hers, and Tim watched her as she made the attempt. He saw how carefully she handled the apple, how carefully she used the fruit knife, her blind eyes behind the dark glasses not lowered but looking straight ahead, her little frown of concentration evident.

'You're winning,' he said, as peel curled and fell. It was a little thick, but what did that matter? The humdrum act was a challenge to her and she won at a slow steady pace, even if she did somewhat reduce the size of the fruit. She cut it into slices. Irregular slices.

'Say something,' she said.

'What's there to say except congratulations?' said Tim. His admiration, his affection and his watchfulness played about with other emotions, but he kept all his remarks on a light level.

They did the washing-up together. Tim washed the dishes, Felicity took careful hold of each one he handed her, and dried it just as carefully. Tim noted the slowness with which she performed every little task, and he knew the medicoes had been right in advising more time for convalescent rehabilitation. The concentration she had given to everything had its effect by the time the washing-up had been done, and Tim took her into his grandmother's parlour and made her relax on the long old-fashioned sofa for half an hour. She said, 'Oh, curse it,' but didn't argue.

At three, however, she was briskly ready for another walk. She was at her best out-of-doors, walking arm in arm with Tim, her feet confident, her coversation full of familiar touches. Her occasional brittle note reminded him of Polly, his stepmother, during the years of her friendship with the family. Polly was a much more relaxed woman now.

'Are we going uphill?' asked Felicity.

'Yes, this is Red Post Hill,' said Tim, 'and we're heading for Denmark Hill.'

'All right for some, including a Commando,' said Felicity, 'but carry on, tiger. Tell me what it looks like.'

'On your left, madam,' said Tim, 'we're about to pass a large three-storey house where Lily Driscoll once slept.'

'Who was she?' asked Felicity.

'Oh, just a girl I used to know,' said Tim.

'Did that make her famous?'

'No, it made her mum keep her in at night,' said Tim. 'Over on your right, madam, is Laburnum Lodge, a high-falutin' monicker for a pile of bricks.'

'Bombed?' said Felicity.

'Incendiaries,' said Tim.

'Those bloody Jerries,' said Felicity. 'Hi, we've passed a tree.'

'How did you know?' asked Tim.

'I can smell trees,' said Felicity. 'I can smell the bark. I can smell you.'

'What's that mean,' said Tim, 'that I've got BO?'

'No, just a man's smell,' said Felicity, her arm

hugging his, her walk almost springy. 'I think I'm developing an acute olfactory sense.'

'Well, how does your olfactory sense rate my man's smell, better or worse than BO?'

'Sexy,' said Felicity.

They walked on, but stopped when they reached Denmark Hill.

'How'd you feel?' asked Tim.

'Same way as you, by touch,' said Felicity.

He smiled. There she was, bare-headed, her striped green and white dress delicate on her lithe body, her expression that of a young woman quite animated. She looked, in fact, as if she had no quarrel with the world. She asked then what he could see from where they were.

'We're fairly high,' said Tim, 'and looking north I can see the sky over the centre of London. It's clear. Can you feel the Sunday quiet?' Perhaps he shouldn't have mentioned quiet, for before Felicity could make her response, the air raid sirens sounded. 'Bloody hell,' he breathed, 'a daylight raid on a Sunday afternoon? Shall we go back and make use of the garden shelter?'

'No,' said Felicity in a strangely positive way, 'let's stay here, Tim, and you can tell me what happens, if it's near enough.'

Dornier bombers, escorted by fighters, came in from across the Channel, passing over the white cliffs of Dover and entering the air space above Kent. It was a reminder from Goering that the *Luftwaffe* was as redoubtable as ever. It was also a recklessly angry response to the RAF's continuous bombing of German strong-points in occupied

France and the factories of war in the western regions of the Third Reich. At their stations in South-East England, Hurricane and Spitfire squadrons were alerted for action.

'Squadron, scramble! South Foreland, nine thousand feet!'

'Squadron, scramble! Hythe, nine thousand feet!'

'Squadron, scramble! North Foreland, nine thousand feet!'

From Manston, Biggin Hill, Kenley, Croydon and other fighter bases, the British planes took wing to meet the oncoming bandits. An American war correspondent, covering the action at Biggin Hill, marvelled at the fact that the pilots were such young men. And what a mixed bag they were. Poles, Czechs, Canadians, South Africans, Australians, Welsh, Scots, English and Americans. Many were survivors from the Battle of Britain.

'Squadron airborne!'

'Airborne!'

'Airborne!'

High, high, high climbed the Spitfires and Hurricanes to make contact with the invaders.

From a squadron leader. 'Hello, squadron! Hello, squadron! Bandits eleven o'clock! Watch for the 109's!'

'Hear you, Leader!'

Suddenly the air battle was joined, and the familiar white trails began to stream across the blue sky above Kent, the Garden of England, the county famed for its cherry orchards, for the profusion of blossom in spring and the harvest of fruit in summer.

'Well, Tim?' asked Felicity. She was conscious only of an intense quiet.

'Can't see or hear a thing,' said Tim.

'Join my club,' said Felicity.

One could never hear the dogfights that took place high in the sky, only watch the white vapour trails, and these, when the aerial battles were fierce, sometimes criss-crossed the blue. From Denmark Hill, however, Tim could see not a single trail. The Hurricanes and Spitfires, alerted by radar, had engaged with the enemy far to the south-east, and the Messerschmitt 109's that had been weaving their protective patterns above the Dorniers, were now mixing it with the RAF fighters. The people of London and its suburbs were in their shelters, breathing fire in fierce resentment of this disturbance on a Sunday afternoon.

'We'll hear something if any of the bombers break through,' said Tim. Some always did, as on this occasion.

It was Felicity who, in the sharp-eared trap of her blindness, was the first to hear them.

'Here they come,' she said.

'Yes,' said Tim a moment later, 'here they come, Puss, and as far as I can see, we're the only people standing about.'

'I'm immune,' said Felicity, 'I've had my bomb. Stick close, chum, and share my immunity.'

The faint drone of the approaching Dorniers took on a stronger note to become a rhythmic surge of noise.

'The buggers are coming straight in,' said Tim.

'Are they visible?' asked Felicity.

'They're too high,' said Tim, 'but I'd guess them to be over Blackheath right now. It'll be Lewisham next, I'll bet, then New Cross and the docks.'

'Not us?' said Felicity.

'Hope not,' said Tim, 'all my closest relatives live around here.'

The surging rhythm created vibrations of noise that travelled and spread through the sky. The first bombs dropped. On Bermondscy, Millwall and the docks. Each one arrived with the bitter compliments of Hermann Goering. Hurricanes arrived over inner London then to drive the bombers to greener pastures before attempting to down them. There were three Dorniers. They turned over the river and dropped low as they headed back home, releasing the residue of their loads as they went. They hit the Borough, Newington Butts, Kennington and Brixton, passing west of Camberwell and Herne Hill, but the huge drone began to buffet the ears of the newly-weds, and Tim glimpsed the planes then, shapes floating at the height of no more than five hundred feet. Low flight was a way of escaping attack, and Tim knew the bombers would attempt to keep at their present level all the way to the Channel, where they could expect protective fighters to shield them home.

'Do I duck?' Felicity, feeling the loudly buzzing Dorniers were almost overhead, raised her voice. 'Or do I let them run me over?'

'No need to duck, Mrs Adams,' said Tim, 'they're leaving us alone.'

The bombers disappeared. In deadly pursuit,

the Hurricanes went after them. In no time at all, Denmark Hill was quiet again.

'Now what?' asked Felicity.

'More walking?' said Tim. 'Down to Ruskin Park and then a bus back? The all-clear will have sounded by then.'

'Good on you, tiger,' said Felicity, 'wear me out and then take advantage of me. No, not on the bus, wait until we reach our weekend home.'

'My grandma would say holy wedlock permits that,' said Tim.

'As far as I'm concerned,' said Felicity, 'holy wedlock tells me to expect it.'

'So?' smiled Tim.

'My expectations can hardly wait,' said Felicity.

Tommy and Vi were sharing their shelter with Chinese Lady and Mr Finch. Tommy was reading a book, and hoping he wouldn't be called on for ARP duties, Vi was knitting, Mr Finch immersed in his Sunday paper and Chinese Lady sounding off.

'I'll never understand what gets into these Germans, they must like wearing uniforms and going to war and making life miserable for other people. And how they can like that man Hitler and bow down to him, well, I'd never bow down to him myself, not if he was wearing six uniforms and sticking both hands up in the air. I just don't know why he has to send bombers over on a nice Sunday afternoon, it's downright criminal and unsociable as well, especially for Tim and his poor young lady when they've only just got married. I just don't know what they must be feeling like. Edwin?'

'Yes, my dear?' murmured Mr Finch. The garden shelter, compact, was large enough to accommodate a put-you-up settee on which they were all seated. When unfolded it provided a bed, similar to makeshift furniture in shelters generally. Sensibly, people had decided there was no point in living too uncomfortably in a refuge, and some had constructed wooden bunks and fitted them with mattresses.

'Edwin,' said Chinese Lady, 'don't you think someone should go round and see if Tim and Felicity are all right?'

'Oh, I think they can take care of themselves, Maisie.'

'I didn't say they couldn't, but suppose a bomb's been dropped on the house? It would be just like the Germans to do that to a young couple just wed. Lor', that poor young lady.'

'I don't think any bombs have been dropped in this area, Maisie,' said Mr Finch.

'Well, I hope you're right,' said Chinese Lady. 'Perhaps Tommy could go and make sure.' Tommy buried himself deeper in his detective story. 'Tommy love?'

No answer.

'Tommy, Mum's talking to you,' said Vi.

'What's she saying?' asked Tommy, who thought the newly-weds should remain free of enquiring relatives, air raid or no air raid, unless an SOS was received.

'Mum's saying that perhaps you could go and see if Tim and Felicity are all right,' said Vi.

'Perhaps you could tell Ma—'

'Vi, is he calling me Ma?' asked Chinese Lady. 'I hope he's not going to get common, like Sammy. I don't know how many times I've told Sammy not to call me Ma. If Tommy's going to start, and if Boots still keeps calling me old girl, well, it'll look as if I wasted my time trying to bring all of them up respectful.'

'Tommy, d'you hear that?' asked Vi.

'Pardon?' said Tommy.

'Mum, he's got his nose in that book of his,' said Vi. 'Still, as soon as the all-clear goes, I could phone Tim, if you like.'

'Well, all right, Vi,' said Chinese Lady, 'but I just hope that while we're sitting here Tim and Felicity aren't lying injured or wounded. Edwin?'

'Yes, Maisie?'

'D'you think they liked the steak-and-kidney pie?'

'I'm sure they did,' said Mr Finch, well aware that his inimitable wife dearly wanted to look in on Tim and his bride herself.

'I'd of made them a banana custard for afters,' mused Chinese Lady. 'It's always been a favourite of Tim's, only you just can't get bananas these days. Edwin, perhaps you could ask the Government about getting some.'

'One can always ask,' murmured Mr Finch, who had obtained the steak and kidney from a Whitehall chef. 'Governments don't always listen,' he added.

'What was that, Edwin?'

'Nothing of any consequence, Maisie,' he smiled. Mr Finch, at this stage of his chequered life, was very much in tune with the spirited resistance of his adopted country and the eccentricities of many of its individuals.

The sirens sounded the prolonged all-clear note, and everyone relaxed.

'Oh, good,' said Vi. 'Now, who'd like a nice cup of tea?'

'Well, I'm sure we all would,' said Chinese Lady.

Mr Finch smiled again.

Tommy's car, driven by Tim, stopped outside the entrance to the hospital at noon on Monday morning. He got out, opened the passenger door, and helped Felicity to alight.

'Is the hospital still standing?' she asked.

'Yes, every brick in place,' said Tim, pulling out her valise.

'You sound cheerful,' said Felicity. 'I hope you're not. I'll send you off with a bomb up your shirt if you are.'

'Well, on a serious note,' said Tim, 'I'd like you to know I've just had a memorable weekend.' He thought Felicity had fought an exceptional fight with everything that represented a hazard. 'It's put me totally in favour of our marriage.'

'I still have a feeling you're wearing a smile,' said Felicity. 'I regard that as treachery. You realize, don't you, that you're dumping me here and chucking me back into the arms of people I love to hate? I appreciate their intentions, but in trying to make a useful woman of me they give me a feeling I'm still pretty useless.'

'Listen,' said Tim, 'all over the weekend you've

been thinking positive. Stay like that, Puss.'

'How can I think positive when you're dumping me and going up to Liverpool in a day or so?' demanded Felicity, who didn't feel at all philosophical about their indefinite separation and didn't care who knew it. The weekend had given her an all too enjoyable experience of what life with Tim could be like. Helpful, caring and very much the lover, he had convinced her that together they could in time make light of her limitations, particularly as she was going to spend further months under the care and guidance of Clara and other staff members, the professional counsellors and teachers of the blind.

'Well, wherever you are and wherever I am,' said Tim, 'hold on to the fact that I love you, and that you were a marvel all over the weekend.'

She made a wry face.

'Sorry about being a little negative now, darling,' she whispered, 'but I've got the rats about you disappearing for God knows how long.'

Clara appeared then, at the entrance to the hospital. Seeing them, she began to advance, crisp uniform rustling.

'Puss, Clara's on her way,' said Tim.

'Write to me,' said Felicity. 'Twice a week at least. And don't be too much of a hero. Fall sick, fall ill. Break a leg if you have to.'

'I'll be rejoining Colonel Lucas,' said Tim, 'and if I know him as well as I think I do, he won't accept a single broken leg as an excuse. I'll have to break both.'

Felicity, her hand on his arm, whispered, 'Must

tell you I loved being in bed with you, both of us in the dark. You've got divine muscles.'

'I'll let you know in a letter what I think of all you've got,' said Tim.

'For Clara to read?' breathed Felicity. 'Don't you dare, you bounder.'

Up came Clara with a swish, a rustle and a smile.

'Hello, lovebirds,' she said. 'I won't ask what you got up to over the weekend.'

'You'll get a thick ear if you do,' said Felicity.

Clara glanced at Tim. He nodded. She understood. He was leaving Felicity chiefly in her care.

'I'll take her bag, Tim,' she said, and he handed it over. He put an arm around Felicity and kissed her. They had agreed not to make their parting more painful by prolonging it.

'You're winning, you know that, don't you?' he said.

'I know you're my lovely lifeline, and I'm hanging on to that,' said Felicity, and emotion disturbed them both. If she found their goodbye painful, so did Tim. But it was said and he got back into the car.

Felicity and Clara were still standing there when he drove away. He saw them as he turned right outside the gate to enter the road. He stopped for a moment, looked back and put a hand out of his open window to make a farewell gesture. Felicity couldn't see him. But Clara spoke to her.

Mrs Felicity Adams lifted a hand and waved.

Chapter Sixteen

'Sammy, Sammy,' Rachel Goodman shook her head at Susie's husband. She was slowly recovering from her own husband's death and tenderly grateful to Sammy for all the sympathetic and practical help she had had from him, which included the job he'd given her. It meant she had the kind of work that was therapeutic, and it strengthened her resolve never to do anything to disturb Susie's trust in her. Rachel could not help her feelings for Sammy, any more than Polly had been able to help her love for Boots. The bomb that killed Emily had given Polly what she most wanted, the chance to marry Boots. The last thing Rachel wanted was for something dreadful to happen to Susie. She was content with the pleasure and exhilaration of being Sammy's general manager. Because of his growing military contracts, his business was booming, and he was at his electric best in his enthusiasm for his newly-formed property company. Yet he was strangely unsettled sometimes.

Rachel was now finding out why, having asked him what was bothering him. Well, in later years, he answered, what was he going to say to his grandchildren when they asked him what he'd done in the war? Could a bloke tell his grandkids he'd supplied official clobber for the men and women of the Services? After all, he wasn't forty yet, and there were men in fighting units who were over forty, and look at Boots, he fought in the last war and he's serving in this one. He couldn't help thinking, he said, that his personal war record was going to disappoint his grandkids and make them forget his birthday.

It was at this point that Rachel shook her head at him.

'Sammy, Sammy.'

'I'm not surprised you agree,' said Sammy.

'I don't agree at all,' said Rachel. 'I should tell my own grandchildren that Sammy Adams didn't pull his weight? Never. My life, haven't you pulled people out of bombed houses, haven't you been called out night after night to brave the bombs with your ARP section? Why, Sammy Adams, all that and your services to our wartime industry, no-one could ask more of you.'

'But I ask myself, could I do more if I joined up?' said Sammy. 'Susie says no, I couldn't, and that she'll break me in half if I offer me talents and me right arm to the Army.'

'Susie's right,' said Rachel, 'and I'd help her. Your talents, Sammy, are very special, and the end products are the best-stitched uniforms and accessories in the country. Why? Because you've got together the best seamstresses and machinists in the rag trade, now up to a hundred and fifty girls and women who gladly do that little bit more for you than they would for any other employer. Whenever you've required extra production from them, they've given it.'

'You know that, do you, Rachel?' said Sammy, looking up at her from his desk.

'Are you forgetting I've always kept up-to-date with the progress of the business and that I'm now in regular touch with Gertie, your faithful charge-hand?' smiled Rachel, and Sammy marvelled at the well-preserved looks of his one-time girlfriend, still a lush female woman at thirty-nine. 'And have you seen the letter from Mr Blenkinsop of the Air Force section of the Ministry of Supplies?'

'I've seen it,' said Sammy. Mr Blenkinsop, in long-winded terms, wished to know if Sammy had an alternative factory available in the event of his Belsize Park workplace being demolished by bombs. 'He's trying to worry me, which I regard as impertinent. Next thing he'll get saucy enough to tell us Air Ministry contracts will only be dished out to firms that can arrange an immediate transfer of production.'

'I'm inclined to believe he's so impressed with the way we carry out our contracts and don't fail on delivery that he simply wants to be sure an air raid won't completely kybosh our production,' said Rachel.

'Where'd you get that lingo from, Mrs Goodman?'

'From you, Mr Sammy.'

'You sure? Sounds Yiddish to me. You speak Yiddish, don't you, Rachel?'

'I know it,' said Rachel, 'but don't speak it. My life, Sammy, should I these days use a language of German origin?'

'It's out, as a matter of principle?' said Sammy.

'Out, Sammy, out.'

'We've all got funny ways when we're upset,' said Sammy. 'As for principles, I've always had some myself. Elastic, of course. Now, about an alternative factory—'

'I'll find one for us, Sammy, one on which we can have a twenty-four-hour option and will be safe from Nazi bombs.'

'No good finding one out of London,' said Sammy, 'too far for Gertie and the girls.'

'Tube to Clapham, say?'

'Clapham? That'll do. Clapham would only get hit by accident unless that fat geezer Goering decided he didn't like the sound of it. Mrs Goodman, I think you've got contacts.'

'Through my daddy, Mr Sammy, I've always had contacts.' Rachel smiled. 'By the way, did you know Lizzy's son Edward and my daughter Leah have begun to write to each other?'

'I heard they had a doorstep chat during Rosie's wedding reception,' said Sammy.

'Now they're pen friends,' said Rachel.

'Hope they'll be happy ever after,' said Sammy, and Rachel gave him a fond look. She knew it wouldn't worry him one little bit, a younger member of the family enjoying a friendly relationship with a Jewish girl.

'I think it's just a harmless boy and girl friendship, Sammy.'

'Like ours of old?' said Sammy.

'Yes, like ours of old,' said Rachel. 'Sammy, are you depressed by what Hitler's Huns are doing to the Russians?'

'Don't get grey hairs, Rachel,' said Sammy, 'I've had it on good authority from my stepdad that Joe Stalin can summon up a million living men for every thousand Hitler knocks off.'

'I should believe that?' said Rachel.

'You can believe that Chinese Lady's better half ain't generally known for telling fairy stories,' said Sammy. 'And on top of manpower by the million, there's all that Russian snow, which I understand can be highly inconvenient. Didn't I learn in me schooldays that Napoleon got stuck in it?'

'Russian snow, yes,' said Rachel, who sometimes had nightmarish dreams that Hitler had conquered the world, and that her daughters were permanently running for their lives. 'Has your stepdad said something about that too?'

'He let me know there's always a lot of it,' said Sammy, 'that it falls by the ton, which makes for a hell of a lot of cold sticky white stuff.'

'But it doesn't arrive until winter, does it?' said Rachel.

'It sits about waiting,' said Sammy, 'and on the first cold day, wallop, down it falls by the ton. It'll bury Hitler's Huns up to their Prussian necks, and their female soldiers up to their Army braziers. Talk about blue bosoms. I got all that in so many words from my stepdad, who's always been a knowing cove.'

'My life, Sammy, Army braziers and blue

bosoms out of the mouth of dear Mr Finch?' smiled Rachel.

'In a manner of speaking,' said Sammy.

'I should question a manner of speaking?' said Rachel. 'No, I think not. Who's going to argue the difference between braziers and brassières as long as we know we're actually talking about bosoms? But can the Russians hold out until the first ton of snow falls?'

'Get old Joe Stalin on the phone,' said Sammy, 'and I'll enquire.'

'I'll do my best,' said Rachel. 'By the way, have you heard from Rosie about when she'll receive her inheritance?'

'She hasn't been in touch lately,' said Sammy.

'I suppose the executors are waiting for probate to be granted,' said Rachel.

'I don't like that word,' said Sammy, 'it's Civil Service lingo and means some clerk is going to Australia in the morning, take a seat until he gets back.'

Rachel laughed.

'Told you,' said Sammy over supper that evening, 'didn't I tell you?'

'Oh dear,' said Susie, 'what was it your daddy told us, Paula?'

'I'm sure I don't know, Mummy,' said little Paula, now nearly six and a half and accordingly acquiring an Adams tongue. 'Blessed if I do.'

'I'm referring, Plum Pudding the Second,' said Sammy, 'to what I've mentioned might happen, the disappearance out of sight of your cousin Rosie.

Much to me sorrow, that's already happened. Very sorrowful.'

'Oh, dear,' said little Paula.

'If Mr Blenkinsop disappeared—'

'Sammy, I don't think Paula's acquainted with Mr Blenkinsop,' said Susie.

'Ministry of Supplies, Air Ministry department,' said Sammy.

'Crikey,' said little Paula.

'Granted, me pet,' said Sammy. 'If he disappeared, who'd mind? But our Rosie, the living light of your Uncle Boots's family, we all mind that we never see her these days.'

'Sammy love, Rosie's only been married a month,' said Susie, 'and it's only been a month since we last saw her, on her wedding day.'

'Is that a fact?' mused Sammy.

'Tell him, Paula,' said Susie.

'Daddy, I was at the wedding, don't you remember me being a bridesmaid?' said Paula.

'So you were,' said Sammy, 'proper little princess too, but when was it exactly, last year?'

'Daddy, course not, it was last month, like Mummy's just told you,' said Paula. 'Oh, there's the phone, could I answer it, please? It might be Lily Davis.' Lily Davis was her best friend at the nursery school.

'All right, darling, you go,' said Susie.

Paula picked up the phone in the hall.

'Hello, I'm Paula, who's that, please?'

'Hello, sweetie, this is Rosie here.'

'Crikey,' said Paula, 'just when we were talking about you and Daddy missing not seeing you.

Are you having a nice wedding time?'

'Very nice, darling,' said Rosie, 'and are you having a nice holiday from school?'

'Oh, yes,' said Paula. 'Rosie, is a nice wedding time the same as a nice holiday time?'

'Not exactly,' said Rosie, 'there aren't any buckets and spades, but it's a lot of fun.'

'Oh, does it make you laugh?' asked Paula.

'Regularly,' said Rosie. 'Darling, could I speak to your daddy?'

'Yes, I'll get him,' said Paula.

Sammy came on the line.

'Rosie?'

'Hello, Uncle Sammy, man of the people,' said Rosie.

'Come again?' said Sammy.

'Yes, you represent the spirit of the masses striving for the good life,' said Rosie.

'Unfortunately, Rosie, Hitler's mucking things up by blowing their shirts off,' said Sammy. 'That's not good, Rosie, life without a shirt. Anyway, how's your one and only better half, General Chapman?'

'He's not a general yet,' said Rosie, 'but at least he's enjoying being on close terms with military engines every day. And I think he quite likes being on close terms with me. Uncle Sammy, about my inheritance. Sir Charles's brother, who inherits the estate, has decided to contest the bequest made to me on the grounds that I'm not Sir Charles's legitimate daughter.'

'Saucy bugger,' said Sammy. 'Does that kind of thing hurt you, Rosie?'

'Not being legitimate?' said Rosie. 'No, I've had

such a lovely life that I'm simply grateful I was born.'

'Well, the brother's riding a loser,' said Sammy. 'You're Sir Charles's natural daughter, Rosie, and it doesn't count for as much as a brass farthing that he didn't marry your mother.'

'Yes, that's what Boots said. But it will still mean, Uncle Sammy, that there'll be a delay in getting the inheritance. Will a delay affect your new property company?'

'Nice of you to think of that, Rosie,' said Sammy. 'but don't worry about it. I can cope with any delay.'

'And if there's an outside chance that I won't get it at all?'

'Well, pick a dark night, Rosie, fix an alibi, and shoot the brother, then he'll get nothing himself.'

'I don't think I'll do that, Uncle Sammy. It's a brilliant idea, of course, but not my style.'

'Well, it shouldn't come to that, Rosie, it should only mean a bit of delay.'

'Yes, and I thought I should let you know,' said Rosie. 'Oh, by the way, Matt and I are on the phone now. We actually had one installed only a few weeks after making our application. Today, in fact.'

'Only a few weeks with a war on?' said Sammy. 'Might I ask if it was an under-the-counter job?'

'Matt knows a fairly influential phone bloke,' said Rosie. 'Would that have led to an under-the-counter job?'

'Who's going to turn their noses up at a useful connection?' said Sammy.

'Oh, very witty, Uncle Sammy,' said Rosie, and gave him the number for future reference.

'Well, your phone's going to help us keep in touch with you, Rosie,' said Sammy.

'Yes, blow the expense,' said Rosie. ''Bye, Uncle Sammy, glad you're not going to worry about any delay. Love to Aunt Susie and Paula. Oh, do you know if Tim and Felicity had a happy wedding weekend?'

'All I know is we had a daylight air raid on Sunday afternoon,' said Sammy. 'Apart from that, I'm in the dark. Ask your dad, he was Tim's best man.'

'Oh, God, that father of mine,' said Rosie, and Sammy thought there it was, the way she always spoke of Boots as if he, and not Charles Armitage, had been her natural father. 'Do you know what he said to me? That the wedding and the reception were both very agreeable, and that when the bride and groom departed for home, the groom looked healthy and capable, the bride unblushing but happily expectant. Uncle Sammy, what can you do with a man like Daddy?'

'Try laughing,' said Sammy.

'I do,' said Rosie, 'I'm long past giggling. 'Bye again, Uncle Sammy.'

''Bye, Rosie, regards to Matt,' said Sammy. Well, he thought, as he put the phone down, that's our Rosie. She's not turning a hair about the fact that someone's trying to do her out of twenty-five thousand quid. She's as airy-fairy as Boots. It's a fact that if anyone in the family is more like Boots than anyone else, it's Rosie, yet she wasn't born to him, even if she talks as if she was.

Susie put in her penny'sworth when he

recounted the phone conversation and mentioned his thoughts about Rosie being so like Boots, although she wasn't born to him.

'For,' said Susie.

'Eh?'

'She was born for Boots,' said Susie.

'Now how could—'

'It was one of those strange things of life,' said Susie.

'I get you,' said Sammy. 'Like you were born for me, Susie?'

'Yes, Sammy, but not as your daughter.'

'Mind you, Susie, I don't call that strange,' said Sammy, 'I call it fateful fortune.'

'Fateful fortune, Sammy?'

'Fateful fortunate fortune,' said Sammy. 'For me.'

'I concur,' smiled Susie.

'Plum Pudding the Second,' said Sammy to the intrigued Paula, 'take a note that when your mum's doing a bit of concurring, your dad's a happy man.'

'Oh, d'you mean you want me to write it down, Daddy?' asked Paula.

'Might as well,' said Sammy, 'it could turn out to be a bit of written history.'

'Um,' said the gynaecologist after Polly had dressed. In view of her need to resolve any doubts she had about her ability to produce the child, her Corfe Castle village doctor had suggested she should consult a specialist. She had elected to consult one whose practice was in Dulwich, close to her family home. 'Um,' he mused again, studying his notes.

'Um what?' said Polly, now nearly five months pregnant.

'Very good, Mrs Adams.'

'No problems?' said Polly, conscious that he'd made prolonged use of his stethoscope.

'None that I can diagnose,' said Mr Rawlinson, well-known at King's College Hospital.

'Why did you say "um", then?'

'Did I? Oh, a habit.'

'You're sure?' said Polly.

'Quite sure,' smiled Mr Rawlinson, 'you're doing a splendid carrying job.'

'Like Carter Paterson?' said Polly.

'I think you'll deliver the parcel safe and sound, Mrs Adams.'

'What happens to the brown paper and string?' asked Polly.

'The midwife will take care of that,' said Mr Rawlinson. 'Um, I'd like to see you again in a fortnight.'

'Just to keep an eye on me?' said Polly.

'Yes, and I'm naturally interested in a patient who's having her first child.'

'At the age of forty-five,' said Polly. Her birthday was only a week away.

'I'd like to keep up with developments,' said Mr Rawlinson, and he and Polly fixed a date for her next consultation.

Polly was smiling as she left. She felt she'd been given the reassurance she needed. Let's see, she said to herself, what do I do next? Boots wasn't with her. His workload was too heavy.

Polly, after reflection, gave in to a strange whim. She had driven up to Dulwich in Boots's private car, and she used it now to take herself to Southwark Cemetery to make her peace with Emily. The well-kept cemetery looked like an oasis of reverent tranquillity, the headstones standing like watchful sentinels. There were flowers in the metal vase set into the base of Emily's headstone, larkspur that looked fresh. Polly was sure that either Lizzy or Boot's mother had placed the sheaf there. She stood in contemplation of Emily's final resting-place, and she read the inscription of remembrance in the light of the cloudy day.

In Loving Memory Of
EMILY
1898 – 1940
Cherished Wife of Robert Alfred Adams

Polly's lips moved in a silent address.

'Are you there, Emily? Are you unhappy about my place in Boots's life? Don't be. He'll never forget you, or all you meant to him, believe me. I'm living with that, so give me your blessing, old sport.'

She stooped and placed a spray of crimson carnations on the grave. She straightened up. The light of the cloudy sky softened the headstone and the brightness of the carnations.

'Rest in peace, Emily,' she whispered, and she knew that was what Lizzy or Vi or Sammy would have said, what any of the Adams family would have said, well-worn and hardly original though it was.

She walked quietly away.

She was an Adams herself, and the first of the wives in pecking order from the day she had married Boots.

What did that mean? That his redoubtable mother, the matriarch, had founded a dynasty, and that she herself would take over the mantle one day?

Matriarch of the whole tribe? Polly silently laughed at herself.

She phoned Boots from her parents' home in the evening, telling him her consultation with the gynaecologist had been a mutually happy one. I'm delighted, said Boots, and did you tell him about your runner beans? Polly asked what was wrong with her runner beans. They're running, said Boots. You're an idiot, said Polly. There's one in every family, said Boots. Happily, said Polly, I like the one I've got. Are you missing me? I'm missing both of you, said Boots. You old darling, said Polly.

She stayed overnight at her old home, her step-mother, prominent in the Red Cross, having joined her there. Lady Simms had been astonished but captivated when informed that Polly was expecting. The following conversation had taken place between them the day after she received the news.

'My dear.'

'Delighted to see you, Mama.'

'How can I express my feelings? I'm happily lost for words.'

'You aren't the only one,' smiled Polly, 'I'm astonished myself.'

'But happy?' said Lady Simms.

'Overwhelmed. And incredulous. How can I, at my age, believe such an achievement? It's almost an impossibility, old thing.'

'Perhaps it would have been for you, with any other man but Boots,' said Lady Simms.

'What shall we say about him?' asked Polly. 'That he's quite unique?'

'I've always found him an adorable man,' said Lady Simms, 'but it's you, my dear, who must be considered unique. Has he suggested you are?'

'He assured me I'm a miracle woman,' said Polly. A little laugh escaped. 'He also suggested that what we've just accomplished, we can accomplish again.'

'That suggestion was made seriously?' said Lady Simms.

'Seriously?' Polly laughed again. 'By Boots? What do you think?'

'He can be very whimsical,' said Lady Simms. 'Does he know just how delighted your father is?'

'Papa left him in no doubt of that,' said Polly. 'If he wasn't before, Boots is now his favourite person. But I'm a little sad, you know.'

'Sad?' said Lady Simms.

'That I wasn't Boots's first love, and able to give him children years ago,' said Polly. 'His first love was Emily, I've no illusions about that. But I still believe that if I'd met him before he came to love Emily, I could have been first and foremost.'

'Polly, my dear, you would have been at college then and Boots in his teens,' said Lady Simms.

'It would have made no difference,' said Polly.

Now, when Polly was five months pregnant, Lady Simms was as fixed as her stepdaughter on successful delivery of the child. Accordingly, she expressed pleasure at being told the gynaecologist had found nothing to worry about.

Polly slept the night at her old home. She woke up midway through the dark hours. London was quiet. There were no bombers making the sky hideous with noise. Dreamily, she murmured and reached to cuddle up. But there were only the pillows. The absence of Boots in her bed was quite painful for a moment.

But she felt at peace with Emily.

Chapter Seventeen

Mrs Mumford, arriving home from her work, found Daisy at the kitchen sink.

'Missy, what are you at?'

Daisy turned and spoke hesitantly.

'Mrs Mumford, I've peeled the pertaters for supper, and I picked some runner beans, and I've done them too. Mrs Mumford, you've got lots of runner beans comin' in the garden.'

'H'm,' said Mrs Mumford, her blouse and skirt looking as stiff as her person. 'Let me see what's in those saucepans.'

''Ave I done them all right?' asked Daisy, showing Mrs Mumford the contents of two saucepans, one containing the white peeled potatoes, the other sliced runner beans of a fresh green. Water covered the contents. 'Mrs Mumford?' Daisy was shyly asking for approval.

'Well, that be a good-looking piece of work, child,' said Mrs Mumford, 'even if supper's a tidy way off. But I don't wish you to be spending time in the kitchen when it's your school holidays.'

'Oh, I 'ad a nice afternoon wiv Posy Goodworvy,'

said Daisy, 'then she went 'ome to 'elp her mum get a chicken meal ready, so I – well, I thought I could 'elp you by doin' the pertaters and beans. 'Ave I really done them all right?'

'I'm happy to tell you they don't need doing again,' said Mrs Mumford.

'Oh, thanks,' said Daisy, looking happy herself. 'I – I like 'elping you.'

'Proper young kitchen missy you are,' said Mrs Mumford, 'but wear an apron next time. Your frock's splashed with water, if I'm not mistaken, and where's the peelings?'

'Oh, they're in the waste dish, look,' said Daisy, and lifted the enamel container out of the sink. It was full of potato peel and runner bean spines.

'I see.' Mrs Mumford actually smiled. 'I'm thinking you might like a cup of tea and a slice of cake now, Daisy.'

'Oh, I would, please,' said Daisy. 'Mrs Mumford, I'll see to the kettle, if yer like.' The old iron kettle was standing on the closed hob of the range, the fire, dusty with ash, burning slowly. Mrs Mumford watched as the young cockney girl lifted the kettle, took the lid off the hob with the hob bar, and replaced the kettle. Then she opened the damper and stirred the fire with the poker. It began to show a red glow. 'Is that all right, Mrs Mumford?'

'I don't be complaining, child,' said Mrs Mumford, setting out cups and saucers. Daisy looked at her, feeling something ought to be said.

'Mrs Mumford?'

'Yes?'

'Mrs Mumford, people's saying things.'

Mrs Mumford glanced at her evacuee. The girl looked awkward and unhappy.

'And you feel you should tell me about these talkative people, missy?'

'Mrs Mumford, it ain't fair, saying things about you and behind yer back,' said Daisy.

'I know about such sayings,' said Mrs Mumford, taking the cake from the larder.

'Crikey, do yer really know?' breathed Daisy.

'It don't take much longer than five minutes or so for everything that's said in Ashleigh to reach every ear,' said Mrs Mumford.

'Are you upset, Mrs Mumford?'

'I don't be over-bothered, Daisy.'

'Well, it still ain't fair,' said Daisy, wondering exactly why there were all these whispers about the grave of the dead dog and about Mrs Mumford having something to hide. 'Mrs Mumford, me and Posy and Stevie, we're on your side, and Posy's been kickin' boys that 'ave talked about yer.'

'I don't wish that girl to do any kicking on my account.'

'No, Mrs Mumford, I'll tell 'er,' said Daisy, and Mrs Mumford, moving to pick up the brown glazed teapot from the dresser, lightly touched the girl's shoulder.

'Thank you, Daisy,' she said.

Daisy wanted to say what a shame that Mr Mumford had gone off on his own years ago. Everyone knew about that. He must have gone in a bit of a temper, because a large old trunk in the spare room was full of a man's clothes, which Daisy supposed were his. She wasn't supposed to go into

that room, but she'd made a nosy exploration a
year ago while Mrs Mumford was at work. Now she
was coming round to thinking Mrs Mumford didn't
deserve to have her husband go and leave her. Well,
she was good at heart really.

Daisy was very touched that the lady had come to
like her.

Eloise was home on embarkation leave, and
Chinese Lady was happy to have her there. She had
never liked what the war had done to the house,
emptied it of her immediate family by putting them
all into uniform. She often thought nostalgically of
the pre-war years, when Boots, Emily, Rosie, Tim
and Eloise had all been around. It was a family that
turned a house into a home. She was thankful for
Edwin's presence during the evenings and weekends. He was always a companion as well as a
husband.

Now, for a while, Eloise was proving a stimulation
and an affectionate granddaughter. She did not ask
to be entertained, and she did not go gallivanting
up West to take in theatre shows. She was happy to
spend the evenings sitting with her grandparents,
and to have long conversations with Mr Finch
about Europe and its peoples. Mr Finch was a mine
of information about the countries of Europe,
especially Germany which, of course, was just about
the most aggravating nation ever as far as Chinese
Lady was concerned. She wasn't sure sometimes
that she approved of Edwin knowing Germany and
the Germans as well as he did. But of course he was
a travelled man.

Eloise went out daily with her grandmother on shopping expeditions or to call on Vi and Susie. She spoke often of her fiancé, Colonel Lucas, whom she thought must have arrived by now in his overseas posting. Regulations did not allow her to name the destination. Such regulations were based on the principle that careless talk cost lives. She also spoke of her own forthcoming time there. She hoped, of course, that she would be able to see Luke from time to time. Chinese Lady said she hoped that didn't mean Eloise would have to be in the trenches with him. Eloise said no, no, the armies weren't figthing this war from trenches, and that she would be doing administration work, anyway, well away from the battles, like all ATS personnel.

'But it's true, Grandmama, I'm so devoted to Luke that if he wished me to drive a tank for him, I would not say no.'

'Lord above, Eloise, I hope I never live to see the day when you do a thing like that. I'm sure it's not what Colonel Lucas would ever want you to do, nor your father or any of the fam'ly. It's not ladylike, nor natural, and I've been saying for I don't know how long that it would of been more fitting if you and Rosie had been nurses instead of women soldiers. I don't like what the war's doing to women, and I don't like what it's done to our fam'ly, your poor stepmother Em'ly dead from a bomb, Tim's young lady wife blinded by one, and your cousin Emma's husband Jonathan crippled by them Germans when he was out in the desert.'

'Grandmama, I'm not dying to drive a tank, no,'

said Eloise. They were in the busy area of Camberwell Green, and lining up for sausages in Kennedy's cooked meats shop. 'I'm only saying I'd do so if Luke wished it.'

'Well, if he did wish it,' said Chinese Lady with asperity, 'I'd having something to say to him which he probably wouldn't like. Boots – your dad – has brought you up to be a lady, like he did Rosie, and it's best if Colonel Lucas knows that.'

'Yes, Grandmama, of course,' said Eloise, hiding a smile.

Chinese Lady, now at the head of the queue, addressed the white-coated assistant.

'Two pounds of your best pork sausages, please.'

'Not today, madam, nor any day till the war's over,' said the assistant.

'This war is getting to be more aggravating than the last one,' said Chinese Lady.

'Yes, bit of a devil, madam. The sausages are made with our best possible filling, but only one pound per person.'

'Well, there's three of us persons at home,' said Chinese Lady, who had hoped to get enough for two or three meals, both Edwin and Eloise being very partial to Kennedy's. 'My husband, my grand-daughter and me.'

'One pound per family, madam.'

Chinese Lady settled for that. Eloise might then have asked for a pound, but Chinese Lady, believing in the shop's fair shares principle, drew her away.

Eloise thought her English grandmother old-fashioned about many things, including what women should and shouldn't do. But being fair to other people, well, that kind of attitude was nice, and everyone should practise it in wartime.

Was Luke in the Middle East now, and already making lightning raids with the LRDG in the desert? Ah, how he would fight the Germans. Ever since Dunkirk he had wanted to give them a beating.

But she hoped very much that his aggression and courage would not lead him into recklessness.

There was Tim too. He was on his way to join Luke.

The war had become more of a worry now, and less of an exciting challenge.

'That's it,' said David.

It was mid-afternoon, and Kate was using a hoe. Not brilliantly, but she was giving it a go, and looking fetching in an embroidered white blouse and dark green skirt.

'You don't have to stand there like an audience,' she said.

'It's not like being in the cinema, I'll admit,' said David, 'but it's not a bad picture.'

'Oh, yes, I'm all the way from Hollywood, I am,' said Kate, digging with the hoe. She'd come to like the garden, to concede it really was a lot nicer than a backyard. 'I could charge you a shilling for watching me.'

'You'd have to do something a lot more spectacular than hoeing,' said David. 'Well, nobody goes to a cinema to see a film of a girl hoeing. Can you do singing and dancing?'

'What, like Betty Grable?' said Kate.

'That'll do,' said David.

'Crikey, you'd like that, wouldn't you, me showing me dancing legs,' said Kate.

'Well, I suppose you've got nice legs, have you?' said David.

'What d'you mean, have I?' said Kate. 'You told me they were pretty.'

'I'm only asking for a reminder,' said David.

'Getting saucier, are we?' said Kate, and poked him with the hoe. David back-pedalled and fell over the lawn. Kate shrieked with laughter, dropped the hoe and jumped on him, straddling him with her knees. 'Got you,' she said, and dug her fingers into his ribs. She tickled him. David went into helpless collapse. Kate pulled his unbuttoned shirt open and tickled his bare ribs. David went into further collapse. Kate laughed in delight. 'Want some more?' she asked.

'Leave off,' gasped David, always helpless when tickled.

Kate gave him a little more, then jumped up. David scrambled to his feet and Kate flew. He went after her, caught her and they fell together. Then they were both laughing, Kate on her back and David leaning over her. They looked at each other. They stopped laughing. Aunt Hilary was out and they had the place to themselves. I'm going to kiss her, thought David. He's going to kiss me, thought Kate.

Sweeping the sky beneath scudding white clouds came six Hurricane trainers, their concerted roar a rolling thunder. Kate saw them high above her, outlined by the clouds and racing in a V formation. David looked up and he saw them too. They held their breath at the awesome symbols of airborne attack, so remindful of what the RAF had achieved during the Battle of Britain. Kate felt emotionally proud. David felt a new ambition, to fly with the RAF.

The planes screamed through the sky and disappeared, taking their rolling thunder with them. David stood up, and Kate came to her feet.

'Oh, blimey, they made me lose me breath,' she said, 'just like the other day.'

'They'll probably give you an idea for another imaginary mission,' said David.

'Crikey, yes,' said Kate. 'Shall we have a cup of tea?'

'You haven't done much hoeing,' said David.

'Still, I did some good tickling,' said Kate, and ran giggling to the back door and into the kitchen.

David picked up the hoe and went to work with it while Kate boiled the kettle. I think I'll write to Uncle Boots, he said to himself, and ask him if a bloke of my age can have serious thoughts about a girl. Uncle Boots knows everything about most things. He's what you might call the family Bible. Well, they say there's everything in the Bible, if you know where to look.

That Kate. What a girl. She's as alive as Aunt Emily always was. Strange that her hair and eyes are just like Aunt Emily's.

It was afternoon of the following day when two men arrived at 'Rose Cottage', home of Mrs Mumford.

'She's at work,' said one man, Amos Penn.

'And young Daisy be running about with Posy Goodworthy,' said Nathan Coote.

'Good time to do the job, then,' said Amos Penn.

'Might as well. We told George Plackford us would.'

Daisy came skipping up the front path at a little after three-thirty, intending to pick some runner beans and dig up some main crop potatoes. She would slice the beans and peel the potatoes, and have them ready for cooking this evening. She was helping Mrs Mumford daily in this way, and Mrs Mumford was being very nice to her about it. Daisy was developing an affection for her prim wartime guardian, who, in turn, was still showing a softer side from time to time. Daisy had a feeling that underneath her strict front, Mrs Mumford was a sort of worthy woman. Yes, that was it, sort of worthy. It had taken a long time to get that feeling, and just as long a time for Mrs Mumford to start being kind instead of fault-finding.

In the kitchen, Daisy poured herself a glass of water from the tap. She was hot from keeping up with the energy of Posy, Abel, Paul and Stevie.

Gulping the clear cold water, she blinked, then stared. Through the window she saw two men at the top of the garden. They were digging, they were actually turning up the earth of the dog Jackie's grave. Daisy recognized them, Mr Penn and Mr Coote, council road men of Ashleigh. Daisy quivered as all the talk and gossip about that grave planted a strange sensation of panic in her mind. She ran out of the cottage and down to the Post Office Store. Outside sat Mrs Mumford's dog. It was always there during her working hours. It was not tied up. It might chase a cat or two, or wander a little way to investigate smells, but it always returned to lie with its head on its forepaws. Daisy looked in from the open door. Mr Pennicot was serving a customer. Mrs Mumford was tidying up a rack that held magazines. From the door, Daisy caught her eye and beckoned in agitation.

'Daisy, what's this you're at?' asked Mrs Mumford.

Daisy beckoned again and stepped from the shop. Mrs Mumford came out.

'Mrs Mumford – Mrs Mumford, there's two men in your garden,' breathed Daisy, face flushed, 'they're diggin' up Jackie's grave. It's Mr Penn and Mr Coote.'

Mrs Mumford's reaction to that was to stiffen and draw a sharp breath.

'Heathens,' she said, 'and nor do they have much by way of good manners. Did you speak to them, Daisy?'

'No, as soon as I saw them when I got in from bein' wiv Posy and Stevie, I come to see you, Mrs Mumford,' said Daisy, unhappy about developments.

'You ran all the way to tell me, child, but not to shout it out in the shop?' said Mrs Mumford.

'I thought—' Daisy stopped as the customer emerged, smiled at them and went on her way. 'Mrs Mumford, I thought—'

'I know,' said Mrs Mumford. 'You be a good and

thoughtful girl, Daisy. Wait there a bit.'

She went back into the shop. She was out again a minute later, wearing her old-fashioned brown straw hat. She took Daisy's hand and walked with her to 'Rose Cottage'. She said nothing. She was stiff and stern, but her grasp of Daisy's hand was warm and reassuring. Daisy's pulse, however, was still erratic. She felt a little frightened about what was to be.

Arriving at the cottage, Mrs Mumford took Daisy through to the kitchen.

'Oh, crikey, there they are,' breathed Daisy. Through the window the men were plainly visible, and so was a great big pile of turned-up earth. But they were no longer digging. They were quite still, and staring.

'Stay here, child,' said Mrs Mumford.

'Yes, Mrs Mumford,' gulped Daisy nervously.

'And don't worry.'

'No, Mrs Mumford.'

The stiff lady opened the back door, stepped into the garden, advanced purposefully along the central path, skirted her vegetable plot and came up with the men and the now open grave. Two spades lay against the large mound of earth, and bones lay close by. Daisy, at the open back door, heard Mrs Mumford speak.

'Might I ask what it is you two be after up here?'

'Ah, well, Dora, 'tis like this, you see,' said Amos Penn, and rubbed his chin. Mrs Mumford looked down into the deep excavation, quite empty.

'I see, do I?' she said. 'Yes, I see a desecrated grave and some bones.'

'The fact is, it were the talk,' said Nathan Coote, shifting about.

'You be inclined by talk and gossip to come here and dig up my garden, nor ask permission?' said Mrs Mumford.

'Ah, well, us thought it best to do it quietly,' said Amos.

'To come digging and looking?' said Mrs Mumford.

Daisy, listening and hearing, was holding her breath.

'There be these bones,' said Nathan.

'Aye, the bones,' said Mrs Mumford.

'Us went pretty deep,' said Amos.

'So I see,' said Mrs Mumford. 'Now you be wishful to take the bones away and have them looked at?'

Both men shifted awkwardly about.

'Us aren't thinking of that, Dora,' said Nathan.

'You know whose bones they be?' said Mrs Mumford.

Daisy shut her eyes and stayed rigid.

'Aye, us knows,' said Amos.

'Dog's,' said Nathan.

Daisy's breath expelled in a long sigh.

'A dog's bones made you stare unbelieving?' said Mrs Mumford.

'Ah, well,' said Amos.

'Or maybe you couldn't believe it were only a dog's bones that were there for the finding?' said Mrs Mumford.

'I'm right sorry I got taken in by talk,' said Nathan.

'George Plackford's talk?' said Mrs Mumford.

'Ah, well,' said Amos.

'It don't be well,' said Mrs Mumford, 'but it'll be to my liking to have you put Jackie's bones back nice and tidy, and then do the filling in. That don't be too much to ask for now and immediate?'

'Fair, I rackon,' said Nathan.

'Fair,' said Amos.

'I'll thank you kindly,' said Mrs Mumford, and left them to it. Entering the kitchen, she gave Daisy a light pat on her shoulder. 'Well, they've done what I thought would be done soon or late, child, either by them or others, but there's no grief come of it, so don't you worry now.'

'Oh, I ain't worried, Mrs Mumford, not now I ain't,' breathed Daisy happily. 'There won't be no more talk, will there?'

'Not by the time everyone's abed tonight,' said Mrs Mumford.

'When they've gone,' said Daisy, 'can I pick some pertaters and beans for yer and get them ready for the saucepans?'

'Why, that you can, Daisy. You be a kind and thoughtful girl.'

That evening, Mrs Mumford called on Mr and Mrs Plackford. Mr Plackford received her with his eyes running about in search of an escape route for his embarrassment, and Mrs Plackford received her with the look of a woman who wished she was somewhere else.

'You've heard from the heathens that were in my garden this afternoon?' said Mrs Mumford.

'Aye,' said George Plackford, inspecting the parlour ceiling.

'It were a silly thing they did,' said Maudie Plackford, flustered up to her eyelashes.

'All on account of talk, so they said,' observed Mrs Mumford, straight-faced. 'Well, most of my life I've minded my own business, and nor did I make it anybody else's when my husband left me. But maybe it's time to make it everyone's business and stop any more talk, though it's shaming for a woman not to be able to keep hold of her husband. You be wondering where Barney is? Kindly read that.'

She put a letter into Mr Plackford's hand.

'Well, Dora, I don't know as—'

'Kindly read it, George.'

Mr Plackford read it. It was from an Exeter address and its date made it over a year old.

> *Dear Dora,*
>
> *I got your letter asking about the cottage. I want to say I'm still right sorry I had to leave you but there it is when a man feels he don't have any standing in his own home, it's one of two things, burn the place down or go quiet like a man should. I know you suffered, more so because I weren't able to make you much of an allowance but I had to start again in a new job and pay for lodgings, and then there were Kitty to look after as well seeing she were willing to throw in her lot with me. I'm thanking you again for agreeing to the divorce and making me free to marry Kitty, which she wanted, and I'm writing this letter to tell you that now I'm earning good money I'm making Rose Cottage*

over to you and you'll get the deeds as soon as they're good and ready. It's what I know I should do. I'm also increasing your allowance from six shillings a week to twelve-and-six which I'll send by way of postal order for two pounds ten every month, and which increase I did promise when I was able. I still don't feel too good about walking out like I did even if I can't ever be minded to take all the blame. I'm sorry it came to what it did and hope life hasn't been a tidy bit too hard on you, and the war not helping. No, I still don't want any of them old clothes of mine. Good luck, Dora.

Yours sincerely Barney.

Mr Plackford cleared his throat.

'Well, that's brought me up short,' he said, and handed the letter to his wife, who took her turn to read it. 'All this time, Dora, keeping things to yourself. See what it's done, made an old fool of me.'

'It were always between Barney and me, nobody else, that and whose blame it were,' said Mrs Mumford.

'Oh, I'm that upset and feeling so foolish,' said Mrs Plackford, handing the letter back to Mrs Mumford.

'Well, there's things you'll want to be telling people, I daresay,' said Mrs Mumford. 'Goodnight, Maudie, goodnight, George.'

'Won't you stay for a cup of tea?' begged Mrs Plackford.

'Not this time, thanking you kindly,' said Mrs Mumford, and left.

Mrs Plackford looked around her parlour.

'Maudie?' said Mr Plackford.

'Yes, I'm looking for something to throw at you,' said Mrs Plackford, 'something heavy that's not too valuable.'

Chapter Eighteen

The recurring dream seemed to hang in space for a moment before plunging into his subconscious and painting its dreadfully unhappy pictures.

Stunned, his ears ringing, he was paralysed for a moment. Then he ran from the store in Streatham, out through shattered glass doors and into the dreadful scene caused by a daylight air raid on London. A bomb had struck the sunlit road, a shopping area, and the road was littered with glass, bricks, masonry, tiles and bodies. The strange terrible quiet was suddenly broken by screams, shouts, cries and desperate appeals for help. Men and women staggered and reeled about, their faces ghastly with shock and horror. He saw Emily, lying on her back at the kerbside. Appalled, he ran and went down on his knees beside her. Shards of glass dug into his trousers.

Emily lay with her dress in shreds, her body broken, her white face covered with dust, her auburn hair sprinkled with tiny glass splinters, her eyes closed.

'Emily? Emily?' He hardly recognized his own voice. 'Emily?' He touched her shoulder.

She opened her eyes, their green cloudy. She looked up at him.

'Dad?' The merest of husky whispers. 'What – what happened?'

'Emily, my dear—'

'Oh, lor'.' A long sigh. 'Aren't I a silly girl?'

Her eyes closed again, and he stayed beside her on his knees, holding her limp hand and, in grief and helplessness, watching her die. She simply slipped quietly away, the woman who had been a renowned godsend to the family in their struggling years.

Amid the ringing of ambulance bells, a policeman placed a hand on his shoulder and gently shook him.

He woke up, his forehead beaded with perspiration, his mind suffering the unbearable. The unbearable came from knowing the dream that attacked him all too often was a frightful image of the truth. He twisted and turned in an effort to expel heart-wounding memories.

'Edwin?' His wife Maisie was awake.

'So sorry, Maisie, that frightful dream again,' said Mr Finch.

'About Em'ly?' said Chinese Lady.

'Yes.'

'It's because you blame yourself, and you shouldn't,' said Chinese Lady, turning to him in the bed. 'You couldn't have known a bomb was going to drop the moment she ran out of the store when the air raid alarm sounded. It was like Em'ly to act on impulse.'

'I told her to run, and I can't help thinking that if I hadn't stopped to pick up her parcel—'

'Edwin, how can you blame yourself for that?' Chinese Lady was warm with sympathy and understanding. 'All the blame belongs to those wretched Germans for dropping their bombs on a place like Streatham, full of people doing harm to no-one. I'll get up and make us some tea.'

'Maisie, there's no need.'

'My dear, I know you won't go to sleep again just yet. It's a cup of tea that'll set your mind at rest, and mine too. We've both got to realize that Em'ly's gone, love, and not any wishes or dreams can bring her back. Boots still grieves a bit, I know he does, and it's a blessing he's got Polly. I always liked Polly, but I never thought she'd turn out such a loving wife like she has.' Chinese Lady was attempting to make homely and reassuring conversation. 'She fits in just as well as Vi and Susie, and not even Em'ly was more affectionate to Boots. You stay there now and I'll get us some tea and bring it up.'

She went down and made the tea. She brought it up on a tray.

'Maisie,' said Mr Finch, 'if there's any woman more of a comfort than you, I've no idea where to find her.'

'Well, I hope you won't go looking,' said Chinese Lady.

* * *

259

Farmers were harvesting in Devon. Aunt Hilary was continuing to get out and about. Daisy was a happier girl all round, Stevie was getting the occasional saucy kiss from her that made him blush, and David and Kate were continuing their enjoyable if mettlesome relationship.

He was mowing the lawn again for her aunt after supper one evening. He'd taken his shirt off, and in just his shorts and sandals was pushing the old mower up and down, creating the attractive pattern.

Kate was sitting on the back doorstep, writing in her exercise book. Her aunt, who'd retired to her study after supper, appeared, a cigarette between her fingers. She eyed the active figure of David with her languid smile.

'That young man already has a superb body,' she murmured.

'Aunt Hilary,' said Kate, 'I don't honestly like hearing you say things like that.'

'Prudish girl, don't be silly,' said Aunt Hilary.

'I'm not silly,' said Kate, 'nor prudish.'

'Jealous, then?' said Aunt Hilary.

'Jealous?' said Kate. 'Me?'

'There's no need,' said Aunt Hilary, flicking ash. 'I'm simply not so old that I can't admire your young man's physique.'

'He's not my young man,' said Kate. 'I don't need one, and anyway, David's still at school, so I wouldn't think of him like that.'

'Why wouldn't you?' murmured Aunt Hilary. 'I can't see why his schooling should matter, not when he's already a young adult mentally and physically. He's left gauche boyhood well behind.'

'Gauche?' said Kate. 'What's gauche?'

'Awkward, simple, adolescent,' said Aunt Hilary.

'Well, gauche doesn't sound English to me,' said Kate, who had an uncomfortable feeling that her aunt actually fancied David.

'It's French,' said Aunt Hilary, 'but it's found its way into our language. Kate, my dear girl, I'd hang on to David if I were you.'

'I happen to be waiting till I can volunteer for the Air Force and meet a Spitfire pilot,' said Kate.

'Ridiculous girl.' Aunt Hilary threw the stub of her cigarette away. 'As for Spitfire pilots, it's a silly war for those young men and for everyone else.' That was voiced a little peevishly, following which Aunt Hilary took herself back to her study.

Kate rose from the step and walked onto the lawn. David stopped mowing. He had to, she was in his way.

'Want me to mow your hair?' he said.

'There's a hairdressing place in Westbury I go to,' said Kate, 'they do it better than that mower would.' She regarded him with new interest. He did have a good body, and very firm legs.

'You're looking me over,' said David.

'Yes, aren't you pretty?' said Kate.

David grinned.

'Well, thanks,' he said, 'that's both of us.'

'Oh, would you like to wear one of me Sunday frocks?' asked Kate.

'No, not much,' said David. He noted her exercise book. 'What've you been writing?'

'Oh, just another one of me stories,' said Kate,

'only with more romance and sex appeal.'

'More?' said David, face dark brown, hair moist.

'Yes, romance has to have a lot of sex appeal,' said Kate.

'That could educate someone as ignorant as I am,' said David.

'You and your innocent talk,' said Kate, 'I bet you know lots more than I do, the way you've grown up. Anyhow, d'you want to come and listen when you've finished your mowing?'

'Can't wait,' said David.

He was sitting on the doorstep with her a little later, his shirt over his shoulder, Kate thinking again that he had the warm smell of summer.

'Ready?' she said, her hip and shoulder touching his.

'Fire away,' said David, thinking he'd give in any moment to the temptation of kissing her.

'Well, I thought I'd write about me as a secret Spitfire pilot ordered to rescue a dashing airman that's been shot down over France and is in hiding waiting for me,' said Kate. 'He's seen photographs of me and is full of desire.'

'Oh, blimey,' said David.

'What's that you said?'

'Oh, blimey,' said David.

'Crikey, are you comin' round to talking natural?' asked Kate.

'I've always wanted to talk natural,' said David.

'Well, keep trying,' said Kate. 'Listen now.' She began to read from her exercise book against the tinny sound of Aunt Hilary's typewriter. '"*My Dangerous Perils* by Kate Trimble Special Secret

262

Pilot. It was just before dawn and our great leader was on the airfield to wish me luck in me mission to rescue an RAF pilot that had been shot down over France and was in hiding waiting for me. Our great leader who was very touched by me bravery placed his hands on me shoulders and said 'Pilot Henry Wilkes the hopes and wishes of your King and country go with you on your courageous mission." I'd better tell you Henry was me dad's name and I had to have a man's name having been trained in secret as a woman pilot that no-one knew about. Of course, it's a bit silly not letting women be RAF pilots, and it means a woman's got to be a secret one.'

'Got you,' said David. 'Go ahead.'

' "I told our great leader he could rely on me and leapt aboard me Spitfire where I took control of the wheel—" '

'The wheel?' said David. 'You sure?'

'Course I'm sure,' said Kate, 'I'm in the pilot's seat, aren't I? Oh, all right.' She made an alteration with her pencil, then resumed. ' "Where I took control of everything and in the grey light of dawn flew up in the air with me propellors turning fast." '

'One propellor,' said David.

'Well, I had two on this Spitfire, so there, stop showing off,' said Kate. 'I was being guided by me compass and me experience and was soon over the Channel and could see the waters of danger below when all of a sudden I heard what sounded like a roll of thunder and there coming towards me were three German fighter planes all at once and all together." '

'Strike a light,' said David, 'did yer do a gorblimey bunk?'

'No, course I didn't,' said Kate, 'I wasn't a famous secret pilot for nothing – here, what're you talking like that for?'

'It's me natural cockney heritage,' said David.

Kate gave him a suspicious look.

'Well, it doesn't sound natural,' she said, 'more like your tonsils need looking at. Still, you can keep trying, if you want, but me dad always said if something doesn't come natural to anyone, they can't ever get the collar on the donkey.'

'I gotcher,' said David. 'Carry on, lovey.'

'Don't be familiar,' said Kate. 'Where was I? Oh, yes. "I could see the German pilots with their eyes gleaming with evil behind their goggles so I didn't waste time, I pulled the triggers of me twelve machine-guns—"'

'Gawd help us, twelve all at once, like?' said David.

'Well, just one wouldn't have been any good, would it?' said Kate. '"I pulled the triggers of me twelve machine-guns and hundreds of bullets smashed into the German planes and they all blew up and fell in the Channel which later made all the RAF pilots call me the Red Baroness after the famous Red Baron that was the daredevil of the skies in the Great War. Well, no-one had shot down three enemy planes all at once like I did through me skill and quick thinking."' Kate expelled triumphant breath.

'Er – shall we discuss?' suggested David.

'Do what?' said Kate.

'Er – talk about this bit of your story,' said David.

'What for?' asked Kate, hair fiery, green eyes challenging.

'Well, could I just say—'

'No,' said Kate.

'Could I just point out—'

'No,' said Kate.

'But if you're flying at three hundred miles an hour, say, and so are the German fighters, and you're going straight at them and they're coming straight at you—'

'You're talking posh again,' said Kate accusingly.

'Oh, sorry,' said David. 'Well, at their gorblimey come-on rate, and you going for them like the ruddy clappers—'

'Here, take that,' said Kate, and hit him with her exercise book. 'Don't you swear at me, David Adams.'

'Beg your pardon, Miss Trimble,' said David, 'but it don't bear thinking about, yer know.'

'What don't?' demanded Kate.

'The closing speed of you and them,' said David, 'especially as you're already so gorblimey close you can see the pilots' mince pies gleaming with evil. I should think the closing speed would be about a thousand miles an hour, which—'

'D'you have to be fussy, like some old woman?' asked Kate.

'I'm just pointing out—'

'Trying to be clever, you mean,' said Kate.

'I dunno why I bother,' said David.

'Oh, that's all right,' said Kate, 'we've all got some faults.'

'Kate?' Aunt Hilary made herself heard.

'Yes, Auntie?' called Kate.

'Are you busy, dear?'

'Yes, I am a bit,' called Kate.

'Oh, well, as soon as you've got a spare moment, could you make some tea?'

'I'll do it in a minute, Auntie,' said Kate.

'There's a sweet girl. I'm parched.'

'All right, I'll make it now,' said Kate. She got up and put the kettle on. 'Would you like a cup, David?'

'Blimey, not 'alf I wouldn't,' said David, 'I dunno I could last out otherwise.'

'I must say you're trying your best to talk natural,' said Kate, 'but it'll give me a headache in a minute.' She frowned. 'Still, I suppose we like each other a bit, don't we?'

'Why shouldn't we?' said David, coming to his feet and joining her as she brought the tea caddy and milk from the larder. 'There's nothing in the way, is there?'

'Well, you probably know by now that I'm not too fond of middle-class blokes,' said Kate, putting out cups and saucers. 'I don't like being snobbish, but I can't help looking down on them. Mind, that's not personal. I mean, I don't look down on you in an unfriendly way, more sorrowful, like.'

'Oh, jolly good,' said David. 'There's hope for me?'

'Well, you're not as bad as some,' said Kate, 'and you do have nice parents that sound very natural.

It's a myst'ry to me why they brought you up middle class. Still, you could sort of fight your way out of it, and if you did you might get someone nice to marry you when you're older, like a Camberwell friend of mine, Olive Glover, whose dad is a bus conductor.'

'Blow me over, I'll do that, then,' said David, 'I'll fight me drawbacks day and night, not 'alf I won't.'

'If I'm around, I'll do my best to help you,' said Kate.

'Is Olive a bit like you?' asked David. 'Is she pretty?'

'Yes, sort of,' said Kate.

'And sexy?' said David.

'No, she goes to church,' said Kate. 'Here, wait a bit, d'you mean I'm sexy?'

'Well, if you don't go to church—'

'Here, hold that,' said Kate, and conked him with a tablespoon. The kettle boiled and she made the tea. She glanced at David. His shirt was still over his shoulder. She frowned. 'Put your shirt on,' she said.

David pulled it on.

'I'll take Aunt Hilary's cup of tea to her, if you like,' he said.

'No, you won't.' Refusal of his offer came quickly from her. She still had this uncomfortable feeling about her aunt's attitude towards David. 'I'll take it.' She did so, her aunt thanked her in an absent way, and then she and David sat on the back doorstep again, drinking their own tea.

'What's the name of the airman you're going to rescue in your story?' asked David.

'Valentine Fitzroy,' said Kate. 'D'you like it?'

'Er, well,' said David.

'Of course, he's not middle class or anything swanky,' said Kate, 'he's come from a nice common fam'ly, actually, and doesn't have any posh airs or graces.'

'Kate, shouldn't his name be something like Fred Simpkins, then, instead of Valentine Fitzroy, which is about as swanky as you can get?' said David.

'Now how could a Fred Simpkins be a dashing RAF pilot?' said Kate. 'You've got to have a sort of 'andsome name. Fred Simpkins is all right for one of the honest workers of the world, but not for a daring airman.'

'See your point,' said David.

'Well, I hope you do,' said Kate, 'I'd like to think you've got a bit of me dad's commonsense.'

'What was your dad?' asked David.

'A bus driver that belonged to his trade union,' said Kate. She looked sad then. 'Poor old Dad, poor old Mum,' she sighed, 'they didn't deserve getting bombed to death.'

'Nor did my Aunt Emily,' said David soberly. 'It's a rotten war, Kate. I'm really sorry about your mum and dad.'

Kate swallowed.

'I'm over the worst, like I told you before,' she said, 'but I do get a bit sad every time I think of them.'

'I know,' said David, and put an arm round her. She turned to him and put her hand on his chest. They looked at each other, misty green eyes meeting sympathetic grey.

'Well, go on, then,' said Kate in an unsteady

whisper. David kissed her. A mutual pressure of lips resulted. 'Crikey,' breathed Kate, pulling away, 'you're a deceiver, you are, the way you talk about not knowing about girls and then kissing me like that.'

'Like what?' asked David.

'All pash,' said Kate. He laughed, so she hit him again with her exercise book. 'Take that. Yes, and that.'

'What for?' asked David.

'For laughing when you shouldn't,' said Kate, 'and for taking advantage of me.'

'Kate?' Aunt Hilary was calling in a die-away voice.

'Yes, Auntie?'

'Is there any more tea, Kate dear?'

'Yes, there's lots in the pot,' called Kate, 'but we're getting a bit short of our ration in the tea caddy.'

'What a lousy silly war. But all right, if I could have another cup from the pot, I'd be grateful. Thank you, Kate.'

'Yes, all right, Aunt Hilary,' said Kate.

'I don't like to say so,' murmured David, 'but your aunt takes advantage of you a bit, doesn't she?'

'No, course she doesn't,' said Kate, getting up, 'so mind your business.'

'Yes, I ought to,' said David. 'Well, I'll get back to the Goodworthys now and listen to the rest of your story some other time.'

'All right,' said Kate. 'Tomorrow,' she added.

'I think I might be a bit tied up—'

'Tomorrow,' said Kate, putting the kettle on.

'I'll see if—'

'Tomorrow,' said Kate again.

'OK,' said David, and left.

Kate gave her aunt another cup of tea, then sat down on the doorstep once more. With David gone, she felt sort of deserted. Oh, blow, she thought. She'd met some of the older village youths, or rather they'd made themselves known to her, but none of them kept her on her toes like David did.

Everything was boringly quiet. The war was going on in many places, and she supposed planes and guns were creating noise and thunder in Russia and Egypt and elsewhere, but nothing was disturbing Devon. All she could hear were flying insects and chattering birds.

She got up, went to the shed, took up a hoe and did a little amateur gardening. She was getting quite fond of the garden.

Evening

In far-off Rotherhithe, south of the river and close to the Pool of London, a terraced house resounded to shouts, yells, curses and blows. Two men were at each other's throat, one a large and beefy London factory worker, the other a husky Canadian soldier, a corporal. The factory worker had left his night shift early, on the pretext of stomach sickness, which proved unfortunate for his fun-loving wife. Thirty-four, a buxom, peroxide blonde, she was entertaining the Canadian, whom she'd met in a West End dance hall. It was a very generous form of entertainment, much appreciated by the Canadian, but not at all by the husband. The sight was like a flaming red rag to a bull. He knocked his wife out first, and then began doing his best to murder the Canadian. The Canadian, not in favour of that, or of the fact that the stupid guy had arrived home far too soon, took umbrage and swapped blow for blow. Furniture crashed and smashed, blood flowed, violence increased, the outraged husband reached a berserk state, and the Canadian began to get by far the worst of the fight.

The police arrived at the scene of the mayhem. Both the wife and the Canadian were taken by ambulance to hospital, and the still raging docker, name of Dan Ricketts, was arrested for causing grievous bodily harm to his wife and for the attempted murder of a soldier of the Empire, something the Government and the law were dead against at this particular time.

Chapter Nineteen

In the Western Desert, Rommel was probing and scouting, looking for weak links in the defensive positions of the British Eighth Army. It could be said that every member of the Afrika Korps knew their Commander by sight, for Rommel was constantly among his troops, including his forward patrols. General Auchinleck, on the other hand, was a thinking but remote Commander, and few Eighth Army men had ever seen him. Rommel was a well-known figure of craft and courage to the Afrika Korps, while to the British troops, Auchinleck was an unknown figure far back at Headquarters in Cairo.

Rommel gave the Afrika Korps confidence. Auchinleck gave the Eighth Army messages of hope but no inspiration. Both commanders were planning late autumn offensives. In the meantime, the Long Range Desert Group and its close associates, the men of the SAS, were initiating their own kind of warfare from the desert base of the SAS.

The place was stony sun-scorched Kabrit, just about as inhospitable as it could be, with Cairo a hundred miles at its back. There, selected officers and men were pitched into training schedules that stretched endurance to the limit and set them up as ravaging night raiders. Night became their friend as they acquired all the necessary skills to mount and carry out raids in the darkness. Blindness was no problem, for they learned how to train their automatic weapons on sound, not sight.

For destructive purposes, they put together a bomb that was both an explosive and an incendiary, a thing of beauty to such men and made of thermite, oil and plastic.

Colonel Lucas was a welcome recruit to this desert group, and so were Tim and other newly-arrived Commandos. If Troon had been hell on frequent occasions, they found Kabrit doubly so, burningly hot by day and freezing by night. Before they could take part in any raids, it was vitally necessary for them to get used to conditions in the desert, and they were pitched into the endurance tests whose purpose was to make or break them.

What was being planned at the moment was a raid deep behind lines into Libya, the intention being to destroy three of Rommel's air support bases at Sirte, El Agheila and Agedaiba.

That appealed to Colonel Lucas, and he also liked the leading figures of the LRDC and the SAS, men tanned to teak-brown and as hard as the rocks of Kabrit. They were lethal when in action. Colonel Lucas, happy when Tim caught up with him, infected him with his own kind of enthusiasm, and they took on all the back-breaking conditioning exercises with the purposeful confidence of men already tried and tested, and determined to be part of the destructive raiding force in a month or so.

Green Devon was a far far cry from the burning desert.

'Look, Mrs Mumford,' said Daisy, 'I picked the first blackberries off the 'edges this afternoon wiv Posy, Paul and Stevie. Posy took some 'ome to her mum and I brought these for you. Ain't they nice, and ever so black and dry.'

Mrs Mumford had just arrived home from her work. She spent half an hour at the cottage at midday, when she and Daisy ate a light lunch, but by a little after four she was home for the rest of the day. She gazed at the bowl of wild fruit on the kitchen table.

'That's a good girl you are, Daisy,' she said. 'I'm minded to make a blackberry and apple pie, using honey in place of sugar that's rationed.'

'Crikey, can yer get some 'oney, Mrs Mumford?'

'From Mr Pennicot,' said Mrs Mumford. 'He keeps bees.'

'Oh, does 'e treat yer nice, Mrs Mumford?'

'He's a kind man, child.'

'Only I think you deserve to be treated nice,' said Daisy, who for weeks had been having the kind of conversations with Mrs Mumford that she'd never had before.

'Mostly in life, Daisy, we all only get what we deserve,' said the reserved lady. 'You'll be getting what you deserve for picking the blackberries. A pie.'

'Mrs Mumford, would yer like a cup of tea now you've just come in?' asked Daisy.

'You be set these days on making the afternoon pot,' said Mrs Mumford.

'Oh, I'm always pleased to do it for yer, honest,' said Daisy. 'Oh, and I've picked the pertaters and carrots for supper.'

'I'm wondering now who be running this kitchen, Daisy, you or me,' said Mrs Mumford.

'Mrs Mumford, I just like bein' a help to yer,' said Daisy.

'You be coming in early from your afternoon play these days,' said Mrs Mumford, 'and on your holidays too.'

'Oh, well,' said Daisy, then asked a little hesitantly, 'Mrs Mumford, d'you – d'you like me bein' 'ere when you come in from your work?'

'Yes, child, but you're entitled to your hours of play,' said Mrs Mumford.

'Oh, I get lots of time wiv Posy and Stevie ev'ry day,' said Daisy, 'and – well –' She stopped.

'Speak your mind, Daisy.'

'Well, I just think ev'ryone that's been at work ought to 'ave someone to come 'ome to most times,' said Daisy, and Mrs Mumford guessed the girl had known an empty house and blank walls all too often on arriving home from her school in London, a city noted for an abundance of churches and an abundance of heathens. Heathen parents like Daisy's should never have children.

Mrs Mumford bit her lip. Barney had wanted children, but nothing had ever come about. There was always a dog, however, to fuss over.

'Make the tea, Daisy,' she said, 'while I go and pick off dead fuschia flowers.'

'Yes, Mrs Mumford,' said Daisy.

'How be your young lady, David?' asked Beth Goodworthy over supper.

'Well, I have to tell you, Aunt Beth, she's waiting to be old enough to volunteer for the Waafs and meet a daredevil Spitfire pilot,' said David.

'Oh, my,' said Beth.

'That be one in the eye for Davy,' said Posy.

'He'd be better off keeping ferrets,' said Paul.

'Some ferrets be little devils,' said Jake.

'Well,' said Abel, looking at Posy, 'some girls—'

'Don't 'ee say it,' said Beth, 'not about your own sister.'

'Are there any daredevil Spitfire pilots in Devon for Kate to meet now?' asked Alice.

'I aren't met one myself,' said Jake.

'Nor me,' said Posy.

'There's Billy Crump,' said Abel, 'he be a daredevil. Went after Lucy Fisher up in the squire's big barn, he did, and Lucy come running out yelling for her dad.'

'Billy Crump be on the way to getting a belting from his own dad, I reckon,' said Jake.

'And better soon than late,' said Beth. 'Ah, well, about Spitfire pilots, I'm thinking there aren't enough for every girl to have one.'

'That's right, Aunt Beth, there aren't,' said Alice. 'I might even be unlucky myself. So if Kate misses out, there's still hope for you, David.'

'What a relief,' said David, 'I'll be able to sleep tonight.'

Beth laughed. Posy giggled. Jake winked.

Saturday night

It was just after ten and the dance at Ashleigh's village hall had finished. Out came teenage boys and girls, young country nobs such as farmers' sons, Land Army girls, and a few off-duty soldiers. Out came Kate and David, Kate delivering some choice words to David.

'Listen, who decided to make that last waltz a "Ladies-excuse-me"?' she said. 'A last waltz shouldn't be an "Excuse-me". You had six girls all taking their turns with you, after the first one took you away from me. I never saw anything more disgusting, it looked as if you'd brought your village harem along. It was a wonder they weren't all dressed in harem flimsies that you could see through.'

'I don't think their mums would let them go to a dance dressed like that,' said David. 'Anyway, there's always these "Ladies-excuse-me" numbers because there's always a lot more ladies than men.'

'Some ladies, I don't think,' said Kate, inhaling the night scents as she walked beside him in the dark. 'Your lot were all like clinging ivy, and not just in the last waltz, either. I've got suspicions about you when you say you don't know anything about girls. Anyway, that's the last time I'm going to let you go dancing. Dancing? Come into me boudoir, more like. Crikey, none of them could've been more than fifteen.'

'Country girls grow up quick,' said David.

'Oh, you know that much, do you?' said Kate.
'Anyway, you can stay away from them in future.'

'Pardon?' said David.

'Or you'll get kidnapped, you poor bloke,' said
Kate. 'I don't know why the girls in this village like
a Lord Muck so much that they can't keep their
hands off him. Don't they know you're supposed to
be me faithful boyfriend?'

'How did I get to be that?' asked David, turning
a corner with her.

'It happened, didn't it?' said Kate. 'Mind you, it
wouldn't if I'd known you'd got a village harem. All
this time and you never said a word.'

'Never gave it a thought,' said David. 'By the way,
could I point out you spent most of the evening
dancing with farmers' sons?'

'I couldn't stop them coming up and asking me,
could I?' said Kate.

'All the same,' said David, 'perhaps you'd better
keep away in future.'

'I'd better what?' said Kate, stopping outside her
gate.

'You'll get kidnapped,' said David, 'and it might
be by someone with evil designs.'

Kate burst into laughter.

'All right, quits,' she said, 'and thanks for taking
me. I'd best go in now. I expect Aunt Hilary's back
from her day out and would like a bedtime cup of
tea. You go off to your harem.'

'It's a hard life for a sultan,' said David. ''Night,
Kate, see you.'

'Tomorrow,' said Kate, and went in. Her aunt, apparently fatigued from one more day out, was draped along the sofa in the front room, all languid limbs.

'Oh, there you are, Kate dear,' she drawled. 'Happy dancing?'

'Lovely,' said Kate.

'How nice. I'm fagged out myself. Do you think—?'

'Yes, a cup of tea and a sandwich,' said Kate.

'Thank you, sweetie.'

'Where've you been that tired you out?' asked Kate.

'Dartmoor.'

'All that way?' said Kate. 'David told us it's a good twenty-five miles.'

'I didn't walk,' murmured Aunt Hilary, 'my bike carried me. It carried me around Paris. My friends and I all used bikes to get about. It was the thing to do.'

'Well, I'll get about on me legs now and do the tea and sandwich,' said Kate.

'There's a good girl,' said Aunt Hilary.

Monday in a magistrates' court in London west-central

The chairman of the bench regarded the defendant keenly. The man's head and face were heavily bandaged. Only his eyes, nose and mouth were visible, but it had to be said that his eyes still held a bit of a glare.

'Is your client fit to plead, Mr Gower?' asked the magistrate.

'Yes, Your Honour,' said the defendant's lawyer.

'How does he plead?'

'With difficulty,' said the lawyer, forgetting himself for a moment.

'What was that?'

'His injured jaw prevents coherent speech for the moment, Your Honour, but I'm instructed to say he pleads not guilty.'

'Very well.'

The defendant, Ben Ricketts, was on a charge of grievous bodily harm and attempted murder. His lawyer thought the latter charge could be reasonably reduced to attempted manslaughter. In any event, he was committed for trial by jury at the Old Bailey, and ordered to be remanded in custody. Bail was denied and he was taken back to Pentonville Prison, where he was existing as an out-patient of the prison hospital.

His battered wife and the Canadian soldier were in-patients at Guy's Hospital, the latter in a humiliated condition, but set for recovery.

Polly kept her appointment for a second consultation with her gynaecologist in Dulwich Village. Midway through his examination, she asked a question.

'Is that some kind of gramophone trumpet you're using?'

'Not at all, Mrs Adams,' said Mr Rawlinson. 'It's a very sensitive stethoscope.'

'Is someone playing a tune?' asked Polly. 'And are you listening to it?'

'Um?' said Mr Rawlinson, concentrating.

'I thought Jack or Jill might be playing a violin,' said Polly.

'Jack or Jill, h'm,' said Mr Rawlinson, and went on with his examination. At the end, he made some notes while Polly dressed in a room next to reception, where Boots was waiting. Sir Henry had excused him from duties for the day so that he could go with Polly this time. When she re-entered the consulting room, Boots was with her. Mr Rawlinson looked up at them from his desk. 'Sit down, Mrs Adams, Colonel Adams.' Polly and Boots seated themselves. 'I'll be writing to Mrs Adams's doctor in Corfe Castle.'

'To let him know everything's as it should be?' said Boots.

With the hint of a smile, Mr Rawlinson said, 'Your wife, Colonel Adams, spoke of Jack or Jill.'

'Yes, boy or girl,' said Boots.

'I'd like one or the other,' said Polly.

'What would you say, Mrs Adams, if I suggested there's a possibility of Jack and Jill?' asked Mr Rawlinson.

'What?' gasped Polly.

'What?' said Boots.

'I suggest,' said Mr Rawlinson, 'that there's—'

'No, don't repeat it,' said Polly, quivering, 'or I'll create a precedent in the stiff upper lip Simms family and faint. You're not serious, are you?'

'I have to tell you that there is a possibility that you're carrying twins,' said Mr Rawlinson.

'I think I'm hearing things from far-off,' said Boots.

Polly was sure that what she had heard herself

had come out of a book of frightful jokes, the effect of which made her feel she had lost her voice and was never going to recover it. However, she fought the feeling, went in gritty search of her tongue, found it and used it, albeit faintly.

'Mr Rawlinson, this can't be true.'

'The possibility of a Jill as well as a Jack? Or two Jills or two Jacks? It exists, Mrs Adams. What you called a trumpet is actually a Pinard Foetal Stethoscope, an extremely sensitive listening device, and although I can't be absolutely sure at this stage, I think I've detected two heartbeats and symptoms of activity that are exaggerated when twin embryos are present. And you're a little – um – larger than if it were a single embryo.'

'I'm going to have twins?' breathed Polly.

'I repeat, the possibility does exist, Mrs Adams.'

'Oh, my God,' said Polly, 'don't you know how old I am?'

'I've patients much younger than you, Mrs Adams, but no healthier and no better equipped for childbirth than you,' said Mr Rawlinson. 'For instance, your pelvic structure is excellent.'

'Blow my pelvic structure,' said Polly, feeling that hysteria was going to make its mark. She glanced at Boots. His expression didn't help her in her dizzy belief that a bomb had dropped. He looked like a man for whom the unexpected was in the nature of a happy surprise.

'Fascinating,' he said.

'Is this the time to be airy-fairy?' said Polly. 'Didn't you hear Mr Rawlinson tell me I'm probably due to have twins?'

'I did hear,' said Boots, 'what a woman.'

Polly, halfway to going off her head, picked up a hollow cardboard roller from the desk and hit him with it. Twice.

'It isn't amusing, you stinker,' she said, 'it's giving me heart failure.'

'Bear in mind I did say I can't be absolutely certain,' observed Mr Rawlinson.

'But if it turns out to be true,' said Boots, 'how will you really feel, Polly?'

'Paralytic,' said Polly. 'Twins? Oh, my God.'

'Shall we pray?' suggested Boots.

Mr Rawlinson coughed. Polly looked at Boots. He made a valiant attempt to show that he shared her sense of frightful confusion, but failed, chiefly because his own feelings were the reverse of hers. He burst into laughter. Polly hit him again with the cardboard roller.

But then she was laughing too. Not because she was amused, no, not at all. Hysterics had overtaken her.

Mr Rawlinson felt one did not often meet a husband and wife of this kind. He did not laugh himself, however. He was sure Mrs Adams wouldn't expect or want him to. So he coughed again.

'Mr Rawlinson,' said Boots, 'my wife has taken to gardening. Would the exercise of nurturing and mothering her runner beans be good for her pelvic structure?'

Polly shrieked and whacked him again. Mr Rawlinson cleared his throat and spoke.

'Um – Colonel Adams – Mrs Adams—'

'So sorry for my giddy behaviour, Mr Rawlinson,'

said Polly, 'but I've lost my head and I've got a frightful feeling it's gone for good.'

'Polly, you're a wonder woman,' said Boots. 'Twice over,' he added slyly. 'Mr Rawlinson, you've made my day.'

Polly said then to her husband what Susie would have said to Sammy if the circumstances had called for it.

'Wait till I get you home.'

Nothing was more typical of an Adams woman than that.

There were further comments from Mr Rawlinson on the symptoms and movements he'd detected, to which Polly listened in a dizzy condition and Boots with the interest of a husband genuinely fascinated. And from Polly's family history emerged the fact that her paternal grandfather had been a twin.

When they left, she was still not herself, but by the time they reached their cottage, the hysterical overtones of her reactions had taken wing. It had proved impossible during the three-hour journey to resist the infectious nature of Boots's own reactions, which were charged with the delight of a man who considered his wife had surpassed all expectations. She kept reminding him that Mr Rawlinson hadn't been absolutely sure. Boots said if the medical gent hadn't been fairly sure, he wouldn't have committed himself to a complimentary mention of pelvic structure.

'You're delirious,' said Polly.

'Lightheaded,' said Boots.

'You realize, do you, that if it is twins, I'm going to get hideously fat,' said Polly.

'I've nothing against fat women.'

'Large and fat,' said Polly. 'I'm already stout.'

'Not everywhere,' said Boots, 'only in the right place.'

'Twins, oh, my God,' said Polly for about the tenth time, 'but you really are delighted, aren't you, you old stag?'

'Proud of you, Polly, you famous woman,' said Boots.

'But not a word to the family, not yet, just in case,' said Polly, who had another appointment in three weeks.

'Agreed,' said Boots.

When they entered the cottage, they stood in the hall. In the kitchen, Lance-Corporal Higgins was preparing supper. Boots and Polly took a long silent look at each other. Boots's lurking smile began to surface. Polly's fine grey eyes took on a challenging light.

'Now what's on your mind?' she murmured.

'Twins, by God.' Boots mused on that. 'If they come about, I'll buy you a grand piano.'

'And what am I to play on it?' she asked.

'Hallelujah?' said Boots.

'Look here, as I've got to face up to a demanding four months, I think you'd better keep your fingers crossed for me.'

'I will,' said Boots, 'and if you fancy anything special in the way of food, I'll see if Higgins can oblige.'

'It's too late to ask for anything special this evening,' said Polly, 'but I know what I'd like for tomorrow's breakfast.'

'And what's that?' asked Boots.

'Fried fish and chips,' said Polly.

Well, bust me trouser buttons, said Higgins to himself a moment later, me lady's back with the Colonel, and I think she's just told him a naughty story.

Boots was laughing out loud.

Chapter Twenty

A Saturday afternoon in Mitcham, and Sister Louise Caldwell entered a small surgical ward of the hospital's military wing. She halted beside a patient's bed. He was sitting on it and reading a newspaper, taking in reports from the war fronts of Russia and the Middle East.

'Up, up, Jonathan, come along,' she said crisply.

'Don't I be up?' said Jonathan.

'I mean walkie-walkies,' said Sister Caldwell, dark, good-looking and efficient. 'Self-imposed therapy. Come along, come along.'

'Blowed if you don't be a fair old fusspot,' said Jonathan, coming to his feet and reaching for his sticks.

'Well, let this fair old fusspot remind you that your wife will be here in five minutes, and you want her to see you on your feet and dancing a rhumba, don't you?'

'Ah, that's a point,' said Jonathan. 'I'll take her walkie-walkies into Mitcham. Yes, so I will, I reckon.'

'You'll do nothing of the kind,' said Sister

Caldwell, 'and if you try it, soldier, I'll come after you and knock your brains out. Short walks, do you hear?'

'Outside?' said Jonathan.

'Around the hospital green, no farther.'

'Sister, I'm thanking you kindly, and I'll wait for Emma outside.'

When Emma arrived in the sunshine of the afternoon, the first person she saw was Jonathan himself. In his dressing-gown, he was standing outside the hospital's military wing, his supportive sticks taking the weight off the knee that had lost the sensitive edge of its post-operative condition and was coming along very nicely, thank you, doctor.

'Jonathan, you're walking!'

'Just this minute, Emma, I be standing still and looking at you, and I reckon you be about the prettiest wife this side of the stars.'

Emma, in a summer dress on this warm September day, smiled happily. Her Jonathan was in good form and actually on his feet.

'Thank you, Jonathan,' she said.

'And who's the lucky chap, I wonder?' asked Jonathan.

'You, you're the lucky chap,' she said, and looked around. There was no-one about except for a nurse walking to her quarters, and she had her back to them. 'Hold up, Jonathan.'

She put her arms around him and kissed him warmly, ardently. It was their first real kiss for ages.

'Emma—'

'Another,' said Emma, and kissed him again.

'Emma—'

'Love you,' said Emma.

'Well, I be tickled about that, Emma, but I think I'm standing on the wrong leg.'

'What?'

'I think I've got my weight on the wrong knee,' said Jonathan.

'Oh, no,' said Emma, immediately fraught. She let go and stood back. Jonathan, wearing slippers, tested his left foot.

'No damage,' he said.

'But, Jonathan, it's your right knee, isn't it?' said Emma.

'Well, durn me, so it is,' said Jonathan. 'Forgot which one it was. I know what caused that. Kisses. Fair sent me cock-eyed.'

'Oh, you don't improve,' said Emma, 'you're still a village idiot. Still, as village idiots go, you're easily my favourite.'

'I'd throw this old leg away if I weren't,' said Jonathan. 'Come on, let's walk through the hospital to the green. It's my therapy, walking.'

They walked through to what was called 'the green', a grassed area of modest size at the rear of the hospital. Emma was delighted to have Jonathan on his feet, exercising his repaired knee. If he limped a bit, who cared? They walked about for fifteen minutes, then sat down on a bench, Jonathan with his right leg stretched out. He wanted to know how her close relatives were. He knew her parents were fine, for they'd been to see him, but how about her brother Bobby and so on? Emma began to bring him up-to-date with news of the people he knew best.

Her brother Bobby was serving somewhere with his French girlfriend. Jonathan asked were they serving in a tent for two beside the English Lakes? Emma said that kind of question was typical and accordingly not worth answering. Nick, her sister Annabelle's husband, she said, was abroad with his squadron, cousin Tim was thought to be in the desert, and so was Colonel Lucas, the fiancé of cousin Eloise.

'There's a colonel going to be one of the family?' said Jonathan.

'Well, there's already Uncle Boots, he's a colonel now,' said Emma, 'and you're going to be a sergeant. We don't mind colonels or sergeants. We aren't sniffy or proud. Eloise, by the way, has recently gone overseas herself, and hopes to see something of her beloved.'

'Colonel Lucas, he be her beloved?' said Jonathan.

'Ar, that he be, I reckon,' said Emma, then laughed at herself. 'Oh, blowed if you don't always get me talking like you.'

'Yes, proper little devil you still are, Emma, taking me off the way you do,' said Jonathan.

'Well, your Sussex talk is imitative,' said Emma. 'Oh, help, suppose that that and your potty ways turn me into a village idiot myself?'

Jonathan laughed.

'Two of a kind are better than two who don't match up,' he said.

Emma smiled. She still felt extraordinarily blissful that her happy-go-lucky Jonathan was going to remain in the UK as a sergeant-instructor of artillery recruits.

'Oh, we'd match, Jonathan, whatever,' she said.

'How's Tim's wife?' asked Jonathan.

Emma said Felicity was still in convalescent hospital, that only Uncle Boots and Aunt Polly had met her so far, but Grandma and Grandpa Finch were going to visit her soon. Uncle Sammy and Aunt Susie were the same as ever, Aunt Susie always one too many for South London's sharpest businessman, which proved women actually had a lot more up top than men. Jonathan said he couldn't argue about that, seeing he himself was only a simple country chap and Emma smart enough to knock wise old owls off their perches.

'Never mind, darling, we can't all be brilliant,' said Emma, 'and I did take you for better or worse. Mind you, if you think you're fooling me, you're not.' She went on to say Uncle Sammy and Aunt Susie were missing their children who were still living in the country, that Uncle Tommy and Aunt Vi were missing theirs too, but still saying bless you to each other. As for darling Uncle Boots and Aunt Polly, it wouldn't be all that long before Uncle Boots became a father again and Aunt Polly a first-time mother.

'Well, that's one thing old sourface Hitler hasn't been able to do himself, nor stop other people doing,' said Jonathan.

'And what's that?' asked Emma.

'Begetting,' said Jonathan.

'Begetting?' said Emma.

'To beget is begetting, according to my Sunday

School Bible that ever was,' said Jonathan. 'It's something that Sussex birds and bees get up to.'

'Oh, we've got our share of those where I live,' said Emma. 'That reminds me, Jonathan, I was thinking that when we're living down in Somerset – well, I was thinking about that.'

'About begetting?' said Jonathan.

'I want you to be serious,' said Emma.

'Begetting's pretty serious, Emma.'

'Well, then,' said Emma, 'do you think it would be nice if we started our own family while we're young?'

'And never mind this old war?' said Jonathan.

'Yes, never mind it,' said Emma.

'Zummerzet-born children, you reckon?' smiled Jonathan.

'Yes, I reckon, Jonathan.'

'Well, the first would be born down by Zummerzet way if we started right now,' said Jonathan.

'Now? Now?'

'Under this old bench?' said Jonathan.

'I'm not letting you do any begetting under a bench here or anywhere,' said Emma, 'and I didn't mean starting a family immediately, anyway. I meant after a year of just you and me.'

'Well, that could be a year, Emma, of country larks in Zummerzet hay,' said Jonathan.

'Lovely,' said Emma. 'Hurry up with that there old knee.'

It was by arrangement, the visit of Chinese Lady and Mr Finch to the convalescent hospital outside

Farnham in Surrey. Mr Finch drove there and he and Chinese Lady waited at reception while an orderly went to advise Clara of their arrival. Clara, after making herself known to them, went to look for Felicity.

A stick was tapping the floor of a corridor. The taps were positive. Clara came to a stop and watched the advance of Felicity, who had just emerged from the recreation room. Clara smiled. Her favourite patient was almost brisk in her walk.

'Felicity?'

'Hello, are you standing in my way?' asked Felicity, dark glasses shielding her scars as usual.

'I've come to tell you Tim's grandparents are here,' said Clara.

'Oh, bloody hell, must I?' said Felicity.

'Meet them?' said Clara. 'You agreed to.'

'Must have had one of my daft days,' said Felicity. 'What're the old codgers like?'

'She looks a little like old Queen Mary, very proud and upright, but not so large-bosomed, and he—'

'God, Queen Mary's a hundred, isn't she?' said Felicity.

'Not yet, my dear,' said Clara. 'Nor is Mrs Finch. Nor Mr Finch, who looks very civilized and distinguished.'

'Lead me to the Holy Inquisition,' said Felicity, 'but don't go away.'

At reception, Clara made the introductions. Chinese Lady, sensitively conscious that this young woman in a simple blue dress and dark glasses was

293

the blind wife of Tim, her cherished grandson, spoke gently.

'I want you to know that my husband and me can't help saying thank you for letting us meet you – er—'

'Felicity.'

'Yes, Felicity, such a nice name,' said Chinese Lady, and Felicity caught the slight cockney overtones. She knew from Tim that his grandmother came of a cockney family.

'We thought Tim might like some of us to visit you from time to time,' said Mr Finch, and Felicity thought it very odd that the husband of the cockney grandmother should sound like an educated and cultured gentleman.

'To keep an eye on me?' she said, but with a smile.

'To let you know we care about you,' said Mr Finch.

Oh, hell, thought Felicity, is there going to be a lot of this?

However, the meeting and the subsequent get-together around a table in the extensive grounds proved unexpectedly entertaining. It didn't take Felicity and Clara long to realize the grandmother was a Victorian matriarch with a fund of eccentric opinions on life, people and everything in general. She was a character unwittingly amusing, referring to Tim, for instance, as a nice young man who had always honoured his parents, treated girls very respectful and gone regularly to church except on the Sundays when he played cricket.

The well-spoken grandfather, the matriarch's

second husband, had a quiet sense of humour and offered no opinions at all, except when invited to. To Felicity, his voice and his manner were remarkably soothing. To Clara, he was as distinguished in his looks and bearing as Tim's father, Colonel Adams. She knew Felicity was finding both grandparents quite tolerable, for she suddenly asked if a pot of tea for four could be arranged.

'Yes, I think so,' said Clara, and spoke to an orderly.

'Well, I must say a cup of tea would be nice,' said Chinese Lady, 'which reminds me I took it on myself to bake you a cake, Felicity. Mr Finch brought me home some dried fruit from the Government. He works for the Government, don't you, Edwin?'

'We all have a cross to bear,' smiled Mr Finch.

'Mind, there's no butter in the cake,' said Chinese Lady, 'but there's a nice amount of dried fruit to keep it moist. I do hope you like fruit cake, Felicity.'

'It sounds as if it'll put the hospital's currant buns to shame,' said Felicity. 'I'm touched. Shall we each have a slice with the tea?'

'It's here in my shopping bag,' said Chinese Lady. Mr Finch extracted a large tin from the bag, placed it on the table and released the lid. The exposed cake, with a golden-brown top to it, looked enticing. 'There,' said Chinese Lady.

'Where?' said Felicity.

'In front of you,' said Clara, and Chinese Lady sat silent as she watched Tim's wife put out a hand to reach and search. She found the tin and she lightly touched the cake.

'Hello, fruit cake, you're among friends,' she said.

Chinese Lady, a sudden lump in her throat, swallowed it and glanced at Edwin. He was looking at Felicity, his expression not one of pity or anything like that. In fact, he was smiling. Not broadly, no. It was just a little smile.

'Looks like the fruit cake of Old England,' said Clara, and buzzed off to make sure plates and a knife were brought out with the tea.

When the tray arrived, a large plate accompanied the small plates, and it was then left to Chinese Lady to lift the cake out of the tin and rest it on the large plate.

'Cake's at the ready, Felicity,' said Clara, and handed her the knife from the tray. Felicity took firm hold of the handle, and reached to touch the cake.

'Hands up those who'd like a slice,' she said. 'No, correction. Shout.'

'No, you're not deaf,' said Clara. 'Mrs Finch?' she smiled.

'A small slice, please,' said Chinese Lady.

'Mr Finch?'

'A little larger than small,' said Mr Finch.

'Same for me,' said Clara, and they watched Felicity apply herself. Using one hand to touch and feel, she carefully cut four slices, three of a modest size and a smaller one.

'Well, I never,' said Chinese Lady, 'I must say I'm very admiring.'

And that was the only reference to Felicity's blindness throughout the hour Chinese Lady and

296

Mr Finch spent with her. Mr Finch had suggested that by now the young lady had probably endured an overdose of pity and sympathy. After all, according to Tim, she had made quite a name for herself as an outgoing and competent ATS officer attached to his Commando group. She would not want people to make her feel she was now pretty helpless. Better not to mention her blindness at all. Chinese Lady took this advice.

The fruit cake proved a triumph, and much to Felicity's surprise, the hour passed in a fashion she actually found agreeable. Clara was pleased for her. The event would give her something to mention to Tim in her next letter. She wrote to him every other day, irrespective of how often she heard from him, and Clara, who unfailingly did the actual writing, knew all too well that they were the letters of a young woman who would always regard Tim as her best reason for living and striving.

The eventual goodbyes were spoken in a very friendly way, and on the drive home, Mr Finch said, 'Well, what did you think of her, Maisie?'

'Well, I must say she was very cheerful, considering,' said Chinese Lady, 'and it's very pleasing to find she's so ladylike.' That was the ultimate seal of approval from Tim's grandmother, and Mr Finch knew it. 'Edwin, what are you smiling at?'

'Life, Maisie, is very much a matter of ups and downs, but you never fail to show me there's always something to smile about.'

'Edwin, I don't think you should smile about Tim's wife, poor young lady.'

'I think we can be optimistic about her, Maisie, and that's worth a smile.'

'Well, if you think so, Edwin.'

'I do,' said Mr Finch, but refrained, naturally, from touching on the lethal risks Tim ran as a Commando operating against the tough, experienced men of the Afrika Korps.

'Well, say something,' said Felicity.

'I'm waiting for you,' said Clara. 'It's your opinions that count.'

'The grandmother, what an old-fashioned old dear,' said Felicity, 'she's still living in a world that's gone.'

'Perhaps she feels it was a more gracious world,' said Clara, 'and perhaps it was.'

'Not bloody likely,' said Felicity, 'Dickens and Dr Barnardo let us know it was hell for the poor. But I think she'd stand up to all the shot and shell of powerful argument, and not yield an inch on any of her beliefs and convictions.'

'And her husband?' said Clara. 'How did you rate him?'

'He sounded a sweet old love,' said Felicity.

'He gets your vote ahead of her?'

'I didn't say that. Listen, you blighter, any woman who can bake a fruit cake like that in a war like this, and let go of it to someone she's never met before, is my kind of old lady.'

'Happy is the day,' murmured Clara.

'It will be when Tim comes home and his dear old grandma bakes a cake for both of us,' said Felicity.

*　　*　　*

'Your aunt leaves you alone a lot,' said David. He and Kate were sitting on the back step, which had become their favourite seat.

'Well, she has to go out and about,' said Kate. 'It's what she calls research for the books she writes.'

'She doesn't seem to do much writing,' said David.

'Yes, she does,' said Kate.

'She's not doing any now,' said David.

'Well, of course she's not,' said Kate. 'How could she be when she's not here? Crikey, your brains could do with a lot of improving. That's a shame, that is. I mean, you've grown up all right, tall and all that, but your brains haven't kept up with you.'

'I'll make an effort to remedy that,' said David.

'Well, it would help, y'know,' said Kate. 'Anyway, I'm out meself in the mornings at the Red Cross, helping to make up parcels. When you going to mow our lawn again?'

'Now,' said David, 'that's why I'm here.'

'Oh, thanks very much,' said Kate, 'I see I'm still second to that old mower.'

'No, you're not,' said David. 'A mower's not the same as a girl.'

'Well, fancy that,' said Kate.

'I mean, who wants to kiss a mower?' said David.

'Listen, if that means you're thinking of taking advantage of me because me aunt's out, you can think again,' said Kate.

'Stop pursing your lips, then,' said David.

'You're suffering wishful thinking, poor bloke,' said Kate.

299

'I'll start the mowing,' said David. School holidays were nearly over and he was making the most of what time was left.

'I'll get some tea when you've finished,' said Kate, and watched him at his work. He whistled cheerfully as he went up and down with the mower, making her think he was always a bit too pleased with himself. Still, his usual shirt and shorts outfit suited him, giving him a nice open-air look.

She'd have liked it if he'd been able to meet her mum and dad.

A little sigh escaped her.

Chapter Twenty-One

Polly received a letter from Mr Rawlinson in which he suggested she might like to consider having an X-ray. The result might clearly establish whether or not she was carrying twins. He could arrange an appointment for her at King's College Hospital when she next came to see him. Perhaps she would let him know.

She muttered over the letter.

'Something up?' asked Boots. They were at breakfast.

'Read that,' said Polly, and passed the letter to him. Boots perused it with interest.

'Is an X-ray what you'd like?' he asked. 'I mean, d'you want to know for certain either way?'

'I'm tempted, naturally,' said Polly.

'Is it common to X-ray a pregnant woman?' asked Boots.

'Darling man, I've never studied pregnant women,' said Polly. 'I'm the first one I've been interested in. But I can understand how useful an X-ray photograph would be if there was something special about the condition, something that needed to be confirmed.'

'There's something very special about yours,' said Boots. 'I'm proud of it.'

'Well, old love, you continue being proud and I'll continue getting bigger,' said Polly. 'Will you still think affectionately of me when I'm as big as a barrel? God, I'll hate myself.'

Lance-Corporal Higgins called.

'Pot of tea comin' up, ma'am.'

'Welcome, pot of tea,' said Polly, and Higgins brought it in, covered by its cosy. He placed it on the table.

'Beg to report good news, ma'am,' he said.

'Welcome, good news,' said Polly.

''Appening to be in the garden a minute ago, ma'am, I can inform you the first runner beans look ready to pick,' said Higgins importantly. 'Permission to pick 'em for supper tonight?'

'Certainly not, don't you dare,' said Polly.

'Do I impute they ain't for eating, ma'am?' asked Higgins.

'I think, Corporal Higgins, they're not for picking except by Mrs Adams,' said Boots.

'Absolutely,' said Polly, pouring hot tea.

'Ah,' said Higgins.

'Fair's fair,' said Boots.

'Absolutely,' said Polly. 'They're my beans and the privilege of picking them is to be mine alone.'

'Understood, ma'am,' said Higgins, 'and might I compliment you on how they look?'

'How do they look?' asked Boots.

'With me 'and on me heart, sir,' said Higgins, 'I can tell yer I've never seen runner beans that looked more like the real thing.'

'They are the real thing,' said Polly, 'and all my own work. But I shall share them out and find some for you and Mrs Higgins.'

'Ma'am, you're a real lady,' said Higgins.

'As real as her runner beans,' said Boots.

Polly smiled, the pretty pictures on the wall seemed to reflect her self-satisfaction, and Higgins returned to the kitchen to grill more toast. His lady captain was consuming quantities at breakfast. And dry, would you believe. Butter made her throw up, and marmalade aroused a look of distaste. Good signs of a healthy pregnancy they were, so Mrs Higgins said, although how she knew, considering she was ignorant of the condition herself, was a mystery. Or natural knowingness. Women had a lot of that.

Polly, reflecting, said, 'I've an appointment with Dr Coburn this morning before I attend his ante-natal clinic.' Dr Coburn was the village doctor whom she'd consulted in the beginning, and she was in regular attendance at his clinic. She was determined to do all that was recommended. 'He's a wise old bird, and I like him.'

'Ask him about the suggested X ray,' said Boots.

'Well, he may be only an old-fashioned village doctor,' said Polly, 'but I think I will.'

'An X-ray?' said Dr Coburn, portly, grey-haired, whiskered and fatherly. He had finished his examination of Polly.

'Here's Mr Rawlinson's letter,' said Polly, handing it over.

Dr Coburn read it.

'H'm,' he said.

'That's not saying much,' smiled Polly.

'Far be it from me to disagree with such an excellent specialist as Mr Rawlinson,' said Dr Coburn, 'but I'm not altogether in favour of pregnant ladies being X-rayed.'

'Why?' asked Polly.

'I'm not sure I like the embryo being subjected to the rays,' said Dr Coburn. 'Put that down to the fact that I'm getting old and fussy. In any case, it's not necessary in your case.'

'Not necessary?' said Polly.

'Not according to my Stone Age stethoscope, Mrs Adams. It tells me you're definitely carrying twins, but of course—'

'Definitely?' said Polly, voice slightly under strain.

'That's my diagnosis, but of course you'll want Mr Rawlinson to confirm it,' said Dr Coburn. 'I suggest that since you last saw him, the symptoms have become more obvious.'

'Oh, my God,' breathed Polly, 'no wonder I'm swelling up.'

'You're still in a very healthy condition, Mrs Adams,' said Dr Coburn, a paternal beam of sunshine lighting up his face and whiskers. 'I hope I'll be among the first to congratulate you after delivery.'

'Be there,' said Polly faintly. 'As I told my husband, if twins arrive, I'll need a doctor.'

Ye gods, she thought, I waited years and years for Boots, and look what he's done to me for my patience. What a fiend. What an old darling. I'll knock his head off.

She let a little laugh escape.

'What's amusing you, Mrs Adams?' asked Dr Coburn.

'My husband,' said Polly. 'When I've finished with him, he'll need a doctor himself.'

Boots at this moment was observing the manoeuvres of an armoured division over a restricted area near Boscombe Downs. He was in company with Sir Henry. Sir Henry looked as if his sharp eyes were concentrating wholly on the movements of new tanks.

However, he suddenly said, 'How's Polly getting on with Dr Coburn, I wonder? By God, Boots, if he backs up the suggestion of an X-ray and it shows twins, how will she react?'

'She'll clout me,' said Boots.

'Come to me for a field dressing,' said Sir Henry, then exploded. 'Damn that tank squadron! It's losing formation.'

'Clout the squadron commander,' said Boots, 'he's got his own field dressing.'

'You swine,' said Polly to Boots the moment he arrived home that evening.

'Runner beans no good and you're blaming me?' said Boots.

'My runner beans are first-class,' said Polly. 'I'm the one with a complaint. God, what a reckless fool I was to marry an Adams.'

305

'Is this a preamble to a divorce?' asked Boots.

'You'll be lucky,' said Polly. 'As the father of twins, your future is going to be one dedicated to the changing of nappies. Do you hear that, you old stallion? Dr Coburn's confirmed my frightful fate. Twins, for God's sake, twins. Where's Higgins' rolling-pin? I'm going to knock your clever head off.'

'Are you saying our village doctor has done an X-ray job of his own on your tummy?' asked Boots. 'And that you really are a wonder woman? We're going to have twins?'

'No, me, I'm having them,' said Polly. 'Bloody hell, it's true according to Dr Coburn. Don't stand there looking like a St Bernard wagging its tail – oh, no, you don't—'

Too late, she was in his arms, all of her, and there was a lot more of her than there had ever been before.

'You darling woman,' said Boots, and kissed her. 'Love every inch of you, specially the extra inches.'

Polly leaned back and looked up at him. There he was, with his lazy left eye and the smile that always surfaced so easily, the man who had never failed to amuse her, delight her and make her weak with wanting.

'Oh, you old sport,' she said, 'if you're pleased, then I am too. But to save me being fussed over by the whole family in advance, say nothing to any of them until the event itself. Promise?'

'Promise,' said Boots.

*   *   *

It was a few minutes after midnight, when darkness always seemed as if it was never going to give way to light. Men of the guard detachment of a certain WD complex were hoping for quiet patrols of the perimeter and some profitable hands of cards in between.

'Where's Sergeant Fox?' asked the man whose turn of patrol duty was coming up.

'Gone off,' said another man.

'Gone off? Gone mouldy, you mean?'

'Sergeant Fox? Not him. Said he was going to collect a permanent member of the guard.'

'Some silly sod wants permanent guard duty?'

'Didn't say.'

Sergeant Fox, guard commander for the night, appeared then. He entered the guardhouse with a dog at his heels.

'Wassat, Sarge?' asked a man.

'Satan.'

'Eh?'

'Dog. Wicked as the devil. Just released for guard duty from the pound. New on the pay-roll. Got his own AB64.' Army pay book. 'Know what his pay is, Dusty? A leg a day, starting with yours if you don't get it out of the way. Down, Satan.'

The dog, a sleek Alsatian in the prime of health, sniffed around at legs, then settled down. New to the routine but well-trained, it awaited orders while listening for the suspicious.

Two intruders who had been as silent and stealthy as cats in search of mice began to hasten. One had been an observer of night guard routines, the other a general observer by day. Their planned job was now done and they were on their way back to the wire perimeter. The nearness of its release point, allied to the excitement of having completed a nerve-racking mission, tempted them to quicken their steps. One stumbled, only slightly, but the guard dog alerted immediately. Its coat bristled and its ears went stiff. It came up on all fours, growling deep in its throat.

'Sod me, is something happening?' The guard commander, about to send the waiting man on patrol, threw his question as if inviting discussion.

'Doesn't Fido know nothing ever happens here?' said one of the detachment.

'Satan, I said, didn't I?' growled the guard commander, and opened the door at which the dog was scratching. 'Go, Satan.'

The animal issued one ferocious bark, then away it went, silent and menacing. In the quiet of the darkness, the intruders heard the bark and pinpointed a distant gleam of light coming from the open guardhouse door. They began a frantic rush for the perimeter, for the long entry and escape gap they had cut in the stout wire of the high fence.

'You missed it, you missed there was a bloody dog!' hissed one.

'So did you, but it's new, I swear it!' panted the other.

Their exchange was in French.

Out of the guardhouse at a run came the guard commander, followed by two of his men. A torch sprang its light. The silent but tenacious dog was far ahead, the intruders shapeless in the darkness, but the animal was going straight for them. They could not hear it, and it was instinct alone that warned them not to stop. They ran pell-mell.

The gap in the fence was camouflaged by a large holly bush. The intruders raced for it, for the space between the fence and the stiff prickly leaves of the bush. The dog caught them. It leapt, took one by his sleeved arm and pulled him down. The other intruder turned and kicked at the dark mass of a snarling, worrying Alsatian. The dog whirled about, barked a signal, and leapt again.

When the beam of the guard commander's torch illuminated the scene, the dog had both intruders trapped. An immediate interrogation took place. It brought forth expletives concerning an interfering and repulsive dog, but nothing else, and the apprehended pair were taken to the guardhouse to await the arrival of a summoned officer. His first action was to make them surrender all they had on their persons. Five minutes later, a specialized workshop, a hundred yards away, blew up with a roar. The guardhouse shuddered.

An Army officer and a mild-looking civilian were waiting for Kate when she arrived at 'Yewtree Cottage' from her morning's work with the Westbury branch of the Red Cross. They were waiting in a car, from which they emerged as soon as she opened the gate to the front path.

'A moment, please,' said the officer, 'are you Miss Kate Trimble?'

'Yes.' Kate was curious. 'What d'you want?'

'I'm Captain Johnson.' He was an Army security

man. 'Sorry to bother you, Miss Trimble, but we should like to talk to you.'

'What about?' asked Kate, feeling that eyes were peering from behind the curtains of dwellings across the street.

'If we could talk to you inside?'

'Well, I don't know you can,' said Kate. 'I mean, I don't know you – or him –'

'Mr Smith.'

'Oh, yes?' said Kate. 'Well, I still don't know either of you, and if you want to come in you'll have to ask my aunt.'

'Miss Trimble,' said Captain Johnson, 'I think you'll find your aunt isn't at home.'

'Oh, that's nothing special,' said Kate. 'She goes out a lot on 'er travels, and told me before she went out yesterday afternoon that she wouldn't be back until today. If she's still not back, that means I'm on me own, and when I'm on me own I don't like lettin' in people I don't know.'

'I assure you, Miss Trimble,' said Captain Johnson, 'you've nothing to fear, although you may not like the reason for our arrival here. It's very necessary for us to speak to you, and I ask again, may we do so inside?'

Two village boys had stopped to gawp. Kate fidgeted and felt uneasy about what it was that she might not like.

'All right, come in,' she said.

They followed her up the path and into the cottage. There, in the parlour, she did not merely dislike what she was told, she hated it and refused to believe it. Her aunt had been apprehended in company with a confederate late last night inside a prohibited area, and subsequently charged with sabotage of an extremely serious nature. Her confederate was discovered to be an expatriate Dutchman who had been working for German interests since arriving in Britain in 1937. British Intelligence had been after him for some time. Miss Hilary Martin had known him during her time in Paris in the early Thirties. (She had confessed much under interrogation, all with a languid smile of contempt for what Captain Johnson represented, a decadent Britain.) The Dutchman was, Captain Johnson informed Kate, one of her aunt's lovers. She had also known German and French acquaintances with Nazi leanings, and had twice attended Nazi Party rallies in Nuremberg before the war. Was Miss Trimble aware of any of these facts?

'No. No.' Kate was finding it difficult now to sustain her disbelief, so quietly convincing was Captain Johnson. 'I thought she was a writer of travel books, and she was. She showed me some. I don't know anything about what else she did, but she couldn't be working for the Germans, she couldn't.'

'I'm afraid she was,' said the mild-looking man, Mr Smith, and Kate thought wildly, I bet his name's not Smith. 'Her travel books and her travel were a cover for the work she did on behalf of Germany. Here in Devon, she's been meeting her confederate, still her lover, and they've been making surveys of military installations. With your permission, Miss Trimble, we'd like to search this cottage

311

from top to bottom. In fact,' added Mr Smith gently, 'we must.'

'Oh, this is awful,' breathed Kate, pale with dismay and shock, 'and I don't like the way you're both looking at me.'

'I assure you, Miss Trimble, you're not under suspicion,' said Captain Johnson. 'We know you did not begin living with your aunt until your parents died in an air raid. A London colleague of ours spoke to old neighbours of your late parents this morning, and the information given confirmed that which your aunt told us about you while we were interrogating her during the night. That helped us to believe her in her insistence that you were and are innocent of her special activities.'

'D'you mean you might not have believed her if those old neighbours of me mum and dad had said the wrong thing?' asked Kate bitterly. 'Well, thanks very much, it's nice to know I might've been arrested meself.'

Captain Johnson apologized for giving her that impression, then asked her questions about her aunt's comings and goings during her time in Ashleigh. Kate said she simply believed that all the comings and goings were to do with a travel book on Devon that her aunt was supposed to be writing, that she'd mention she'd been to a famous beauty spot or an ancient monument or something like that. A thought struck her. Her aunt often took binoculars with her. Was that so she could spy out that Army place where Captain Johnson had said she and her Dutchman had committed sabotage and been caught? Should I tell on Aunt Hilary, should I tell Captain Johnson about the binoculars? No, I can't. After all, Aunt Hilary did take me in when my mum and dad were killed, and Captain Johnson knows enough about her already. Oh, I'm so sorry for you, Aunt Hilary, I remember now you didn't think much of Britain going to war. That was because you sided with Hitler. A new thought struck her, one with a slightly hysterical note to it. I've got a real story to write now, not an imaginary one.

'Miss Trimble?' Captain Johnson imposed himself on her reflections.

'Oh, that's all I know,' said Kate. 'I honestly just thought all my aunt's outings were to do with her writing.'

'They were mainly to do with her espionage activities and her sabotage mission,' said Captain Johnson. 'Would you know if she ever brought a man, her confederate, back to this cottage?'

'I know I never saw her with any man, here or anywhere else,' said Kate.

'Did she receive letters?'

'Yes, now and again,' said Kate, 'but she never told me who they were from.'

'Thank you, Miss Trimble, you've been extremely helpful,' said Captain Johnson. 'I'm really very sorry I've had to bring you such distressing facts about your aunt.'

'It feels just like I've been stabbed,' said Kate, green eyes dark with sadness and pain. 'But I'm sorrier for my aunt than for meself.'

'Your aunt, I'm afraid, was a woman infatuated with the glittering might of Nazi power and all its trappings,' said Mr Smith, whose eyes seemed to be in constant search of everything around him.

'And with men who represented that power,' said Captain Johnson. 'Men set on helping Germany to enslave the conquered.'

'Poor Aunt Hilary,' said Kate, pale, shaken and suffering.

'Miss Trimble, do we have your permission to search this cottage?' asked Mr Smith, the bloodhound of the duo.

'I don't think I can say no, can I?' said Kate. 'And I don't suppose I should. So yes, help yourselves.'

She wished then that David was here to stand beside her.

It was an hour and a half later. Captain Johnson and Mr Smith had gone, taking papers, letters and files with them. Kate sat at the kitchen table, sipping a glass of water, her face drained of colour, her thoughts stark with misery. She had no-one now, no parents, no aunt, no guardian of any kind. Somewhere there were distant cousins, but she had seen little of them and they had seen little of her. Captain Johnson had been kind, very kind, promising that her circumstances would be referred to a suitable authority. To Kate that meant a superintendent of a home for the homeless. Something like an orphanage. Orphanages had had to cope with an intake of children whose parents had been killed by bombs. She would be just one more inmate. No, never. She wasn't a child. She was sixteen. Her thoughts took a brighter turn, a typically resolute turn. She could

get a full-time job easily in a big city. There was work
for anyone not yet old enough to be called up or
directed into industry. Yes, she could get a job, rent
a room and look after herself with no trouble at all.
And she and David could write to each other. Oh,
Lord, what was he going to say when he found out
she was bearing the guilt of having an aunt who was
a traitor to her country? She must go and see him.
He was the only one she could talk to.

The brighter moment lapsed then, and she
thought of her dead parents, her misguided aunt,
the emptiness of this cottage, and life without
anyone close. A noise intruded on her aching
mind. She jumped up and through the window saw
David bringing a hoe out of the shed. She opened
the back door and rushed out.

'David!'

'Hello,' said David breezily, 'I've got time now
to—' He checked as green eyes, swimming with
moisture, begged for his serious attention. 'Kate?
What's up?'

She told him everything in quick, staccato
fashion, emotion making her swallow repeatedly.
David, stunned, was a study in incredulity.

'You can't believe it, can you?' she said. 'I
couldn't, either, at first, and it took me ages to – to
sort of feel it was true. I remembered Aunt Hilary
never liked us being at war, she said it was silly, and
I realized when Captain Johnson was talking to me
that she meant silly to be at war with Hitler. Not that
she praised him or said anything nice about him.
Well, that might've made me wonder about her.
Captain Johnson told me, just before he left, that

she'd go to prison for years, and that the man she was caught with might be executed. David, d'you feel sorry for her?'

'In a way,' said David.

'So do I,' said Kate.

'Come on, sit down,' said David, and they seated themselves on the back step, where the sun of calm September encompassed them in a mellow way. 'I'm nowhere near as sorry for your aunt as I am for you,' said David, wishing his equable and comforting mum would appear. He felt someone kind and motherly was Kate's real need at the moment. He also thought someone as thinking and unflappable as his Uncle Boots was just the one to find the right answer to the crisis. 'Kate, what a lousy blow you had to stand up to by yourself.' Coming not all that long after the death of her parents, it must have knocked her sideways. It was a wonder she wasn't on her bed, crying her eyes out. No, blow that, she wasn't the kind of girl to collapse, she was made of better stuff, like his cousins Rosie, Annabelle and Emma. 'I just wish I'd been here with you,' he said.

'David, except for when me mum and dad died, I've never been more sad,' she said.

'I know,' said David.

'Thanks for being here now.'

David said he'd stay as long as she liked, that he'd make a pot of tea in a minute. His mum and his grandma, he said, always reckoned a cup of fresh hot tea could work wonders. Kate said in a rueful way that she qualified now for an orphanage, that Captain Johnson had told her he'd see that something was done about her circumstances. David said he didn't like the sound of that, it might mean some big woman in a uniform knocking at Kate's door. Kate said she'd fight that.

'I'll fight it with you,' said David.

'I'm going to have to think about finding a job and lodgings in a big city somewhere,' said Kate.

'Well,' said David, 'I'm going to have to think about going home and—'

'Oh, no,' breathed Kate in sudden panic, 'please don't do that, David, please don't go.'

'I didn't mean—'

'You're the only one I've got.'

'Kate, I meant I ought to go home and talk to my parents about you,' said David. 'I think the Goodworthys could put you up for a little while, but with Alice, Paul and me there, as well as Posy and Abel—'

'I'll be all right here,' said Kate, 'except you won't go 'ome for good, will you?'

'My parents wouldn't let me stay while there are still air raids,' said David. 'Kate, have you got money to pay the rent?'

'Oh,' said Kate, and made a face.

David said he had any amount of savings that would help. Kate said no, she couldn't take money from him. She could if they were married, she said, but of course they weren't old enough for that, or to be even thinking about it.

'Thinking about marrying?' said David, blinking.

'We're just not old enough,' said Kate, 'and, anyway, we're not really suited. I know it would sort

317

of grieve me late dad if I married – well, beneath me, like.'

'Oh, right,' said David.

'You do see that, don't you?' said Kate.

'Yes, of course,' said David, feeling that in her melancholy she was wandering a bit. 'Still,' he said, going along with her abstraction, 'thinking about it later on, when I might have improved, is something to look forward to.'

'Yes, but with all this worry on me mind, I don't want to get confused about the future,' said Kate.

'Round here, there's going to be a lot of confusion about you and your aunt,' said David, 'and curiosity as well. I mean, when this story gets out, the whole village'll start steaming.'

'No, it mustn't get out,' said Kate. 'Everybody for miles will get to know about the explosion, but not about Aunt Hilary, unless I tell people, and Captain Johnson said he would rather I didn't. He said I mustn't, in fact. So I won't, and you mustn't, either, not even to the Goodworthys or your fam'ly.'

'Listen,' said David, 'there'll be people asking you every day where your aunt is and what's happened to her. You're going to be up against any amount of talk, gossip and questions. We've got to make sure you escape that. Now why did I talk about going home to see my parents about you when all I need to do is use the public phone box outside the Post Office Store this evening? I'll do that, I'll talk to them.'

'About me?' said Kate.

'About getting you away from curiosity and about being on your own,' said David. 'I can't let a girl like

you live alone, and I'm dead set on making s
someone doesn't come and cart you off to an
orphanage, not at your age. I mean, you're not ten.
So we've got to get you away from here pretty quick.
But I don't suppose you want to go back to London
and the air raids.'

Kate remembered the hideous sounds of air
raids, she remembered the bombs and the death of
her parents, and she winced.

'I miss London and Brixton and Camberwell
Green and some of me friends,' she said, 'but I
don't want to go back yet. I thought a job in somewhere like Exeter would be best.'

David felt certain his parents wouldn't think
twice about offering Kate a home, except they
wouldn't like her having to suffer air raids again.
Still, he could phone his dad and talk to him about
some kind of solution.

Some kind of solution.

Well, of course, the whole family knew who had
solved every really worrying problem over the years.

Uncle Boots.

True, he had a very responsible position on the
staff of Aunt Polly's father, General Sir Henry
Simms, and that would be taxing him every day, but
David would bet his savings on him handing out the
right kind of advice and help.

Yes, he'd phone Uncle Boots first.

'Kate, I'm not going to let you go off by yourself
to find work and lodgings, I'm going to see something's done before you get carted off to a place
for the homeless. We've got to get you out of the
village in quick time. I'll talk to an uncle of mine

... s evening when he ought to be at ... the Army, but he lives in a cottage ... t's what they call a billet, and near the ... orfe Castle in Dorset. If he can't help, ... ur lawn mower.'

... stared at him. She swallowed.

'David, could you really do that for me?'

'Could? I'm going to,' said David, 'so let's both of us cheer up. Tell you what, let's have that pot of tea now.'

'Oh, and talk some more?' said Kate.

'That's it,' said David. Quite sure she didn't want to be left alone, and shouldn't be, he added, 'I'll stay and have supper with you, shall I?'

'Oh, yes, please,' said Kate. 'I've got some sausages, if you like sausages.'

'Love 'em, even wartime ones,' said David. 'When we've had the tea I'll get a village kid to leg it down to Mrs Goodworthy and let her know I'm having supper with you. There needn't be any mention of your aunt.'

'David, I'm ever so glad you came,' said Kate.

'Me too,' said David. 'Let's concentrate on all your troubles for a bit until they're sorted out, and then I'll think how I can best improve myself.'

Kate, her smile weak, said, 'Oh, that can wait.'

Chapter Twenty-Two

David used the public phone that evening to speak to Uncle Boots. He had his address and phone number. The operator charged him a tanner for the call to Dorset. He slipped the coin in, pressed button A, and Boots came on the line.

'Hello?'

'Hello, Uncle Boots, David here. I'd like to talk to you. Oh, first, how's yourself and Aunt Polly?'

'It's a long story,' said Boots, 'but I think there'll be a happy ending, David.'

'Well, I wish Aunt Polly all the best,' said David, who knew, as did all the family, that an infant was in the offing.

'Thanks,' said Boots. 'Now, what's on your mind?'

'Did you know I've met a girl here?' said David.

'Your dad mentioned you're on very friendly terms with a girl called Kate when he last spoke to me on the phone,' said Boots. 'I gather she's a peach.'

David smiled to himself. It would have been unusual if the whole family hadn't heard of Kate by now. Family phones were always buzzing.

'Camberwell peach, Uncle Boots.'

'I think I've heard about Camberwell roses,' said Boots, 'but peach seems fair enough.'

'Actually, I was thinking of writing to you to ask if blokes of my age ought to have serious feelings, Uncle Boots, but I'll pass that one up now,' said David. 'Look, it's like this.' He talked in detail about Kate and her Aunt Hilary, and his relationship with them. He emphasized the fact that her aunt was frequently out and about on her bike to visit places of interest for a travel book on Devon, she said. She'd written travel books about foreign countries while living in Paris.

'She sounds poles apart from her Camberwell niece,' said Boots.

'Oh, I think she's got a bit of a liking for Kate,' said David, 'but unfortunately—'

The operator broke in.

'In ten seconds, caller, another sixpence must be inserted if you wish the line to remain open.'

Boots took a practical step.

'Reverse the charges, operator, please.'

'A moment, sir.' An interval of silence obtained and then she said, 'Please go ahead, caller.'

'Thanks for that, Uncle Boots,' said David.

'Take your time now,' said Boots, and David completed the picture relating to Kate, her aunt and himself, which included quite a cameo of Kate. Boots, given this well-drawn picture, listened with interest to all that came next. David decided that although Kate had said he mustn't tell anybody about her aunt's secret activities and arrest, he could confide everything to Uncle Boots. Well, he was an Army officer on a general's staff, and not just anybody.

Accordingly, David gave him the full story.

'Can you believe that, Uncle Boots?' he said at the end.

'Nothing surprises me, David. You're telling me, are you, that Kate, having lost her parents, has now seen the last of her aunt, her only real relative, for a good many years?'

'She's shocked all over, and so sad,' said David. 'She's got no-one, nor any home. She could stay in the cottage for a while as I offered to pay the rent out of my savings, but she didn't want that.'

'The officer who visited her told her he'd do his best to get something done for her?' said Boots.

'Kate can see herself in a place for the homeless, or an orphanage,' said David. 'Can you imagine that for a girl of sixteen? She deserves something a lot better than that, and what I'm wondering, Uncle Boots, is if you can help to get her out of this village before someone in authority arrives and before the villagers bombard her with kindness, questions and curiosity. I know Mum and Dad would have her, I'm certain they'd offer, but she's still got too many painful memories of air raids and the bombs that killed her parents, to go back to London yet. Dad would be the first to say she needs a safer place, that he wouldn't ask her to face up to air raids again.'

'You're particularly fond of her?' said Boots.

'She's a great girl,' said David, 'even if she is as scatty as a cuckoo at times.'

'She's fun?' said Boots.

'A laugh a minute usually,' said David.

'Well, David,' said Boots, 'I can't think of any descendant or in-law of your grandmother who can't relate in some way to cuckoos. I'd say, in fact, that we've all got a liking for the barmy side of people. And for each other's.'

'Can you think of how we can help Kate?' asked David.

'Hold on for a minute or so,' said Boots, and David held on, knowing the family's thinking man was conferring with Aunt Polly. Boots came back on the line after three minutes. 'We've room here, David, in plenty. Your Aunt Polly will be delighted to have her as a companion, and we'll be more than happy to save her from wagging tongues and the arrival of authority. Tomorrow's Sunday, so I'll be able to come and collect her myself, which is as soon as any of us could arrange. How's that?'

'Can you really come tomorrow?' asked David.

'It's a promise,' said Boots.

'Marvellous,' said David. 'I just don't know how to thank you and Aunt Polly except to say you're both heroes. By the way, everything I told you about Kate's aunt is supposed to be confidential. Captain Johnson said he'd be obliged if she kept it to herself.'

'Understood,' said Boots. 'That kind of activity isn't for public knowledge, and the trial won't be open to the public. So what do we tell the rest of the family?'

'Oh, that she's got herself into a spot of trouble that means Kate is all alone for a while,' said David.

'I'd suggest that because of her knowledge of French and France, she's been directed by the Government into work that has taken her out of the country,' said Boots.

'Well, what she's been up to, Uncle Boots, has certainly taken her out of sight,' said David. 'Yes, OK.'

'And let's say that Kate prefers a home with us to some Government hostel,' said Boots.

'I'm beginning to wonder what all of us would do without you, Uncle Boots.'

'You'd all do very well,' said Boots. 'Your grandmother would see to that. Incidentally, as soon as she finds out about Kate, she'll be writing to you asking what your intentions are.'

'At my age?' asked David.

'Those three words, David, have been spoken in my hearing about personal relationships by your Uncle Sammy, your cousins Annabelle and Emma, your Uncle Ned and your Aunt Lizzy. Aunt Lizzy was in a personal quandary when she was only fourteen. Don't worry about your age. Simply let things happen.'

'Well, if they happen in a way that causes a problem, I'll phone you again,' said David.

'There's always your dad,' said Boots. 'He'll always hand out the right kind of advice, David.'

'Dad's a sport,' said David.

'I think you'd better tell him about all this,' said Boots.

'Yes, I'll phone him now,' said David. 'What time would you be arriving tomorrow at Kate's cottage? It's "Yewtree Cottage", about a hundred yards after you pass the Post Office Store, and this phone box is just outside the shop.'

'I'll be at the cottage about midday,' said Boots.

'Thanks,' said David. 'You'll like Kate, I know you will.'

'Tomorrow, then,' said Boots.

'Great,' said David. 'Goodbye, Uncle Boots, and thanks again.'

'Goodbye, David.'

David then phoned home. The trunk call cost him a shilling, money well spent, he thought, when his dad came on the line.

'Hi there, Dad.'

'That's you, David,' said Tommy.

'Yes. How's your evening there? Is it quiet?'

'Yes, so far,' said Tommy, 'and most of the news is about the Russian Front. Your grandma's takin' a poor view of that, I can tell you. She says after what's come out of her wireless about Hitler for years, she'll go potty if it now keeps on about Stalin. She's no fonder of Bolshevik Joe than she ever was of loudmouth Hitler. Anyway, what's brought you to the phone, my lad? Don't tell me Paul's landed 'imself in trouble.'

'No, we're OK, Dad,' said David. 'It's Kate. You remember meeting her?'

'Me and your mum have got a very nice memory of meetin' that young lady,' said Tommy. 'But is there a problem?'

'Well, it's her aunt,' said David, 'she's Kate's only relative and she's had to go off to do some kind of work for the Government. They want to make use of her French and her knowledge of France.'

'That's got to be work with the Free French lot, I suppose,' said Tommy.

'Something like that, I suppose,' said David, 'but it's left Kate by herself, all alone. She's got no other relatives.'

'Well, my lad, she can come and live with us, if that's what you're thinking about,' said Tommy.

'I thought you'd offer, Dad, and thanks, but she's got too many rotten memories of air raids to face up to them again,' said David. 'If you remember, she lost her parents in one raid.'

'I remember,' said Tommy. 'Tragic. Won't someone give her a home in the village?'

'The trouble is that the Government, knowing her circumstances, might want to place her in an orphanage,' said David. 'Could they do that to a sixteen-year-old girl?'

'If someone filled in a form about her, some bloke in a bowler hat might turn up with an orphanage in mind,' said Tommy. 'Your Uncle Boots would tell you that once someone's filled in a form about you, blokes in bowler hats 'ave got you. Well, that's what he told me once.'

'Yes, and he's just told me much the same thing,' said David, and went on to recount the better part of his conversation with Boots. 'So he's saved the day, Dad, and I thought I'd let you know.'

'I'm glad you did, sunshine,' said Tommy, 'and I like it that you care for the welfare of that girl. Losing parents and an only relative, that's like a ton of bricks falling on her head. She doesn't need any bloke in a bowler hat, she needs friends and a home. Well, she'll get all that from your Uncle

Boots and your Aunt Polly. Proud of you, me lad, for using your head.'

'Well, good on you, Dad,' said David. 'I'll keep in touch with you and Mum.'

'And I'll be talkin' to your Uncle Boots,' said Tommy. 'So long now.'

'So long, Dad, love to Mum.'

Polly, of course, had been talking to Boots. Lance-Corporal Higgins, off duty, was home with Mrs Higgins.

'We're doing the right thing, do you think, old sport?' Polly still used the euphemisms of her years as a flapper.

'Well, you know David,' said Boots, 'as straight-forward as his father, and just as sensible. If he's sure the girl needs to escape from the village, I believe him. And if she's sixteen, she's no infant and won't need us to hold her hand. And it's not such a bad idea, a companion for you. What's more, the time will come when you'll need someone to look after your little kitchen garden.'

'I already need someone to hold my hand,' said Polly.

'Not you, Polly,' said Boots, 'you're a big girl now.'

'Don't make jokes like that,' said Polly, 'tell me one that's funny.'

David walked back to the cottage. Kate was waiting for him and looking a little uncertain. He gave her the gist of the phone conversations with his dad and his uncle, and finished by telling her that she had to be packed and ready to leave by midday tomorrow. Kate stared at him, and he thought again how her green eyes reminded him of his late Aunt Emily. So did her gorgeous auburn hair. Crikey, he thought, what's Uncle Boots going to say when he meets her and sees Aunt Emily's green eyes looking at him? No, that's a silly thought. Barmy, in fact.

'Well, what d'you think about going to live with my aunt and uncle, Kate?' he asked.

'David?' she said in disbelief at the offer of a home.

'Yes, it's all arranged,' said David, 'and if I know my Uncle Boots—'

'Uncle Boots?' said Kate. 'Boots?'

'A nickname he got stuck with from an early age,' said David, 'and no-one calls him anything else. You'll like him, and you'll like Aunt Polly too, who made a name for herself as a jazzy flapper about the time I was born. She's over forty now, but she's expecting a baby, would you believe?'

'What?' said Kate.

'Fact,' said David. 'She's Uncle Boots's second wife. His first wife, Aunt Emily, was the one who was killed in an air raid. She had auburn hair too, like yours. Anyway, Uncle Boots and Aunt Polly can't wait to give you a home. That's why Uncle Boots is coming to collect you tomorrow.'

'David, I just don't know what to say,' said Kate, perceptibly happier. Sixteen she might have been, and accordingly almost an adult in her own opinion, but the realization of having no-one and nothing had given her a fright. To know she had somewhere to go and people to turn to, people who were close relatives of David, lifted her.

'You'll make a fine companion for Aunt Polly,' said David.

'Oh, crikey, it's lovely to know your aunt and uncle can be so kind,' she said, 'but what about you, David? You won't have me to come and talk to no more. Don't do anything silly, will you?'

'Eh?' said David.

'Well, I expect you'll get desp'rate without me,' said Kate.

'I'll miss you and that's a fact,' said David, 'but I'll have to put up with it, or look for someone else, say a girl more suited to me.'

'What?' said Kate.

'There's Dr Marshall's daughter Jenny,' said David. 'She's a bit middle class—'

'She's fat and toffee-nosed,' said Kate.

'I wouldn't say fat. We might suit each other.'

'You and her?' said Kate. 'Don't make me spit.'

'Not that I feel I need to get serious about this kind of thing yet,' said David.

'If anyone got serious about Jenny Marshall, he'd need a special kind of doctor to examine his 'ead,' said Kate. 'Look, you can write to me, if you like.'

'I could catch a train and come and see you some Saturdays,' said David, pleased that she had perked up.

'Oh, would you do that?' she asked.

'I'd like to,' said David, 'and each time I visit perhaps you'll have a new story to read to me. I didn't get to hear the rest of the last one you wrote.'

'Well, you put me off when you said me 'ero's

name ought to be Fred Simpkins,' complained Kate.

Alice arrived then. She'd come to find out what was going on, and exactly what was keeping David. She was given the story suggested by Boots in regard to the departure of Aunt Hilary, and she listened to the details of David's phone conversations with his uncle and dad. Alice, sympathetic, agreed with the outcome. She said Aunt Polly and Uncle Boots would be lovely for Kate to live with until she was old enough to look after herself.

'Oh, I do feel cheered up,' said Kate. 'Alice, would you like to 'ave a cup of tea with me and David?'

'Oh, thanks,' said Alice, 'then I'll have to take David back home to the Goodworthys.'

'I can usually get there by myself,' said David.

'Kate,' said Alice, 'I'm sure if you came with me and David, that Mr and Mrs Goodworthy would put you up for the night.'

'No, I'll be all right just for this one night,' said Kate.

'Mrs Goodworthy could easily find room for you,' said Alice, and Kate thought about being alone in the cottage that now had its memories of her unhappy aunt and the prowling, searching men who had turned everything over.

'Yes, come with us, Kate,' said David.

'Well, if you're sure the Goodworthys won't mind,' said Kate.

Beth and Jake, far from minding, gladly put themselves out to make the girl welcome once they'd been given details of what had happened, although Jake said it were a mite strange that Kate's aunt hadn't made some kind of provision for her before going off. That comment, thought David, was probably typical of what Kate would be up against from enquiring villagers if she stayed.

'Ah, I heard there were a car and two men at the cottage early this afternoon,' said Beth.

'Well, my aunt went out yesterday,' said Kate, 'and the men called to tell me she wouldn't be comin' back on account of being wanted for a special kind of work.'

That's the stuff, it's pretty near the truth, thought David. What a girl, she was all there. It occurred to him then that he really was going to miss her. It's going to put me off thinking about my future as a self-made bloke. I wonder, did Uncle Sammy ever get put off making a name for himself when he had serious thoughts about Aunt Susie?

Kate shared Alice's bed that night, and with the natural aid of some cosy chat before they went to sleep they got to know more about each other.

Chapter Twenty-Three

On Sunday morning, Kate was ready by eleven o'clock. She had packed everything of her own, and everything belonging to her aunt, except the typewriter. David, who usually attended church with the Goodworthys and his brother and sister, was ducking the service for once to be with Kate. He had helped her to tidy up the cottage, and watched while she wrote two letters, one advising the owner that she and her aunt had to leave, the other notifying the Red Cross branch in Westbury that she had to give up her morning work for them. David took both letters from her, saying he'd stamp and post them. Then he gave her two pounds, insisting she had to have some money in her purse, seeing she wouldn't get pocket money from her aunt any more. The gesture turned Kate's eyes misty.

'Oh, that's ever so kind of you, David, and I'll pay you back one day, honest I will,' she said.

'Kate, I don't want it back,' said David, 'it's yours from me.'

Kate swallowed and said, 'Thanks ever so much.

Oh, I'm sorry about having to say goodbye to the garden. Well, I think it's nicer than a backyard, after all.'

'Aunt Polly and Uncle Boots have got their own garden,' said David. 'You'll be able to show them you can help a bit now that you can handle a hoe. Listen, what about your aunt's typewriter?'

'There wasn't room to pack that in her case, nor in my handbag,' said Kate, 'and it's not much good now, anyway.'

'Yes, it is, you could learn to use it and type your stories on it,' said David. 'Uncle Boots'll find room for it in his car.'

'Crikey, what a good idea,' said Kate. 'David, I know I've made fun of you a bit, but I want to tell you you're the best friend I ever had.'

'Same here,' said David. 'You're tops, Kate. Have some photographs taken, and send me one.'

They talked while they waited. At eleven-twenty there was a smart knock on the front door.

'That's your uncle, I expect,' said Kate, and they went to the door together. David opened it. Two men were on the step, one a well-dressed man who looked about forty, the other a sergeant who looked well-seasoned.

'Good morning,' said the civilian gentleman. 'Miss Kate Trimble?'

'Yes,' said Kate, 'but who are you?'

'I'm Mr Fortescue of Government Welfare, and this is Sergeant Amos, my driver,' smiled the gentleman. 'My department was advised yesterday of your unfortunate predicament, Miss Trimble, and we've arranged a place for you at a Government hostel near Torquay. All expenses will be taken care of. Oh, and Sergeant Amos and I will be happy to wait while you pack your things.'

Kate looked taken aback. David interceded.

'Well, it's very good of your department,' he said, 'but Miss Trimble has already made other arrangements. She's going to be looked after by an aunt and uncle of mine.'

'Ah,' said Mr Fortescue.

'Tricky,' said Sergeant Amos.

'Under the circumstances and in view of the confidential nature of the matter that created the predicament,' said Mr Fortescue with a kind smile, 'my department requests that the responsibility of Miss Trimble's welfare be theirs.'

David decided to be ignorant of what was confidential.

'All I know is that her aunt had to go away, and that my aunt and uncle are going to look after her,' he said.

'Yes, and who wants to live in a Government hostel, whatever that is?' said Kate. 'I don't.'

'May we come in?' asked Mr Fortescue.

'What for?' demanded Kate.

'To wait while you get packed, Miss Trimble.' Mr Fortescue issued a gentle cough. 'I have a form authorizing me to take you to the hostel, a very comfortable establishment and all found, I assure you.'

A form. David remembered his dad telling him about people with forms. He also remembered he hadn't yet brought down the packed luggage cases from the upstairs rooms. What with that and

335

the feeling he and Kate weren't going to be able to get these men off the doorstep, he decided the best thing was to play for time. Uncle Boots had promised to be here by midday, and he'd keep that promise, David was sure. What he wasn't sure of was why the men were insisting it was their responsibility to look after Kate when a home with his aunt and uncle was obviously preferable to her.

'Excuse me,' she said then, 'but I don't have to go where I don't want to.'

'You'll be well looked after, and you'll like Torquay,' smiled Mr Fortescue. 'Please get packed. Take your time, of course. Sergeant Amos and I don't intend to hurry you.'

'All right, let them come in, Kate,' said David, 'then we'll go upstairs and I'll help you get packed.'

Kate shot him an angry glance. He gave her a wink that was unseen by the men. Kate caught on.

'Oh, all right,' she said, and addressed the men. 'Come in, then.' She took them into the room her aunt had used as a study. 'You can sit down, and while I'm packing, I'll think about if I want to go with you or not.'

'Who is the young man?' asked Mr Fortescue.

'My best friend,' said Kate.

'Does he know the truth about your aunt?'

'Captain Johnson told me not to tell anyone the truth about her,' said Kate.

'Well, discretion is everything at this stage,' smiled Mr Fortescue.

'I won't be too long,' said Kate, and whisked out to rejoin David. They went upstairs, and there David suggested their best bet was to hang out the time until his Uncle Boots arrived. Uncle Boots was the kind of bloke who wouldn't play second fiddle to anyone waving a form about, even if he was wearing a smart suit and had a sergeant with him.

'I never thought someone in authority would come here on a Sunday,' said Kate. 'What a cheek. D'you think your uncle can really get rid of them?'

'I'm living in hope and confidence,' said David.

'I don't know if I'm ever going to stop you talking posh,' said Kate.

She set about tramping the floors of bedrooms, creating the kind of sounds which the men could relate to someone packing. David placed himself at the window of the main bedroom to keep a lookout for the arrival of his Uncle Boots. He noted a standing car in the road. An Austin Cambridge saloon. The Government bloke's, of course.

He didn't have to wait long at his observation post.

Boots arrived at eleven-fifty. His car pulled up behind the Austin. Down went David at speed, and was out through the front door in a matter of seconds. Boots, alighting, saw his nephew hastening down the front path.

Kate, now at the window, observed a very arresting, long-legged man in the uniform of an Army officer. Oh, good, she thought, he might have been a short, fat bloke, but he's not. I don't think a short, fat bloke would get a lot of change out of that Government man. If this is David's uncle, crikey, he looks a bit like Gary Cooper in uniform.

She watched as David began to talk to him. Down

she went while they were still conversing, and she put her head into the study.

'Me friend's uncle, he's here,' she said.

Mr Fortescue, seated, smiled up at her.

'I'll be delighted to explain things to him,' he said.

'I'll bring 'im in,' said Kate, and out she went through the open front door just as David and his uncle began to move from the car. She had an immediate impression of a fine-looking man with a very relaxed air. Again she thought of Gary Cooper.

'Uncle Boots,' said David, 'would you like to meet Miss Kate Trimble?'

'I'm here for the privilege,' said Boots. 'Hello, Kate.'

Kate gulped.

'Oh, pleased to see you, sir,' she said.

Boots looked into wondering green eyes, and looked again. The green evoked instant memories, and so did dark auburn hair touched with tints of fire by the morning sun. Shades of Emily, he thought, here's a girl who could be her daughter. For a moment he experienced something like confusion. It was quickly replaced by a whimsical acceptance of life's quirks, of its ungovernable tendency to surprise and confound.

'I'm delighted to know you, Kate,' he said, 'and to say my wife and I will be more than happy to have you with us. Let me add that David gets full marks for phoning me. Take a bow, David. I've spoken to your father and we both agree you're as bright as your grandma's best Sunday pearl buttons. That said, how near are you to being ready to leave, Kate?'

Oh, me gawd, thought Kate, is he really true? I've met David's mum and dad, and his Uncle Sammy and Aunt Susie, and they all sounded like my kind of people, but his Uncle Boots, he sounds and looks like a born gent, except without any swank. I don't know that me dad would have wanted me to live with someone like this. He'd have wanted it to be someone more like that Russian bloke Trotsky. He'd often said Trotsky was the only real champion of the working classes.

'Kate?' said David.

'Beg pardon?'

'Uncle Boots is asking if you're ready to leave.'

'Oh, sorry,' said Kate. She gulped again. 'Mr Adams – oh, I mean Captain or something – I just don't know how to thank you for giving me a home. I'm all ready. Only there's two men here. Has David told you?'

'He's told me,' said Boots.

'They want to take me to a Government hostel,' said Kate.

'I thought that might be on the cards,' said Boots. He smiled. 'I understand one of them has a form.'

'Yes, he said it authorized him to take me to a hostel near Torquay,' said Kate.

'Well, let's do something about what you'd prefer to do yourself,' said Boots. 'I'll talk to them.'

'This way, Uncle Boots,' said David, and took him to the room in which Mr Fortescue and Sergeant Amos were waiting.

'You keep Kate company, David,' said Boots, and entered the room by himself. Eyebrows went up at the arrival of the unexpected, the distinguished figure of an Army colonel, and the two men came to their feet.

'Mr Fortescue, I believe?' said Boots. 'Good morning. Good morning, Sergeant.'

Sergeant Amos came to attention and saluted smartly.

'I'm Colonel Adams,' said Boots. 'Let's see. I understand you're here to remove Miss Trimble. Is that correct, Mr Fortescue?'

'Quite correct, Colonel Adams,' said Mr Fortescue.

'Her destination is a Government hostel near Torquay?' said Boots.

'Quite so.'

'Is this because of her circumstances?'

'Yes, naturally,' said Mr Fortescue. 'May I ask if you know the exact facts?'

'Miss Trimble was asked by the investigating officer to keep them to herself,' said Boots.

'Yes, that was Captain Johnson,' said Mr Fortescue.

'However,' said Boots, 'I insisted on being told.'

'Ah, yes, you have some standing as a senior Army officer, of course,' agreed Mr Fortescue. 'I should like you to understand my department is taking a compassionate view of Miss Trimble's misfortunes.'

'And your department is—?'

'Welfare, Colonel, a new department of the Home Office.'

'And you have Army personnel to assist you?' said Boots, glancing at Sergeant Amos. Sergeant Amos came to attention again.

'We have the Army's co-operation,' said Mr Fortescue.

'Well,' said Boots, maintaining a laid-back approach to the dialogue, 'until Miss Trimble's circumstances change for the better, I've arranged for her to stay with my wife and myself. She's a close friend of my nephew David, the young man you've met. I felt the death of her parents followed by the unfortunate events involving her aunt, called for whatever help I could give.' He offered his next comment in a confidential way. 'I suppose, of course, that as well as being concerned for her welfare, you need to keep her under surveillance because of her close relationship with her aunt. Am I right?'

Mr Fortescue made the obvious response of a man unexpectedly disconcerted. He coughed. However, the apparently imperturbable Sergeant Amos let a fleeting grin come and go.

'Ah, Miss Trimble isn't under suspicion,' said Mr Fortescue.

'But one can't be too careful,' said Boots, who knew he had scored a hit.

'True,' said Mr Fortescue, 'true.'

'And then there's the question of making sure she's available in the event of being required to attend her aunt's trial as a witness,' said Boots.

'One must allow for that,' said Mr Fortescue.

'Have no worries,' said Boots, 'I'll stand by my promise to give her a home.' He smiled. 'And I'll keep an eye on her.' Having met the girl, he thought that would not be necessary.

Mr Fortescue coughed again.

'I'm not sure—'

'Mr Fortescue, I'm on the staff of General Sir Henry Simms,' said Boots. Again, Sergeant Amos released a fleeting grin, much as if he found this relaxed-looking Army officer more entertaining than Mr Fortescue.

'General Sir Henry Simms?' said Mr Fortescue.

'You can check my credentials,' said Boots. 'Thank your department for their interest in my nephew's young lady friend, and let them know she'll be staying with me and my wife indefinitely.'

'I'm still not sure—'

'You can be very sure,' said Boots.

'Time to go, guv'nor,' said Sergeant Amos.

'Very well,' said Mr Fortescue. 'Colonel Adams, if we need to communicate with you—?'

Boots quoted his address and phone number, and having noted this, Mr Fortescue departed, along with Sergeant Amos.

Boots acquainted David and Kate with the outcome, and David said what a famous victory.

'But how did you manage to win?' asked Kate, enthralled.

'Fluked it,' said Boots. 'Now, are you still ready for the off?'

'Oh, would you like some refreshments first?' asked Kate. 'There's still some tea and milk, and some biscuits.'

'Thank you, Kate,' said Boots, 'but shall we get going and perhaps stop in Dorchester? There's a teashop there where we might enjoy a break and some tea and toast.'

'Oh, I'll just put me hat on,' said Kate and fluttered upstairs to her room.

'What d'you think of her, Uncle Boots?' asked David.

'That no girl of sixteen should lose both parents at once,' said Boots. 'I also think, David, as your Aunt Polly does, that if the power-mad idiots of this world could be discovered and eliminated at birth, it would be a happier place for the rest of us, and especially for young people like you and Kate. She's sweet. Your Aunt Polly and I will take good care of her. Where's her luggage?'

'Forgot,' said David, and dashed upstairs. He passed Kate as she emerged from her room carrying a small case and wearing a round white hat that had growing feminine girl written all over it. The wartime fashion for female adults had military squares and corners to it, and perched awkwardly on the head. Down the girl came, and Boots took the case from her.

'There's me big case to come,' she said, as they went out to the car, 'and me aunt's as well. I thought it wouldn't be right to leave all her clothes and other belongings.'

'No, it wouldn't,' said her new guardian, stowing the case in the car boot.

'There's her typewriter too, is it all right to bring it?' asked Kate.

'As right as your hat,' said Boots.

'Oh, d'you like it? It's me Sunday one.'

'Delicious,' said Boots.

'Well, I think you're nice,' said Kate.

343

'You'll have plenty of time to change that opinion,' said Boots. Out came David with Kate's large case. Boots took it, and David went back for Aunt Hilary's. Having dealt with that, he then brought out the typewriter in its cover.

'That's the lot,' he said. 'Kate writes stories, by the way, Uncle Boots, and she'll read them to you if you're keen.'

'Oh, I promise not to,' said Kate, going a little pink.

'We'll see,' said Boots, and stood well aside to let the boy and girl speak their goodbyes.

'All right now, Kate?' asked David.

'Oh, 'elp,' said Kate, 'what do I say now?'

'Anything you like,' said David.

'David, could I just say I'm ever so glad I met you?'

'Mutual,' said David, and suddenly felt parting was going to be more of a wrench than he'd imagined.

'You – you won't forget me, will you?' said Kate.

'How could I do that?' said David. 'I couldn't.'

'Will you write to me?' she asked.

'Yes, and come and see you,' said David.

'Well, you can give me a kiss, if you want,' she said.

He kissed her on her pursed lips, and Boots did not miss the quiver of her lashes, nor the advent of a little mist in her eyes, as green as Emily's had been.

''Bye, Kate,' said David.

'Oh, it's not goodbye,' said Kate, a lump in her throat, and then ran to the car. Boots, holding the passenger door open for her, let her slide in. He closed the door gently on her. Then he said goodbye to David, shaking hands with him.

'Thanks again, Uncle Boots.'

'Well, old lad, if your Aunt Polly and I couldn't lend a hand in a crisis, your grandma would disown us,' said Boots. 'And I've an idea the better part of the arrangement will be ours. The girl's very sweet. I'll be in touch. So long now, David.'

'So long, Uncle Boots.'

David watched as the car moved off. Kate wound her window down, waved and called.

'Don't forget me.'

'I won't.'

David went back into the cottage when the car had disappeared. He sat on the kitchen doorstep, as he had so often with Kate. It was empty now, the cottage, except for the ghost of that strange sexy-voiced woman, Aunt Hilary. The garden lay still and quiet, and was going to be neglected again unless new tenants came. Not that he was bothered one way or the other, for nothing was going to be the same without Kate, without her lively presence and the sound of her perky voice.

Blowed if he didn't feel lonely.

'David?' Alice was there. People were out of the church. 'Has she gone, has Uncle Boots taken her?'

'Yes, they left five minutes ago, Alice.'

'David, are you missing her already?'

'I am a bit, Alice, and that's a fact.'

'Well, I expect she's missing you too, and I don't

345

think much of her aunt for going off without her,' said Alice. 'She could have made some arrangements, surely. Still, we know Kate will get to be happy with Uncle Boots and Aunt Polly. Come on, let's go home to Aunt Beth and Uncle Jake.'

Chapter Twenty-Four

Boots drove east towards Dorset, saying nothing for the moment. Kate couldn't say anything herself. Little tears were seeping. Boots wondered if they were for her aunt or for her parting from David. Tommy's elder son was singularly advanced for his age. His extrovert outlook, his gift for repartee and his physical appearance would make most girls see him as far more adult than most of his contemporaries. But then other members of the family's younger generation such as Bobby, Annabelle, Emma, Rosie and Tim, had all grown up early.

Kate used her hankie to dab at her eyes and nose.

'D'you mind me being a bit sad and silly, sir?' she said, slightly throaty.

'I don't think sadness is at all silly,' said Boots, 'It's the most natural of emotions in certain circumstances. Don't worry about showing it, Kate.'

'It's just that on top of everything else, I'm goin' to miss David,' said Kate. 'He's been lovely to me, even when I've pulled his leg something rotten. Excuse me, sir, but are you a captain?'

'Oh, a colonel, I believe,' said Boots in throw-away style.

'A colonel? Oh, crikey.' Kate blinked. 'That's ever so high and mighty, isn't it?'

Boots, heading for Honiton and Dorchester, with traffic at a Sunday minimum, laughed.

'Not quite as high and mighty as Everest, Kate, no, not by a long shot,' he said. 'Nor even as high as Brixton Hill.'

'But a colonel,' said Kate, 'you must be a bit important.'

'Perhaps to a nervous recruit, Kate, but not to too many other people. If you so much as suggest I'm high and mighty in front of my wife, she'll collapse laughing.'

'David said your wife is – well, he said—'

'That she's an expectant lady?' smiled Boots.

'Yes,' said Kate, 'so I'll be ever so pleased to be a help around the house, and in the kitchen.'

'If you try to get into the kitchen, Lance-Corporal Higgins will draw blood,' said Boots.

'Beg pardon?' said Kate, startled.

'Lance-Corporal Higgins is my batman,' said Boots, 'and regards the kitchen as exclusively his. He stands guard over it with a meat axe. Not even General Rommel of the Afrika Korps could get into it without the risk of losing his head.'

'You're joking,' said Kate.

'Well, young lady, I'll give you a couple of days only to find out that Lance-Corporal Higgins and his meat axe are no joke.'

'You are joking, you must be,' breathed Kate. She essayed a glance at this fascinating Army officer who was David's uncle. Boots returned it and delivered a smile and a wink, a lazy wink of his almost blind left eye. Kate, relaxing, fell in with his sense of the absurd, and expelled a little series of giggles. 'I think I'm going to like your home,' she said. 'And even Corporal Higgins. Is a batman a kind of servant?'

'Let's say Higgins and I have come to an agreement that his responsibilities help me to carry out mine,' said Boots, 'which means I try not to pull rank on him.'

'You're sort of equal?' said Kate.

'That's the accepted point of the agreement,' said Boots.

'But a corporal's not really equal to a colonel, is he?' said Kate, as the little hills and slopes of green Devon travelled serenely by.

'Between you and me and the cowshed,' said Boots, 'no, not quite equal. Not a word to Higgins, of course.'

'Oh, no, not a word,' said Kate, and felt an onset of happiness at finding him so amusing and so easy to talk to. A warm liking for him was born, and so was an idea for a new imaginary report on how Kate Trimble, Special Secret Agent, together with a daredevil Army colonel, captured a hated German spy, brought him to the Tower of London to be executed, and afterwards went to a tea dance at the Ritz.

Boots drove on at a controlled speed, and Kate, further relaxing, participated freely in the kind of conversation that was both entertaining and informative. She spoke about her late mum and dad,

349

and confided the fact that her dad had been a trade unionist who sang 'The Red Flag' whenever he happened to be passing Buckingham Palace. Did that mean, asked Boots, that he would have liked to do away with the Royal Family?

'Oh, no, just the middle classes,' said Kate.

'That's a lot of people,' said Boots. 'Where would he have buried them?'

Kate thought.

'Oh, at sea, I should think,' she said.

'At sea?' said Boots.

'Yes,' said Kate. 'Well, there's a lot of that too.'

Boots smiled.

Kate wondered if David really would miss her.

On arrival at the pretty half-timbered cottage on the outskirts of Corfe Castle village, Kate, alighting, saw climbing roses on each side of the front door, the blooms vivid splashes of scarlet. The door opened and a lady appeared, a lady in a maternity smock, her dark brown hair styled in clustering curls that eschewed the wartime trend of tight rolls, which she thought artificial and unflattering. Polly had given up her piquant Colleen Moore bob some time ago in favour of a style more suited, she informed Boots, to a woman who had seen thirty come and go. Thirty, yes, my compliments, said Boots, and refrained from mentioning forty. There were still occasions when Polly asked to be looked at as Mrs Peter Pan.

'My wife Polly,' he said to Kate as he lifted out luggage.

Kate advanced a little tentatively along the front path.

'Hello, young sport.' Polly's greeting was bright, welcoming and typical of her idiom, but she blinked when Kate reached her. Green eyes and dark auburn hair leapt to her startled gaze. Oh, my God, she thought, who's brought shades of Emily to me if not Boots, the stinker? She blinked again, then said, 'So you're Kate.' She smiled. That was an effort of will. 'I'm Polly.' That was typical of her inclination to discourage being addressed in a way that advertised her maturity.

'Oh, howd'you do?' said Kate. 'I wish I knew just how to thank you and Mr – Colonel Adams – for having me.'

The cockney accent was no surprise to Polly. David, when talking on the phone to Boots, had said Kate was a Camberwell cockney who thought the middle classes a bit inferior. Polly's years among the Tommies of the Great War and her years of close association with the Adams family had made her regard all talk of class divisions as utter piffle. People were people, either worthwhile or bloody boring.

'Dear girl, it's a pleasure to welcome such a good friend of David's,' she said. Boots jostled up beside them, a luggage case in each hand.

'Good, you've met,' he said. 'Where's Higgins, Polly?'

'Higgins,' said Polly, 'has committed the un-forgivable by falling off a stepladder and breaking his leg.'

'What!' said Boots. 'He did that here?'

'No, in his billet, an hour ago,' said Polly. 'Mrs Higgins came to inform me in person.'

'Oh, what a shame, I am sorry,' said Kate, 'I was looking forward to meeting him after hearing all about him.'

'Dear girl, we were all to look forward to rabbit baked in style for supper,' said Polly. 'I've no idea what to do with it now. Did my husband tell you Corporal Higgins has never allowed me into the kitchen, and that I'm consequently a frightful duffer at cooking?'

'Oh, I can cook,' said Kate, 'I did all the cooking for me and my aunt, and I know how to bake a rabbit so that it comes out tasting like chicken. I'll be pleased to help, especially in the kitchen.'

'Eureka!' said Polly. 'Arrival of a wizard in the wilderness. Sound the trumpets, Boots.'

Help, she talks upper class, and I'm sure she is, thought Kate. What a funny family all round, cockneys, middle class and now upper class. Did it work, that kind of mixture?

'Shall we first get Kate off the doorstep and up to her room before we take advantage of her offer and throw her at the kitchen?' suggested Boots. 'Tomorrow, I'll arrange to commandeer a replacement batman.'

'Oh, you don't have to get a replacement,' said Kate, eager to be useful in return for a kindness that touched her every chord. 'I'll do everything Corporal Higgins did, honest.'

'Ducky, you're a guest,' said Polly gently, 'not a servant.'

'But, Mrs Adams,' said Kate, 'I could have an agreement with you and your husband, the same kind he told me you had with Corporal Higgins, so that we're all sort of equal.'

Boots laughed. Polly smiled. Kate looked from one to the other in the hope of being accepted on her merits rather than as someone who needed a home.

'Well,' said Polly, 'I really—'

'The kitchen at least is Kate's,' said Boots, 'and that'll make her more equal than us to start with.'

'I can't argue with that,' said Polly, 'so come along, Kate, let's climb the ancient stairs of this rural Saxon retreat. I daresay you'd like to enjoy ten minutes to yourself before anything else. This way, dear girl.'

Kate entered the home of her new guardians, thinking the colonel's wife moved in a very elegant way, which upper class ladies did, of course, even if this particular one was a bit heavy with child.

Boots led the way up to the bedrooms, Kate and Polly following. The bedroom selected for the girl was colourful with its radiant bedspread, its old-fashioned but well-preserved wallpaper patterned with cherry blossom, and its chintzes.

'Oh, crikey,' breathed Kate, 'I never saw a prettier room.'

'All yours,' said Boots, setting the cases down, 'but put your head under the pillows if the dawn chorus wakes you. The birds here sing a lot louder for their breakfast than their supper.'

'Oh, I won't mind, I'm sure,' said Kate, 'and as soon as I've unpacked I'll come down and see when

I ought to start preparing the rabbit. Mrs Adams, a broken leg must be hurtful for Corporal Higgins, so I hope me using the kitchen won't add uncomfort'bly to 'is suffering.'

'I'll visit him, take him some flowers and say nothing about the kitchen,' said Polly.

'But suppose he asks?'

'I'll take the coward's way out, ducky, and go deaf,' said Polly.

Kate laughed, and Polly thought it extraordinary that the girl should be so remindful of Emily. Kate, laughter still bubbling, glanced at Colonel Adams. His lazy eye delivered another wink. Then he and Polly left the girl to herself.

Downstairs, after Boots had fetched Kate's small case and the typewriter from the car, Polly took the opportunity to speak to him.

'I can't believe it. We've got a young replica of Emily under our roof. That hair, those eyes. David should have warned us.'

'If he had,' said Boots, 'what would we have done?'

'Asked if we could change her for another orphan in serious need of a home,' said Polly.

Boots mused on the matter.

'Is it a problem?' he asked.

'Yes, and disconcerting,' said Polly.

'I admit I felt confused when I first saw her,' said Boots.

'I admit I felt disbelief when she reached our front door,' said Polly. 'I ask you sincerely, dear man, are we going to think of Emily every time we look at her?'

'We might for the first week or so,' said Boots.

'Let's be frank,' said Polly. 'We will, and not just for the first week.'

'But do we like her, Polly?'

'Do we?' asked Polly.

'I can say yes for myself,' said Boots.

'She's bright, engaging and extremely pretty,' said Polly.

'A Camberwell peach, according to David,' said Boots.

'And very willing to be helpful,' said Polly. A little smile touched her mouth. 'I've an idea Higgins might fall over and break his other leg when he finds out her interest in his kitchen is outdoing our cowardice.'

'So exactly how do you feel about her?' asked Boots.

'I can't help myself, I like her, very much,' said Polly.

'Can we live, then, with her hair and eyes?'

'I can, yes.' Polly smiled. 'I've made my peace with Emily.'

'How?'

'That, my dear old love, is not for publication,' said Polly.

Boots did not press her.

'By the way,' he said, and recounted details of his encounter with a Mr Fortescue, who claimed to be working for some innocuous department of the Home Office, but was obviously a security man who wanted to keep Kate close to his chest in a manner of speaking.

'I'm delighted you floored him,' said Polly.

'Your father's name and rank helped,' said Boots.

'But we're to keep an eye on our Miss Trimble in case she's been hand in glove with her aunt?' said Polly.

'What do you think?' asked Boots.

'Fiddlesticks,' said Polly.

'I'll go along with fiddlesticks,' said Boots, and switched on the radio to catch the five o'clock news.

The broadcast mainly concerned Hitler's war with Russia, and Rommel's intended offensive in the Western Desert. On the vastly long Russian Front, Hitler's generals had set in motion the massive advance aimed centrally at Moscow, a great roar of guns preceding the onslaught of tanks and infantry. The Russians, however, were not now in the mood to be intimidated, and the battles were on a terrifying scale.

In the Western Desert, it was estimated that General Rommel was ready to move in a finely calculated attempt to overrun Egypt and establish himself in Cairo.

Polly and Boots knew Eloise was presently in Cairo, from where she'd written to say that she and all other ATS personnel were pinning their faith in Britain's desert army.

The broadcast also dealt with the continuing siege of Malta, the war in the Atlantic, and American Aid sponsored and approved by Roosevelt, who seemed to have a liking for Winston Churchill. Churchill, of course, knew the need Britain had for all the help America could give. It was his good fortune that Roosevelt could see what the isolationists of the USA would not, that Hitler's Germany posed a menace not only to Britain and Russia, but the whole world. Complete victory for Hitler would see Germany as an ironclad colossus bestriding the globe.

The mention of Malta made Boots think of Nick Harrison, Annabelle's husband. Nick wrote to him now and again, as he did to Lizzy and Ned. He'd written recently, and the letter, although guarded, left Boots in no doubt that Nick's RAF squadron was involved in the defence of Malta. What, thought Boots, was the life span of a fighter pilot in the air war over that beleaguered island?

Kate's voice intruded.

'Here I am again.'

The girl, refreshed, entered the bright living-room.

'Well, sit down, Kate, and tell us something about your friendship with David,' said Polly.

'It's a bit of a scream, our friendship, and you'll laugh when I tell you about it,' said Kate, 'but could I see the kitchen first?'

'It's almost a stranger to us,' said Boots, 'but I think we can lead you there.'

He and Polly introduced her to the domain of the batman, and Kate thought it the tidiest and cleanest kitchen she had ever seen. She explored wall cupboards, the electric cooker, the vegetable racks and their contents, and the larder. There, on a large plate, was the rabbit, freshly skinned and gleaming.

'Well, you dear girl?' said Polly.

'Oh, I can manage the cooking easily,' said Kate.

'I did Domestic Science at school, and me mum always encouraged me.'

'So sorry you lost her, and your father as well,' said Polly.

'David's been a great help' said Kate. She looked at David's uncle, such a good-humoured man, and at his upper class lady wife. Since she had never suffered from an inferiority complex, she had no thoughts of not being able to fit in. She simply hoped they would like her. 'And you're both so kind. Thanks ever so much for having me.'

Polly, regarding the girl and her luminous green eyes with a slightly fixed smile, thought well, I've made my peace with Emily, but has she made her peace with me?

Has she come back to haunt me because I'm going to present Boots with twins?

Chapter Twenty-Five

Mrs Marshall, wife of Dr Marshall and chairman of the committee that looked after the interests of Ashleigh's evacuees, called on Mrs Mumford at four-thirty on Monday afternoon and, on the doorstep, expressed a wish to speak confidentially to the reserved lady. Daisy, as usual at this time of the day, was in the kitchen helping to get things ready for the preparation of supper. Mrs Mumford told her to busy herself on her own for a little while, then joined Mrs Marshall in the parlour.

'Mrs Mumford, this concerns Daisy,' said Mrs Marshall. 'I have a letter from London, from the Rotherhithe council. Perhaps you would like to read it.'

Mrs Mumford did so. Her lips tightened. The letter explained the dreadful position in which Daisy's father had placed himself by an act of grievous violence on his wife and a Canadian soldier. He was to stand trial for attempted murder, although it was expected the judge would accept a plea of attempted manslaughter. Mr Ricketts, if found guilty on that charge, would undoubtedly be sent to prison for several years. The Public Prosecutor, however, was now in a dilemma. The Canadian soldier, on the way to recovering, was insisting that his worst injuries had been caused by falling on the hearth and fender, and that he would not give evidence against Mr Ricketts. It was a fair fight that went a bit wrong, he said. Mrs Ricketts, having recovered from her own injuries, had decided to separate from her husband and move to Tooting. She wished Daisy to join her there. The council was concerned mainly with the interests of the girl. A speedy reply was requested.

'I be wanting to know why Daisy's father committed violence,' said Mrs Mumford, returning the letter.

'I've been on the phone to the writer,' said Mrs Marshall, 'and it seems, regrettably, that Mr Ricketts came home unexpectedly from his factory work and found his wife and the Canadian soldier together.'

'Together?' said Mrs Mumford.

'If you know what I mean.'

'I know what you mean, but it don't be what I like to hear,' said Mrs Mumford. 'It's Daisy's misfortune to have heathen parents, and it'll be her worse misfortune to be told about this. Must she be told?'

'If her father is sent for trial, she may read about it in a newspaper or hear about it on the wireless,' said Mrs Marshall.

'Well, until that happens, I'll not have her told,'

said Mrs Mumford. 'All I be willing to do is ask her if she'd like to join her mother, though she don't be the kind of mother a good girl like Daisy deserves. Will you wait a few minutes, Mrs Marshall, while I speak to her?'

'Of course,' said Mrs Marshall.

Mrs Mumford returned to the kitchen.

'Daisy?' she said.

'Yes, Mrs Mumford?'

'I have to tell you your mother and father have parted,' said Mrs Mumford, who rarely beat about the bush. 'Is that upsetting to you?'

'Oh, I ain't surprised,' said Daisy, 'me mum and dad don't get on.'

'Would you like to go and join your mother?'

Daisy stared, her mouth open.

'Mrs Mumford, I – I –' She stumbled on words, then said in a faltering way, 'D'you mean this week?'

'I mean, child, is it what you would like, to go and live with her in a place called Tooting?'

Daisy did look upset then.

'Mrs Mumford, don't you like me livin' 'ere wiv you?' she asked.

'That be another question you don't need to ask,' said Mrs Mumford. 'You be a good girl, and welcome company for me. The dog, well, does a dog count for as much as a girl? But you be fond of your mother?'

'Oh, I like 'er a bit,' said Daisy.

'Then is it your wish to go and live with her?' asked Mrs Mumford, persisting.

Daisy swallowed.

'Please, Mrs Mumford, couldn't I stay 'ere livin' wiv you?' she asked.

'You would like that better than going home to your mother, child?'

'I – I like it 'ere wiv you best,' said Daisy.

'I see,' said Mrs Mumford, and showed a faint smile. 'Then you shall stay here, Daisy, and go home only when you wish to.'

'Oh, I won't be no trouble,' said Daisy, letting happy relief surface. 'I'll be ever so good all the time.'

'Girls your age be entitled to scamper about with their rapscallion friends sometimes, and be good other times,' said Mrs Mumford. 'That be the way to grow up natural.'

Daisy, a little pink and a little breathless, said, 'Mrs Mumford, could I – could I—' She stumbled again.

'I'm not going to bite you, Daisy,' said Mrs Mumford gently.

'Then could I grow up 'ere?' asked Daisy.

'I don't think certain council people will say no, Daisy, and nor will I,' said Mrs Mumford.

'Oh, thanks, Mrs Mumford,' said Daisy.

'It don't be one-sided, child,' said Mrs Mumford, and went to acquaint Mrs Marshall with Daisy's decision. Mrs Marshall did not argue about it. She said, in fact, she believed it was in Daisy's best interests to stay, and she'd inform the council officially to that effect.

'But I wonder,' she said, 'if her father isn't prosecuted, will he turn up here and claim her?'

362

'Only over my dead body,' said Mrs Mumford.

'I hope it won't come to that,' smiled Mrs Marshall, and said goodbye. As she left she heard Daisy singing in the kitchen. It sounded like 'Happy Days Are Here Again'.

'Daisy?' said Mrs Mumford, rejoining the girl.

'Yes, Mrs Mumford?' said Daisy.

'On Saturday, perhaps Mr Pennicot will let me finish early, say at three. That will give me time to take you into Westbury.'

'What for?' asked Daisy, nervous again.

'I be thinking you need a new frock, a nice one for Sundays, and maybe one or two other little things.'

'But, Mrs Mumford, you—'

'We have a little money to spare, child, enough to dress you nice and pretty on Sundays,' said Mrs Mumford.

'Oh, lor',' breathed Daisy in bliss. 'Mrs Mumford, I do like yer, ever so much.'

Mrs Mumford smiled and gently patted the girl on her shoulder.

'It don't be one-sided, Daisy,' she said.

Chinese Lady, listening with Mr Finch to the wireless that evening, winced as the announcer gave details of a mass raid on Berlin by formations of Britain's newest bombers, the four-engined Stirlings and Halifaxes. Hitler's capital suffered such tremendous damage and loss of life that the leading German newspaper called the raid 'rotten and disgusting', which was a bit thick considering the multitude of destructive raids the *Luftwaffe* had carried out on London, Coventry, Plymouth and other towns and cities of Great Britain. Unfortunately, twenty of the British aircraft failed to return. That announcement made Chinese Lady wince again.

Among other war news was the account of a Commando-style raid on the Norwegian island of Spitsbergen by a combined force of British, Canadian and Norwegian soldiers. Spitsbergen's rich coal mines were a valuable fuel source for Germany. The landing was unopposed, for there was no sign of German troops, and every mine was destroyed, while sappers blew up the power station. Seven hundred Norwegian miners and their families volunteered to leave with the raiders, and sailed with them to the shores of Britain.

The destruction wrought enraged the Germans and convinced Churchill once and for all that these kind of raids unsettled the enemy and dented his morale.

However, the fact that the striking force had enjoyed an unopposed landing would not have appealed to Colonel Lucas. His war was one in which he could get in among Hitler's robots and make them wish they'd never joined. He was presently establishing himself as a potentially lethal threat to Rommel's men. So was Tim. They sweated, they took salt tablets, they lost every ounce of surplus flesh and turned into brown wolves of the desert, along with SAS men and fellow Commandos, while waiting for the moment when they would be asked to strike at Rommel's Libyan airfields.

Chinese Lady, knowing nothing of what was happening in the Western Desert, was wondering if she had ever heard of Spitsbergen.

'Have you, Edwin?' she asked, thinking aloud.

'Have I what, Maisie?'

'Have you ever heard of that place?'

'Spitsbergen? Yes, it's about two hundred and fifty miles north of Norway, and freezing cold in winter.'

'Does anyone ever go there?'

'Only if they have to.'

'Well, did those soldiers have to go?'

'Only after Mr Churchill promised they wouldn't have to stay. So off they went, smashed it up to prevent the Germans making use of it, and home they came. Now I'll make you a promise, Maisie, a promise that I'll not take you there for a holiday.'

'Edwin, is that a joke?'

'Certainly not, Maisie, it's a promise of a sincerely serious kind.'

'Well, I liked the holidays we had with the fam'ly at Salcombe best, Edwin, I must say. But I don't know I like the way bombs are dropping everywhere.'

'Germany must be hit, Maisie, in every way possible.'

'But all those airmen of ours in the planes that we lost, it upsets me.'

'It's a heavy price to pay, Maisie, but one the people of this old country have to endure.'

'Well, Edwin, I just hope this fam'ly doesn't have to pay heavy by the time the blessed war is over.'

'Amen to that, Maisie.'

'Shall we have a nice cup of tea, Edwin?'

'I'm not going to say no, Maisie.'

Chinese Lady switched off the aggravating wireless on her way to fill the kettle.

'Dear Mrs Newly-Wed,' began Clara.

'Oh, great,' said Felicity, 'I need to be reminded I'm actually married. I can now understand why some sane-thinking lovers choose not to get spliced in wartime.'

'Not many, my dear,' said Clara. 'Most sprint to the altar.'

'They're the daft ones,' said Felicity. 'Look at me, sitting here abandoned and bereft, like a forgotten cricket ball on the playing fields of Eton at dusk.'

'I'm happy to tell you, you don't look in the least like a forgotten cricket ball,' said Clara, and continued reading Tim's airmail missive. *'I'm hardly given time to write my name, let alone a letter, and there are some really fanatical types here who think only pansies need sleep. Still, I've got five minutes to myself so how are you, Puss, my angel and number one woman?'*

'If that means there's a number two somewhere,' said Felicity, 'find her and cut her head off.'

'I'm missing you a hell of a lot, believe me. That's because there's a lot more mileage between us than there ever was before, although I'm with you in spirit every minute of the day and night, more so at night, if you remember what our nights were like. Few but memorable. Yes, thanks for the memory. I'll never forget—'

'Is the next bit indecent?' asked Felicity.

Clara's eyes skimmed.

'Redhot,' she said.

'When that bounder was a growing boy, I'll wager schoolgirls ran screaming from him,' said Felicity. 'But all right, let's have the next bit, but keep your voice down.'

'Yes, righty-oh,' said Clara, and continued in a murmur. *I'll never forget how late the breakfasts were. What were we doing, staying in bed until midday? If you can remember what, let me know. How's the Braille coming along? Can you get books of bedtime stories in Braille?'*

'Hold on,' said Felicity, 'where's the redhot stuff?'

'That was it, the late breakfasts,' said Clara.

'Oh, very funny,' said Felicity, and listened to the rest of the letter. It was typically light and pithy, an attempt to entertain her. From the day when he said he fancied her something chronic, he'd chosen to be entertaining instead of heavy-breathing. Felicity's sense of humour responded to that.

There was no real information in the letter, nothing to tell her exactly where he was or if he'd been in action. Censorship of military mail was always strict. However, the last paragraph was full of affection, and Felicity lapped it up. Then she sat with her imagination drawing pictures that blindness could not restrict.

'Felicity?' said Clara.

'I'm looking at a ship coming home,' said

Felicity, and Clara thought that for the first time her favourite patient had indulged in a comment frankly sentimental.

'Understood,' she said, and Felicity, with a quick change of mood, responded in typically brittle fashion.

'I hope the bloody thing doesn't sink,' she said.

Chapter Twenty-Six

'Permission to go off duty for the afternoon, ma'am?' said Captain Rosie Chapman, intercepting Major Robbins, the senior ATS officer, outside Brigade HQ.

'Granted, so push off, Rosie,' said hearty Major Robbins. 'No, half a mo', is today's bumph all cleared up?'

'All of it,' said Rosie.

'Good man,' said Major Robbins, jacket and shirt proudly in line with her tiptop bust. 'Can't think what I'd do without you. I've just come back from the wilds of Dorset. Did you know your father's out there with the Brigade's troops today?'

'Yes, he's making the rounds again with General Sir Henry Simms,' said Rosie.

'Damned fine example of meritorious manhood,' said Major Robbins.

'Sir Henry?' smiled Rosie.

'Eh? No, your father. Ought to have been a cavalryman. Bloody shame they've done away with horsed men. Nothing more exciting to the eye than a man like your father going at full gallop for the enemy. What was it you asked me, Rosie?'

'Permission to go off duty for the afternoon,' said Rosie.

'So you did. Yes, push off.'

'Thanks,' said Rosie.

Boots, out in the country with other staff officers and Sir Henry himself, had promised by phone to call on her this afternoon if she could get time off, and Rosie in turn had promised she would. Major Robbins, she said, was a bit of a warhorse, but could be sweetened by a few lumps of sugar. Raid your ration store, said Boots.

Rosie, who always considered a visit from her adoptive father to be special, would have wangled time off somehow. However dedicated servicemen and servicewomen were to the necessity of winning the war, there were times when dedication took a back seat. Some men at Brigade HQ had been known to slip off for an unauthorized weekend with their families, and risk the charge of being AWOL on their return.

At two-thirty she was at the cosy cottage she called her home. While waiting for Boots, she was preparing a tea tray. The door knocker sounded, and she was quick to answer it. The caller wasn't Boots, however, it was a woman in country tweeds and a brown velour hat. Rosie judged her to be in her forties, with fine, well-preserved looks and deep blue eyes.

'Forgive this unannounced call, but I was passing by and couldn't resist stopping.' The voice had an aristocratic lilt and was accompanied by an engaging smile. 'Would you be Rose, known as

370

Rosie, daughter of the late Sir Charles Armitage?'

Rosie studied the woman in earnest, and had a strange feeling that there was something familiar about her. That was strange indeed, since she was sure she had never seen her before.

'I'm Rosie, yes,' she said, passing over the reference to her natural father. 'May I ask who you are?'

'Mrs Beatrice Freeman, a widow, alas, and Charles's sister. I'm staying with friends near Dorchester, and I'd very much like to talk to you. Well, I'm your aunt, you see, and the mother of two sons who are cousins to you.'

Curiosity made its mark on Rosie, but she was too much like Boots in her self-control to be flustered.

'Come in, yes, please do,' she said. She noticed a car parked in the road, an ancient open roadster, with a large bonnet, and a man in a peaked cap at the wheel. 'You have someone with you?'

'Only Albert, my chauffeur,' said Mrs Beatrice Freeman. 'Invaluable, of course, as the guardian of my heap of old iron, but irrelevant at the moment. He'll be all right there.' She called. 'Albert?'

'Yes, mum?'

'You'll be all right there for ten minutes or so?'

'Be all the same if I wasn't,' said Albert Figgs, the chauffeur.

'Don't fuss,' said Mrs Freeman, and stepped in. 'Albert's a law unto himself,' she murmured. Rosie took her into the living-room, newly furnished and in a style that favoured relaxation.

'Please sit down,' said Rosie.

'My word, you're a very self-possessed young lady,' said Mrs Freeman, and seated herself. She regarded Rosie with extreme interest, noting the immaculate lines of her tailored khaki uniform and her exceptionally attractive looks. 'Do you realize that if I were twenty years younger you and I could be taken for sisters? My dear, Charles was right, you are undeniably an Armitage.'

'Sir Charles was always positive about that,' said Rosie, who knew then why she had felt there was something familiar about this lady. In appearance, she was a maturer edition of herself. 'But I must tell you, as I often told him, that my feelings are for my adoptive family. They're feelings that will never change.'

'Oh, I don't myself quarrel with that,' said Mrs Freeman. 'Charles, however, when telling me a great deal about you, made it plain that he hoped your feelings would favour him one day and induce you to take up your rightful place as his natural daughter. Such a sad event, his death.'

'You may believe me when I tell you I was desperately sorry about that,' said Rosie. 'I found him an entirely likeable man, and had a sincere affection for him.'

'A great pity he never knew about your birth, Rosie.'

'But would he have married my mother?' asked Rosie.

'What exactly was she like?' asked the intrigued Mrs Freeman.

'She would never have made the right kind of wife for Sir Charles, but apart from that, I prefer not to discuss her,' said Rosie. It was the first time she had ever spoken unkindly of her mother.

Throughout her life with the Adams family, she had simply never spoken of her at all. From the moment when Boots and Emily took her into their home to give her love and devotion, she had detached herself from memories of the shallow woman who had conceived her. But because she had lived such a happy life with her adoptive parents, she was grateful for being born, and silently acknowledged she was in debt to her mother for that. And to her natural father.

'I think I understand,' said Mrs Freeman, 'and I think I also understand why Charles made generous provision for you in his will. One of the reasons why I decided to stop in the hope of finding you at home was to tell you not to worry about my other brother, Bernard. A hopeless case of idiocy. One wonders why the two sons of my parents should be so different, one intelligent and charming, the other simply an idiot. You've been advised your Uncle Bernard is disputing your inheritance?'

'Yes,' said Rosie.

'You're fighting it?'

'No,' said Rosie. 'My father, Colonel Adams—'

'Your father, Rosie?' Mrs Freeman raised an eyebrow at the unqualified reference.

'As long as I live I shall always regard my adoptive father as my natural one,' said Rosie.

'Is the bond so strong?' asked Mrs Freeman gently.

'I always think of him as the father I was born for,' said Rosie, 'but please don't infer my affection for Sir Charles was casual.'

'My dear, I don't,' said Mrs Freeman, 'but exactly how did you see him?'

'As a treasured friend,' said Rosie.

'I'm sure he was touched by that. However, although he accepted that your filial feelings were all for your adoptive parents, he really did hope you'd come to spare some for him. You were going to say?'

'That my father and I, in regard to the dispute, both agree it would be silly to line the pockets of lawyers,' said Rosie.

'How right you are,' smiled Mrs Freeman. 'Bravo. I think I'm going to like you, and can tell you there's no need for you to fight. Bernard's counsel advise him he hasn't a leg to stand on. He's had to concede. You'll receive your inheritance any day now. Does that make my call a welcome one?'

'Mrs Freeman, your call would have been welcome, in any case,' said Rosie.

The fine-looking lady made a little face.

'If not Aunt Beatrice, then Beatrice, please,' she said. 'Don't stand off from me, my dear. I'm not a stuffy old biddy, and certain conventional attitudes don't bother me in the least. I take people as I find them. That may be hackneyed, but it's a sound principle in the establishment of compatible relationships. Because Charles has gone, I'd like to take his place as your closest Armitage relative.'

'But you hardly know me,' said Rosie.

'My dear, despite your uniform, I think I knew you as soon as you opened the door to me,' said Beatrice. 'How do you like the Army?'

'Not as much as I like my husband,' said Rosie.

374

'By the way, Sir Charles never spoke of you as a widow.'

'That unwanted state, Rosie, came about fairly recently,' said Beatrice. 'My husband, a Naval man, went down with the *Hood* in May. A ghastly day for all concerned. A sad year for me, losing my husband and brother Charles within a short time of each other.'

'I'm sorry, very sorry,' said Rosie. 'I lost my mother in a daylight bombing raid a year ago.'

'Your adoptive mother, yes,' said Beatrice sympathetically. 'Charles mentioned that in a letter to me after receiving the news from you.'

The front door knocker sounded again.

'I think that's my father,' said Rosie. 'I'm expecting him.'

'Then I'd better go,' said Beatrice, rising, 'I've already stayed too long and that will earn me a ticking-off from Albert.'

'Before you go, you must meet my father,' said Rosie, and Sir Charles Armitage's sister did not miss the insistent reference to 'father'.

'I can't deny I'd like to,' said Beatrice, and Rosie answered the knock. Boots smiled at her.

'Hello, poppet,' he said, and glanced back at the roadster. 'Who owns the vintage job?' he asked.

'Mrs Beatrice Freeman, the sister of Sir Charles Armitage,' said Rosie.

'Who?' asked Boots.

'Yes, that's the lady,' said Rosie. 'She's here, she called on the off-chance of seeing me, and you might as well meet her.'

Albert made himself heard from the vintage job.

'Would someone let Mrs Freeman know I'm still 'ere and gettin' cramp in me backside?'

'She won't be long,' called Rosie.

'Try a cushion,' said Boots.

'Ho-ho, very comical, I don't think,' said Albert.

Boots followed Rosie into the living-room, and there he came face to face with her natural father's sister. Beatrice visibly blinked, and her fine features took on an expression of lively interest. Boots looked into eyes as deeply blue as Rosie's.

'Daddy old love,' said Rosie, 'enjoy the pleasure of meeting Mrs Freeman, my Aunt Beatrice. Aunt Beatrice, meet Colonel Adams.'

'Heavens,' murmured Beatrice, 'this is very unexpected.'

'For my part, I'm delighted,' smiled Boots.

'I hope so, Colonel Adams,' said Beatrice.

'Believe me,' said Boots.

Beatrice took him in, an Army officer of distinction and not at all as she had imagined him. Charles had said he'd been a sergeant during the Great War, and likeably civil. She had drawn a mental picture of a pleasant and homely man, with a Great War sergeant's waxed moustache. He was far from homely. He had style. Charles, perhaps, had not wanted to say so.

'So, Colonel Adams, you're the gentleman who is Rosie's adoptive father,' she said.

'Fortune, now and again, is exceptionally kind to some of us,' said Boots, and a little smile touched Rosie's mouth.

'Well, my dear man, I'd like to talk to you at length one day about your family and mine,' said

Beatrice. 'Rosie is our happy link. But I don't have time now, and I'd be reluctant, in any case, to outstay my welcome. Rosie has been very indulgent of my impromptu arrival. Perhaps I could have the pleasure of seeing both of you again in the near future. As it is, if I don't leave at once I'll lose the goodwill of Albert, my chauffeur, a fidgety old fusspot. Goodbye, Rosie, I'm so happy to have made your acquaintance at last. Goodbye, Colonel Adams.'

They both saw her out. They heard a distant mutter from Albert. But he slipped from the car and opened the door to the back seat for his elegant employer. She murmured something to him.

'Oh, don't mention it, mum, I ain't the Lord Mayor,' he said. He fished into the car, brought out a starting handle and used it. The engine fired, he eased himself into the driving seat and the car moved off. Beatrice fluttered a hand. Rosie and Boots responded with a goodbye wave.

'Well?' said Rosie, when they were back in the cottage.

'One could call her charming,' said Boots.

'And what would she call you, I wonder?' smiled Rosie. 'I didn't fail to notice you made your usual impression.'

'What's my usual impression?' asked Boots.

'Something you achieve with all women without even trying. Heavens,' said Rosie, 'you did it to me when I was only five, I remember. And I do remember. Oh, Beatrice was sweet enough to tell me Sir Charles's will is no longer being disputed by his brother, and that I'll receive the money quite soon.'

'You'll receive a confirmatory letter from the solicitors first,' said Boots, 'but when the cheque does arrive, it'll give your Uncle Sammy all the extra financial backing he needs for his new venture, the property company. He'll fizz.'

'Well, he's always been like a newly-opened bottle of champagne,' said Rosie.

'Yes, corks fly when Sammy's fizzing,' said Boots.

'Shall we make do with tea, old thing, and some happy talk?' suggested Rosie.

'That'll suit me as a welcome way of relaxing,' said Boots. Staff work made its demands on mind, body and soul, and there was little let-up in view of the country's need for building the kind of army that one day would have to attempt an invasion of France, to say nothing of first disposing of Rommel and his Afrika Korps. 'You can tell me how Matt's getting on, and all about the three bears and who pinched their porridge.'

'That's nursery stuff,' said Rosie.

'Well, let's see how much you remember,' said Boots, 'and then I'll tell you all about Kate, your cousin David's girlfriend.'

'Family gossip?' said Rosie. 'Are we into that?'

'As a change from slaughter on the Russian Front,' said Boots, and thought of Polly and her twins and the delight he could take in mother and infants if only Hitler and Nazi Germany could be cast into oblivion. Little whispers were coming out of holes in scientific walls concerning something

called nuclear fission, and Sir Henry had one of his
ears to one of the holes.

'Well, mum?' enquired Albert.

'Sir Charles was right,' said Mrs Freeman from
the back seat. 'His daughter is a striking and
cultured young lady.'

'And who was the milit'ry bloke?'

'Her adoptive father.'

'The character that did Sir Charles in the eye?'

'That's the gentleman. But my word, what a
delightful man. One could almost forgive him
for his bad form in hanging on to Sir Charles's
daughter. I must arrange a more intimate
meeting.'

'Who gets to handle the oof, 'im or 'er?'

'It's in her name, Albert, and she's over twenty-
one. And yes, a perfect Armitage. Still I can
understand her attachment to Colonel Adams.'

'You told me the gent was a sergeant.'

'That, apparently, was only during the Great
War. I had no idea he was such a fascinating man.'

'I trust you don't 'ave ideas you shouldn't 'ave,
mum.'

'Ideas, like dreams, Albert, are permitted to all
of us,' said Beatrice. 'Colonel Adams lost his wife
through a bombing raid. Sir Charles advised me so
in a letter from the Middle East after receiving the
news from Rosie. I don't imagine he's married
again, not yet. Of course, he may have his eyes on
some lady. If not, well, who knows?'

'I'll 'ave to watch you, mum,' said Albert.

Chapter Twenty-Seven

'Sammy?' said Rachel.

'Ah, my good woman,' said Sammy from his desk, 'what can I do for you?'

'You can stop calling me good woman unless you want a hole in your head,' said Rachel, her well-constructed female figure clad in a grey costume and white blouse. The jacket was square-shouldered, a wartime fashion that hurt Sammy's eyes. Fashion to Sammy was something that had been invented to make feminine females feel good and look good, and to please the eyes of discerning blokes. Whoever put square shoulders on feminine females to make them look ready for a punch-up ought to be chucked to the lions. The rag trade called it the wartime military look. The rag trade was off its rocker. 'I'm nobody's good woman,' said Rachel.

'Slip of me mind,' said Sammy, 'for which me apology is sincere, and genuine as well. Have you just got back from somewhere?'

'Yes, from seeing Mr Blenkinsop in his Ministry office,' said Rachel.

'Of course,' said Sammy. 'Good of you to go and see him, Rachel. What's he like in person?'

'Sweet,' said Rachel.

'Eh?' said Sammy.

'Sweet,' said Rachel.

'Blenkinsop?'

'Oswald Blenkinsop.'

'Eh?' said Sammy.

'Oswald,' said Rachel.

'Oswald Blenkinsop, Grade One Civil Servant?'

'We had tea and biscuits,' said Rachel. 'My life, buttery shortbreads, would you believe.'

'He's human?' said Sammy.

'Sweet,' said Rachel.

'Don't start that again,' said Sammy, 'I'm feeling faint.'

'You'll feel a lot better when I tell you Oswald sent you his compliments for our reliability and our excellent fulfilment of contracts,' said Rachel. 'And, of course, he was delighted when I let him know we now have an option on an alternative factory in Clapham.'

'For which I hand you the credit,' said Sammy.

'Sammy,' said Rachel, 'I think Oswald is actually quite fond of you. He spoke almost affectionately of the relationship.'

'Here, hold up,' said Sammy. 'Rachel, that's not the kind of clean-living talk I like. I don't want Osbert to be fond of me or regard our business relationship with affection.'

'Oswald,' said Rachel.

'Never mind dotting his eyes,' said Sammy, 'I can go up to his office and do that myself. Listen, suppose it gets about that there's affection coming my way from someone in trousers? Bang goes me business reputation and me peace of mind. And Susie'll divorce me.'

'Sammy, he spoke of coming to Camberwell to see you,' said Rachel.

'That's done it, I'm joining the Army,' said Sammy. 'Tomorrow. Or could I ask you to make sure all his fond affection is pointed at you? Would you do that for me, Rachel?'

'I should say no, Sammy?' said Rachel. 'How could I? I'll do it, even if he is bald. And it was good business for me to arrange a meeting with him. I gave him such positive confidence in us that he's promised us automatic renewal of existing contracts. Oh, and there's a new contract. For WAAF's tropical kit and lightweight tropical necessities.'

'Ne-what?' said Sammy.

'Knickers,' said Rachel.

'Same to you, Mrs Goodman,' said Sammy. 'Wait a minute, are you telling me you came away with extra business from Oscar?'

'Oswald,' said Rachel.

'Leave off, will you?' said Sammy. 'Just confirm I'm hearing you correct.'

'Quite correct, Sammy,' smiled Rachel. 'I slipped in an encouraging word about our production potential, and ten minutes later I signed the extra contract on behalf of Adams Enterprises. I've a copy for our files, and I'm also in possession of the relevant specifications.'

'Well, bust my shirt buttons,' said Sammy, blue

eyes electric with elation and his smile an acknowl-
edgement of her worth. 'Who's a clever girl, then?'

'I am,' said Rachel. Outwardly, she was light and
teasing. Inwardly, she was delighted she was
proving an asset. 'All for the firm, Sammy.'

'Help yourself to a bonus, Rachel,' said Sammy.
'Further, your executive position here is yours for
the rest of your working life, if you want.'

'I do want, Sammy,' said Rachel.

'All yours, Rachel, and it's the firm's gain,' said
Sammy.

'The bonus, Sammy, shall we say a hundred
pounds on my director's fees?' murmured Rachel.

'Rachel, I think you said that without moving
your lips.'

'So kind of you, a hundred pounds,' smiled
Rachel.

'I think I'm feeling faint again,' said Sammy.

Rachel laughed. Sammy never failed to be entertaining. If she envied anybody, it was his wife Susie.

'If Winnie Churchill could only drop a bomb on
Hitler, or if Bolshevik Joe could flatten his army,
the war could be over by the weekend,' said Sammy
to Susie over supper that evening. 'Then with Boots
back, I'd have a team that could help the firm go
public inside a year. I tell you, Susie, Rachel's a
natural.'

'Go public?' said Susie. 'What's that mean?'

'Floated on the Stock Exchange, with shares
on offer to the public at a price you'd only dream
about,' said Sammy. 'Turn you into a duchess,
that would, Susie, and Plum Pudding the Second

into a débutante at Buckingham Palace.'

'Oh, and would we be able to go to Margate on a steamer?' asked little Paula.

'Margate?' said Sammy. 'New York on the *Queen Mary* more like.'

'Crikey, wait till I tell my teacher,' said Paula, still attending the nursery school for young children not evacuated.

'Don't tell her just yet, darling,' said Susie, 'Daddy's running a bit ahead of himself. Still, we're pleased, aren't we, that Aunt Rachel is helping him to look after the firm's profit, which Daddy would have married if he hadn't married me.'

'Mummy, how can anyone marry profit?' asked Paula.

'Oh, lots of businessmen manage it,' said Susie.

'Mummy, in church?' said Paula.

'No, in their offices,' said Susie. 'Then they take it home with them, bring it to bed with them, and call the doctor in if it loses weight.'

'Loses weight?' said Paula.

'Umpteen pounds at a time,' said Susie. 'I saved Daddy that kind of worry by making him keep his profit locked up in his offices.'

'With the overheads,' said Sammy.

'What's them?' asked Paula.

'Frightening,' said Sammy.

'Like witches?' said Paula.

'That's it,' said Sammy.

'Mummy, what did you say this was that we're eating?' asked Paula.

'Baked sheep's heart,' said Susie.

'Well, Mummy, I hope you don't mind me saying mine tastes like my shoes,' said Paula.

'Oh, dear,' said Susie, and looked at Sammy. Sammy looked at Paula.

'Might I ask when you last tasted your shoes, Paula me pet?' he enquired.

'I forget,' said Paula, 'and I'm only saying, that's all.'

'I'm not saying anything,' said Sammy.

'You'd better not, either,' said Susie, 'there's a war on and our butcher's getting ratty with finicky customers.'

'Well, I'll talk to a bloke I happen to know,' said Sammy. 'He's got a nose for things that fall off the backs of lorries. He might lately have seen a side of beef fall off.'

'Sammy Adams, you're talking about black market,' said Susie, 'so you can forget the bloke. He sounds like a spiv to me, and we don't talk to spivs.'

'Well, all right, Susie, roast Paula's Sunday shoes for tomorrow's supper,' said Sammy. 'I'll have a sole.'

Paula giggled.

Later that evening, Lizzy and Ned were talking about Bobby and Helene.

'Bobby didn't really tell us much in his last letter except that he and Helene were waiting to go overseas,' said Lizzy. 'I wonder where?'

'Middle East, I should imagine,' said Ned. 'That's the only place I can think of where the Army would post servicewomen. But I can't think why Helene, as a FANY officer, should get posted with

385

Bobby, who's a gunner. Artillery regiments don't use FANY personnel as admin. FANY personnel are a bit special.'

'Well, so's Bobby,' said Lizzy, then sat up, stiffening. 'Oh, Lord,' she said.

'Oh, hell,' said Ned.

The air raid alarm sirens were blasting the quiet of the September evening.

Goering's bombers were not long in arriving, passing through a barrage of ack-ack fire. Searchlights swept the cloudy sky, endeavouring to pinpoint any low-flying aircraft. High explosives began to drop the moment the raiders reached the outskirts of London. Goering, in an attempt to restore his waning prestige, was demanding extra efforts from his bomber squadrons. He still had hopes of reducing London to rubble and of persuading its people to demand an end to Britain's war with Germany. He also needed to convince the German people that the *Luftwaffe* bomber squadrons could outdo those of the RAF, busily pounding Germany's industrial centres to smithereens, and attacking heavy water plants whose remote locations had been discovered by British Intelligence.

Tommy, out on ARP duty, rushed home to make sure Vi had tucked herself safely up in their garden shelter and hadn't forgotten to take a warm blanket and the usual flask of hot tea with her.

Lizzy and Ned were quickly in their own shelter, and Chinese Lady and Mr Finch were hurrying to theirs, Chinese Lady going on about the aggravation that that man Hitler was causing.

386

Sammy saw to it that Susie and Paula were comfortably bedded down within their earthbound Anderson shelter before mentioning his ARP responsibilities.

'It sounds as if I'll be called out tonight, Susie,' he said amid the frightening sounds of the invading bomber squadrons.

'Well, wait till the call comes,' said Susie. In the light of a rigged-up electric light, little Paula had her head under a pillow. She was used to these disturbances, but although she felt safe in the shelter, she always tried to shut out the noises. If a raid began late at night while she was in bed, she could sleep through it when carried to the shelter, but this one was early.

Distant rumbles were perceptible. Explosives and incendiaries were raining down on Barking, Dartford, Bromley, Croydon and other places as the raiders converged on central London. The indiscriminate nature of the targeting was one more gesture of anger for the frequency of the RAF's assaults on Germany.

The stream of aircraft passing over Bromley reached south-east London, and a bomb, rocketing down, smashed its way through the front bedroom of a house on Denmark Hill. It plummeted down to the foundations and the explosion was a roar of noise. The house, blasted, blew up. Bricks, tiles, glass and shattered chimneys fountained upwards and cascaded down. The garden shelter, solidly earthed though it was, shivered. Its door split, its light went out. Falling bricks and chunks of torn timber thudded down on its earth-covered roof.

Within seconds, a river of rubble formed like spewed rocks of a volcanic eruption, extending from the devastated house to the lawn.

'Christ,' breathed Sammy, switching on his torch to view the split door and his shaken wife and daughter. Beneath the shelter the ground itself seemed to be vibrating.

'Daddy, Daddy.' Paula sat up in her bunk, face pale, mouth quivering. Sammy wrapped his arms around her and brought her onto his lap. The child emitted frightened little sobs.

'That was a noisy one, eh, sweetie, but we're all right. Don't worry now, we're as safe as—' Houses? Christ, no. 'Yes, safe as heaven's angels.'

'But it was a big one, Daddy, wasn't it?' she gulped against his chest, and he held her tighter.

'Noisy, my little love, noisy, that's all.' He looked at Susie over the top of Paula's fair head. She was white. He knew she was as sure as he was, that it was their own house that had been hit.

'Better that than us, Sammy love,' she said, voice shaky, and took the torch from him.

With one warm arm wrapped around Paula, he reached and took Susie's hand. He squeezed, gently, and Susie returned the pressure. Bricks and mortar, what did they matter? The finest house was a trifle compared to little Paula, to having her safe, sound and close to them. Susie wondered numbly if she and Sammy should send Paula to join her sister and brothers in Devon, despite her being so young.

A flicker of light was seen through the split in the door. Sammy, Paula's arms around his neck, leaned from the low stool on which he was sitting and peered through the narrow gap. He glimpsed flames leaping up from points almost at ground level. Bloody hell, the house had been flattened, it had vanished.

'Don't go out there, Daddy,' whispered Paula.

'Little Plum Pudding, I'm not going anywhere without you and your mum,' he said. 'You're here, Mummy's here, and so am I, and we're all staying put for the moment.'

'Sammy, someone's out there,' said Susie.

That someone was shouting.

'Here, men, here! Come on! They'll be in the shelter, I hope. Come on!'

Feet rushed. The burning remnants of the large house gave light to the ARP team heading around it to the garden. Sammy and Susie heard men clambering over what sounded like gravel. Torches were spouting beams over the river of rubble that covered the garden's central path, the shelter itself at the end of the path set halfway into the earth. Steps led down to the door. It was the rubble that Wellington boots were treading.

Again a shout.

'Susie! Sammy! You there?'

It was Tommy. He had rushed to head the rescue team the moment he realized whose house had been hit. Appalled by its complete destruction, he was nevertheless as much the Adams family stalwart as Boots was its peacekeeper and Sammy its driving force. He was first down the steps to kick in the damaged door.

The beam of his torch looked into the blinding

389

eye of another. The other went out, and his own bright light held sway. There they were, all three of them.

'Thank Christ,' he breathed.

'Pleased to see you, Tommy,' said Susie, dry-throated.

'Always welcome,' said Sammy.

Paula looked up at her uncle.

'Uncle Tommy, wasn't it a noisy bang?'

'Nearly sent me deaf,' said Tommy, and turned his head. 'Back off,' he growled to the man behind him. The growl covered his emotion. 'Give 'em air.' He looked into the shelter again. 'Susie love, you all right?'

'Yes, all of us,' said Susie.

'Then take your time,' said Tommy. 'There's no hurry.' The immediate area was quiet now, the bombers swarming above central London, discharging their loads quickly, for the RAF night fighters were among them, aiming to tail them and shoot them down on their way home.

Sammy let his tense nerves relax. Susie lightly stroked Paula's hair. Paula emitted a dry sob.

'Daddy, can we go out now?' she asked huskily.

'Take her, Tommy,' said Sammy.

'Come on, precious,' said Tommy. He handed his torch to Sammy, stooped from the bottom step and took Paula up into his arms. She snuggled.

Out came Susie, and Sammy followed. Shifting clouds had uncovered the full moon, and the night sky was brilliant, the flames of the burning remnants of the house flickering and dying. But by their light and the light of the moon, Susie and Sammy were able to see that their handsome house and everything in it had been completely destroyed.

'Flat as a burnt pancake,' said Sammy quietly.

'Sammy love,' breathed Susie, 'isn't it a sad sight?'

Tommy, cuddling Paula close, said, 'You can rebuild a house, Susie.'

I know, thought Susie, I know. It's lives that can't be, once they've gone. A little shiver ran through her body. Sammy put an arm around her.

'No worries, Susie, except about a few bricks,' he said, and thought what a treasure of a woman she was. No hysterics, no breakdown, just a few tremors.

'Tommy?' a warden called. 'Any First Aid wanted, any ambulance? There's a phone on offer across the road.'

'Susie?' said Tommy.

'If there's some hot tea going, that's all we need just now,' said Susie.

'Pots of it,' said Tommy. 'Vi will make it at home. There's whisky and brandy too. We'll go there. And there's beds to spare.' His own house was only sixty yards away.

'Tommy?' called the warden again.

'No ambulance needed, Johnny,' said Tommy. Not yet, anyway, he thought. Later, when delayed shock arrived, Sammy, Susie and Paula might need sedatives. He'd phone the doctor as soon as he got home.

Susie looked at the burning embers again. She felt numb apart from thankfulness that they'd been spared themselves.

'Everything's gone, Sammy, everything.'

'That's going to be trying for a while, Susie, but we'll manage,' said Sammy. 'We'll start again from nothing.'

Paula, still up in Tommy's arms, stopped shivering and turned her head.

'Daddy, not nothing,' she said. 'I've still got my teddy, he's in the shelter.'

That from a little girl of six, thought Sammy. Brave as a king's trooper in the front line of battle.

'I'll get him, me pet,' he said.

From that moment on Sammy's Plum Pudding the Second became just that little bit dearer to him than his other children.

Chapter Twenty-Eight

A coded radio message reached the man called Paul in Carbonne, Vichy France.

POSTPONED FLIGHT ARRANGED FOR THIS EVENING LYNETTE AND MAURICE ARRIVING AT AGREED TIME AND DESTINATION MEET THEM BBC WILL CONFIRM IF DEPARTURE ON BY TRANSMITTING SIGNAL MRS EVELYN RICHARDS THANKS MICHAEL FOR NEWS OF HER SON STOP ENDS.

The transmission was made during the one o'clock overseas news broadcast.

The Whitley bomber, flying low in the light of a full moon, was east of the Garonne river and four miles south of Lys when the dropping zone was reached. Its two passengers departed into space, one after the other, and pulled on their ripcords. Their parachutes unfolded fast, billowed out and floated above them. They descended, gently swinging, heartbeats erratic, adrenalin running, eyes on a single light that drifted away to the west as the prevailing breeze took them off course to the east.

A Frenchman, awakened by the noise of the bomber, was at his bedroom window, binoculars to his eyes, the moonlight giving him vision.

Bobby landed first, the ground hard on impact. He was ready for that, and he rolled over, going with the forward motion of his body. His parachute flopped and dragged. Helene landed forty yards farther on, contact with unyielding terra firma driving the breath from her. They saw each other clearly in the moonlight, but neither called to the other. It was not to be supposed that the lush countryside of Garonne lacked ears, quiet though it was well after midnight. They both felt the noise of the Whitley's engines must have woken some people, all of whom might be supporters of old Marshal Petain, Hitler's puppet President of Vichy France. Petain, of course, would have disputed such a contemptuous title.

The night brightness that had assisted pilot and navigator to locate the dropping zone was no friend now, thought Bobby, and he made quick work of releasing his parachute, bundling it up and looking for a place in which to make it disappear. Helene came running up, folded chute held close. Bobby pointed to a copse, thick with the verdant growth endemic to the South of France. Helene hurried along with him, and they hid themselves in the friendly cover of the copse. Bobby selected a tree that invited a climb into its thickly leafed branches.

He unstrapped a small valise from his back, opened it, took out a fashionable little hat and handed it to Helene. She removed her helmet, dropped it, put the hat on, slipped off her denims, smoothed her dress down and took on the look of a young lady closely acquainted with attractive millinery and stylish clothes. Bobby took off his own denims to disclose jacket, shirt, tie and trousers, then took a soft trilby from the valise. All clothes had French labels. Helene breathed in the scent of the pines of her native land and watched Bobby as he climbed. They were both too keyed-up and too sensitive to the incautious to say anything. Bobby reached down from his perch, Helene reached up, and he took one tightly folded parachute from her. He stuffed it out of sight within the cradling embrace of an upper branch, took the second chute she handed up, and made that disappear too. The denims and their helmets, packed into the valise by Helene, followed, Bobby taking his time to ensure nothing could be seen from the ground. Then down he came. Helene gave him the soft trilby and he put it on at a jaunty angle befitting a journalist. Spare clothes, nightwear and accessories would be found in their allocated apartment, according to Major Buckmaster.

'So far, so good,' whispered Bobby.

'I'm glad to hear you say something,' whispered Helene.

'Let's find our contact man,' murmured Bobby, and they moved cautiously out of the copse to observe the area in front of them. Bobby estimated that the central point of the dropping zone, marked by a flare, was well over two hundred yards away. With the land bathed by the ghostly light of the moon, they could not, at this distance, discern even a tiny impression of flame. The flare had been clearly visible from the bomber, but was difficult to make out at ground level.

'Where is our contact?' breathed Helene.

'He must be here, or who else placed the guiding light?' said Bobby. 'No, not just here. We went off course a bit in our drop. We'll have to do some walking, and perhaps he'll come to meet us. Hell, this moon makes me feel there's a searchlight on us.'

They began walking, nerves at a pitch, the night bereft of all sound. They were in Vichy France, the territory allowed to Petain and his Government by Hitler as long as collaboration on certain matters was forthcoming. Certain matters included a gradual round-up of all Jewish citizens. In this kind of silence, however, one took hold of a feeling that Himmler's secret assassins had made ghosts of every man, woman and child, Christian or Jew.

Where was the contact, the man known as Paul?

They strained their eyes, looking and searching, and they peered ahead for sight of the flare that had helped the Whitley to pinpoint the rendezvous. Helene shot out a hand and clutched Bobby's elbow.

'Listen!'

They stopped. There was a road a little way north of the rendezvous, they knew that, and the sound of a speeding car reached their ears. They glimpsed its headlights as it rounded a bend, and they went to ground, flinging themselves flat. A man materialized in a silent rush. Without a word, he dropped beside them, burrowing into the thick coarse grass.

Helene gasped, 'Arc you—?'

'Silence!' It was a rasping whisper from the man.

The car stopped, its headlights went out, and in the pall of silence they clearly heard the sounds of doors opening and closing. They stayed flat and kept quiet. Four men appeared, some fifty yards away. Two were uniformed Vichy policemen, the other two wore belted raincoats and trilby hats. Bobby and Helene knew enough from training catechisms to at once decide the latter were men of the Gestapo, the notorious German security organization allowed by Petain to operate in Vichy France.

All four men were looking to their right, towards the centre of the landing area. Bobby could still not see any sign of the flare. But he felt the man beside him had to be the contact Paul, the man responsible for placing and lighting the signal.

The four men, talking, moved towards the centre of the dropping zone. They had their backs to Bobby, Helene and the newcomer.

'Quick,' hissed the newcomer, and Helene and Bobby were up in a flash, turning and making a fast silent retreat to the copse, their companion leading the way. He did not enter the copse, however, he skirted it and placed himself on the right side of it, Bobby and Helene with him. 'You're late,' he whispered.

'You're early,' whispered Bobby, and the spoken passwords established acceptance of each other.

'Talk no more, they are going to search the area. Stay quiet, stay still.' The whispering man was tall, slender, suited and bareheaded.

Bobby and Helene stayed still, on their feet, and waited. From where they were now, they could see nothing of the four men, who had spread out, but they heard the occasional sound, and after several acutely tense minutes they heard the distinct whispers of men approaching the copse. There followed the sounds of the copse being noisily invaded by men who rushed in, torches issuing beams. Shouts abounded.

'Come out!'

'Show yourselves!'

'You are here, we know that!'

'Show yourselves!'

Helene, Bobby and their contact did not move. Not a muscle twitched. Here and there they glimpsed the moving lights of torches. Suddenly, feet trod brittle undergrowth only fifteen yards from them, and a man cursed as he tripped and almost fell. Another man spoke in lucid French.

'Too late, we arrived too late.'

A response came in guttural French.

'The man who saw them took too long to decide to phone you.'

'But we were only just too late, or the spot where the flare was placed would not have been as warm as it was.'

'A car collected them, of course, and they'll end up somewhere in this area, in Carbonne or Lys.' The guttural French was spoken curtly. 'Enquiries must begin tomorrow morning, you understand?'

Gestapo giving orders to the natives, thought Bobby.

An argument began, but voices were fading, feet taking the searchers out of the copse and back to the car. Bobby, Helene and their contact still did not move. They remained silent until they heard the car's engine fire.

Then Helene breathed, 'Did you hear? Someone saw us dropping.'

'Yes,' said the contact man brusquely. 'There's a vineyard not far from here.'

'Well, curse it,' said Bobby, 'I've just developed a dislike of a full moon.'

'You are?'

'Maurice.'

'You?' The man addressed Helene.

'Lynette.'

'And you?' said Bobby.

'Paul. You were earlier than I expected.'

'But you were early yourself, weren't you?' said Bobby.

'Of course. One must prepare for everything. You missed the dropping zone.' The man Paul was abrupt.

'No, we were wide of the central mark, that's all, and not by much,' said Bobby.

'By a few hundred metres. With conditions so good, I expected a much more accurate landing.'

'You did not expect us to land on the flare, did you?' said Helene, bridling a little.

'It gave me no chance to make immediate contact with you,' said Paul. 'Also, you were seen and the police informed. You gave them time to get here before I could find you. What were you doing?'

'Hiding our parachutes and other items,' said Bobby. 'Didn't you see us yourself?'

'Yes, but I lost sight of you,' said Paul acidly. 'I put out the flare and removed it, then began searching for you.'

'The two men with the policemen, were they Gestapo?' asked Helene.

Paul stared at her.

'What good will you be if you can't be sure of recognizing our most dangerous enemy?'

Helene thought little of that.

'I was asking only for your confirmation,' she said. 'This is our first mission.'

Ignoring that, Paul said, 'You have six kilometres to walk to Lys. Although I never visit it myself, being known there for my religion, I will take you in. It will be safe to go now. Follow me.'

'Thanks for the cheerful welcome,' said Bobby.

'Bear in mind that your country is not as close to Nazi terror as France and Poland are,' said Paul.

'You would not say that if you lived in London amid the bombs,' said Helene.

Paul shrugged, then led the way from their retreat. Helene and Bobby followed their abrasive and quick-moving contact. It took only a few minutes to reach the road, a pale ribbon in the moonlight. Paul turned onto it, striding like a man quarrelling with circumstances. Helene and Bobby, fit and vigorous, stayed on his heels, Helene carrying her French-made handbag.

Paul broke the silence.

'Your French will do, Maurice,' he said.

'Thanks for that,' said Bobby. 'Lynette, of course, is French.'

'The right kind, I believe. We are up against the wrong kind, like Petain and Laval, and the anti-Semitic ones. But we'll be troubled by Germans too. Himmler has his agents all over Vichy France, for the specific purpose of nosing out people of my race and people opposed to the New Order.'

'I should like to kill Petain and Laval,' whispered Helene fiercely.

'Don't be stupid. We need people of intelligence, not assassins.' Without looking back, Paul asked, 'Are you both carrying arms?'

'No, neither of us,' said Helene, who disliked being spoken to as if she had no sense. 'Would a milliner and a journalist carry weapons?'

'I'm not always sure London understands our exact needs. The English are practical, but not very imaginative.'

'That is a lie,' said Helene, suspecting, much to her vexation, that this man, even though Jewish, was among all too many French people who had a dog-in-the-manger attitude towards the British for their success in forcing Hitler to abort his invasion plans. General de Gaulle himself was hardly admiring. 'Yes, a lie.'

'Never mind,' said Bobby pacifically. He felt the arrival of police and Gestapo had been an annoyance to Paul.

'I spoke a lie?' said Paul. Banks of trees on either side of the rural road absorbed their voices and threw no echoes.

'It was also a foolish generalization, and out of

courtesy should not have been spoken in front of Maurice,' said Helene. 'The English think themselves superior, yes, I will admit that, but they are also crazy, and many crazy people are very imaginative.'

'You have lived among the English for how long?' asked Paul, the road, the night and the land all atmospheric of a country brooding in its sleep.

'Since Dunkirk,' said Helene.

'And you've found them to be conceited and crazy?'

'Yes,' said Helene.

'Thanks,' said Bobby.

'Oh, not you, *cheri*, you are only crazy,' whispered Helene. To the back of Paul's head, she said, 'I've also found I like crazy people. There's a happy difference between people who are crazy and people who are maniacs, like Hitler, or psychopaths, like Goering and Himmler. You wish Maurice and I to be intelligent agents. We are, or we would not be here. Also, Maurice is extremely imaginative.'

'Don't mention it,' said Bobby.

'How imaginative?' asked Paul, keeping his eyes on the road ahead.

'That, *m'sieur*, is between Maurice and myself,' said Helene.

Bobby would have laughed if his nerves had not been so much on edge. What was the time? Two in the morning? Three?

'We shall see,' said Paul.

'Can anyone hear this conversation?' asked Bobby.

'The vineyard is well behind us now,' said Paul, then came to an abrupt stop. Behind him, Helene and Bobby pulled up. 'My friends,' he said temperately, 'there's a car coming and we must lose ourselves for a moment. Pardon my irritations.'

He turned, ran over the verge and into the shelter of the trees, Helene and Bobby following at a rush. The car was approaching at speed. It passed at speed, headlamps brilliant. Vichy France was not at war, and did not, therefore, impose a blackout. Bobby and Helene saw the car for a second or so, a police car laden with men.

'More bloodhounds?' murmured Bobby.

'Probably to conduct another and more extensive search for you by the order of a superior,' said Paul. 'A superior being, if he's a Gestapo chief,' he added drily. 'The other men no doubt delivered their report some time ago, and perhaps that didn't satisfy him. Your parachutes are safely buried?'

'Hidden high up in a tree,' said Bobby.

'We'll go on,' said Paul, and went back to the road, Helene and Bobby on his heels again. They walked in single file.

'If we're not found by the time we get to Lys,' said Bobby, 'we can take it, can we, that the mentioned enquiries will begin tomorrow?'

'Yes. That,' said Paul, 'is definitely irritating and a nuisance. You will both have to lie low for a week, perhaps longer, and I will have to watch out for myself in Carbonne. I'm a lawyer, but no safer than anyone else when the Gestapo come prowling.'

'We're to do nothing for a week or more?' said Helene, finding it irksome to be talking to a man who had his back to her the whole time. But she was beginning to feel he knew what he was about. If brusque, he was also positive.

'Lying low for the time being seems sensible,' said Bobby.

'In all things, please do as I say,' said Paul.

'We're briefed to that effect,' said Bobby.

'When we reach the millinery shop, I will give you the keys,' said Paul, 'one for the shop door, one for your apartment. Go through the shop and you will see the stairs to the apartment. Don't put any lights on. Settle in and stay. Do nothing until you hear from me, and do nothing at all that might mean being stopped and questioned. Madame Clair, the manageress, will arrive as usual tomorrow morning. She's a sympathizer, but not an agent. She will deal with any enquiries concerning strangers. We shall have to wait until the police or Gestapo interest in your whereabouts dies down, and only then will I ask you to begin work for us.'

'Understood,' said Bobby.

'You will come to find none of us can be too careful,' said Paul.

'Yes, we understand,' said Helene.

The police car had not returned by the time they reached the ancient little town of Lys. Lys was asleep. Even by day it was sleepy, and had been since Roman times, for it always seemed to snooze in the sun of the South of France. In the still bright moonlight, with not a soul about and a fat marmalade cat curled up on a stone step, they passed through the spacious square, around which stood peaceful-looking houses roofed by

Roman tiles. They entered the Avenue du Parc, and without encountering anyone, went on until Paul stopped outside a millinery shop. Its window contained just a single example of what was designed to look enchanting when placed on a lady's head. As far as Helene could make out, it seemed an absurd concoction with a purple sheen and gauzy trimmings. Helene, however, was a farmer's daughter, not a daughter of Nice or Paris.

'You like it?' she whispered to Bobby.

'Might look pretty on a fancy French poodle,' whispered Bobby.

Paul produced a ring containing two keys.

'Yours,' he whispered to Helene. 'For the shop door and your apartment, as I said. So, for the time being, goodbye to both of you and thank you for coming.'

He slipped away, and suddenly Bobby and Helene were by themselves. Helene steeled herself to be composed, and while Bobby cast glances up and down the deserted street, she found the key that opened the shop door and used it. Quickly, they stepped in, and Bobby closed the door with only the faintest of clicks. The moonlight, filtering in through the shop window's curtain-like backdrop, showed them the way to an inner door straight ahead. It was not locked. Helene opened it and they saw the stairs. Up they went, as quietly as they could, and Helene unlocked the door to the apartment. They glimpsed a corridor, with doors on either side, everything in shadow.

'Where's the moonlight gone?' asked Bobby.

'You think it should have followed us up here?' said Helene.

'It would be a help,' said Bobby.

'*Cheri*, I will always give you all the help you need,' said Helene, 'and you will always give me all I need.'

'Rephrase that sometime,' said Bobby.

They groped about and opened doors. The moonlight helpfully reappeared through unshuttered windows. They examined two modest-sized bedrooms, an attractive living-room, a good-looking kitchen, and amenities, including a shower. In the kitchen larder there was tinned food.

'It isn't at all bad, no,' said Helene.

'Howd you feel?' asked Bobby.

'Mentally drained and physically exhausted,' said Helene.

'I'm tired out mind and body myself,' said Bobby.

'It's the same, isn't it, you lunatic?' said Helene.

Relief at their safe arrival, however, induced a blissful relaxing of nerves and limbs.

'Shall we turn in?' suggested Bobby. 'Which bedroom would you like?'

'For tonight at least, the same as you,' said Helene.

'Well, you'll be safe,' said Bobby, 'I'll be asleep as soon as I hit the pillow. By the way, if we can't go out except into the backyard, what about fresh food and things like milk?'

'I've a feeling Madame Clair will look after us,' said Helene. 'What did you think of Paul?'

'A bit ratty to begin with,' said Bobby. 'Probably because we didn't drop into his lap, and the enemy turned up.'

'But it was unfair to take it out on us,' said Helene.

'He's Jewish,' said Bobby, 'and the Gestapo are sitting on his doorstep.'

'Ah, yes, we must make allowances,' said Helene, and yawned. That set Bobby off.

'I'm giving in,' he said.

They undressed in a bedroom with the aid of a little light peeping in through shutters Bobby had partly closed. The lowering of adrenalin, the release from tensions, and the calming of nerves, allowed extreme tiredness to happily govern their preparations for bed. They did not bother to look for nightwear.

'I'm almost falling over,' sighed Helene.

'I'm losing my legs,' said Bobby. A huge yawn overtook him, and only after his mouth, jaws and cheekbones had settled back into place was he able to murmur, 'Here goes.'

They both fell into bed, Helene in bra and panties, Bobby in his brief pants. Helene sighed with the sheer bliss of a luxuriating body, turned to Bobby and the next moment they took the compulsive drop into sleep.

Yes, they had safely arrived. What lay ahead of them was in the lap of the gods.

First, however, were the days of waiting.

* * *

Lizzy and Ned received a letter from Bobby the following morning, advising them he and Helene were about to embark overseas. He sent love and best wishes from both of them.

Chapter Twenty-Nine

October

The Germans, hugely man-powered and armoured, had taken Kiev, Odessa, and Stalino. They were at the gates of Kharkov and over-running the Crimea, while their central thrust, aimed at Moscow, was making dangerous but costly headway. Russian resistance was total, their armies executing a scorched earth policy that left towns and villages burning in the wake of their fighting retreat.

Malta was still under unremitting air attack, and Annabelle's husband Nick, despite notching up his fourth victory, had been shot down again. He was in the military hospital with burns to his legs, and would be out of action for some time. He wrote to Annabelle, telling her he'd been sun-scorched, which made Annabelle think his squadron was operating from an air base in the Sahara.

In the Western Desert, the Afrika Korps, fully reinforced at last with tanks, planes and men, and the British Eighth Army, almost up to required strength, were squaring up to each other in formidable fashion, the British intent on recapturing

Libya, the Germans planning to conquer Egypt. Eloise and all other ATS personnel at Cairo head-quarters were slimming down under pressure of work. Eloise had seen not the slightest sign of Colonel Lucas, or of Tim, but she had heard from both and was so heart and soul in tune with every-thing demanded of her that she was not making a single complaint. All ATS personnel were dedi-cated to the interests of the fighting men, and something of the camaraderie so prevalent during the Great War was making its binding mark. Eloise raised smiles in sister officers by her constant refer-ences to Colonel Lucas as the man who could not only hang Hitler, but Goering the Nazi hippopotamus as well.

Bobby and Helene were in the little town of Lys, Vichy France, operating in concert with furtive and elusive figures of the French Resistance movement, and gathering information about the routines applied to the delivery of Jews into the French-controlled concentration camp.

Jonathan was in Somerset, a sergeant-instructor at a training camp for artillery conscripts, and if he had a bit of a limp, well, his father-in-law had a more pronounced one. Jonathan had succeeded in finding not only a billet for Emma with a market gardener and his wife, but a job with them as well. They had fields of vegetables and three large green-houses, and Emma was actually working in the fields and the greenhouses. A little fastidious about her appearance and her person Emma may have

been, but the war asked for some kind of contribution from everyone and she adapted herself
willingly to the perspiring demands of field work,
especially as this kind of employment put her into
a reserved occupation and kept her closely in touch
with Jonathan at the nearby training camp. On
Sundays, however, she was allowed time off, and
she and Jonathan were discovering the quietest
retreats of the Somerset countryside.

'Why, Mrs Emma Hardy, don't you be a lovely
girl?'

'Blushing, more like. Me blushing at my age.
Jonathan, oh, Lord, there's a whole flock of
pigeons looking.'

'Somerset rooks, I reckon, Emma.'

'They're still looking.'

'Fledglings, I'd say, Emma, and admiring of
grown up birds like you.'

'Are you calling me a bird? I – oh, help.'

'Is there something you want, Emma?'

'Yes, could someone turn the light out?' said
Emma.

His expertise proving invaluable to REME,
Matthew Chapman was awarded a second pip and
the rank of first lieutenant, which delighted Rosie
who, despite being run off her feet as deputy to
horsy Major Clarice Robbins, never lost her cool.

She had received her bequest, had passed it on
to Sammy, and Sammy had it lodged in the firm's
bank, where it was earning interest. The interest
was to be siphoned off and placed in a special
account for Rosie's benefit, although the capital

would be reduced each time a site for development was purchased.

Polly, laden with her burgeoning twins, still had moments when she told herself she was dreaming, and other moments when reality either made her feel an exceptional woman or induced her to berate Boots for doing to her what no woman of her age should expect. Boots, of course, said he hadn't expected anything like that himself, but would happily come to terms with the end products. Polly threw a cushion at him. They made life entrancing for Kate, who delighted in all that went on between David's whimsical uncle and his vivacious wife in the way of repartee. She was a great help to both, quick and willing in all she did around the cottage and in the kitchen. With Lance-Corporal Higgins hobbling about on crutches, Kate simply took over the kitchen, and did so in a way that belied her sixteen years. She also helped Polly with the vegetable plot, since Polly found bending the kind of activity that caused her twins to kick in protest. They're boys, she told Boots. Boots asked how she knew. The little devils have got leg muscles, she said.

Boots received a letter sent to him by Mrs Beatrice Freeman care of Rosie's address. It was a nicely worded invitation to visit her at her country house near Fordingbridge, Hampshire. He showed it to Polly. Polly put it in an egg saucepan and boiled it. She was up to doing that much in the kitchen.

*   *   *

Felicity was a young woman waiting for the return of Tim while improving her mobility and her usefulness. She was actually under instruction in the hospital kitchens, Clara joyful for her on the day when she successfully mixed and baked a cake. She could handle a kitchen knife, peel potatoes, trim a cauliflower, slice an onion and take the heads off carrots. She could prepare a salad. You're a marvel, said Clara. I know I am, said Felicity, but I still can't see a bloody thing. And she laughed.

Chinese Lady, horrified though she was at the destruction of Sammy and Susie's home, found a happy consolation. Sammy, Susie and little Paula were now under her roof, and she and Mr Finch were delighted to have them. The house was alive again. Sammy and Susie had had a little chat with Paula, asking her if she'd like to join her sister and brothers in the country. It stirred their emotions when Paula said she'd rather stay with them, especially as she liked all of them living with Grandma and Grandpa.

Saturday, late October
Kate was out, walking to the little rural railway station that served the village of Corfe Castle. There was a spring in her walk, the skirt of her coat whisking, the autumn breeze containing a hint of winter. But the day was bright, and the morning news had been cheerful. The Russians had at last emerged victorious from one of their tremendous battles with the Germans, causing them to fall

413

back and straighten out their line of advance on Moscow.

She hurried. She was a bit late. She heard the train coming in. She was still at a distance from the station when David emerged. They saw each other. Kate broke into a run.

'David!' She ran into his arms.

'Hello, me young dearie, 'ow's yerself, blooming?' said David. 'My, ain't yer growin' prettier all the time, like?'

'Why'd you talk like that every time you come 'ere, you dummy?' asked Kate.

'Well, didn't I give yer me solemn promise I'd improve meself?' said David. 'Corblimey, I don't want yer to look down on me year in, year out. So what d'yer think, is me improvement to yer likin', ducks?'

'No, it's not,' said Kate, 'and how dare you call me ducks, you common beast?'

'But I thought—'

'I can't think where you get your silly ideas from,' said Kate. 'I know you're middle class, but you don't 'ave to be ashamed of it. It might be hard luck, but it's not a crime. I can live with it all the time we're best friends, can't I?'

'But will it hurt?' asked David.

'Only a bit,' said Kate. 'Look, I'm going to do hot carrot soup for lunch. Aunt Polly's got a fancy for carrots lately. So come on, don't stand about, come on home with me.'

Home?

David, smiling, put his arm around her and

414

walked there with her, the ruined ramparts of Corfe Castle reaching for the sky.

There was a phone in the cluttered little office of a large workshop at Bovington REME. It rang. A corporal answered it, then called Lieutenant Chapman, the officer in charge.

'It's for you, sir.'

'Right,' shouted Matthew above the grinding noises of repair and maintenance work. He took the call. 'Hello, Chapman here.'

'It's your missus at this end,' said Rosie.

'I'd like it better if you were at this end,' said Matthew.

'Hold your horses for a while, then perhaps I'll be there.'

'Are you telling me you've got a posting to Bovington?' asked Matt.

'No, I'm telling you I'm going to find a place we can rent when I leave the ATS,' said Rosie. 'A place close enough to Bovington for you to be able to persuade your commanding officer to let you billet there. You're too far away from me as things are.'

'Rosie, what's on your mind?' asked Matt.

'Oh, nothing that's uncommon,' said Rosie. 'Or unpleasing.'

'Rosie?'

'Yes, isn't it lovely, Matt? We're going to have a baby.'

THE END

A SELECTED LIST OF FINE NOVELS
AVAILABLE FROM CORGI BOOKS

14447 9	FIREBIRD	*Iris Gower*	£5.99
14537 8	APPLE BLOSSOM TIME	*Kathryn Haig*	£5.99
14566 1	THE DREAM SELLERS	*Ruth Hamilton*	£5.99
14686 2	CITY OF GEMS	*Caroline Harvey*	£5.99
14220 4	CAPEL BELLS	*Joan Hessayon*	£4.99
14599 8	FOOTPRINTS ON THE SAND	*Judith Lennox*	£5.99
14492 4	THE CREW	*Margaret Mayhew*	£5.99
14499 1	THESE FOOLISH THINGS	*Imogen Parker*	£5.99
10375 6	CSARDAS	*Diane Pearson*	£5.99
14577 7	PORTRAIT OF CHLOE	*Elvi Rhodes*	£5.99
14636 6	COME RAIN OR SHINE	*Susan Sallis*	£5.99
13951 3	SERGEANT JOE	*Mary Jane Staples*	£3.99
13845 2	RISING SUMMER	*Mary Jane Staples*	£3.99
13299 3	DOWN LAMBETH WAY	*Mary Jane Staples*	£5.99
13444 9	OUR EMILY	*Mary Jane Staples*	£5.99
13856 8	THE PEARLY QUEEN	*Mary Jane Staples*	£3.99
13975 0	ON MOTHER BROWN'S DOORSTEP		
		Mary Jane Staples	£3.99
14106 2	THE TRAP	*Mary Jane Staples*	£4.99
14154 2	A FAMILY AFFAIR	*Mary Jane Staples*	£4.99
14230 1	MISSING PERSON	*Mary Jane Staples*	£4.99
14291 3	PRIDE OF WALWORTH	*Mary Jane Staples*	£4.99
14375 8	ECHOES OF YESTERDAY	*Mary Jane Staples*	£4.99
14418 5	THE YOUNG ONES	*Mary Jane Staples*	£4.99
14469 X	THE CAMBERWELL RAID	*Mary Jane Staples*	£4.99
14513 0	THE LAST SUMMER	*Mary Jane Staples*	£4.99
14548 3	THE GHOST OF WHITECHAPEL	*Mary Jane Staples*	£5.99
14554 8	THE FAMILY AT WAR	*Mary Jane Staples*	£5.99
14606 4	FIRE OVER LONDON	*Mary Jane Staples*	£5.99
14657 9	CHURCHILL'S PEOPLE	*Mary Jane Staples*	£5.99
14640 4	THE ROMANY GIRL	*Valerie Wood*	£5.99